YASUNARI NAGATOSHI

Thank you for supporting this series!
I'm grateful I got to write Zombie Boy stories
for this long! I'm hoping that I can come back
like an immortal zombie with another story
to share with you soon. Please look out for it!!

ZOMBIE BOY'S METAMORPHOSIS COLLECTION

MINI ZOMBIE BOY

Just as his name implies, he's a miniature
Zombie Boy, about the size of an eraser.
Since he's so tiny, he's hard to spot and can
bite people and turn them into zombies before
they know it. He often hides in pencil cases
or shoes, so you must be very careful.

ZO ZO ZOMBIE

VOL. 11

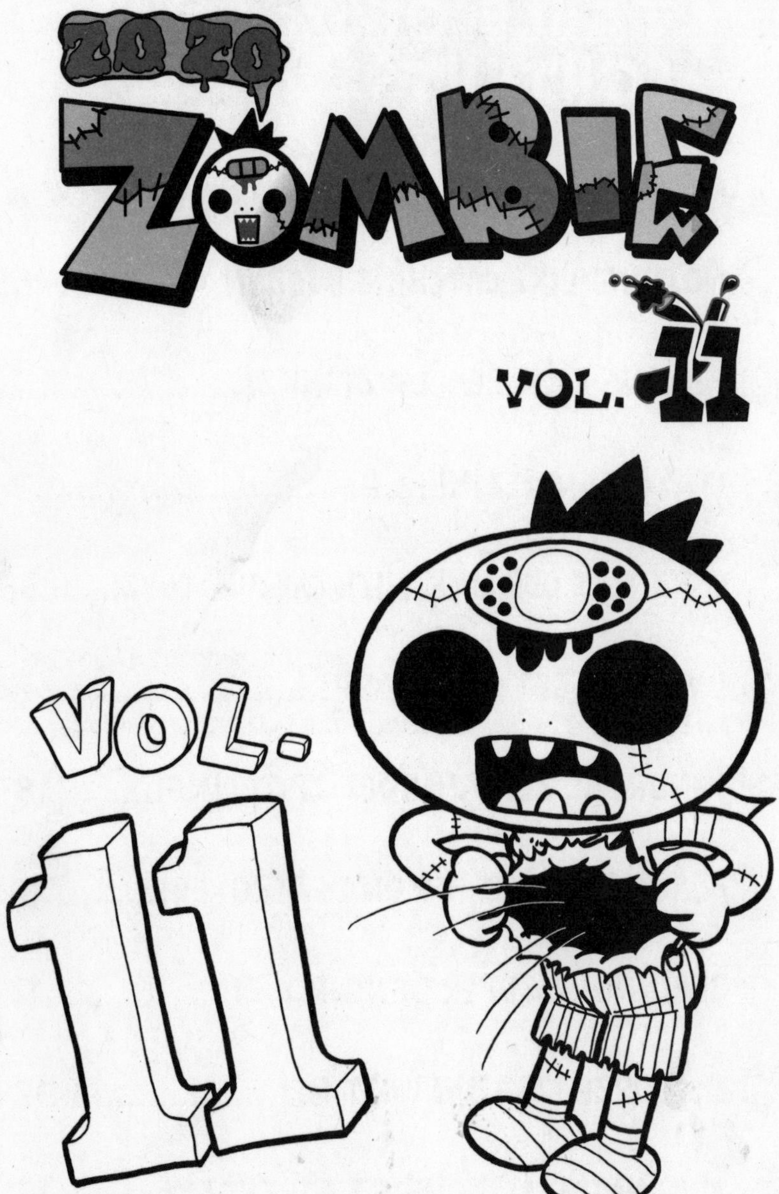

VOL. 11

YASUNARI NAGATOSHI

TABLE OF CONTENTS

BATO

MANGA

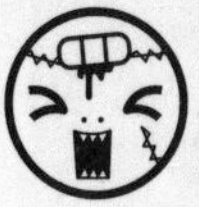

NOTHING LIKE CATCHING BUGZ IN THE ZUMMER!

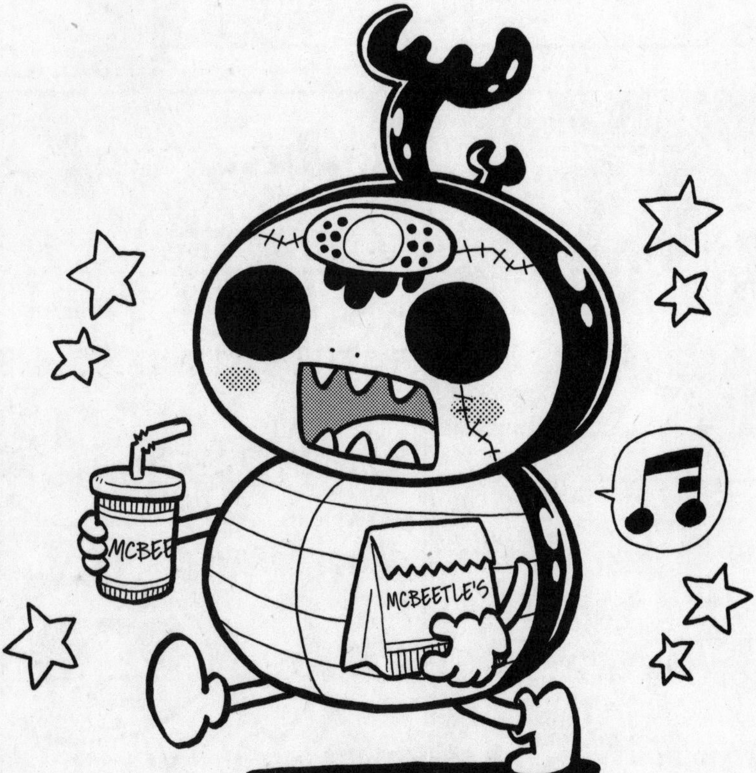
MCBEE
MCBEETLE'S

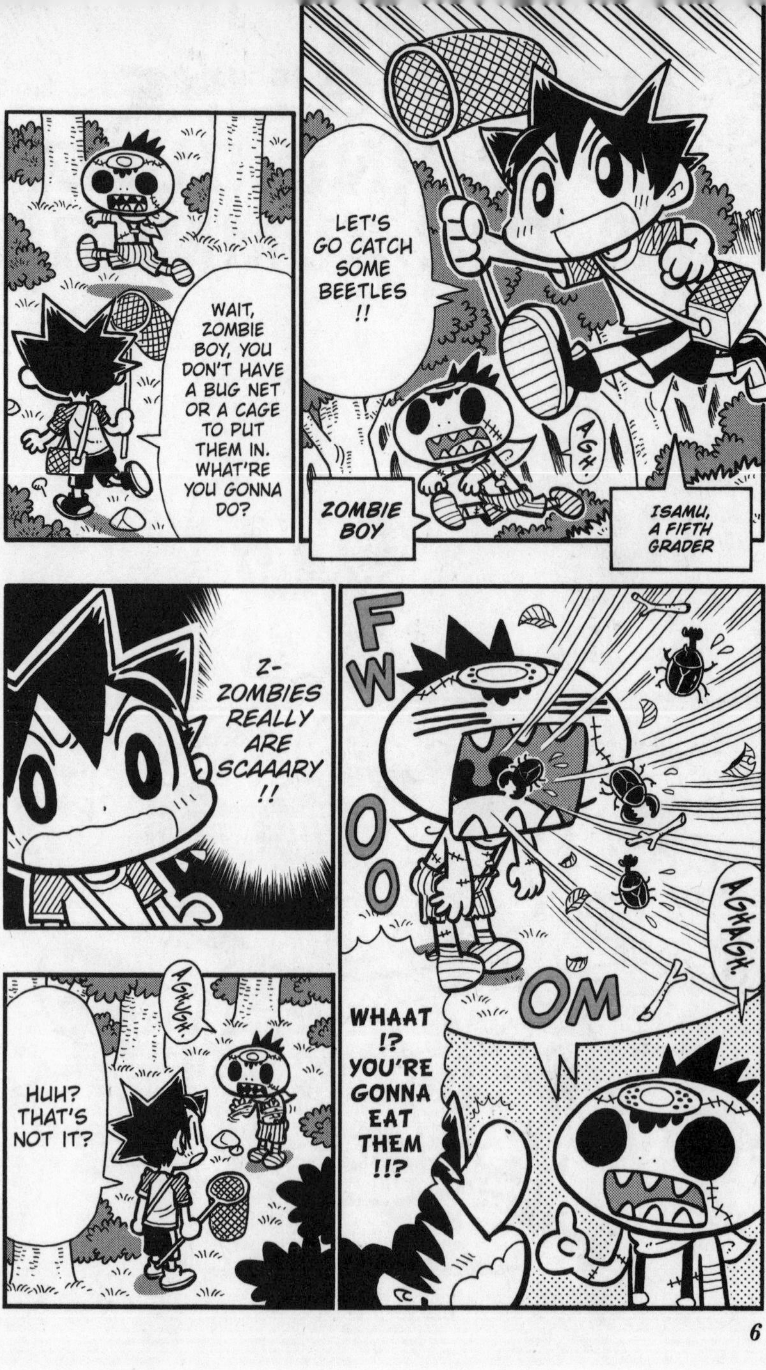
LET'S GO CATCH SOME BEETLES !!
AGH.
ZOMBIE BOY
ISAMU, A FIFTH GRADER
WAIT, ZOMBIE BOY, YOU DON'T HAVE A BUG NET OR A CAGE TO PUT THEM IN. WHAT'RE YOU GONNA DO?
FWOOOOM
AGHAGH.
WHAAT !? YOU'RE GONNA EAT THEM !!?
Z-ZOMBIES REALLY ARE SCAAARY !!
AGHUGH.
HUH? THAT'S NOT IT?

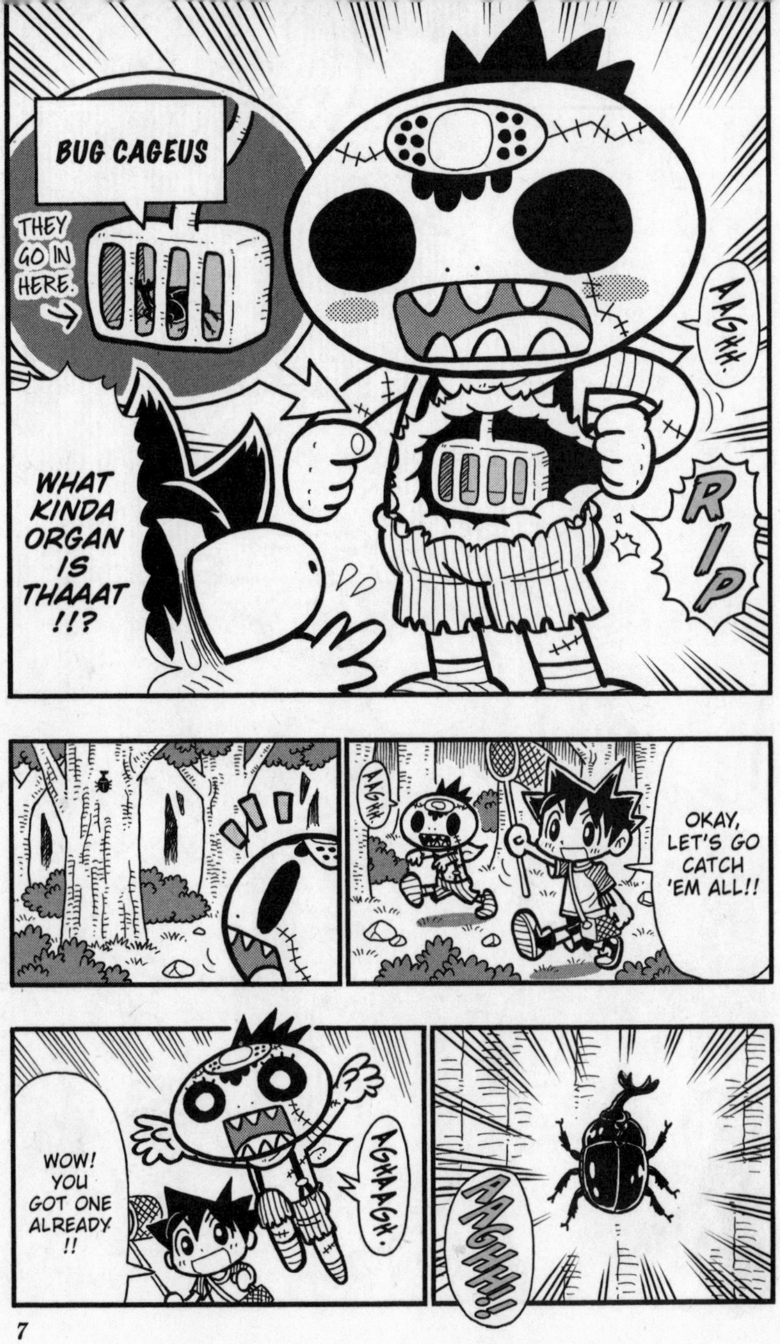
AAGHX.
RIP
BUG CAGEUS
THEY GO IN HERE.
WHAT KINDA ORGAN IS THAAAT!!?
OKAY, LET'S GO CATCH 'EM ALL!!
AAGHX.
AAGHHH!!
AGHAAGH.
WOW! YOU GOT ONE ALREADY!!

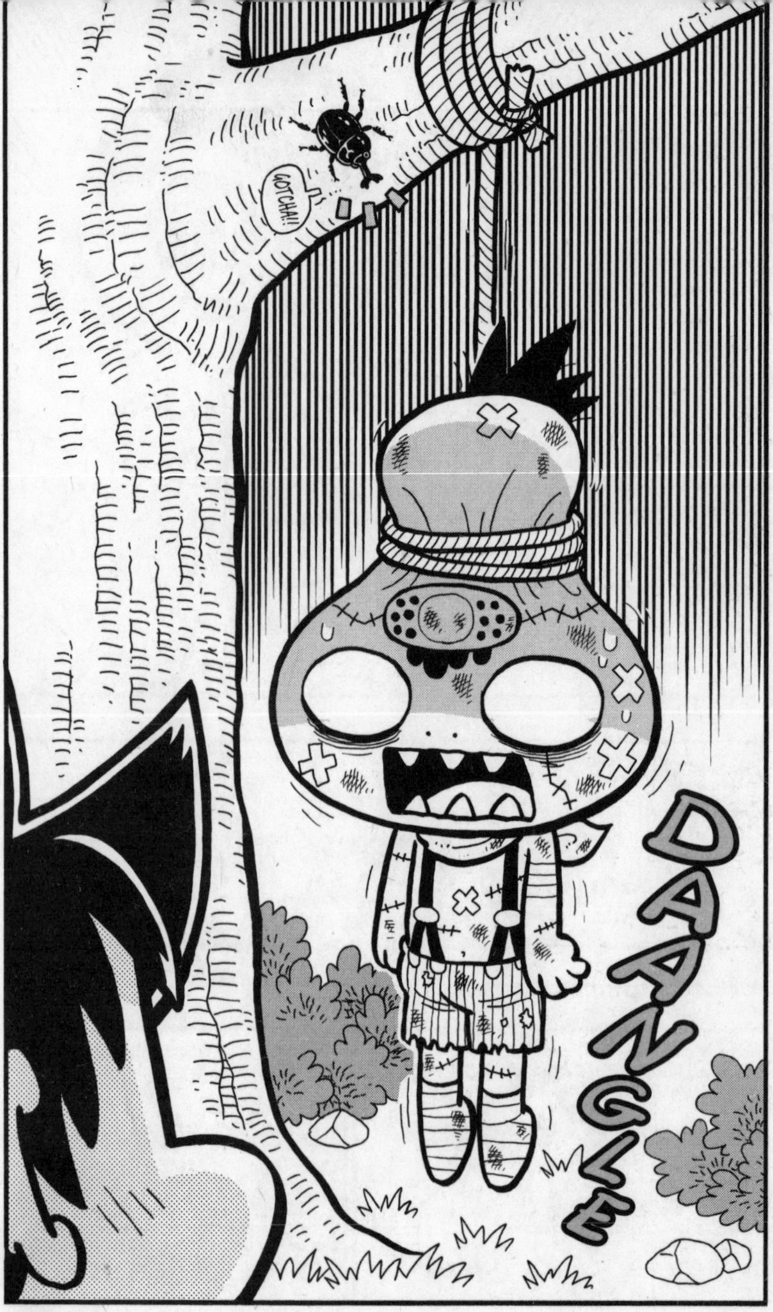
GOTCHA!!
DAANGLE

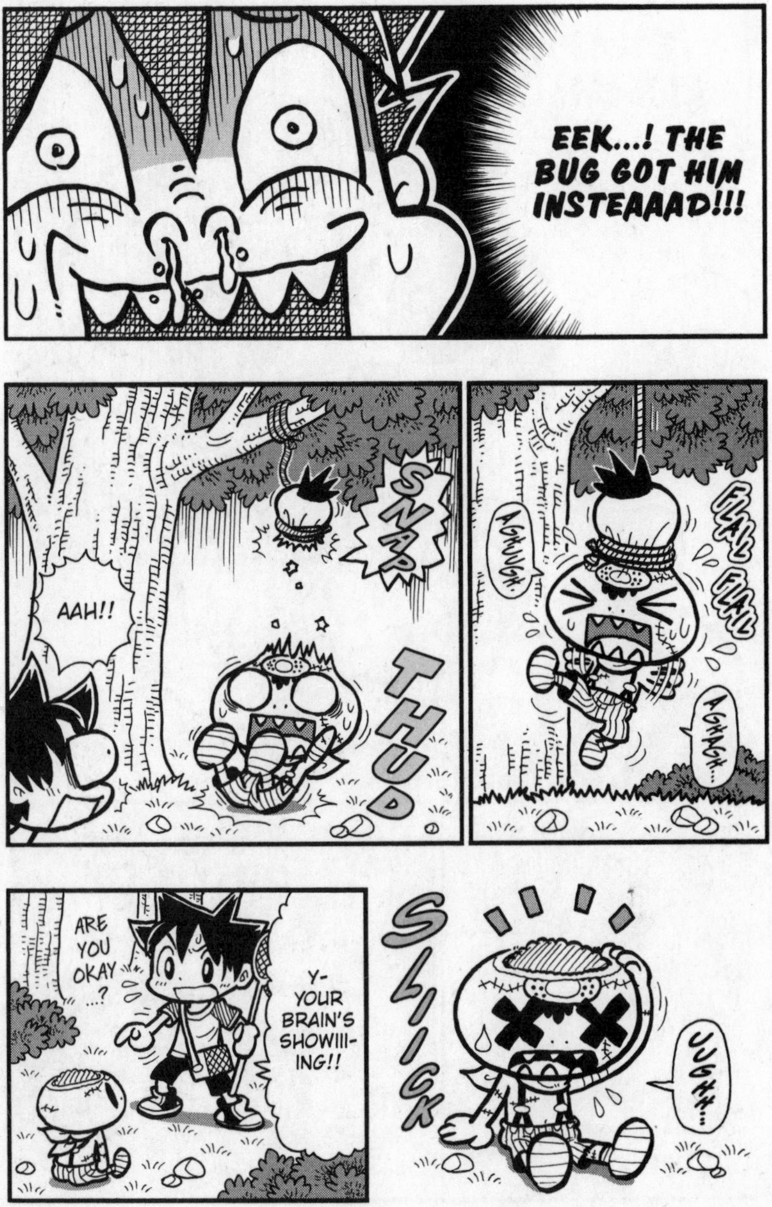
EEK...! THE BUG GOT HIM INSTEAAAD!!!
AGHUUGH.
FLAIL FLAIL
AGHAGH...
SNAP
THUD
AAH!!
SLICK
UGHHH...
ARE YOU OKAY ...?
Y-YOUR BRAIN'S SHOWIIII-ING!!

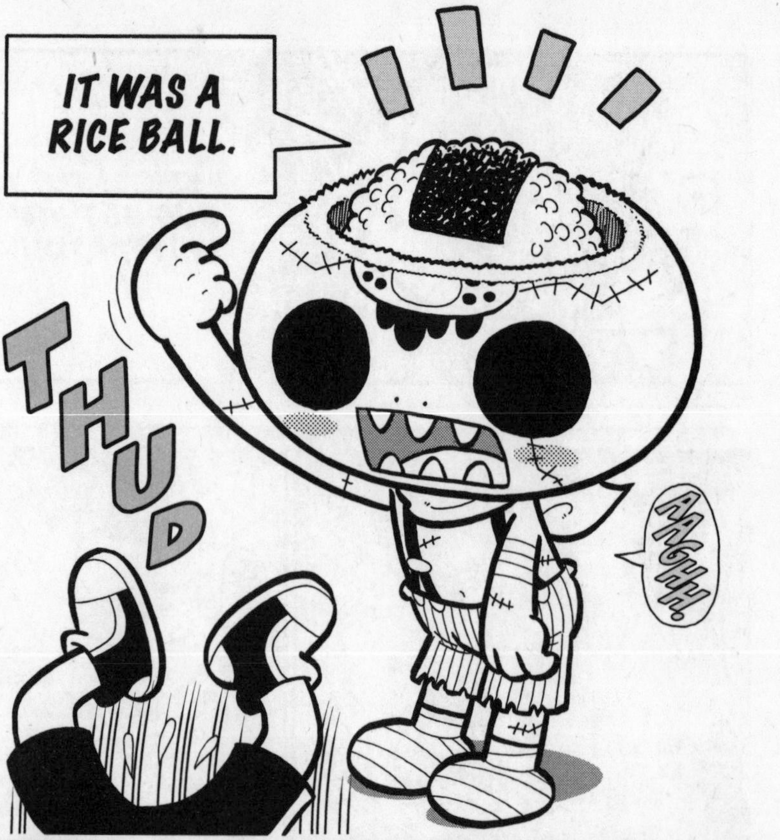
IT WAS A RICE BALL.
AAGHH!
THUD

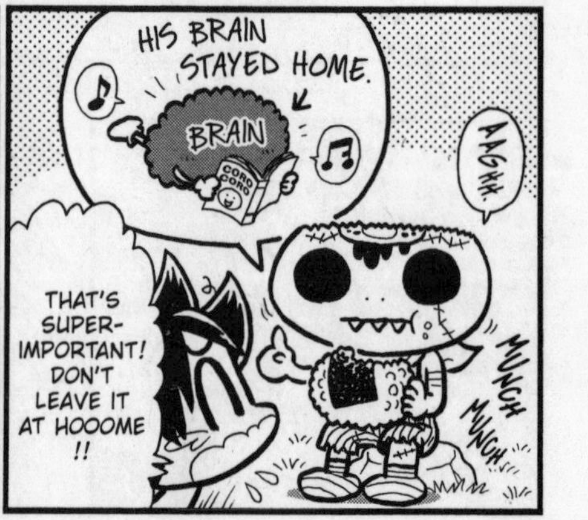
HIS BRAIN STAYED HOME.
BRAIN
CORO CORO
AAGHH.
THAT'S SUPER-IMPORTANT! DON'T LEAVE IT AT HOOOME!!
MUNCH
MUNCH

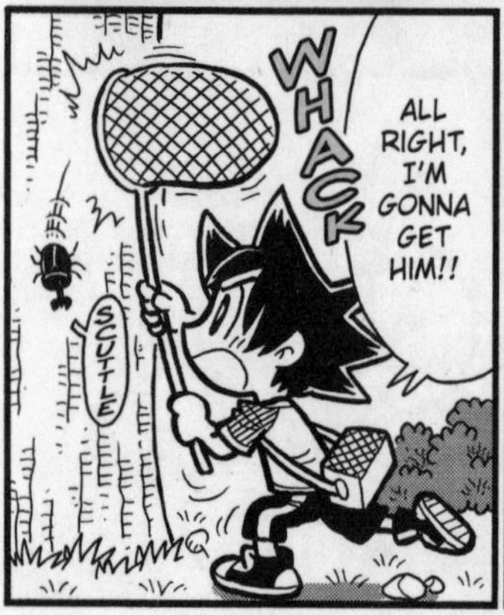
WHACK
ALL RIGHT, I'M GONNA GET HIM!!
SCUTTLE

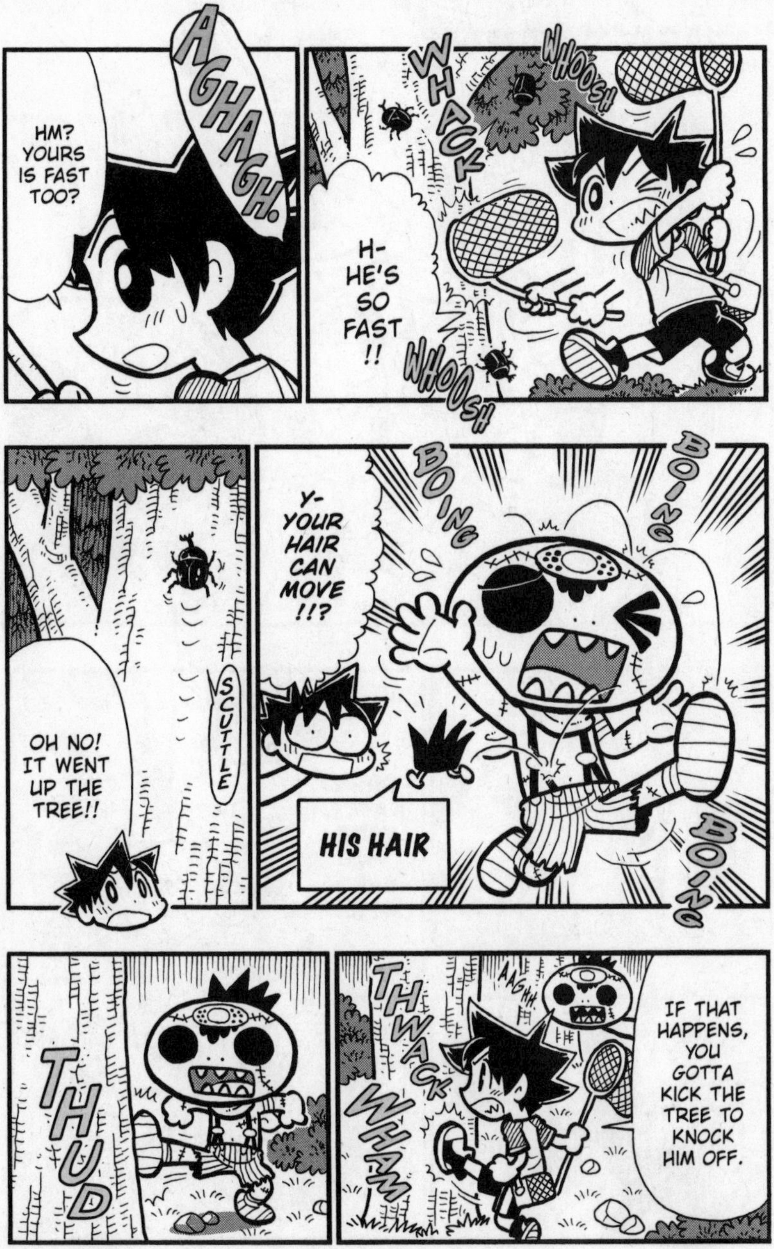
WHOOSH
WHACK
H-HE'S SO FAST!!
WHOOSH
AGHAGH.
HM? YOURS IS FAST TOO?
BOING
BOING
Y-YOUR HAIR CAN MOVE!!?
HIS HAIR
BOING
SCUTTLE
OH NO! IT WENT UP THE TREE!!
IF THAT HAPPENS, YOU GOTTA KICK THE TREE TO KNOCK HIM OFF.
AAGHH
THWACK
WHAM
THUD

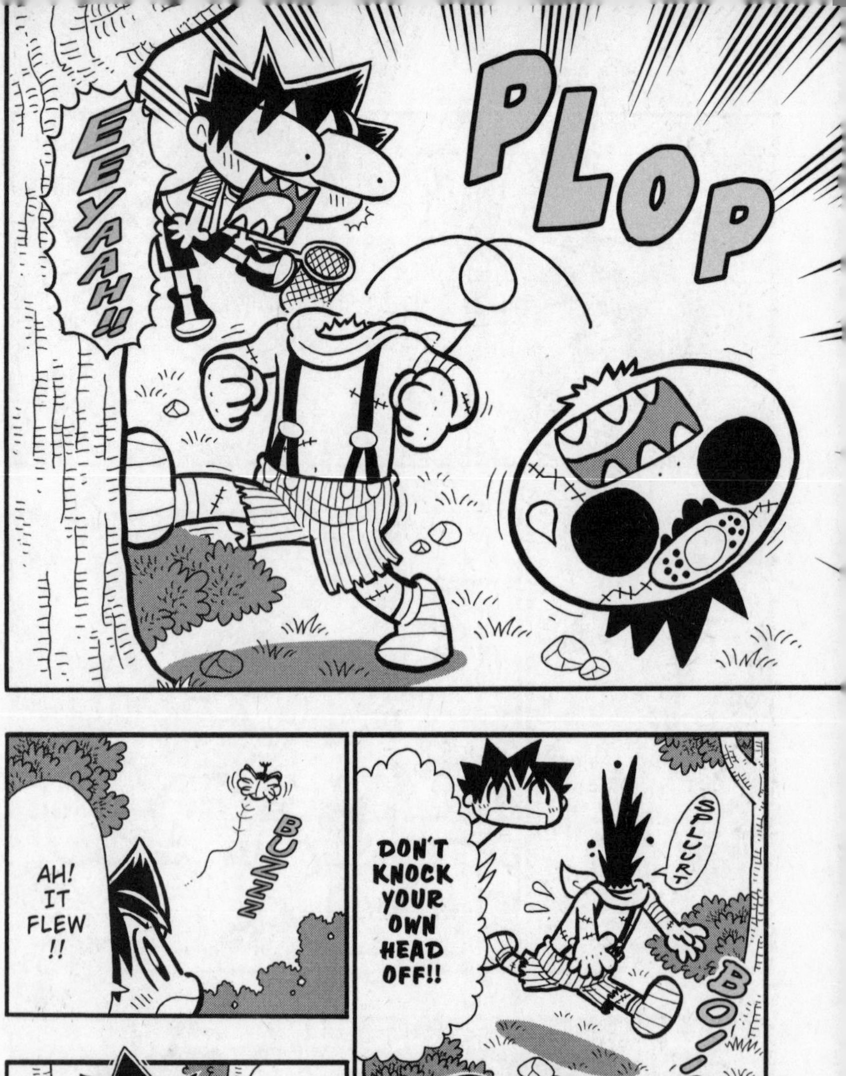
PLOP
EEYAAH!!
SPLURT
DON'T KNOCK YOUR OWN HEAD OFF!!
BOOING
BOOING
BUNNN
AH! IT FLEW!!
CRAP... IT GOT AWAY...

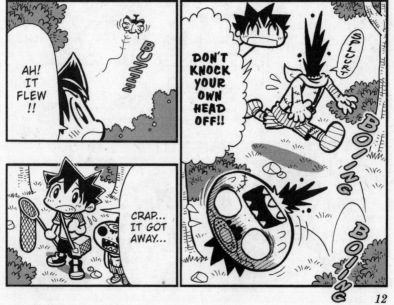

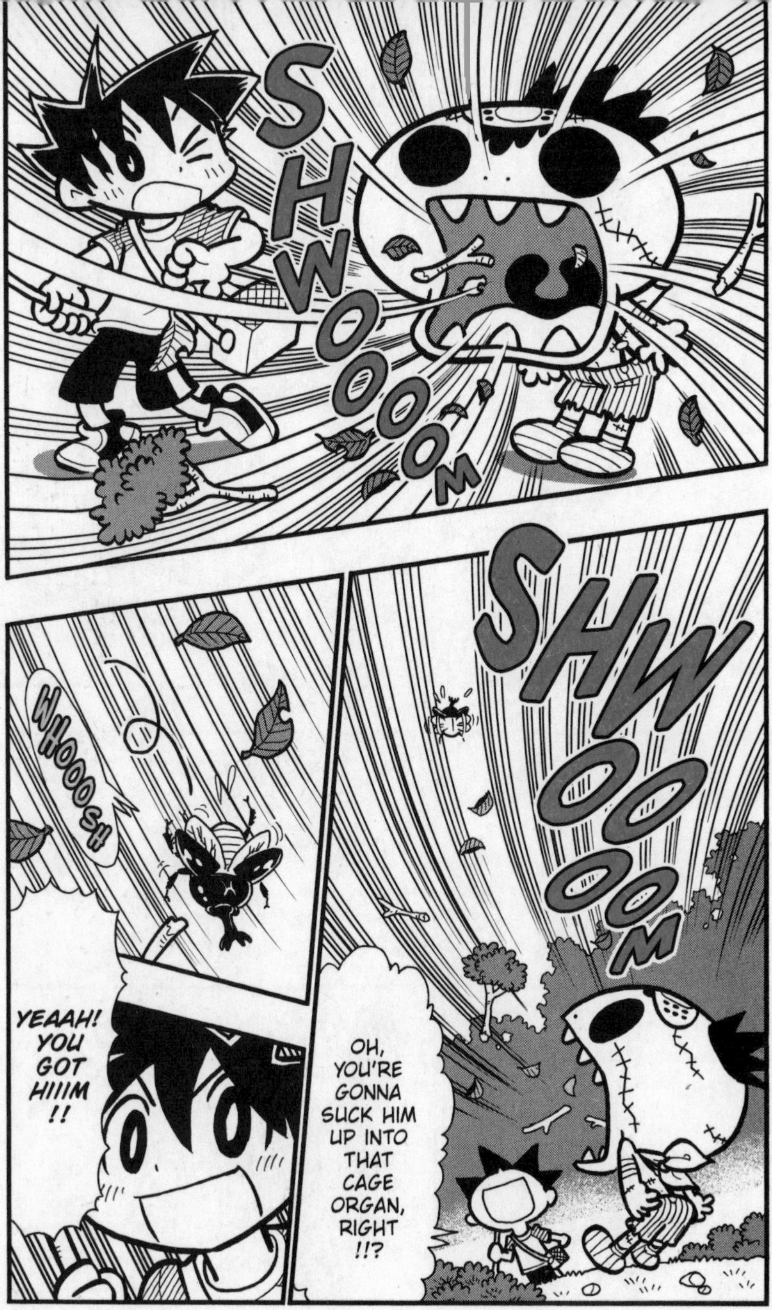
SHWOOOOOM
SHWOOOOOM
OH, YOU'RE GONNA SUCK HIM UP INTO THAT CAGE ORGAN, RIGHT!!?
WHOOOOSH
YEAAH! YOU GOT HIIIM!!

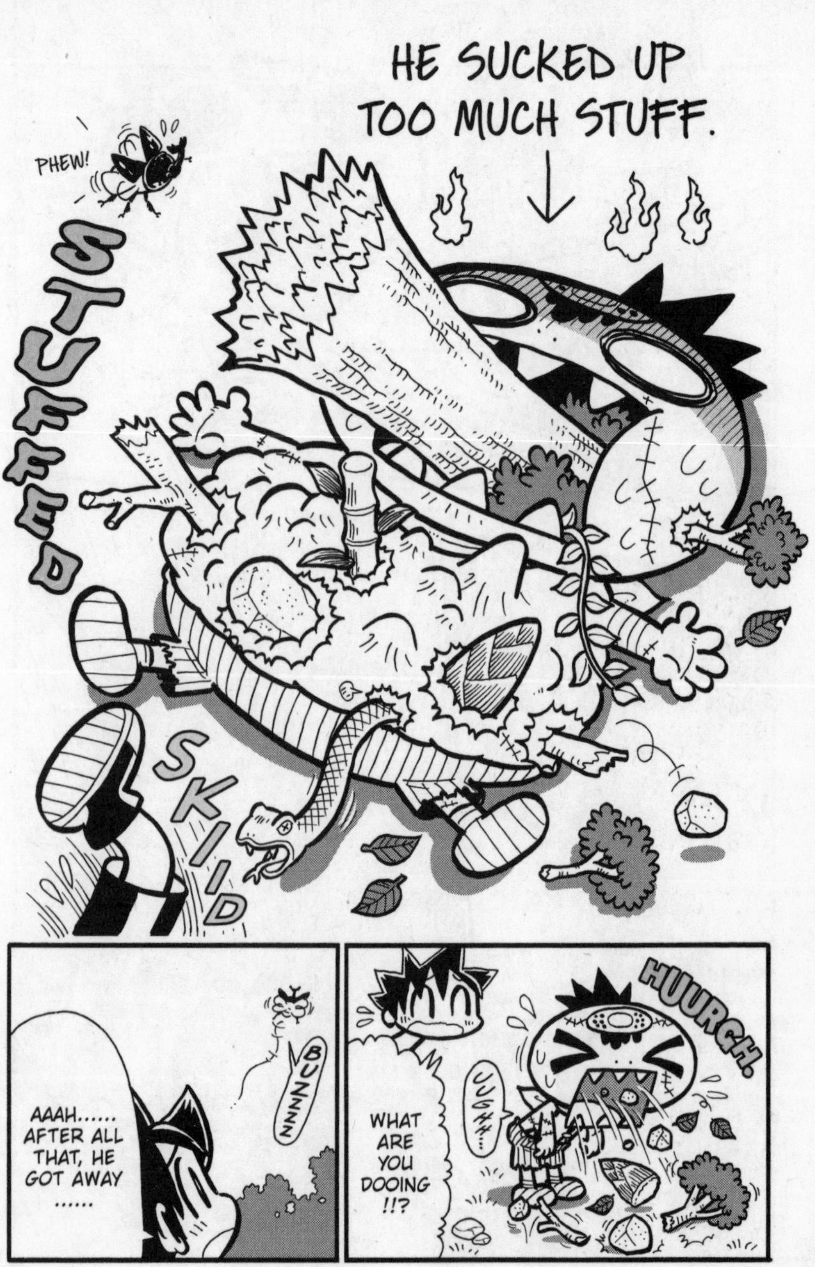
HE SUCKED UP TOO MUCH STUFF.
PHEW!
STUFFED
SKID
HUURGH.
UGGHH...
WHAT ARE YOU DOOING!!?
BUZZNNNN
AAAH...... AFTER ALL THAT, HE GOT AWAY ......

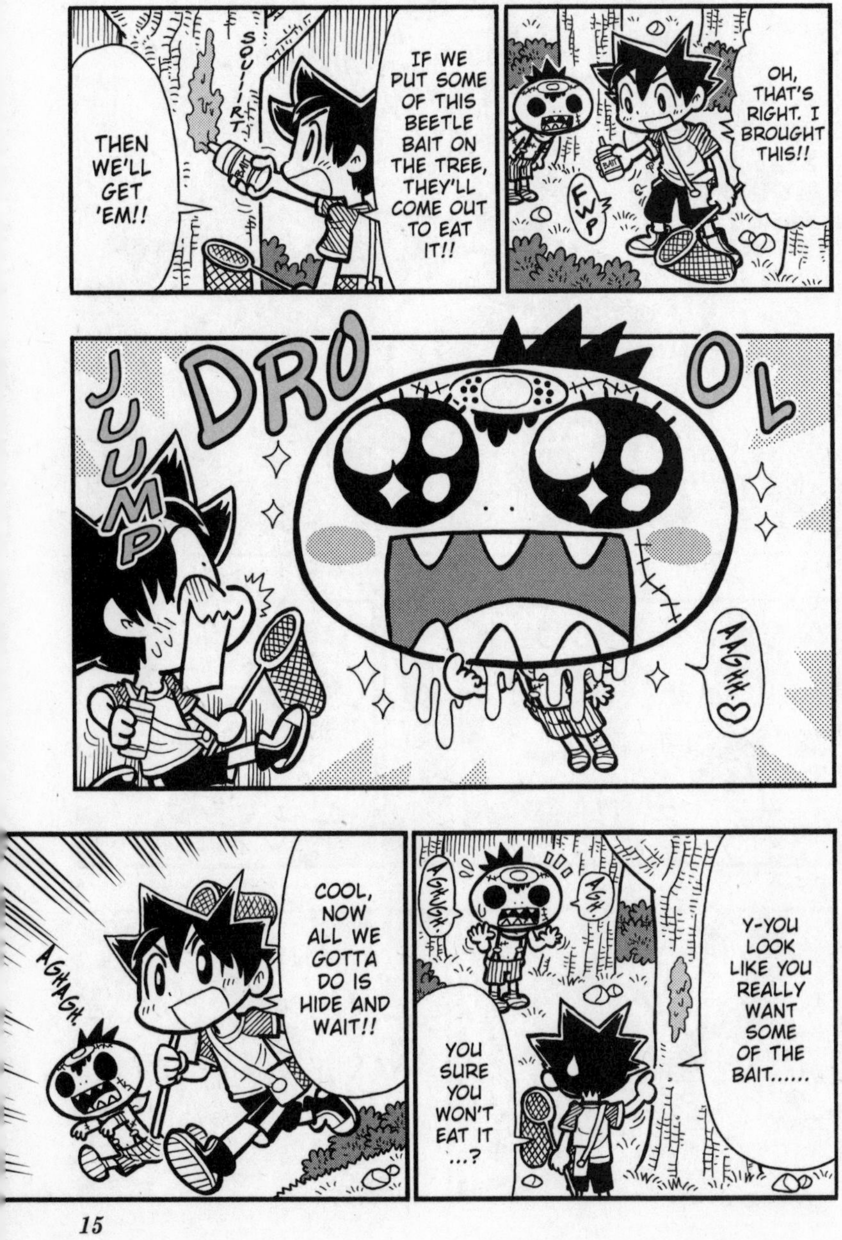
OH, THAT'S RIGHT. I BROUGHT THIS!!
FWP
BAIT
SQUIIIRT
IF WE PUT SOME OF THIS BEETLE BAIT ON THE TREE, THEY'LL COME OUT TO EAT IT!!
THEN WE'LL GET 'EM!!
DRO OL
JUUMP
AAGHH.♥
Y-YOU LOOK LIKE YOU REALLY WANT SOME OF THE BAIT......
AGH.
AGHUGH.
YOU SURE YOU WON'T EAT IT ...?
COOL, NOW ALL WE GOTTA DO IS HIDE AND WAIT!!
AGHAGH.

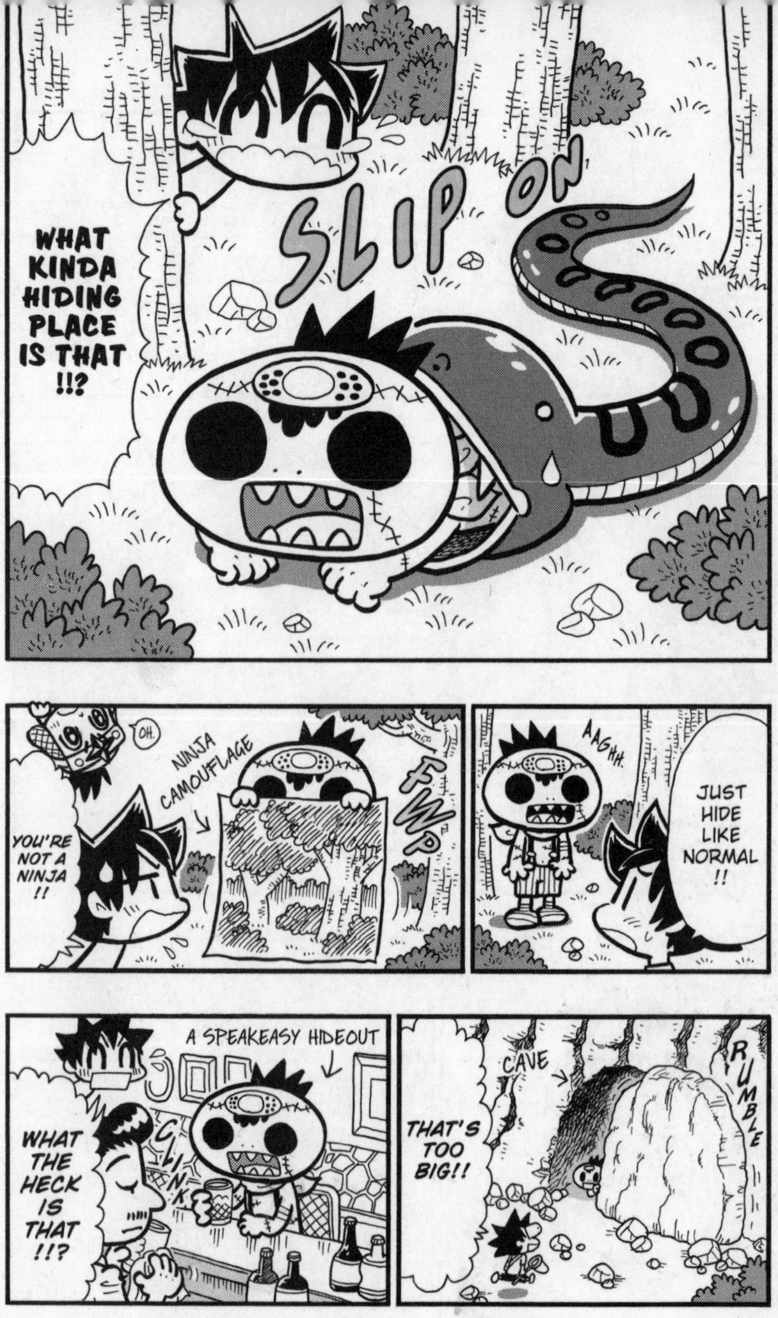
SLIP ON
WHAT KINDA HIDING PLACE IS THAT!!?
AAGHH.
JUST HIDE LIKE NORMAL!!
OH.
FWP
NINJA CAMOUFLAGE
YOU'RE NOT A NINJA!!
RUMBLE
CAVE
THAT'S TOO BIG!!
A SPEAKEASY HIDEOUT
CLINK
WHAT THE HECK IS THAT!!?

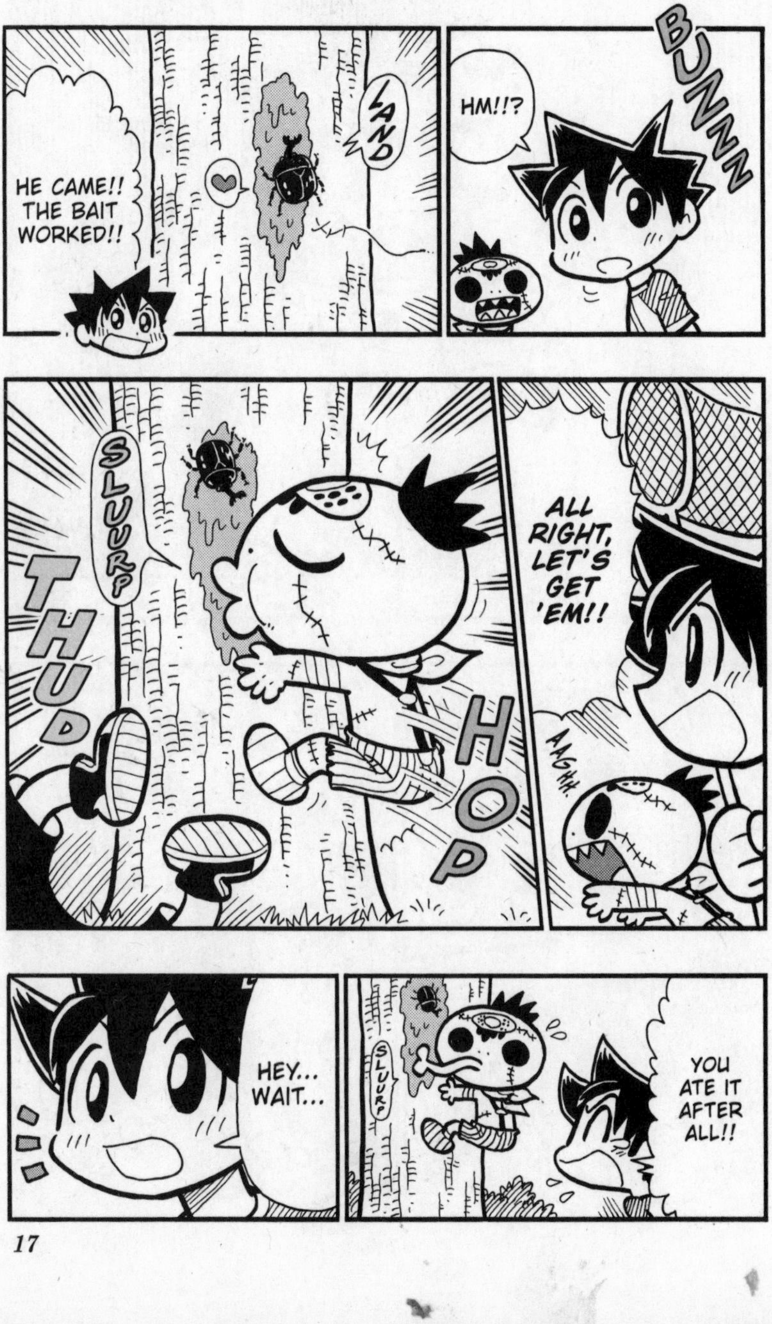
BUNNN
HM!!?
LAND
HE CAME!! THE BAIT WORKED!!
ALL RIGHT, LET'S GET 'EM!!
AAGHH
HOP
SLUURP
THUD
YOU ATE IT AFTER ALL!!
SLUURP
HEY... WAIT...

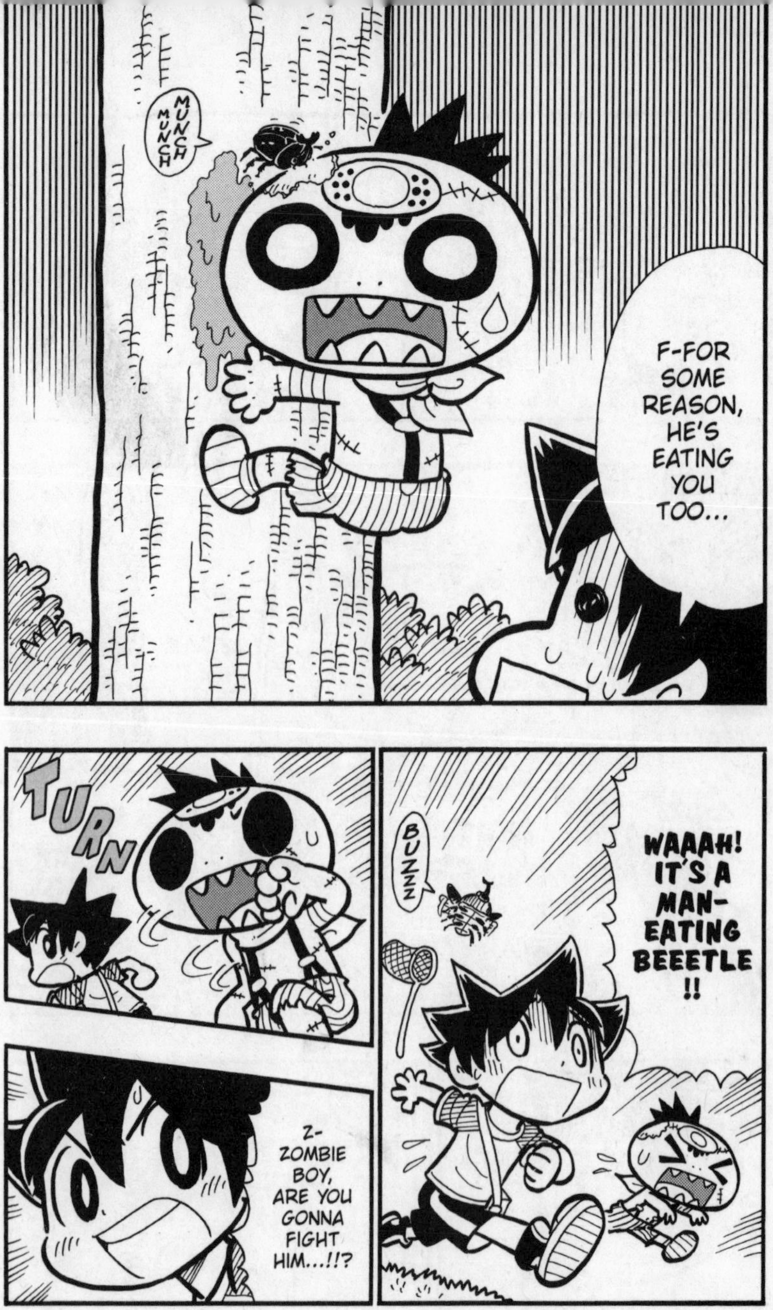
MUNCH MUNCH
F-FOR SOME REASON, HE'S EATING YOU TOO...
WAAAH! IT'S A MAN-EATING BEEETLE !!
BUZZZ
TURN
Z-ZOMBIE BOY, ARE YOU GONNA FIGHT HIM...!!?

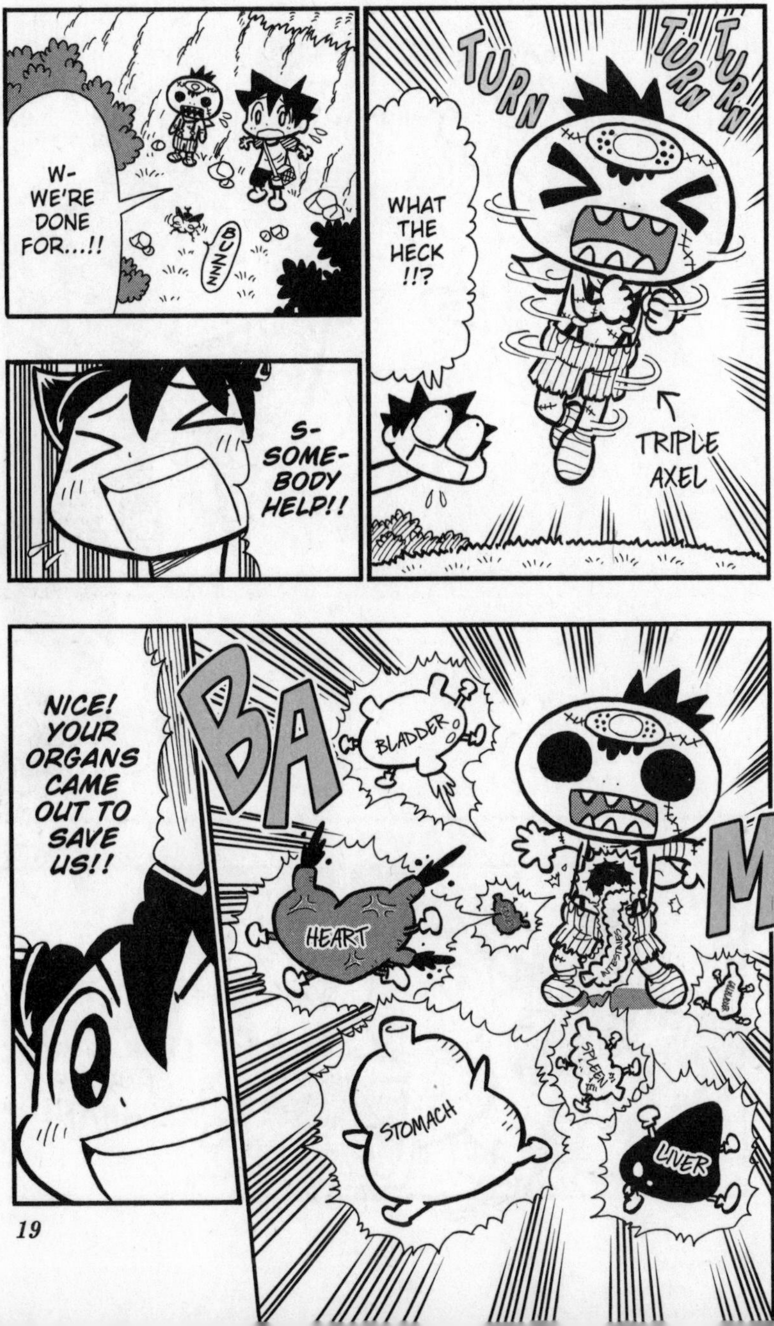

TURN TURN TURN
WHAT THE HECK!!?
TRIPLE AXEL
W-WE'RE DONE FOR...!!
BUZZZ
S-SOMEBODY HELP!!
BAM
NICE! YOUR ORGANS CAME OUT TO SAVE US!!
BLADDER
HEART
INTESTINES
SPLEEN
STOMACH
LIVER

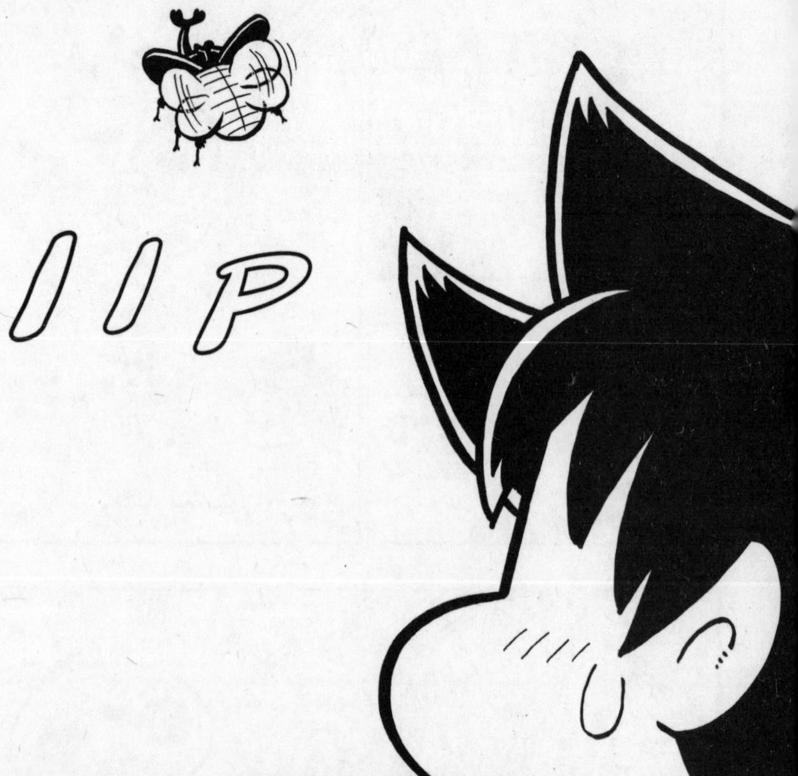
IIP

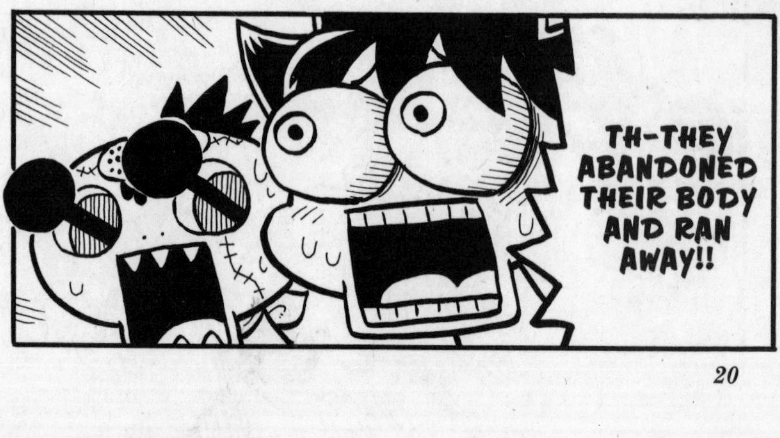
TH-THEY ABANDONED THEIR BODY AND RAN AWAY!!

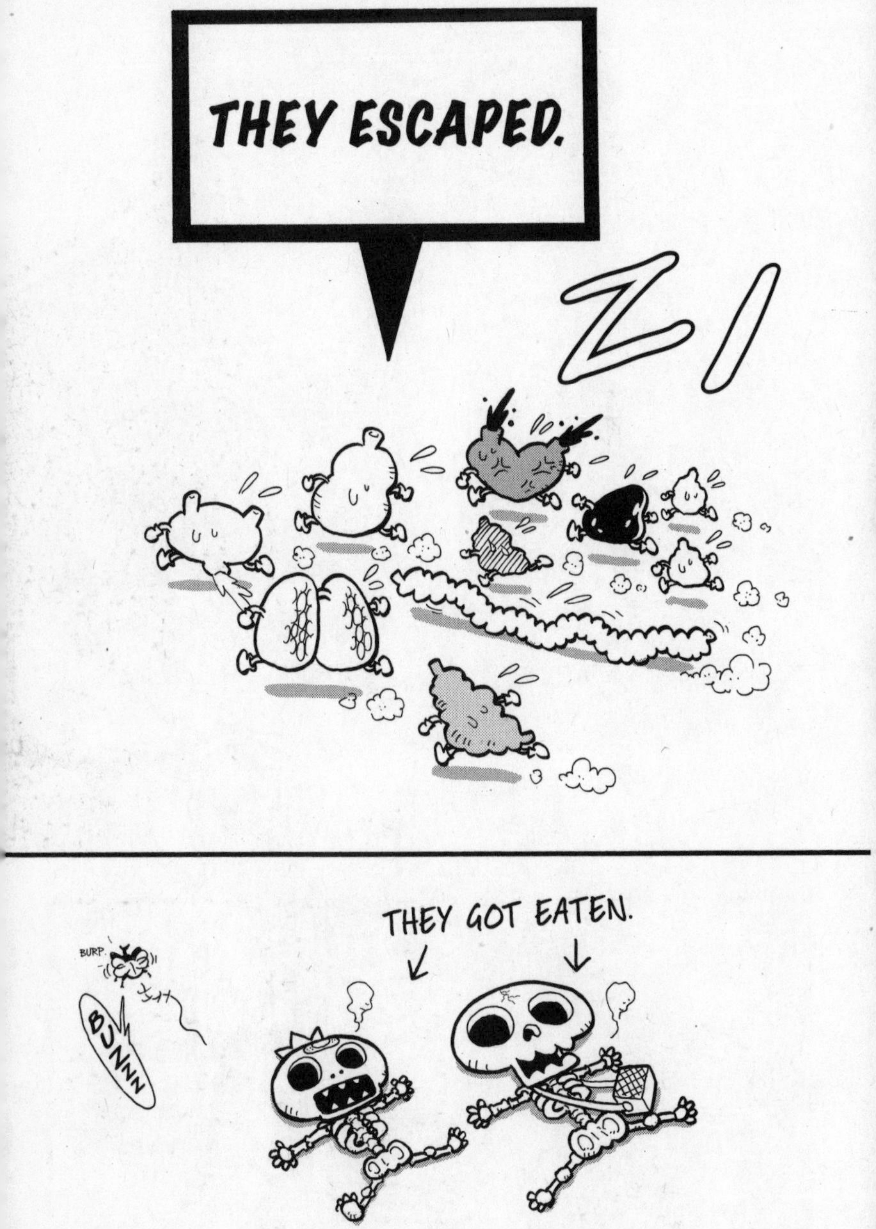
THEY ESCAPED.
ZI
THEY GOT EATEN.
BURP.
BUNNN

CATCH YA LATER!!
OCTOSKY

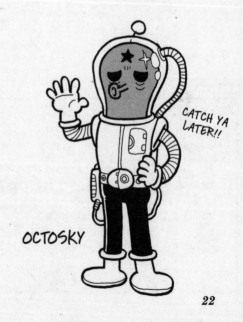

FEELING ZICK REALLY ZTINKZ!

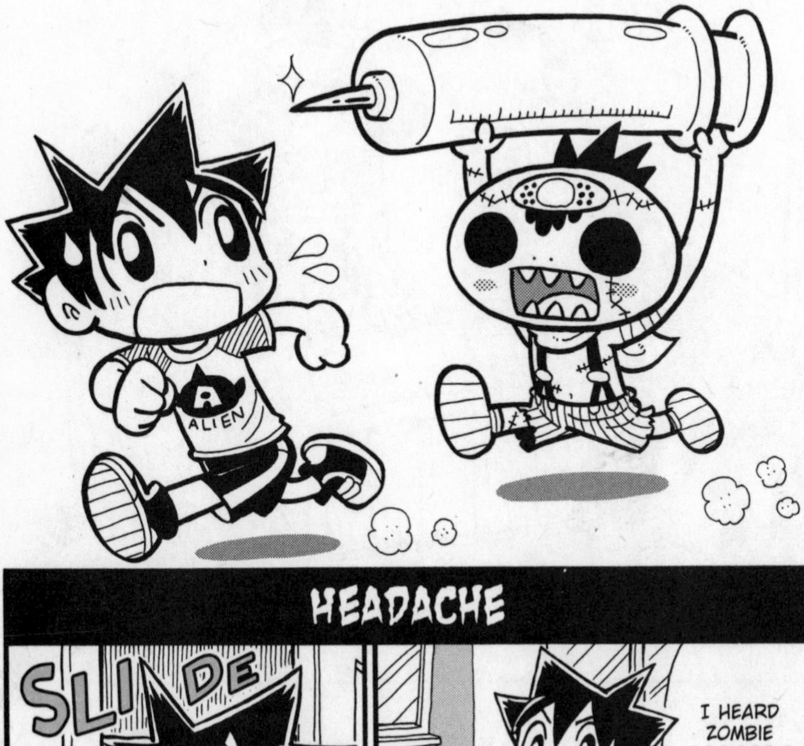
ALIEN

HEADACHE

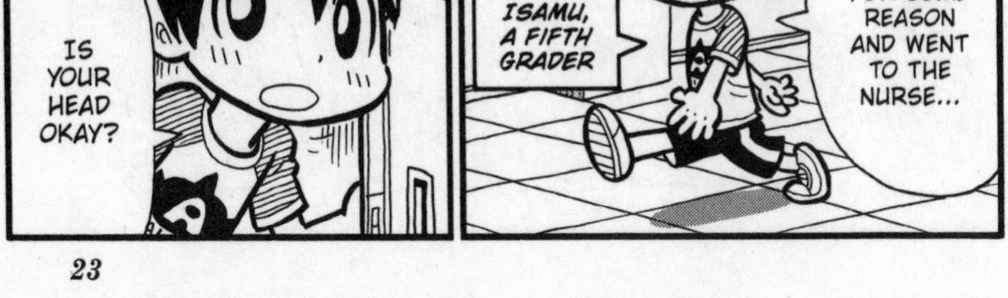
I HEARD ZOMBIE BOY GOT A HEADACHE FOR SOME REASON AND WENT TO THE NURSE...
ISAMU, A FIFTH GRADER
SLIDE
IS YOUR HEAD OKAY?

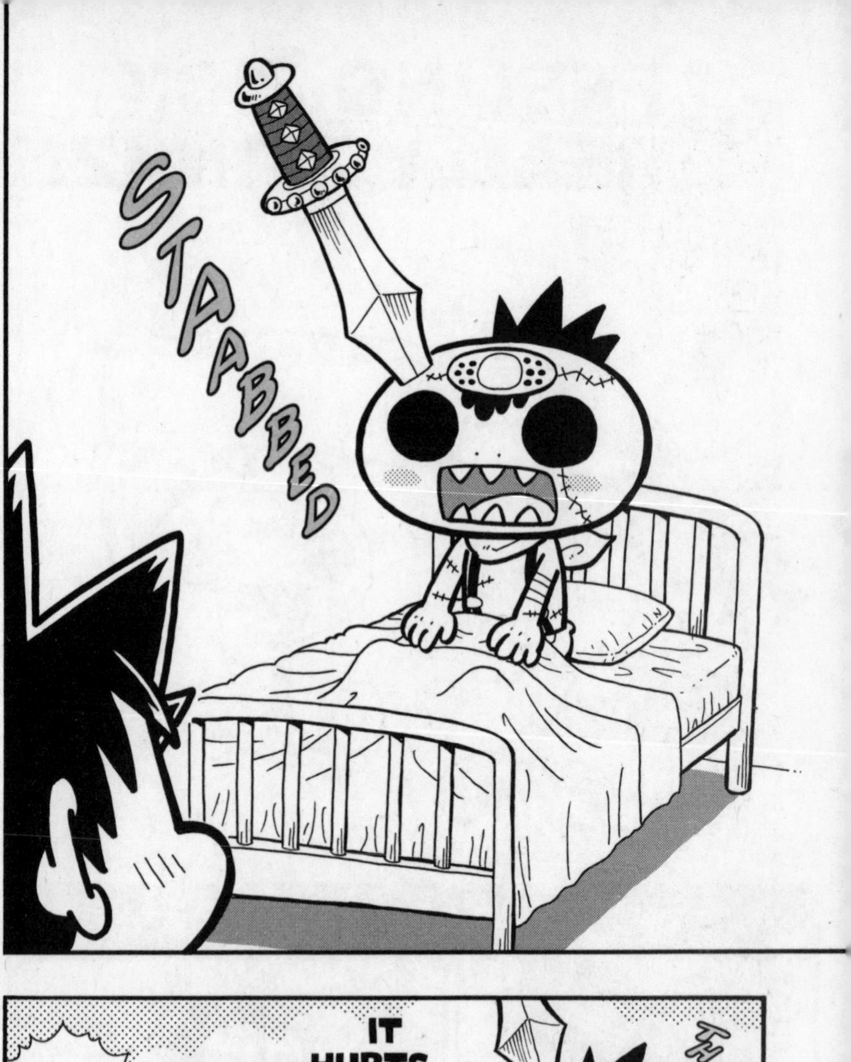
STABBED
THROB THROB
UGHH!
IT HURTS...
TAKE IT OUT!
THE REASON'S SUPER-OBVIOUS!!

STOMACHACHE

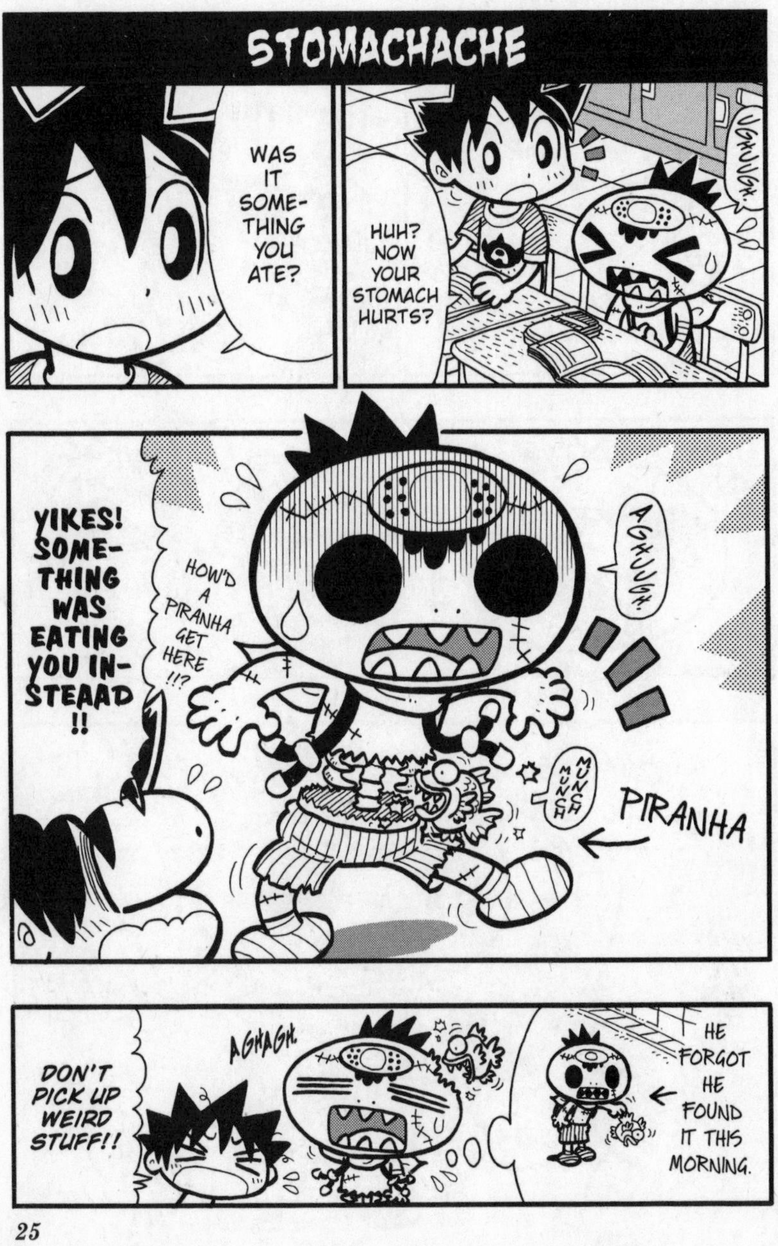
UGXUUGH.
HUH? NOW YOUR STOMACH HURTS?
WAS IT SOME-THING YOU ATE?
AGXUUGH.
MUNCH MUNCH
PIRANHA
HOW'D A PIRANHA GET HERE !!?
YIKES! SOME-THING WAS EATING YOU IN-STEAAD !!
HE FORGOT HE FOUND IT THIS MORNING.
AGHAGH.
DON'T PICK UP WEIRD STUFF!!

BROKEN BONES

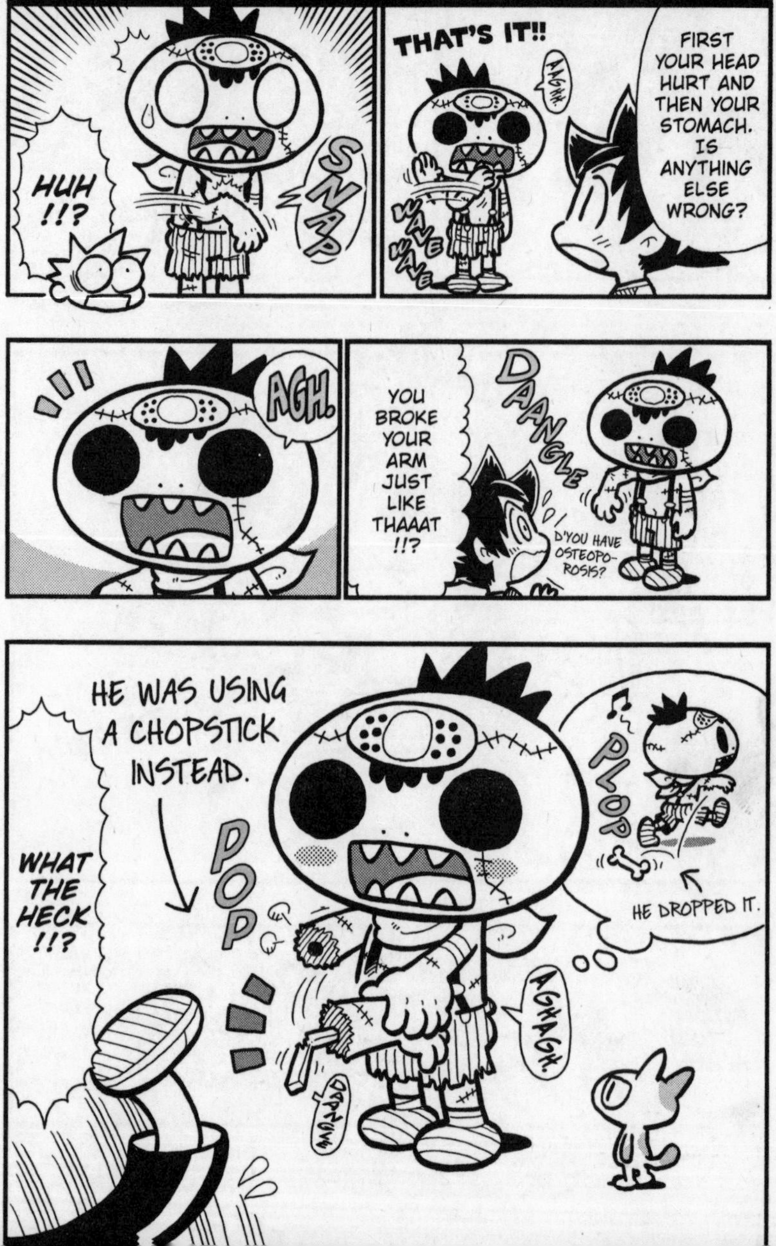
FIRST YOUR HEAD HURT AND THEN YOUR STOMACH. IS ANYTHING ELSE WRONG?
THAT'S IT!!
AAGHH.
WAVE WAVE
SNAP
HUH!!?
DAANGLE
YOU BROKE YOUR ARM JUST LIKE THAAAT!!?
D'YOU HAVE OSTEOPOROSIS?
AGH.
PLOP
HE DROPPED IT.
HE WAS USING A CHOPSTICK INSTEAD.
POP
AGHAGH.
WHAT THE HECK!!?

TIRED EYES

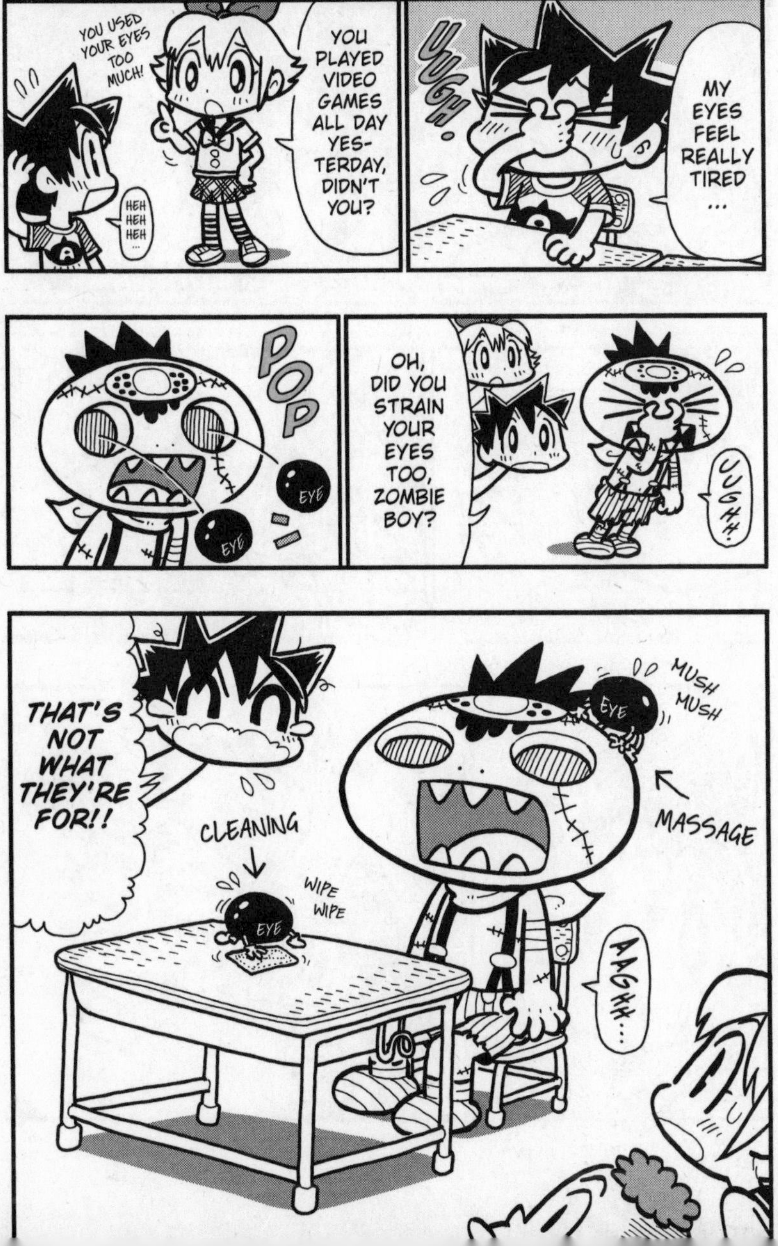
UUGH
MY EYES FEEL REALLY TIRED...
YOU PLAYED VIDEO GAMES ALL DAY YES-TERDAY, DIDN'T YOU?
YOU USED YOUR EYES TOO MUCH!
HEH HEH HEH...
OH, DID YOU STRAIN YOUR EYES TOO, ZOMBIE BOY?
UUGHH!
POP
EYE
EYE
MUSH MUSH
EYE
MASSAGE
AAGHH...
THAT'S NOT WHAT THEY'RE FOR!!
CLEANING
WIPE WIPE
EYE

DIZZINESS

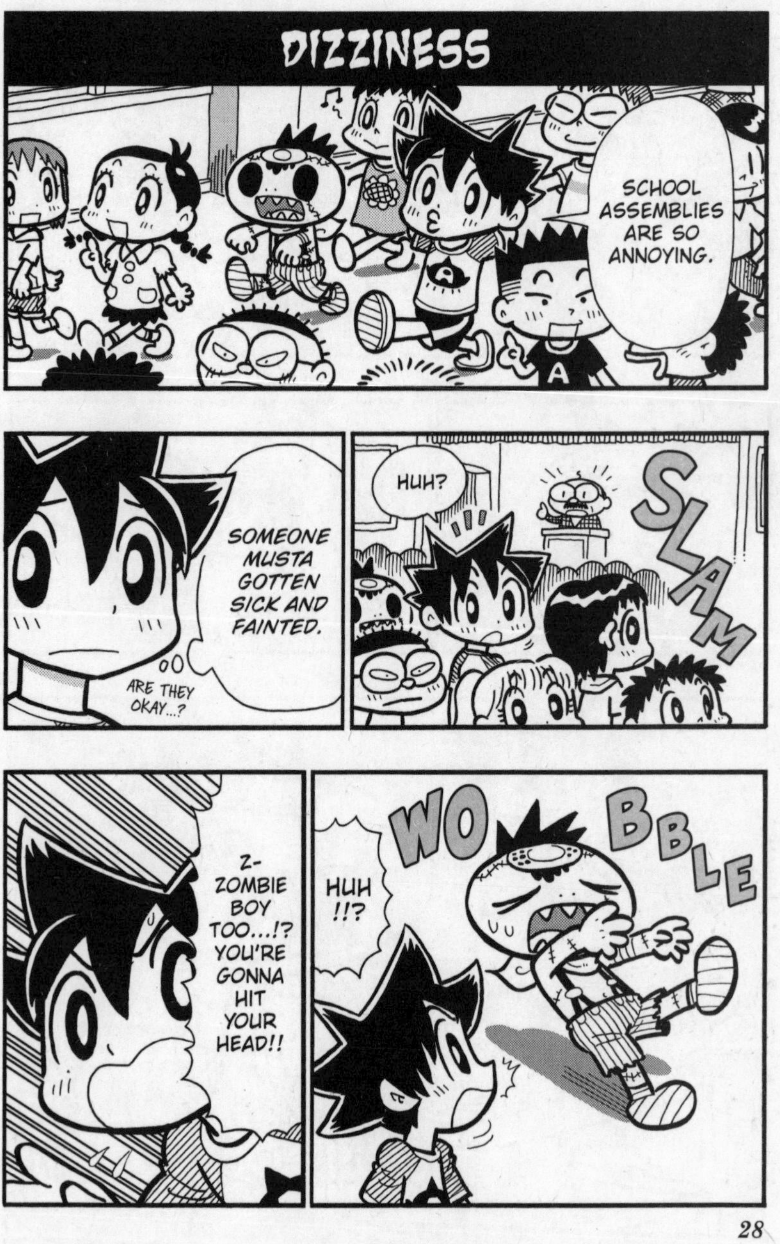
SCHOOL ASSEMBLIES ARE SO ANNOYING.
HUH?
SLAM
SOMEONE MUSTA GOTTEN SICK AND FAINTED.
ARE THEY OKAY...?
WOBBLE
HUH!!?
Z-ZOMBIE BOY TOO...!? YOU'RE GONNA HIT YOUR HEAD!!

RIP
FWOOP
POOMF
YOU'VE GOT AIRBAGS !!?
AIRBAG

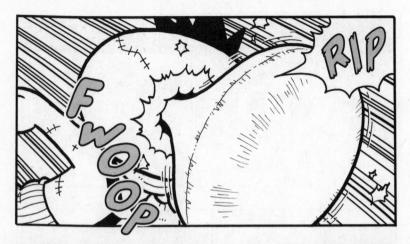

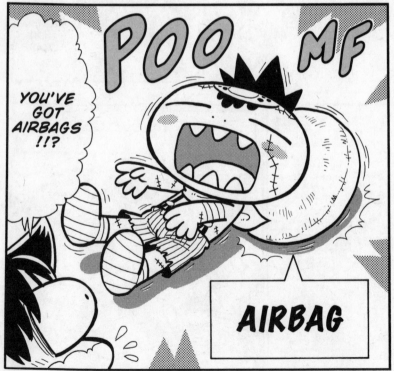

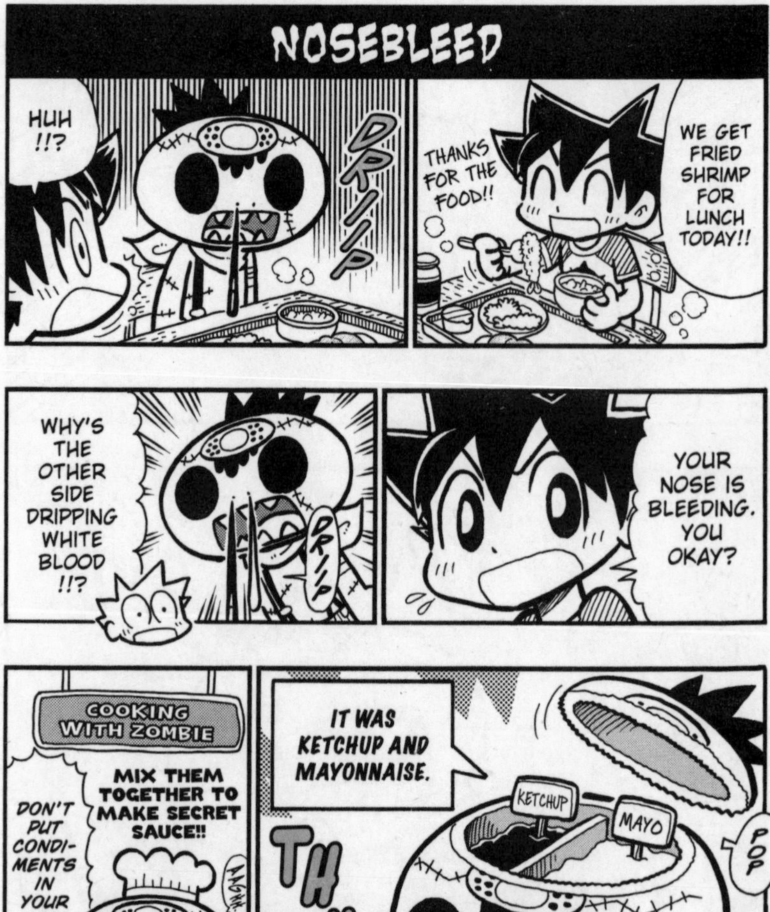
NOSEBLEED
WE GET FRIED SHRIMP FOR LUNCH TODAY!!
THANKS FOR THE FOOD!!
DRIP
HUH !!?
YOUR NOSE IS BLEEDING. YOU OKAY?
WHY'S THE OTHER SIDE DRIPPING WHITE BLOOD !!?
DRIP
IT WAS KETCHUP AND MAYONNAISE.
POP
KETCHUP
MAYO
THUD
PUDDING
COOKING WITH ZOMBIE
MIX THEM TOGETHER TO MAKE SECRET SAUCE!!
DON'T PUT CONDI-MENTS IN YOUR HEAD !!
GOOD ON FRIED SHRIMP!

CAVITIES

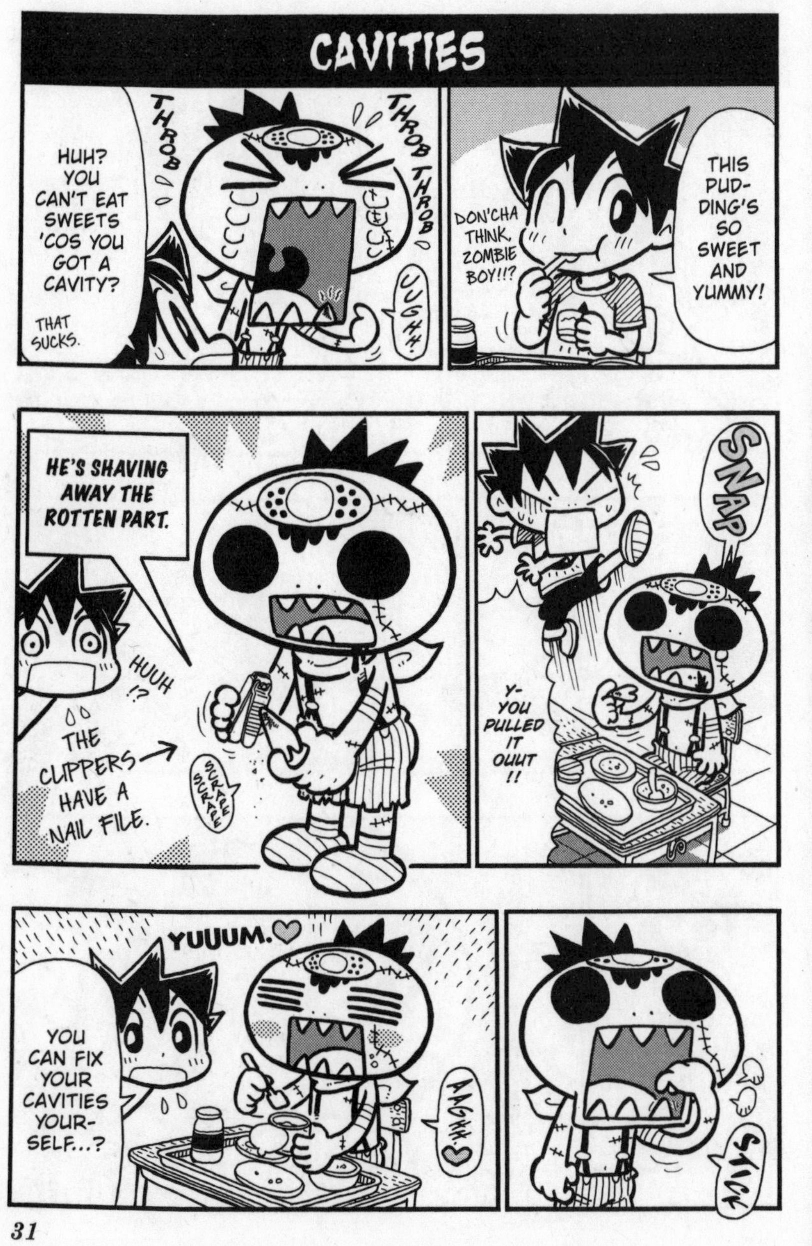

THIS PUD-DING'S SO SWEET AND YUMMY!
DON'CHA THINK, ZOMBIE BOY!!?
THROB
THROB THROB
HUH? YOU CAN'T EAT SWEETS 'COS YOU GOT A CAVITY?
THAT SUCKS.
UUGHH.
SNAP
Y-YOU PULLED IT OUUT!!
HE'S SHAVING AWAY THE ROTTEN PART.
HUUH!?
THE CLIPPERS HAVE A NAIL FILE.
SCRAPE SCRAPE
STICK
YUUUM.♡
YOU CAN FIX YOUR CAVITIES YOUR-SELF...?
AAGHH.♡

SCRAPES

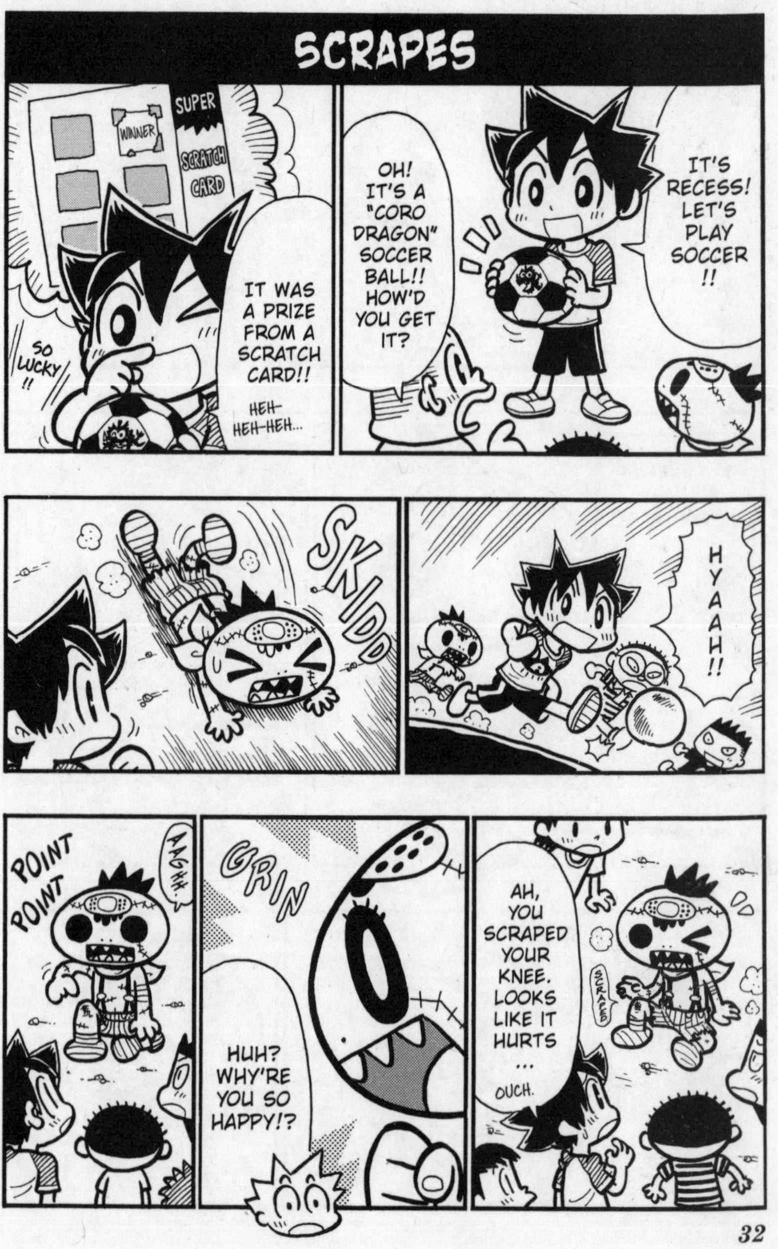
IT'S RECESS! LET'S PLAY SOCCER!!
OH! IT'S A "CORO DRAGON" SOCCER BALL!! HOW'D YOU GET IT?
SUPER SCRATCH CARD
WINNER
IT WAS A PRIZE FROM A SCRATCH CARD!!
HEH-HEH-HEH...
SO LUCKY!!
HYAAAH!!
SKIDD
AH, YOU SCRAPED YOUR KNEE. LOOKS LIKE IT HURTS...
OUCH.
SCRAPED
GRIN
HUH? WHY'RE YOU SO HAPPY!?
AAGHH.
POINT POINT

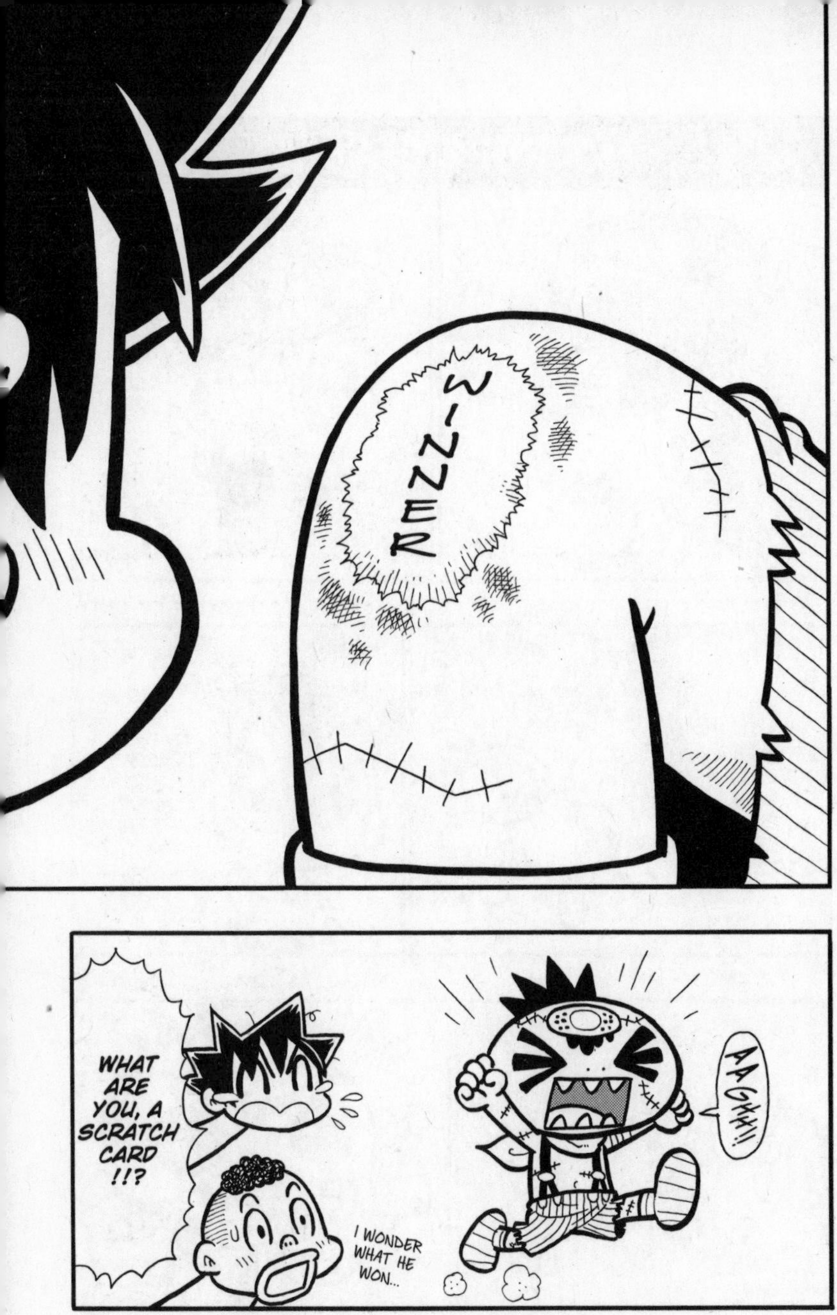
WINNER
AAGHH!!
WHAT ARE YOU, A SCRATCH CARD !!?
I WONDER WHAT HE WON...

MOTION SICKNESS

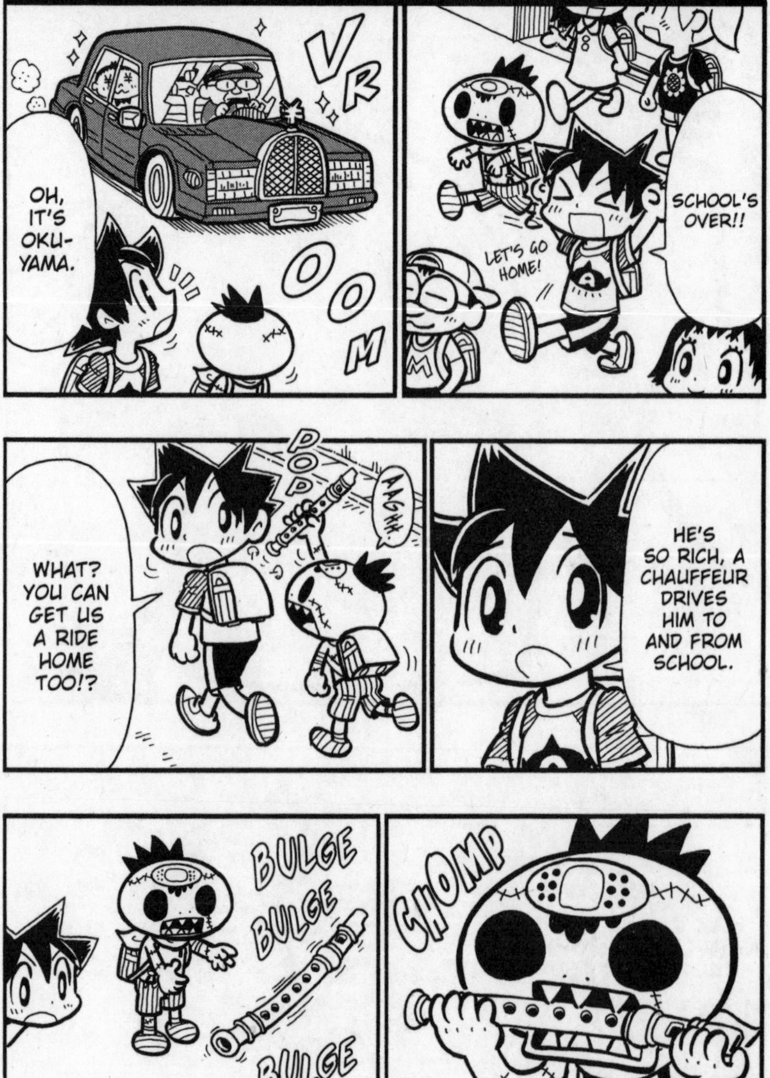

SCHOOL'S OVER!!
LET'S GO HOME!
VROOOM
OH, IT'S OKU-YAMA.
HE'S SO RICH, A CHAUFFEUR DRIVES HIM TO AND FROM SCHOOL.
POP
AAGH.
WHAT? YOU CAN GET US A RIDE HOME TOO!?
CHOMP
BULGE
BULGE
BULGE

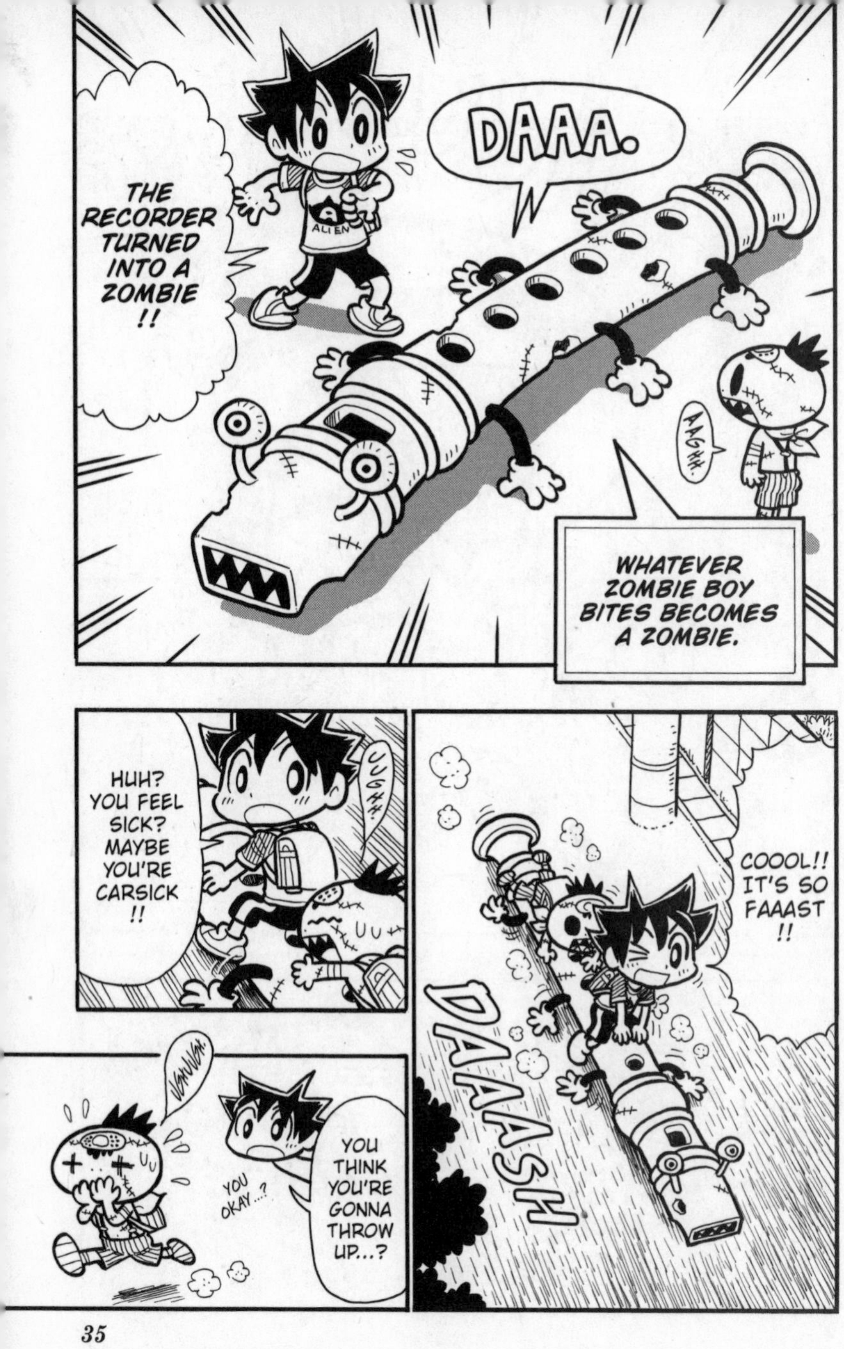
DAAA.
THE RECORDER TURNED INTO A ZOMBIE!!
AAGHH.
WHATEVER ZOMBIE BOY BITES BECOMES A ZOMBIE.
COOOL!! IT'S SO FAAAST!!
DAAASH
HUH? YOU FEEL SICK? MAYBE YOU'RE CARSICK!!
UGGHH.
YOU THINK YOU'RE GONNA THROW UP...?
YOU OKAY...?

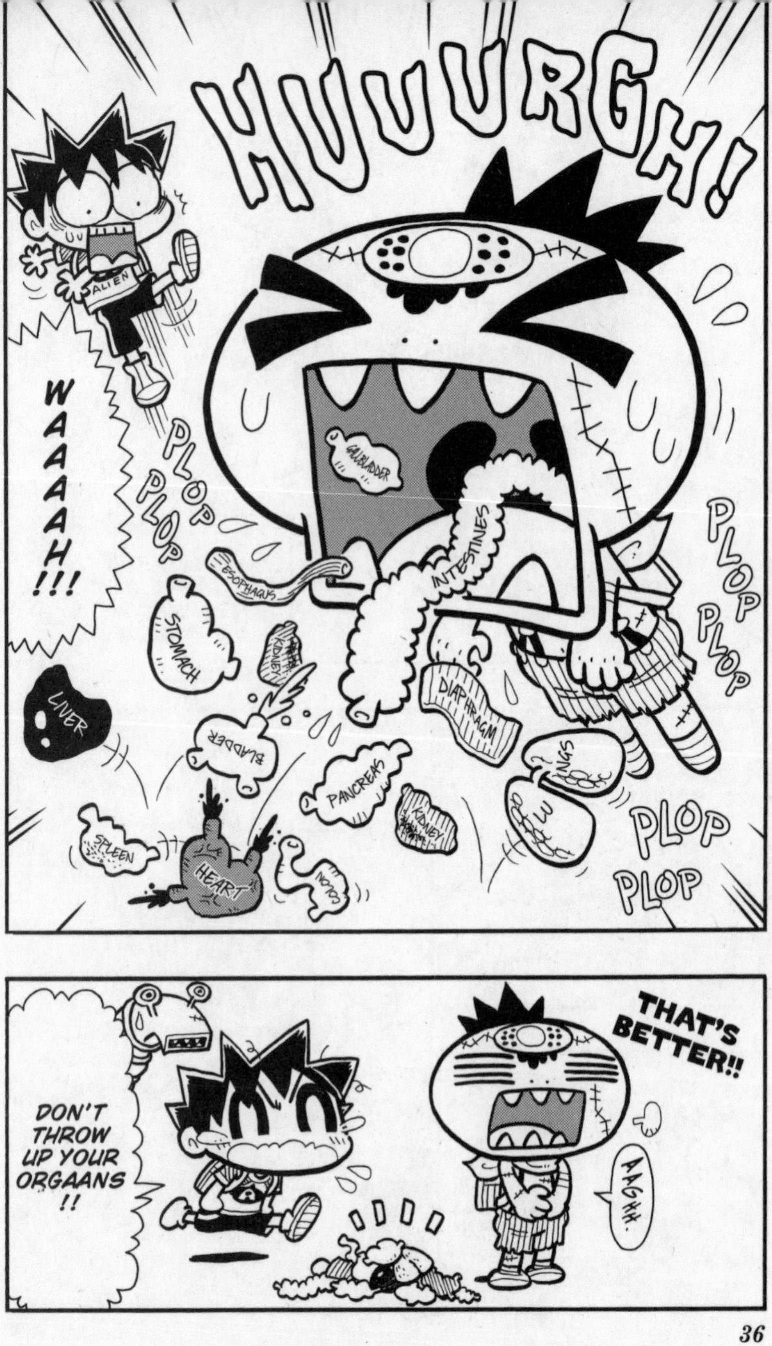
HUUURGH!
PLOP PLOP
PLOP PLOP
GALLBLADDER
INTESTINES
ESOPHAGUS
DIAPHRAGM
KIDNEY
STOMACH
PLOP PLOP
WAAAAAH!!!
LIVER
BLADDER
PANCREAS
KIDNEY
LU NGS
PLOP
PLOP
SPLEEN
HEART
COLON
THAT'S BETTER!!
AAGHH.
DON'T THROW UP YOUR ORGAANS!!

MOSQUITO
SQUITO! HO-HO!
BYE-BYE.
BOXSTER #1

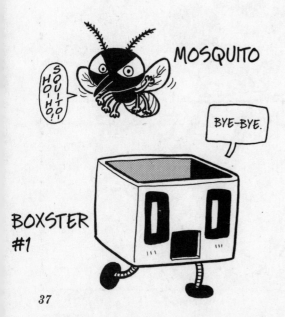

IT'Z CLEANUP TIME!

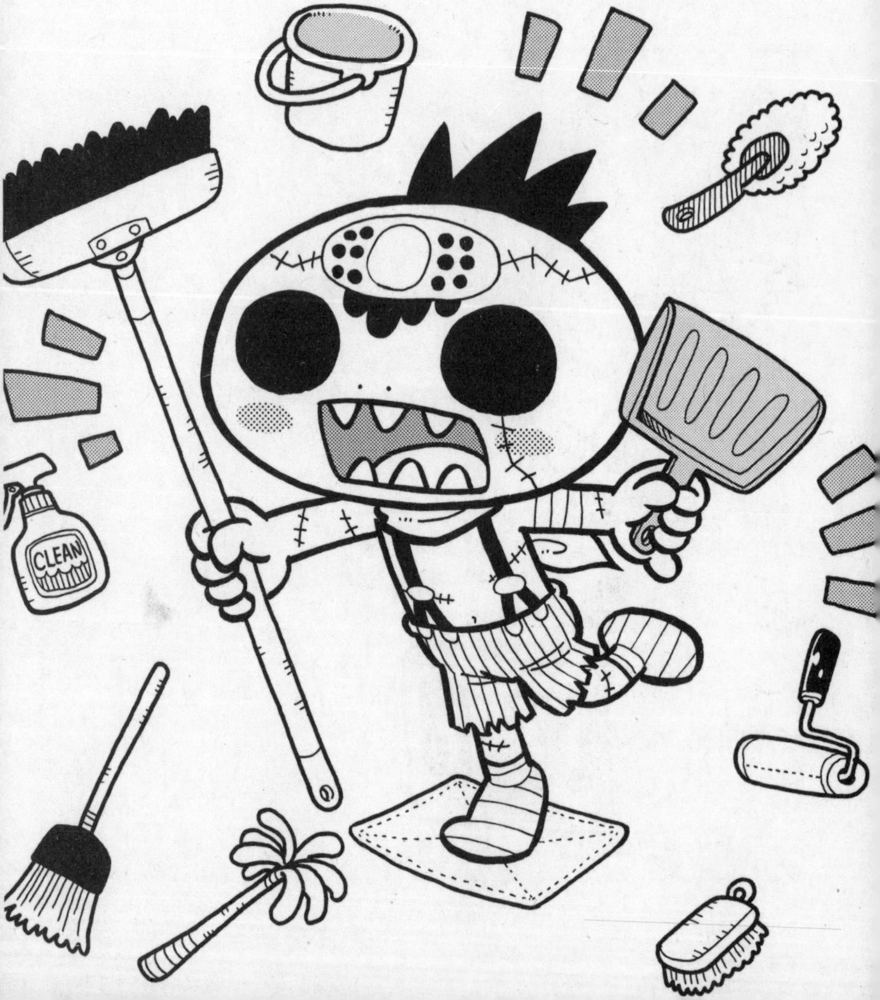
CLEAN

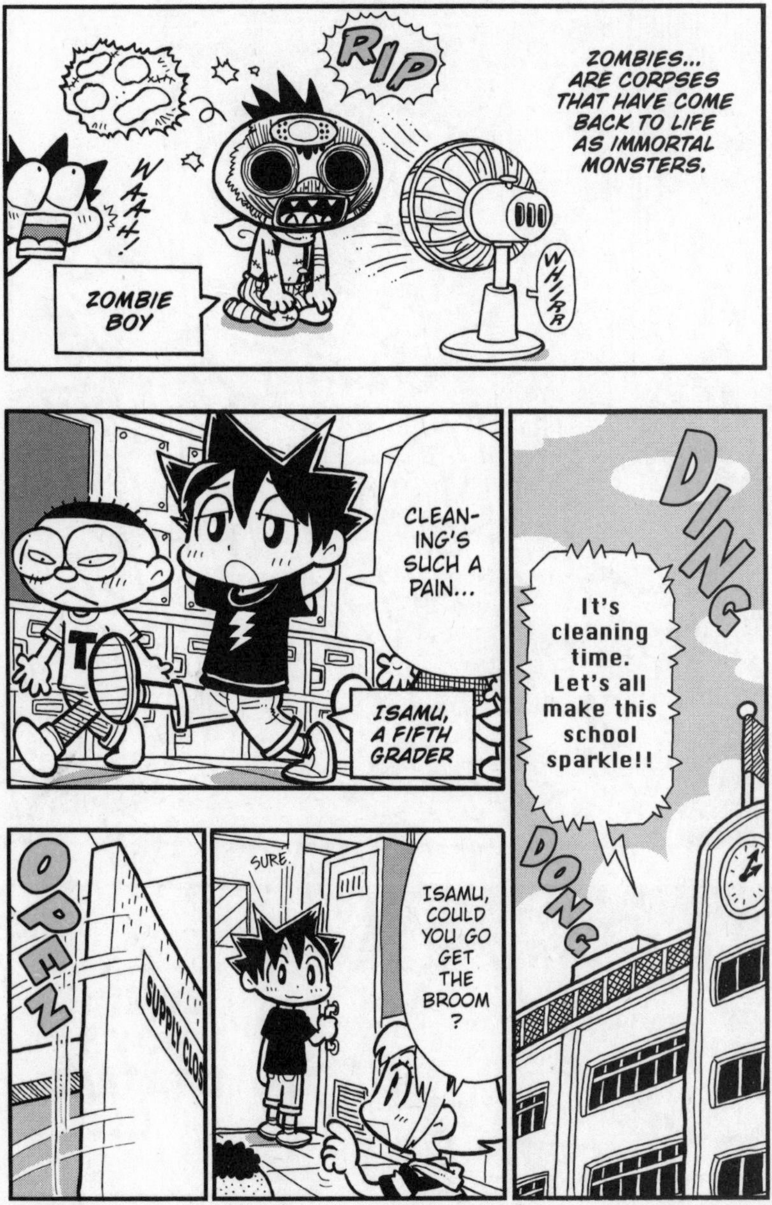
ZOMBIES... ARE CORPSES THAT HAVE COME BACK TO LIFE AS IMMORTAL MONSTERS.
RIP
WAAAH!
WHIRR
ZOMBIE BOY
DING
It's cleaning time. Let's all make this school sparkle!!
DONG
CLEAN-ING'S SUCH A PAIN...
ISAMU, A FIFTH GRADER
ISAMU, COULD YOU GO GET THE BROOM?
SURE.
OPEN
SUPPLY CLOS

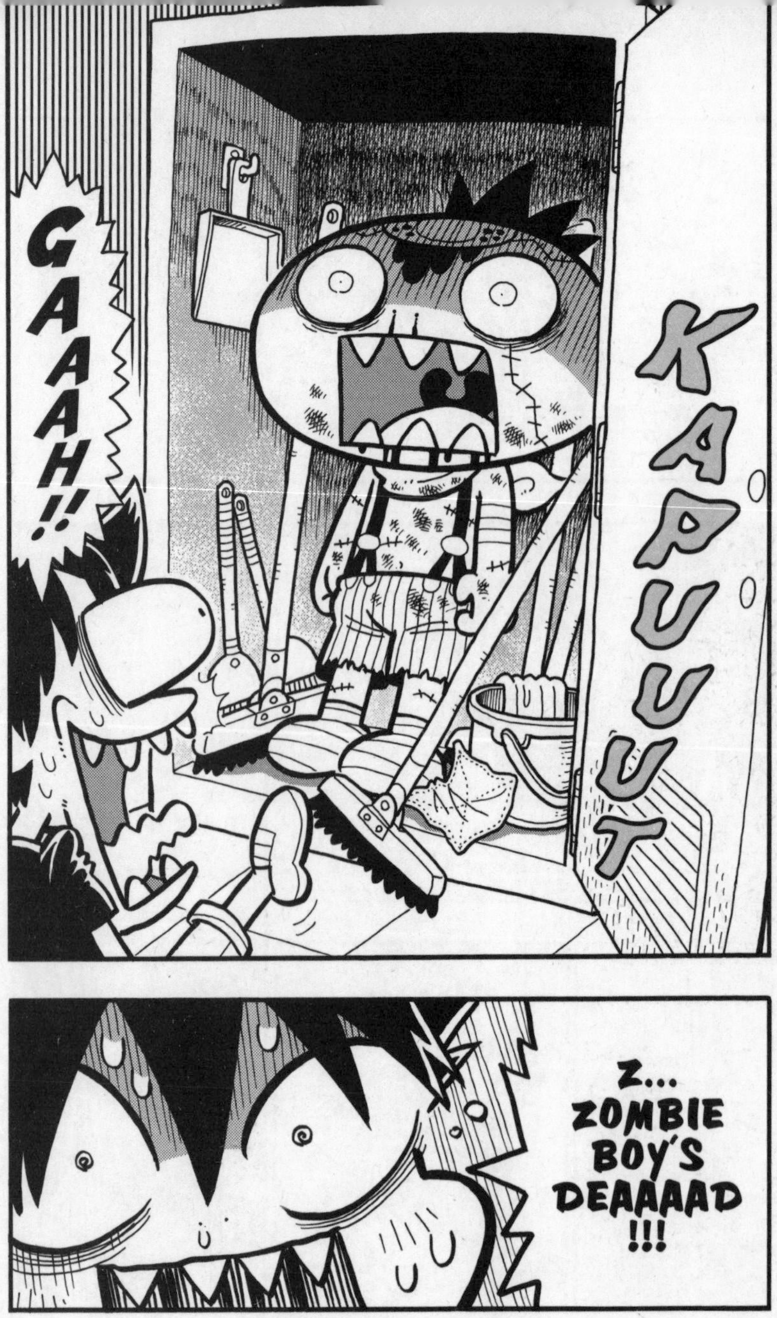
KAPUUUT
GAAAH!!
Z... ZOMBIE BOY'S DEAAAAD!!!

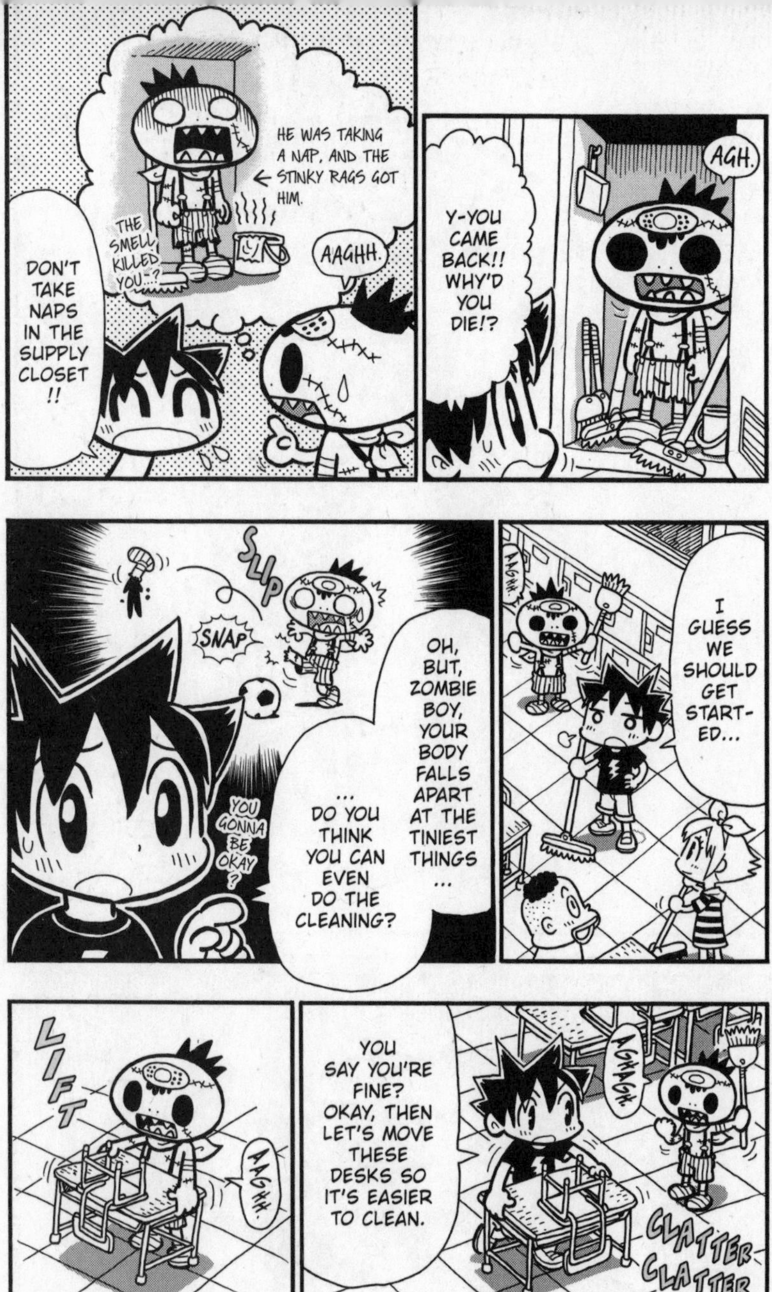
AGH.
Y-YOU CAME BACK!! WHY'D YOU DIE!?
AAGHH.
HE WAS TAKING A NAP, AND THE STINKY RAGS GOT HIM.
THE SMELL KILLED YOU...?
DON'T TAKE NAPS IN THE SUPPLY CLOSET !!
AAGHH.
I GUESS WE SHOULD GET START-ED...
OH, BUT, ZOMBIE BOY, YOUR BODY FALLS APART AT THE TINIEST THINGS ...
SLIP
SNAP
... DO YOU THINK YOU CAN EVEN DO THE CLEANING?
YOU GONNA BE OKAY?
AAGHGH.
YOU SAY YOU'RE FINE? OKAY, THEN LET'S MOVE THESE DESKS SO IT'S EASIER TO CLEAN.
CLATTER CLATTER
LIFT
AAGHH.

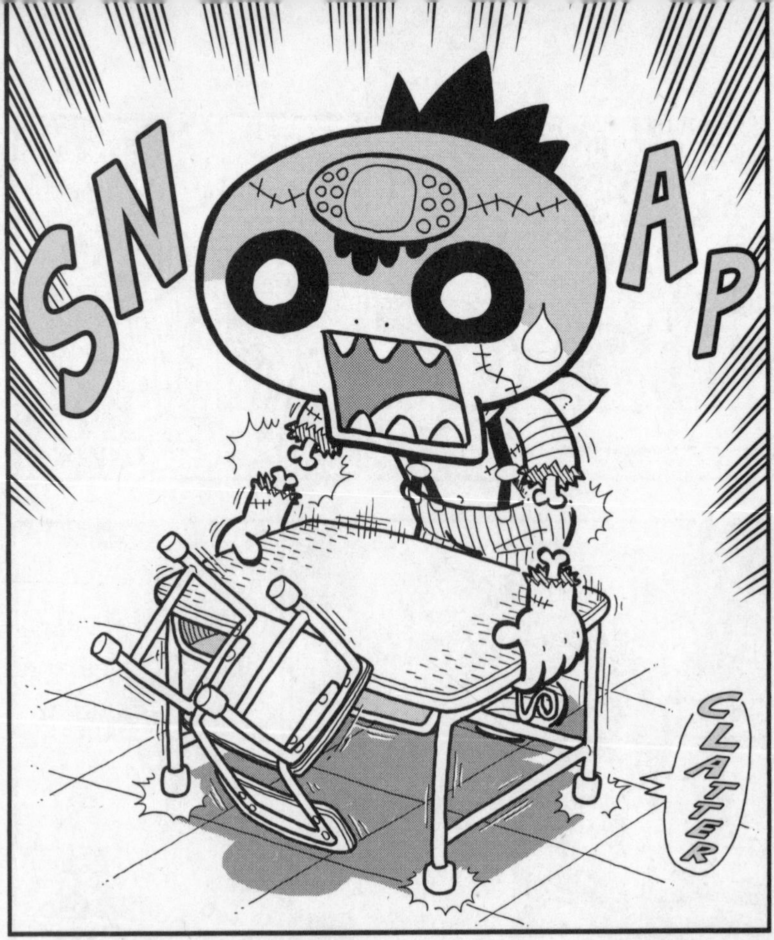
SNAP
CLATTER

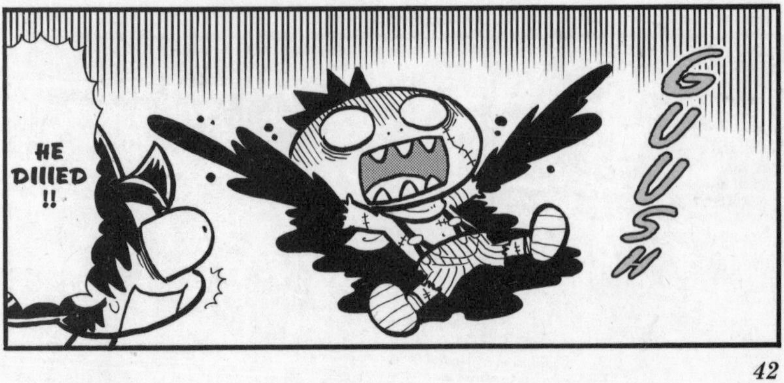
GUUSH
HE DIIIED !!

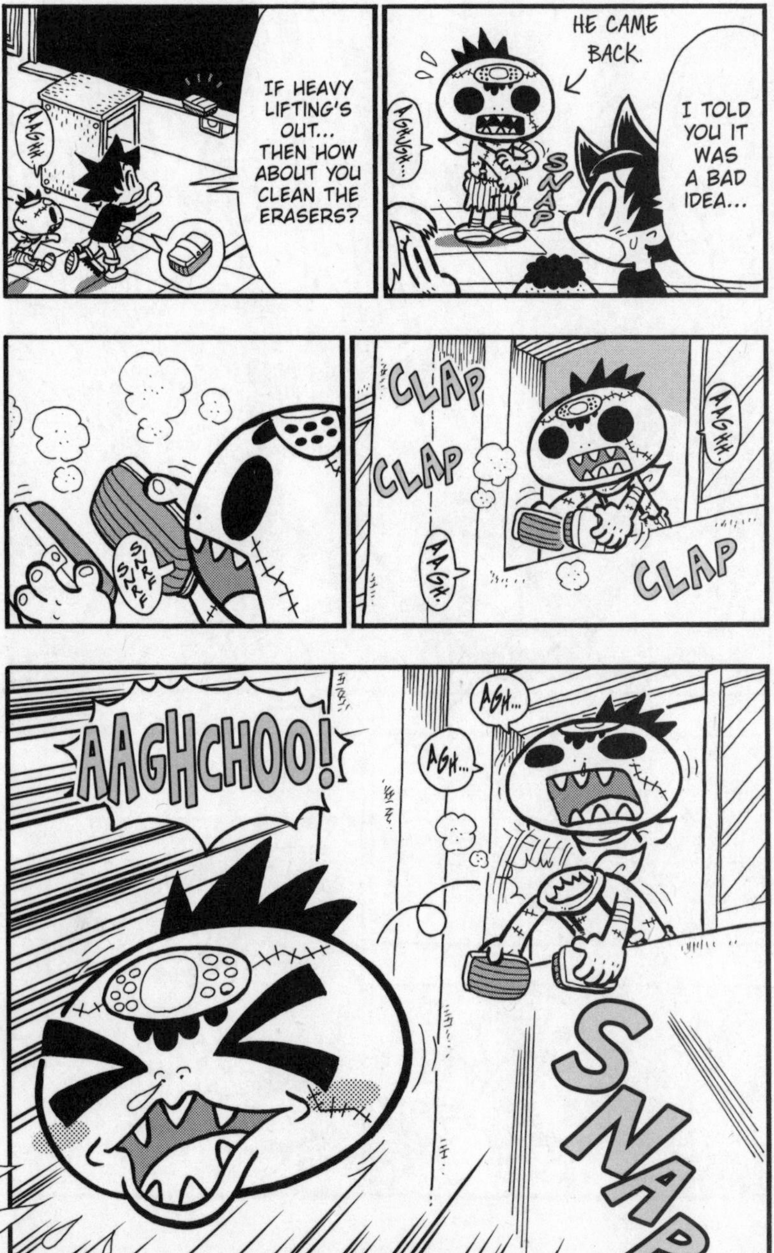
I TOLD YOU IT WAS A BAD IDEA...
HE CAME BACK.
SNAP
AGUGH...
IF HEAVY LIFTING'S OUT... THEN HOW ABOUT YOU CLEAN THE ERASERS?
AAGHH
AAGHH.
CLAP
CLAP
AAGH.
CLAP
SNRF SNRF
AGH...
AGH...
AAGHCHOO!
SNAP

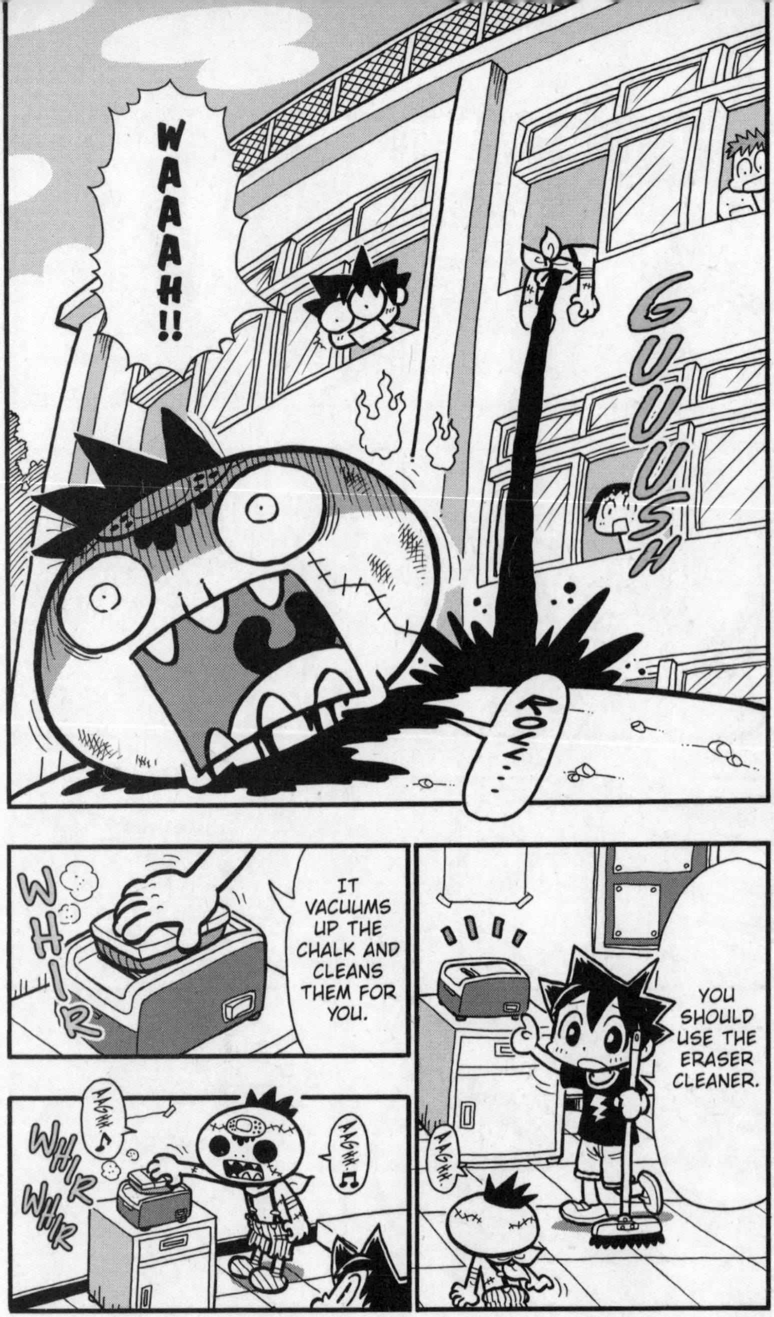
WAAAAH!!
GUUUSH
KOW...
YOU SHOULD USE THE ERASER CLEANER.
AAGHH.
WHIR
IT VACUUMS UP THE CHALK AND CLEANS THEM FOR YOU.
AAGHH.♫
AAGHH.♪
WHIR WHIR

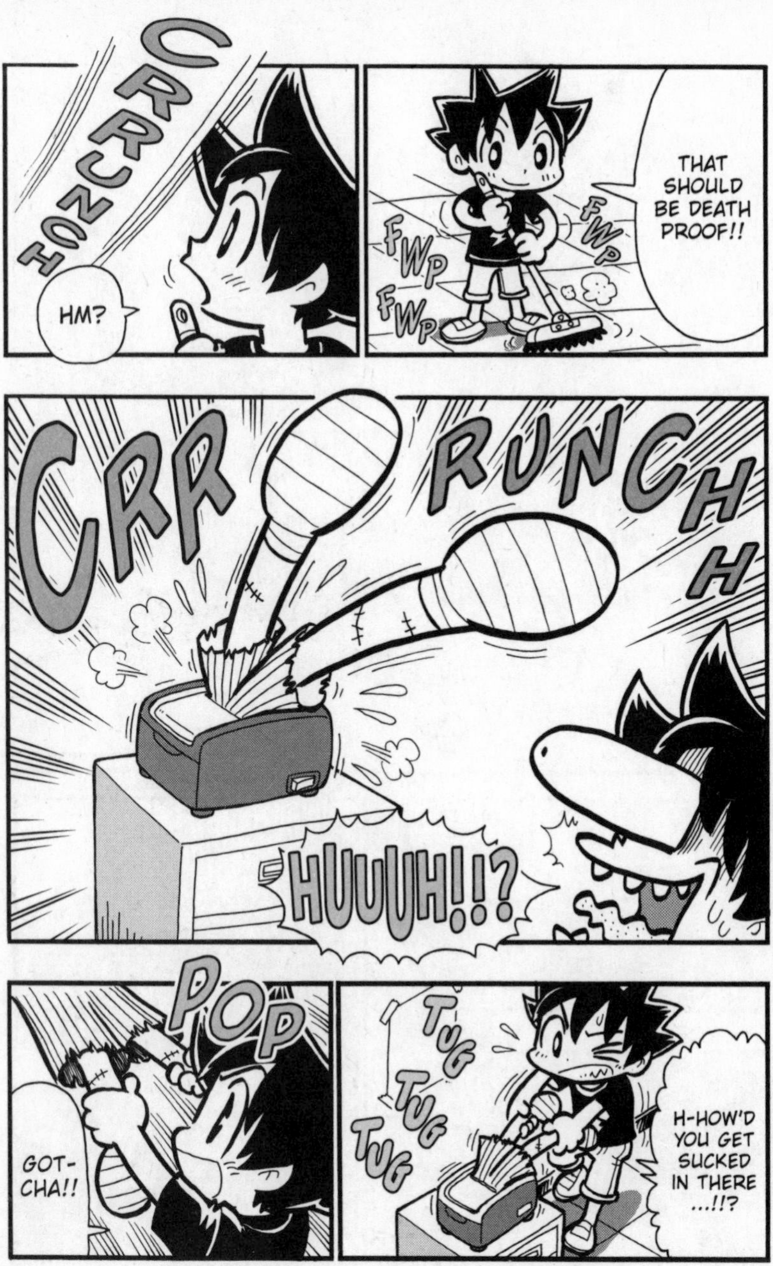

FWP
FWP
FWP
THAT SHOULD BE DEATH PROOF!!
CRRUNCH
HM?
CRRRUNCHHH
HUUUH!!?
TUG
TUG
TUG
H-HOW'D YOU GET SUCKED IN THERE ...!!?
POP
GOT-CHA!!

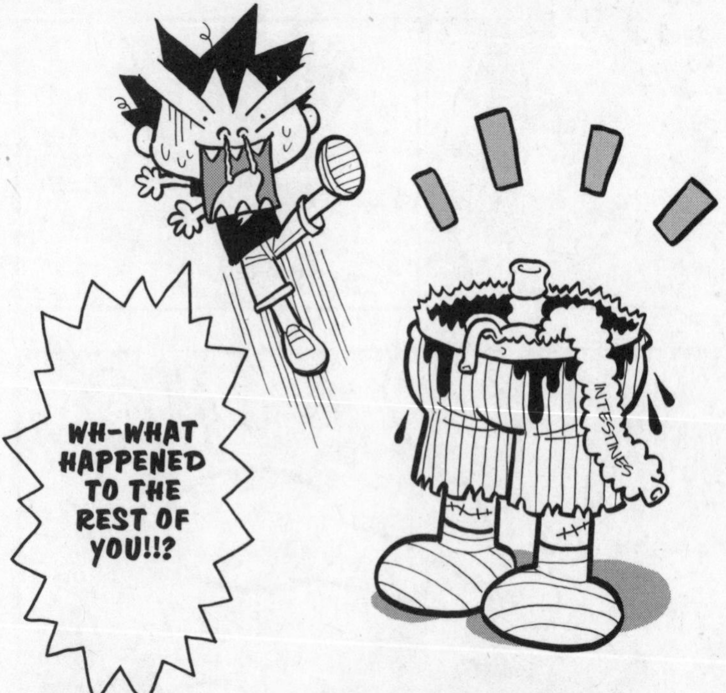
WH-WHAT HAPPENED TO THE REST OF YOU!!?
INTESTINES

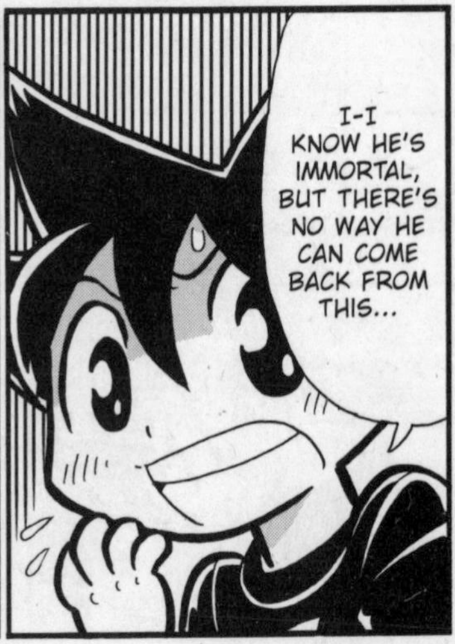
I-I KNOW HE'S IMMORTAL, BUT THERE'S NO WAY HE CAN COME BACK FROM THIS...

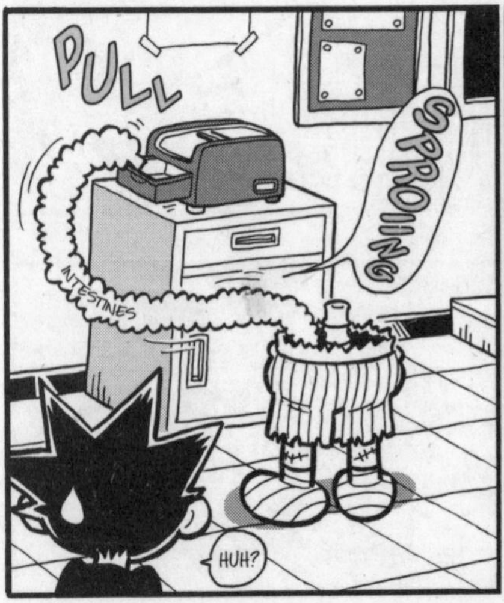
PULL
SPROING
INTESTINES
HUH?

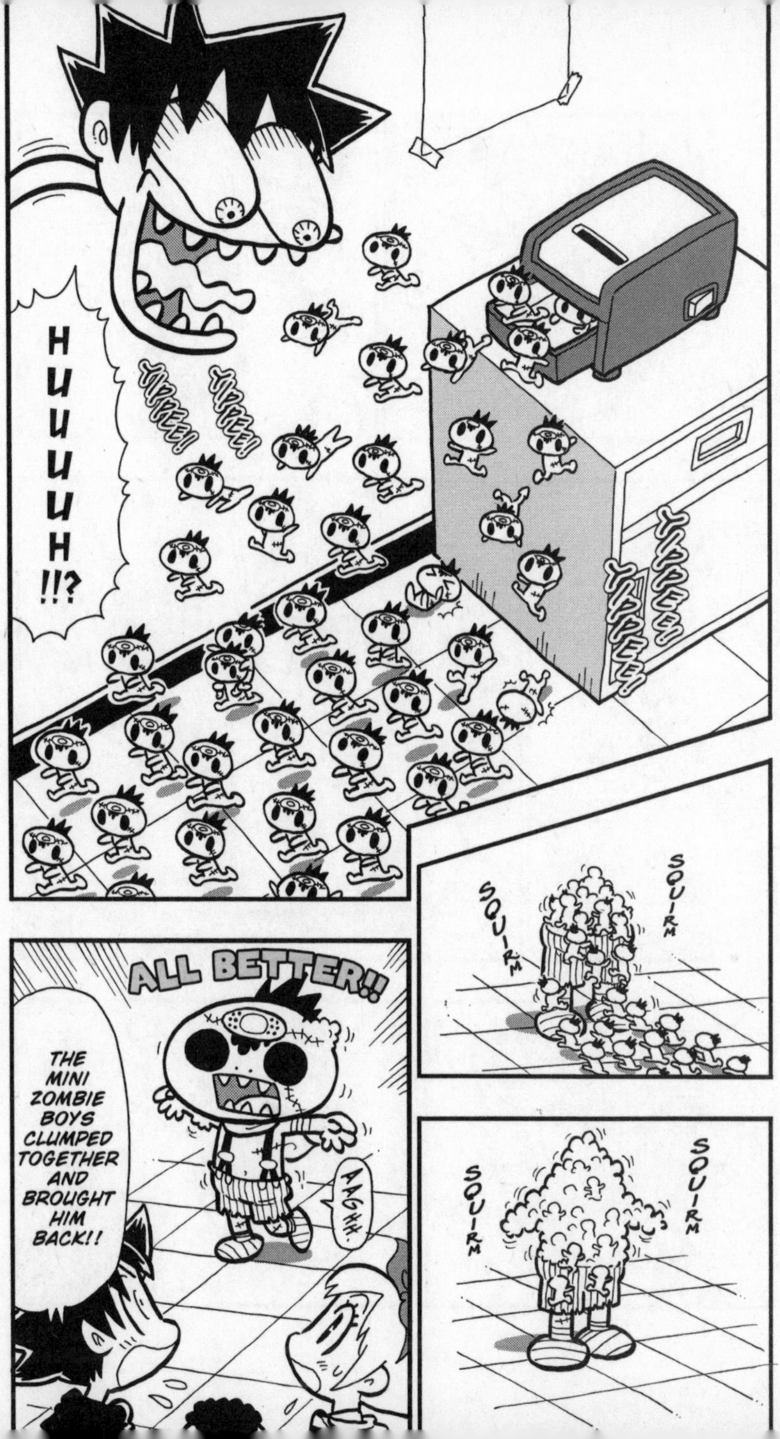
HUUUUUH!!?
YIPPEE!
YIPPEE!
YIPPEE!
YIPPEE!
SQUIRM
SQUIRM
SQUIRM
SQUIRM
ALL BETTER!!
THE MINI ZOMBIE BOYS CLUMPED TOGETHER AND BROUGHT HIM BACK!!
AAGHH

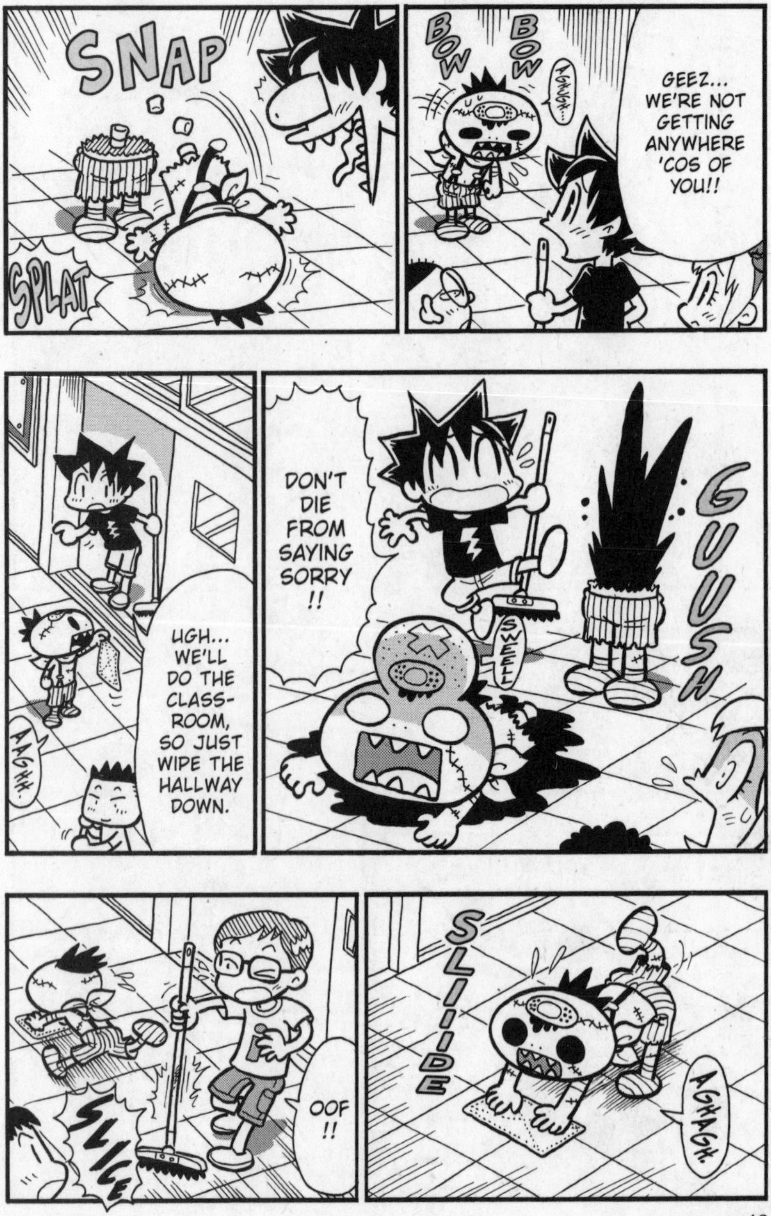
BOW
BOW
AGHUGH...
GEEZ... WE'RE NOT GETTING ANYWHERE 'COS OF YOU!!
SNAP
SPLAT
DON'T DIE FROM SAYING SORRY !!
GUUSH
SWELL
UGH... WE'LL DO THE CLASS-ROOM, SO JUST WIPE THE HALLWAY DOWN.
AAGHH.
SLIIIDE
AGHAGH.
OOF !!
SLICE

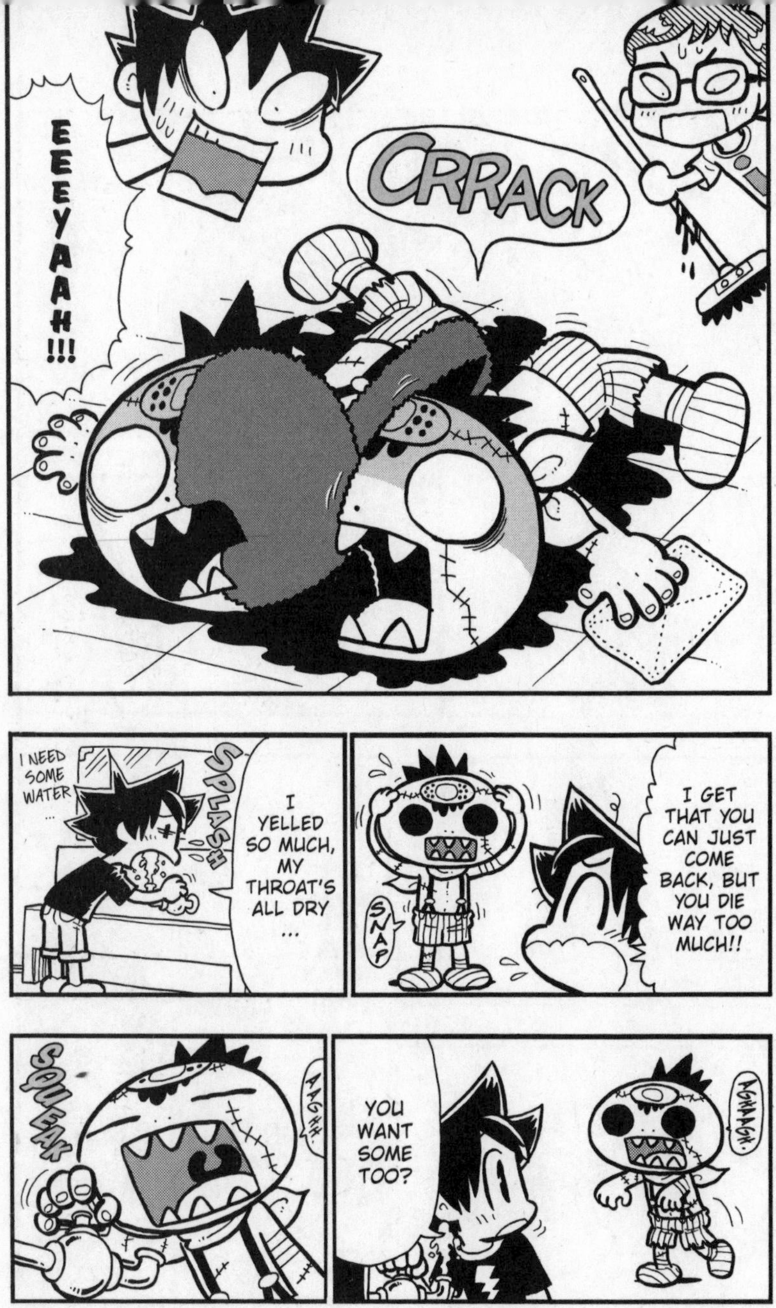
CRRACK
EEEYAAAH!!!
I GET THAT YOU CAN JUST COME BACK, BUT YOU DIE WAY TOO MUCH!!
SNAP
I YELLED SO MUCH, MY THROAT'S ALL DRY ...
SPLASH
I NEED SOME WATER ...
AGHAAAGH.
YOU WANT SOME TOO?
AAGHH.
SQUEAK

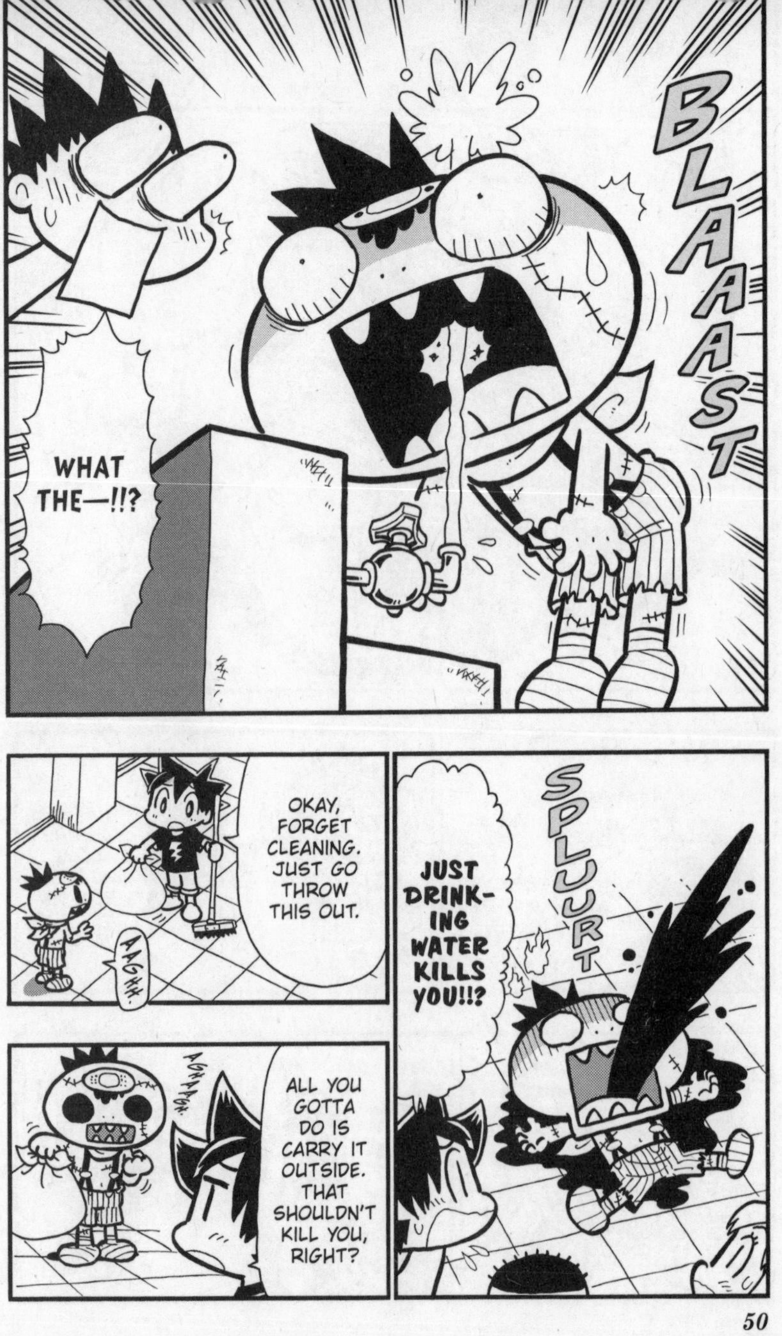
BLAAAST
WHAT THE—!!?
SPLUURT
JUST DRINKING WATER KILLS YOU!!?
OKAY, FORGET CLEANING. JUST GO THROW THIS OUT.
AAGHH.
ALL YOU GOTTA DO IS CARRY IT OUTSIDE. THAT SHOULDN'T KILL YOU, RIGHT?

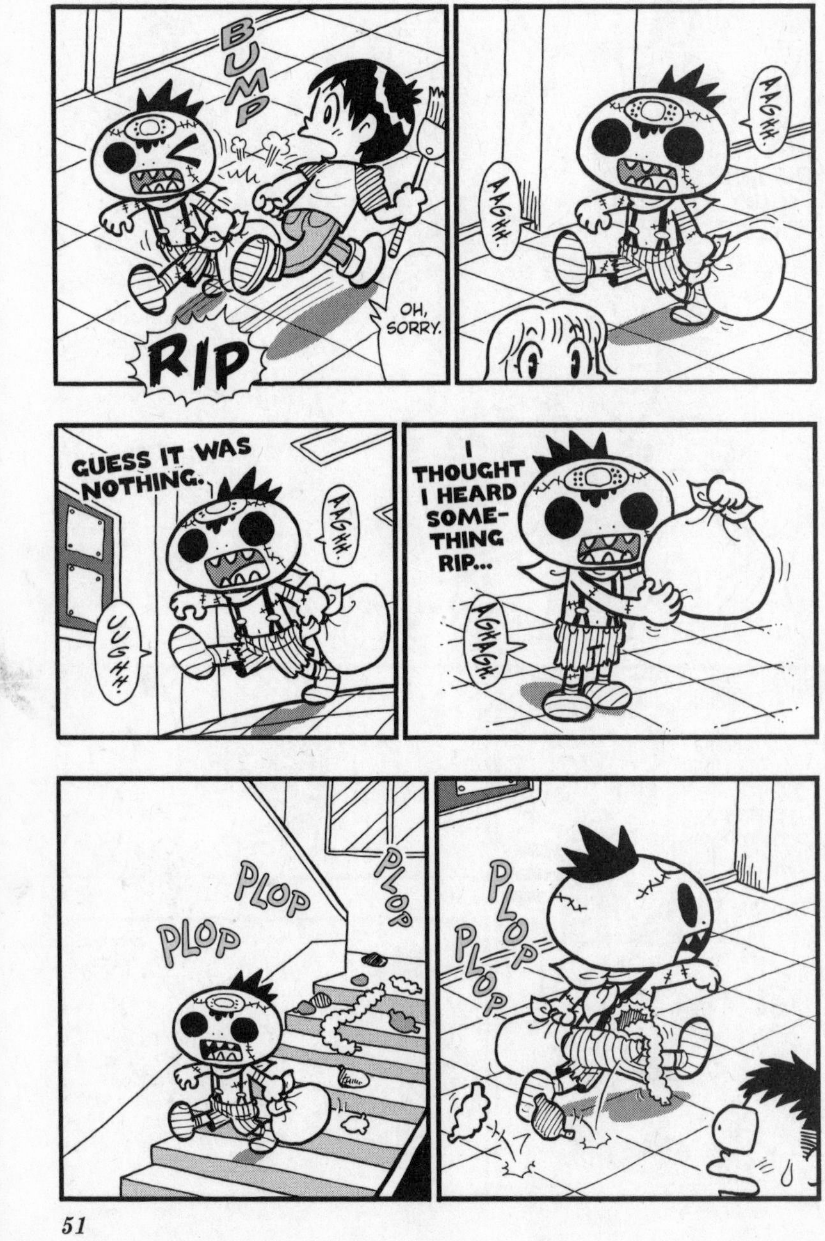
AAGHH.
AAGHH.
BUMP
OH, SORRY.
RIP
I THOUGHT I HEARD SOME-THING RIP...
AGHAGH.
AAGHH.
GUESS IT WAS NOTHING.
UUGHH.
PLOP
PLOP
PLOP
PLOP
PLOP
PLOP

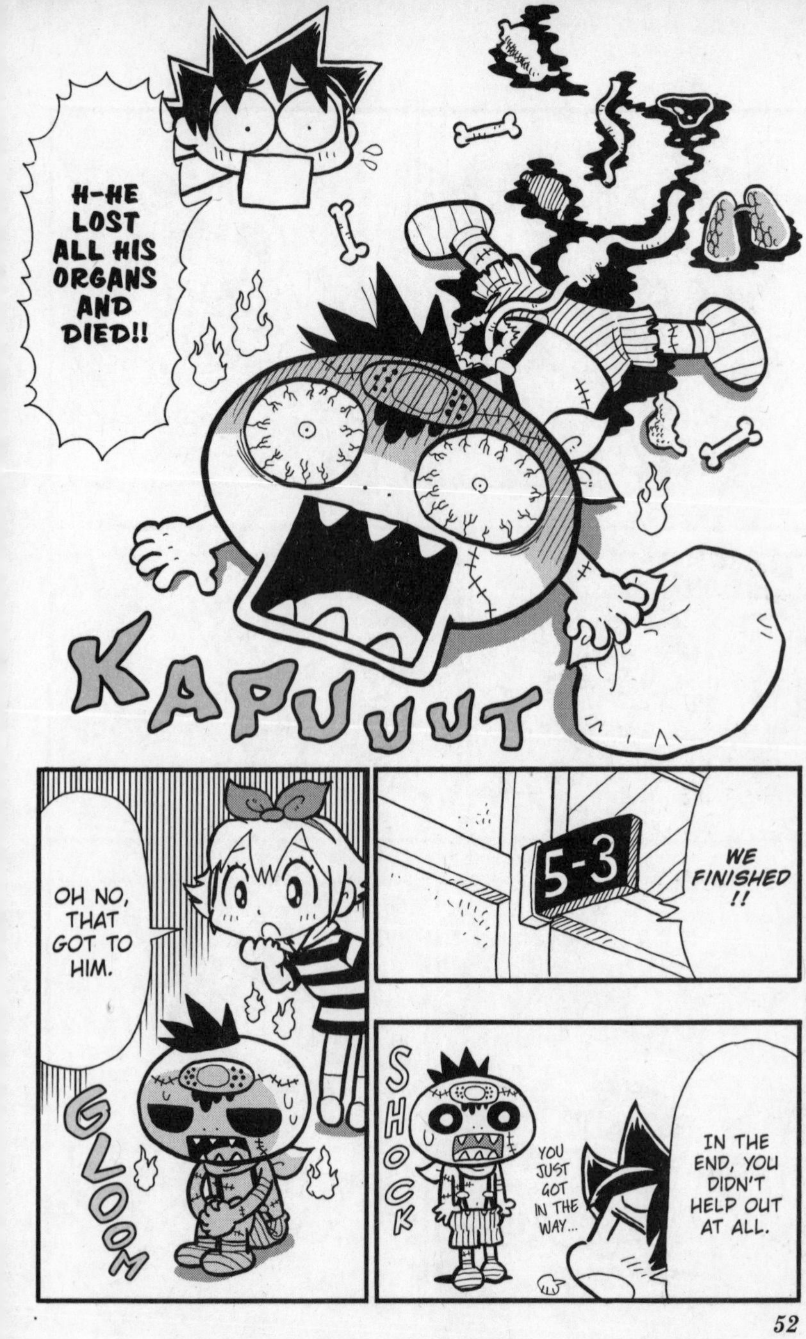
H-HE LOST ALL HIS ORGANS AND DIED!!
KAPUUUT
WE FINISHED!!
IN THE END, YOU DIDN'T HELP OUT AT ALL.
YOU JUST GOT IN THE WAY...
SHOCK
OH NO, THAT GOT TO HIM.
GLOOOM

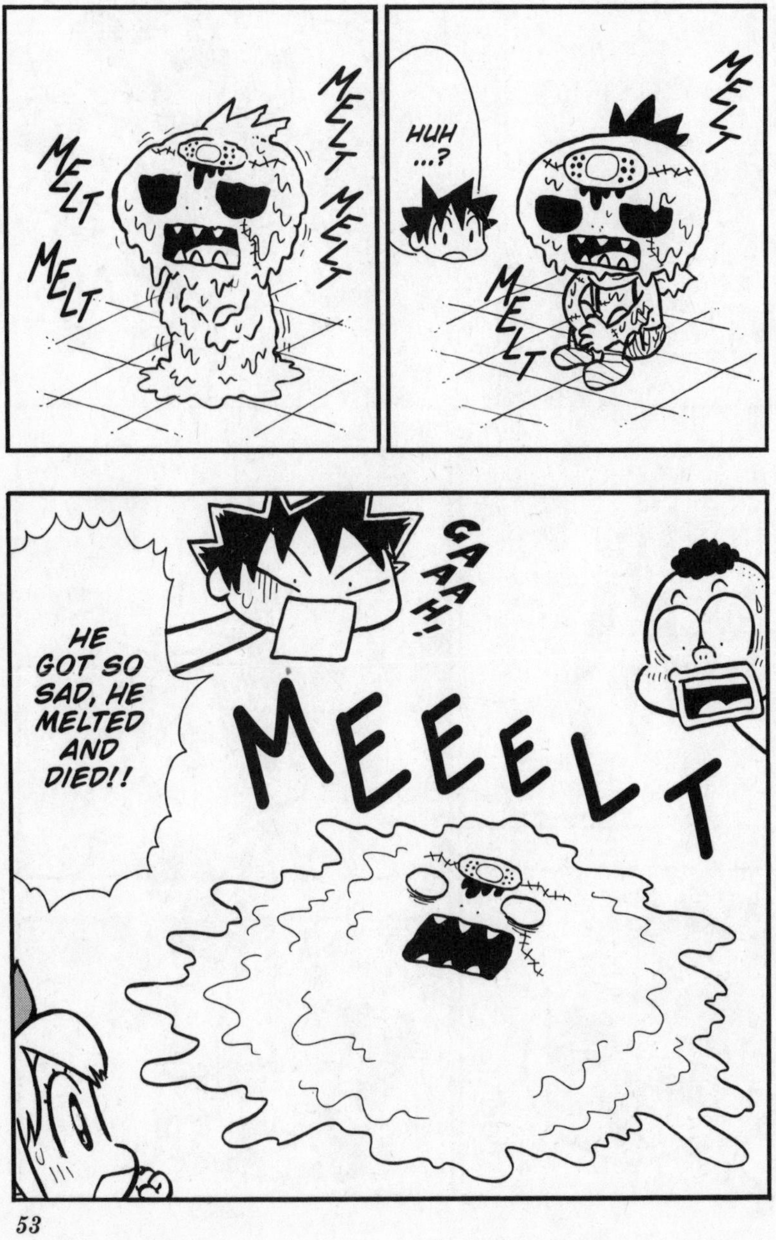
MELT
HUH ...?
MELT
MELT MELT
MELT
MELT
GAAAH!
HE GOT SO SAD, HE MELTED AND DIED!!
MEEELT

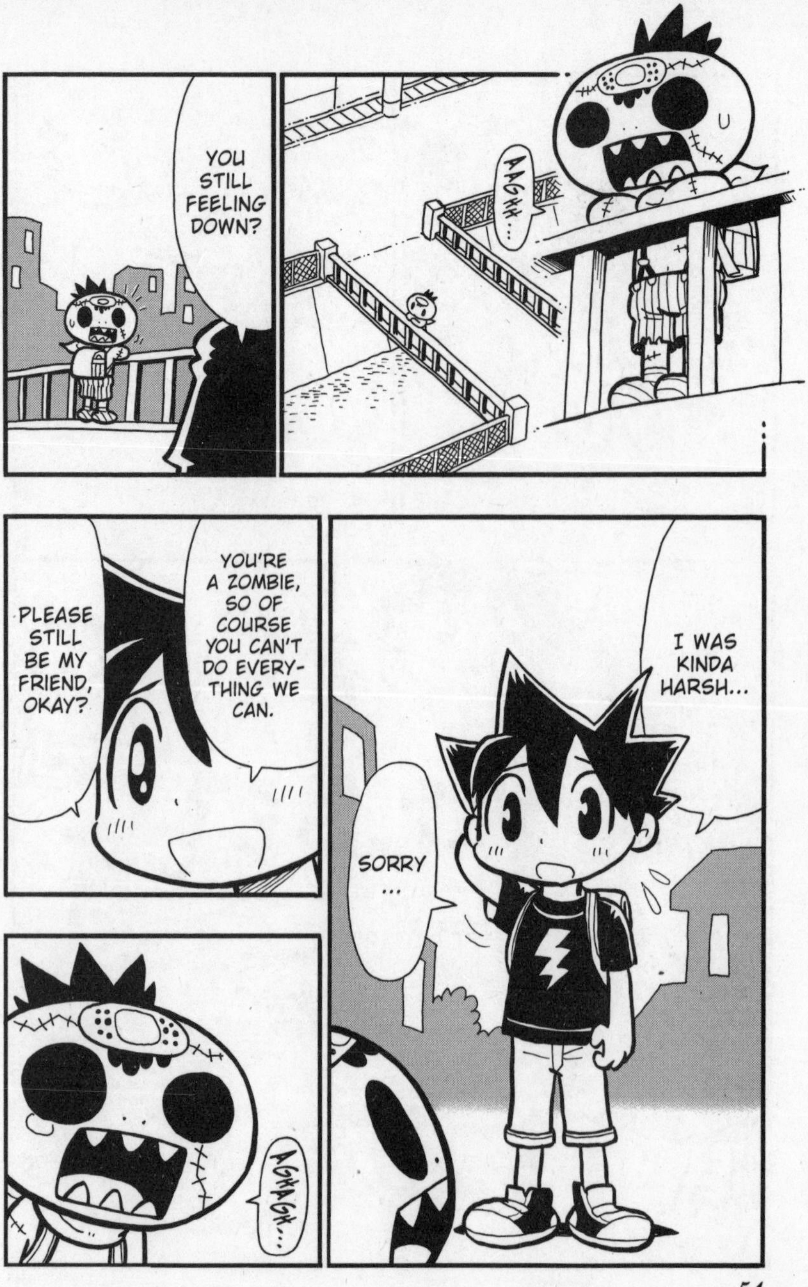
AAGHH...
YOU STILL FEELING DOWN?
I WAS KINDA HARSH...
SORRY...
YOU'RE A ZOMBIE, SO OF COURSE YOU CAN'T DO EVERY-THING WE CAN.
PLEASE STILL BE MY FRIEND, OKAY?
AGHAGH...

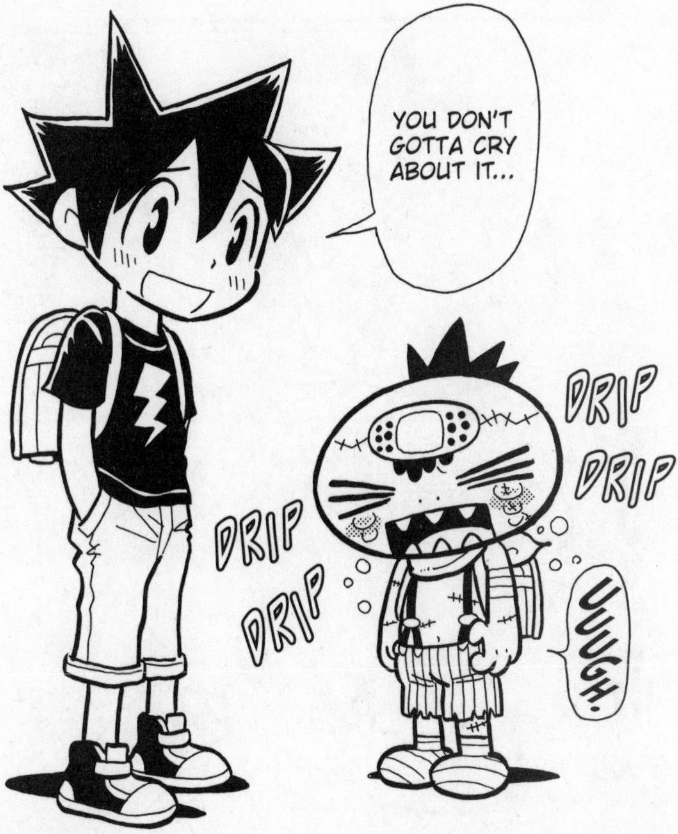
YOU DON'T GOTTA CRY ABOUT IT...
DRIP DRIP
UUUGH.
DRIP DRIP

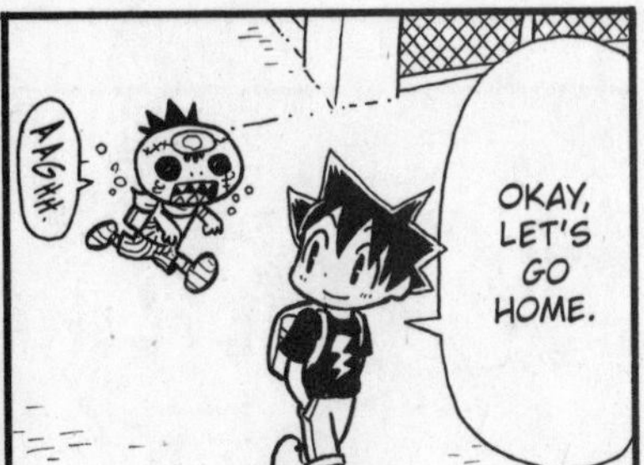
OKAY, LET'S GO HOME.
AAGHH.

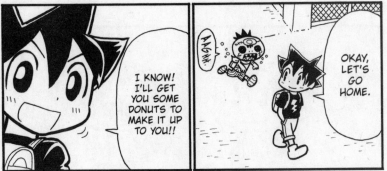

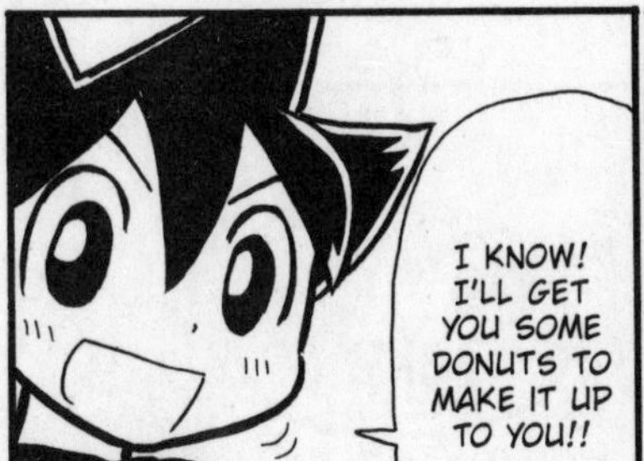
I KNOW! I'LL GET YOU SOME DONUTS TO MAKE IT UP TO YOU!!

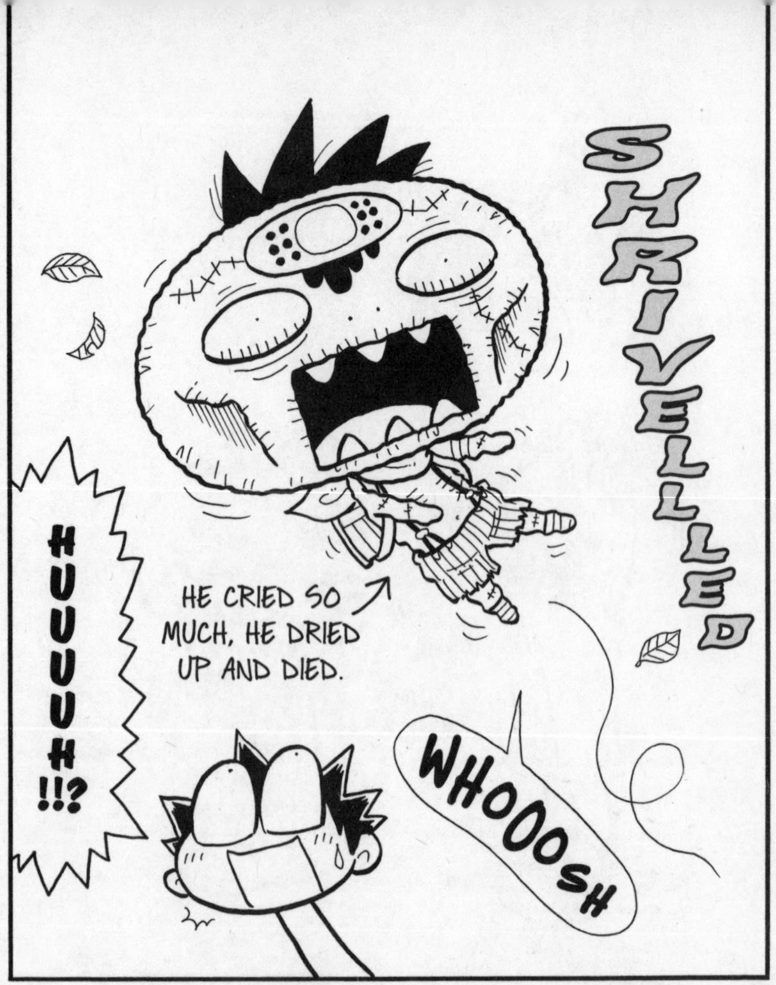
SHRIVELLED
WHOOOSH
HE CRIED SO MUCH, HE DRIED UP AND DIED.
HUUUUUH!!?

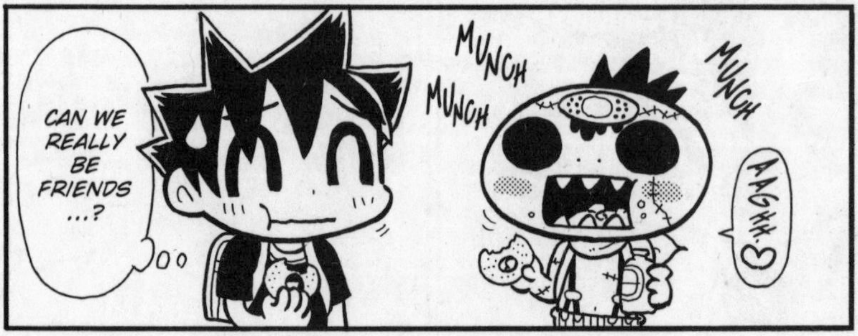
AAGHH.♡
MUNCH
MUNCH
MUNCH
CAN WE REALLY BE FRIENDS ...?

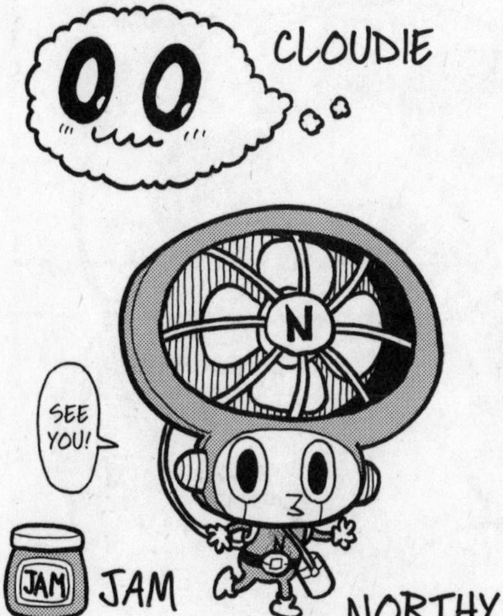
CLOUDIE
SEE YOU!
JAM
JAM
NORTHY

LET'Z TEZT OUR LUCK WITH CAPZULE TOYZ!

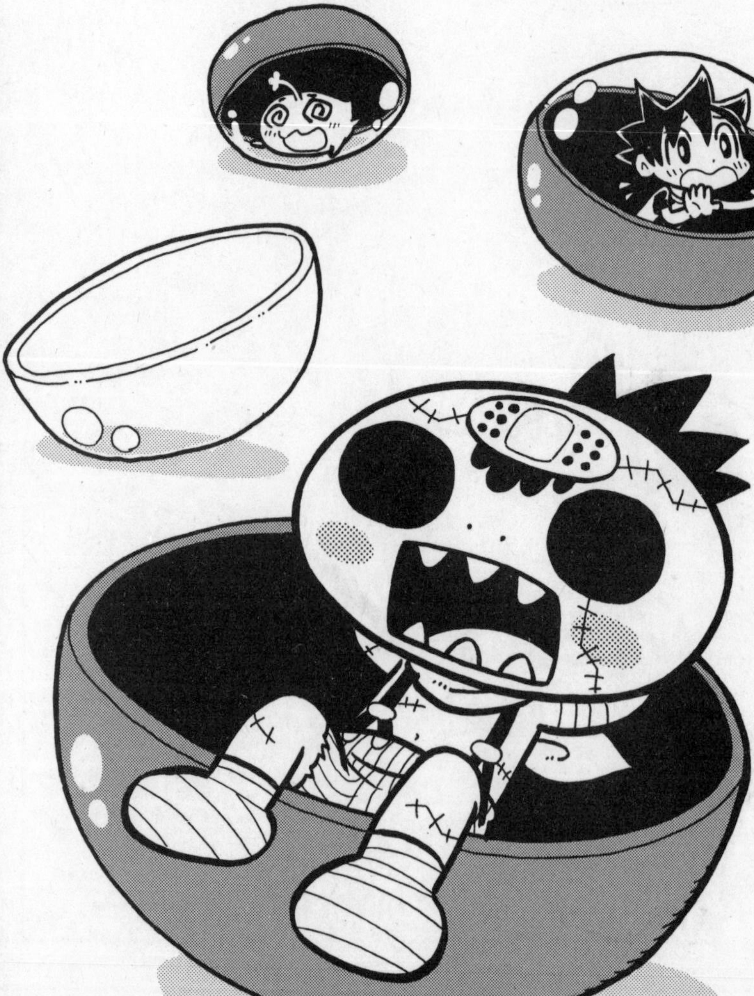

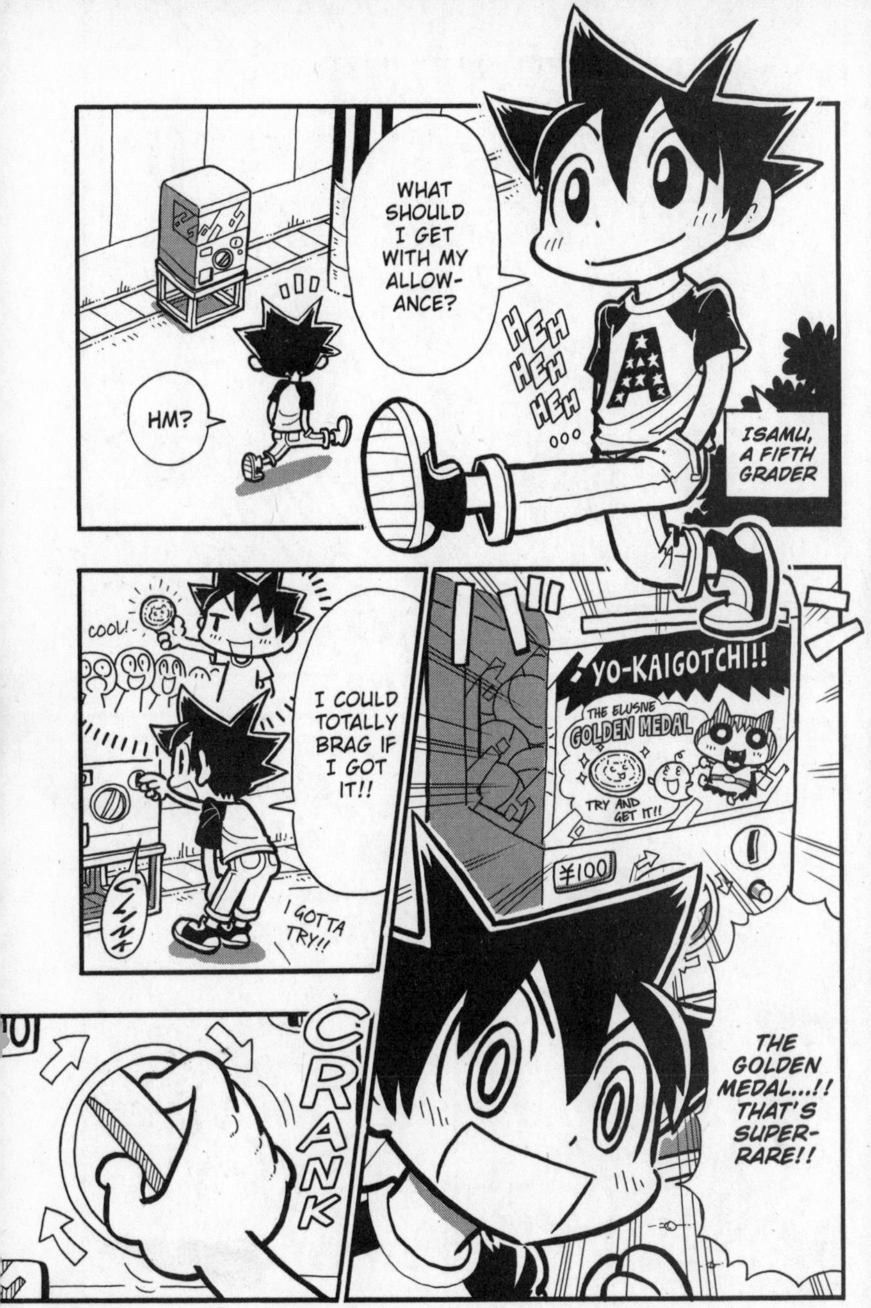
ISAMU, A FIFTH GRADER
HEH HEH HEH
WHAT SHOULD I GET WITH MY ALLOW-ANCE?
HM?
YO-KAIGOTCHI!!
THE ELUSIVE GOLDEN MEDAL
TRY AND GET IT!!
¥100
I COULD TOTALLY BRAG IF I GOT IT!!
COOL!
CLINK
I GOTTA TRY!!
THE GOLDEN MEDAL...!! THAT'S SUPER-RARE!!
CRANK

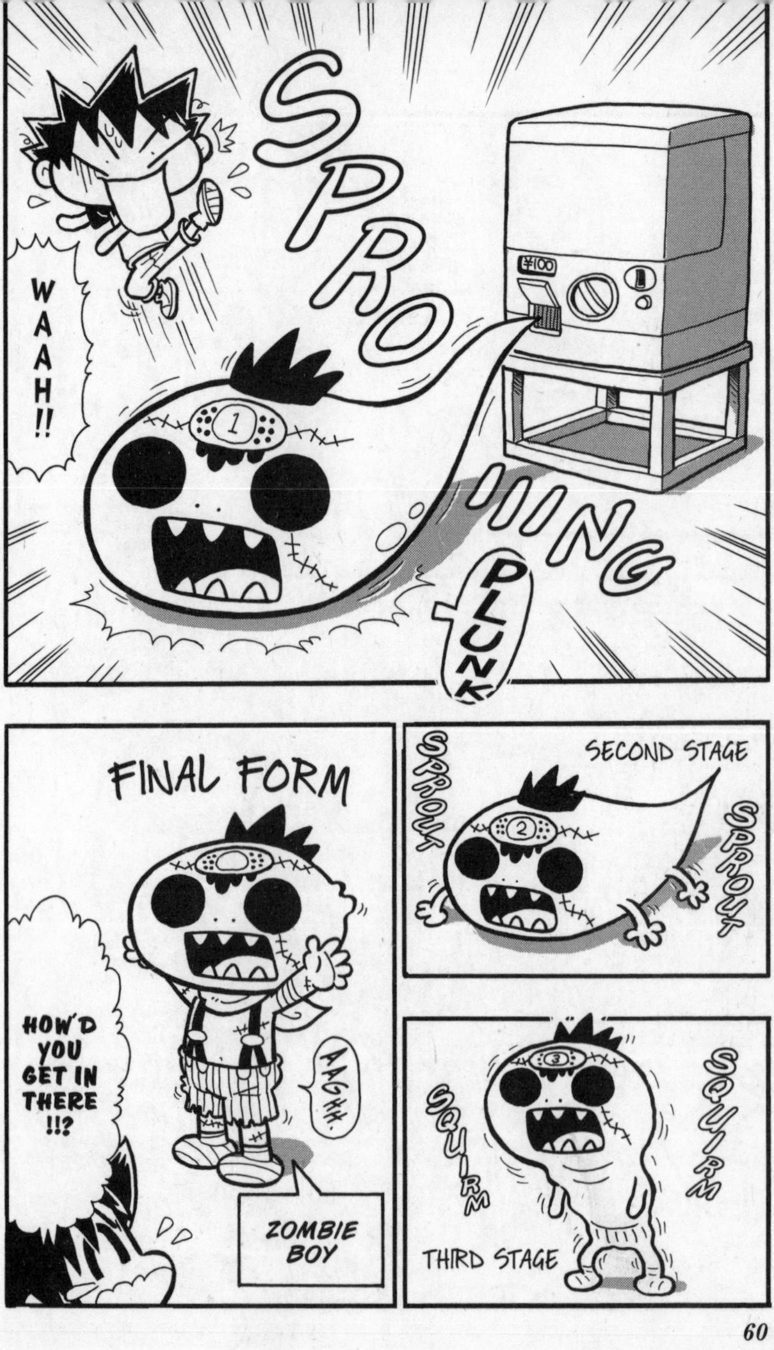
SPROIIING
PLUNK
WAAAH!!
SECOND STAGE
SPROUT
SPROUT
SQUIRM
SQUIRM
THIRD STAGE
FINAL FORM
AAGHH.
HOW'D YOU GET IN THERE !!?
ZOMBIE BOY

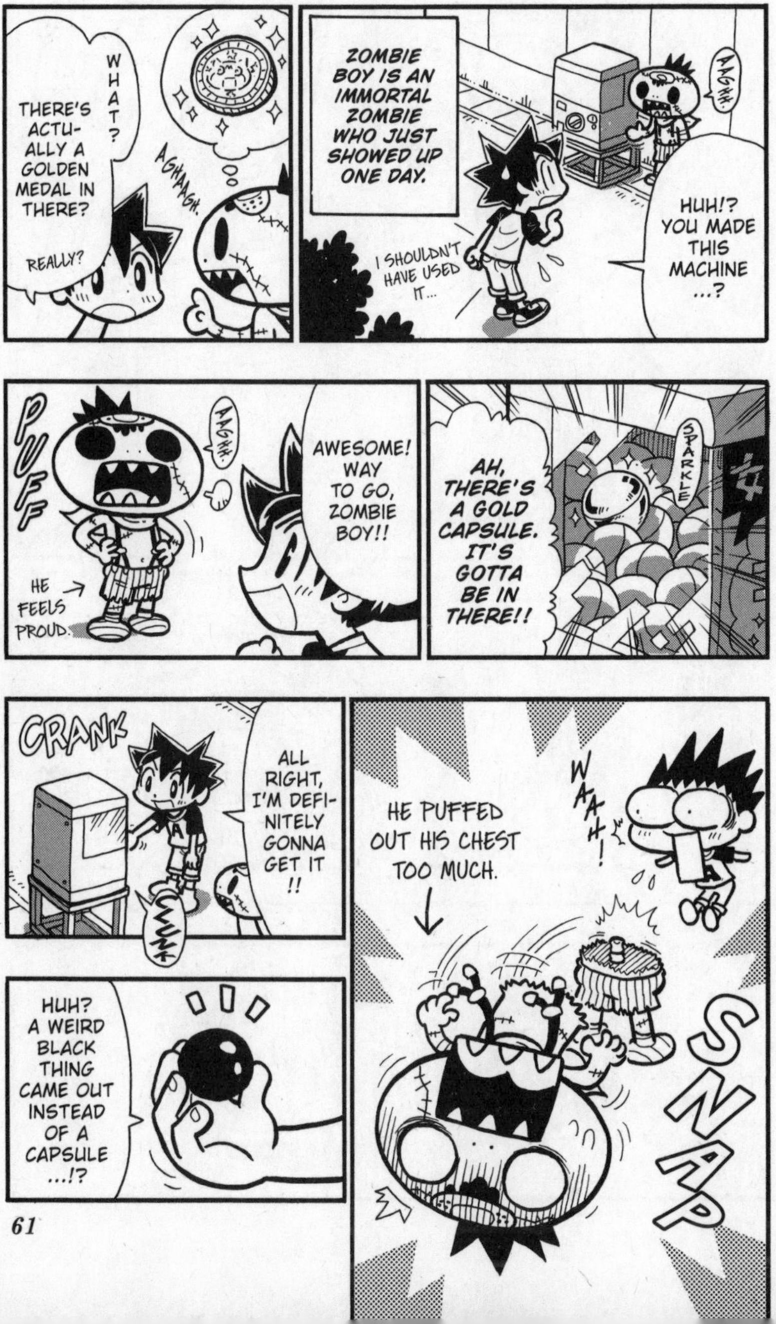
ZOMBIE BOY IS AN IMMORTAL ZOMBIE WHO JUST SHOWED UP ONE DAY.
AAGHH.
HUH!? YOU MADE THIS MACHINE ...?
I SHOULDN'T HAVE USED IT...
WHAT?
AGHAAGH.
THERE'S ACTUALLY A GOLDEN MEDAL IN THERE?
REALLY?
SPARKLE
AH, THERE'S A GOLD CAPSULE. IT'S GOTTA BE IN THERE!!
AWESOME! WAY TO GO, ZOMBIE BOY!!
AAGHH.
PUFF
HE FEELS PROUD.
WAAH!
HE PUFFED OUT HIS CHEST TOO MUCH.
SNAP
CRANK
ALL RIGHT, I'M DEFINITELY GONNA GET IT!!
CLUNK
HUH? A WEIRD BLACK THING CAME OUT INSTEAD OF A CAPSULE ...!?

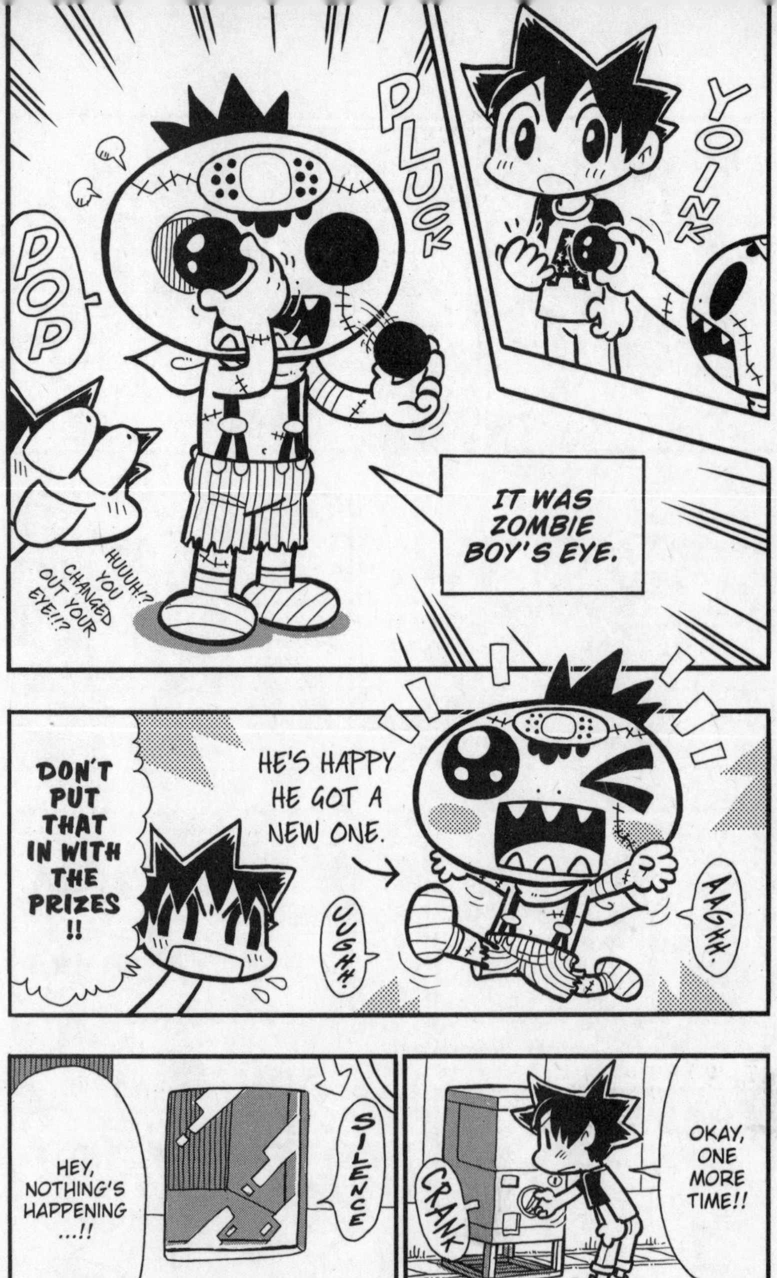
YOINK
PLUCK
IT WAS ZOMBIE BOY'S EYE.
POP
HUUUH!? YOU CHANGED OUT YOUR EYE!!?
AAGHH.
HE'S HAPPY HE GOT A NEW ONE.
UGHH.
DON'T PUT THAT IN WITH THE PRIZES!!
OKAY, ONE MORE TIME!!
CRANK
SILENCE
HEY, NOTHING'S HAPPENING ...!!

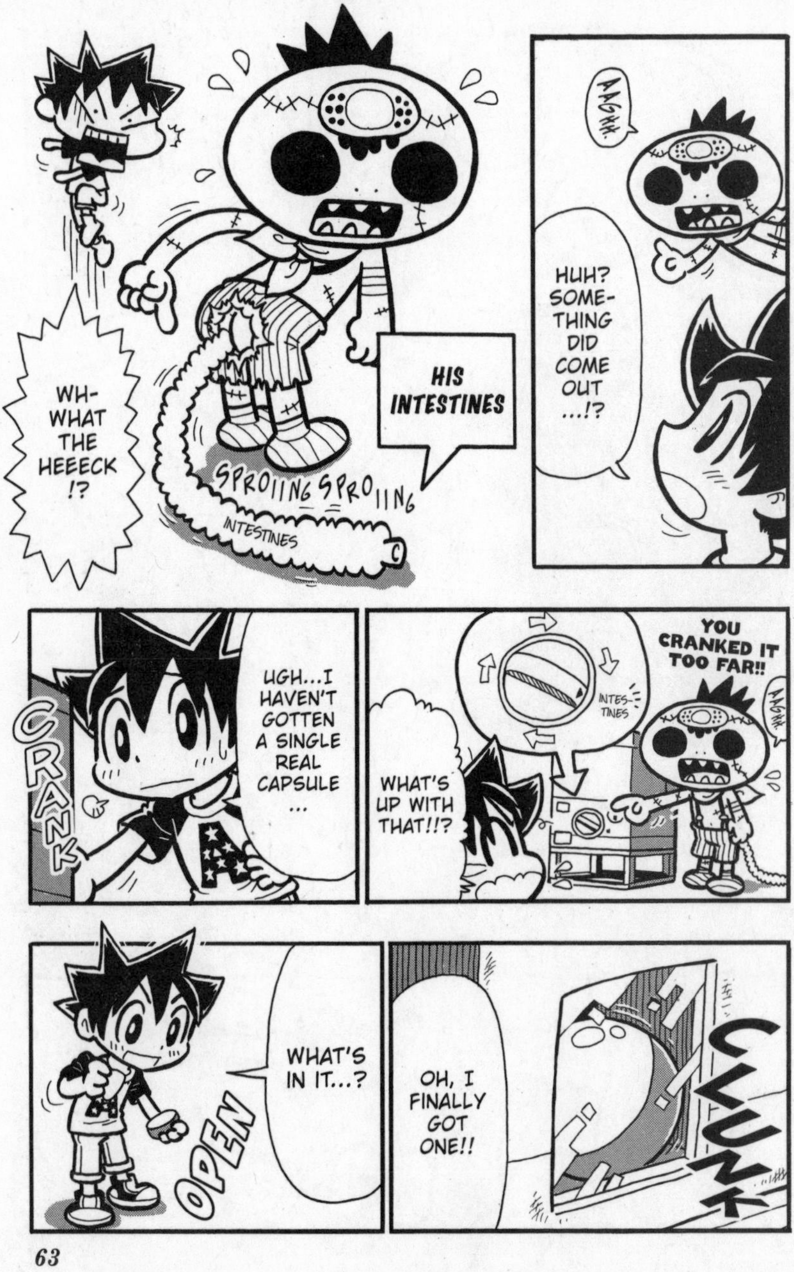
AAGHH.
HUH? SOME-THING DID COME OUT ...!?
HIS INTESTINES
SPROIING SPROIING
INTESTINES
WH-WHAT THE HEEECK!?
YOU CRANKED IT TOO FAR!!
AAGHH.
INTES-TINES
WHAT'S UP WITH THAT!!?
UGH...I HAVEN'T GOTTEN A SINGLE REAL CAPSULE ...
CRANK
CLUNK
OH, I FINALLY GOT ONE!!
WHAT'S IN IT...?
OPEN

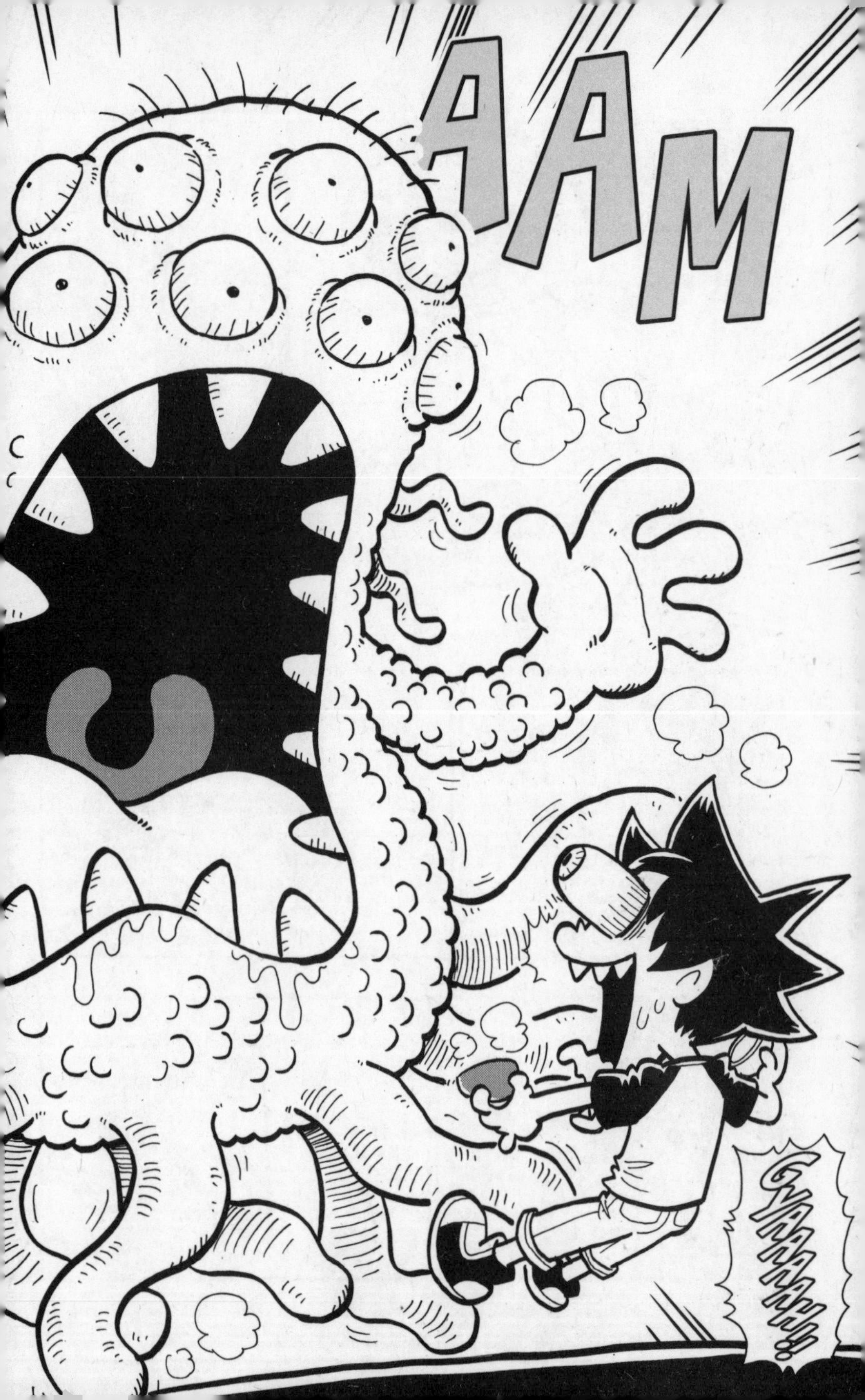
AAM
GYAAAAH!!

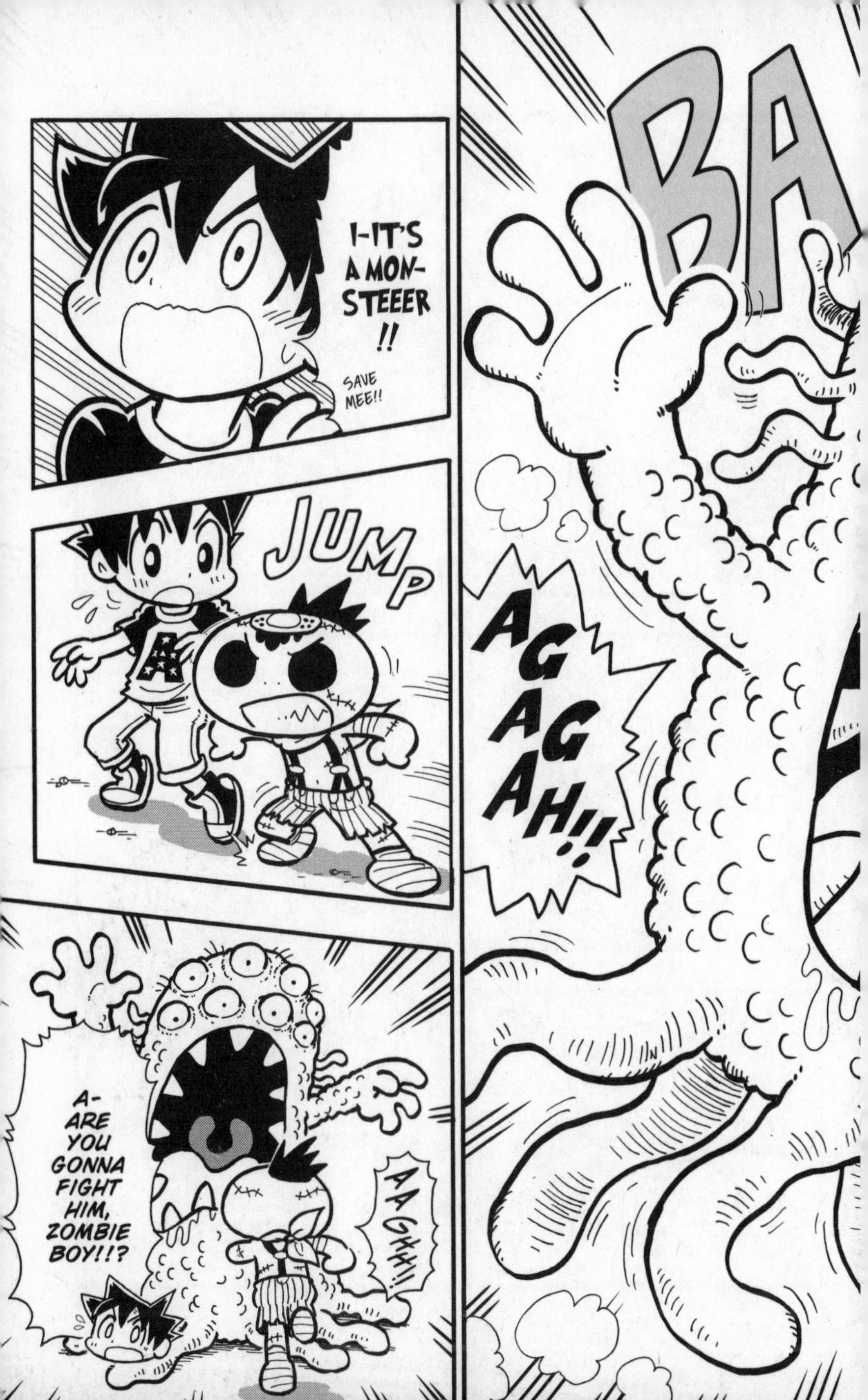
BA
AGAGAGAH!!
I-IT'S A MON-STEEER!!
SAVE MEE!!
JUMP
AAGHH!!
A-ARE YOU GONNA FIGHT HIM, ZOMBIE BOY!!?

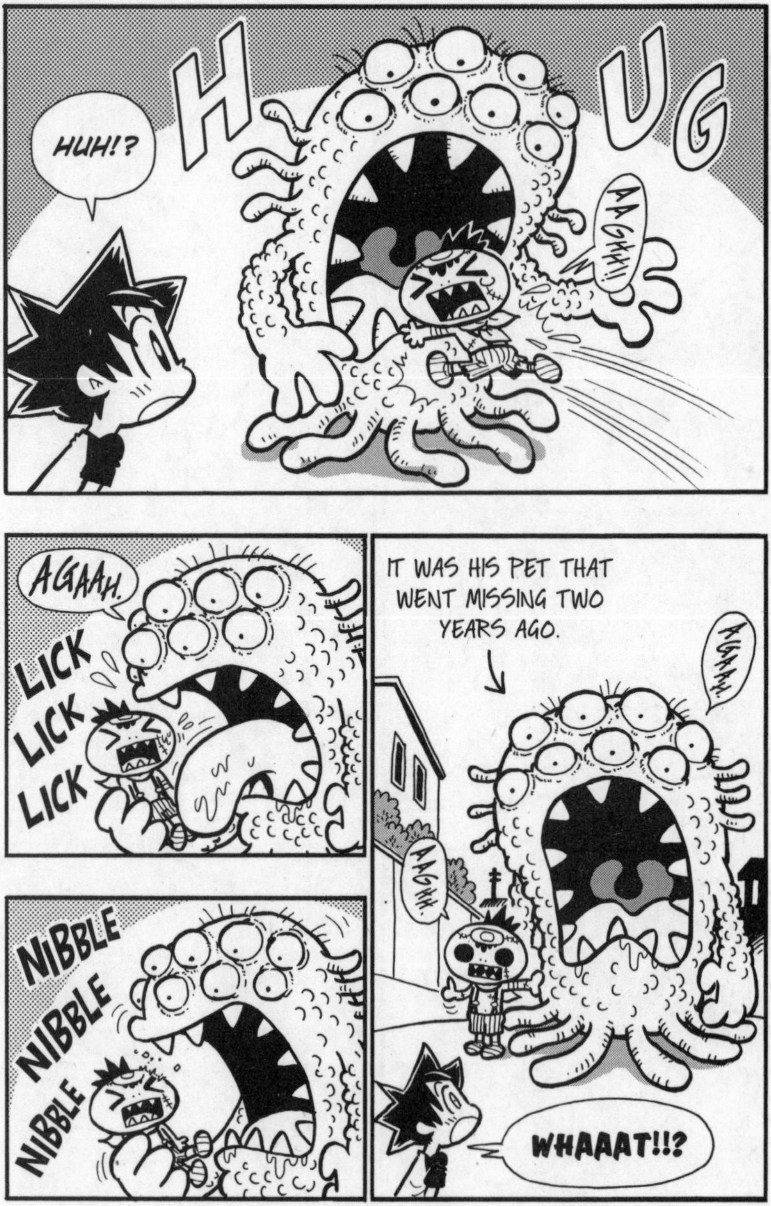

H
UG
AAGHH!!
HUH!?
IT WAS HIS PET THAT WENT MISSING TWO YEARS AGO.
AGAAAH.
AAGHH.
WHAAAT!!?
AGAAH.
LICK LICK LICK
NIBBLE NIBBLE NIBBLE

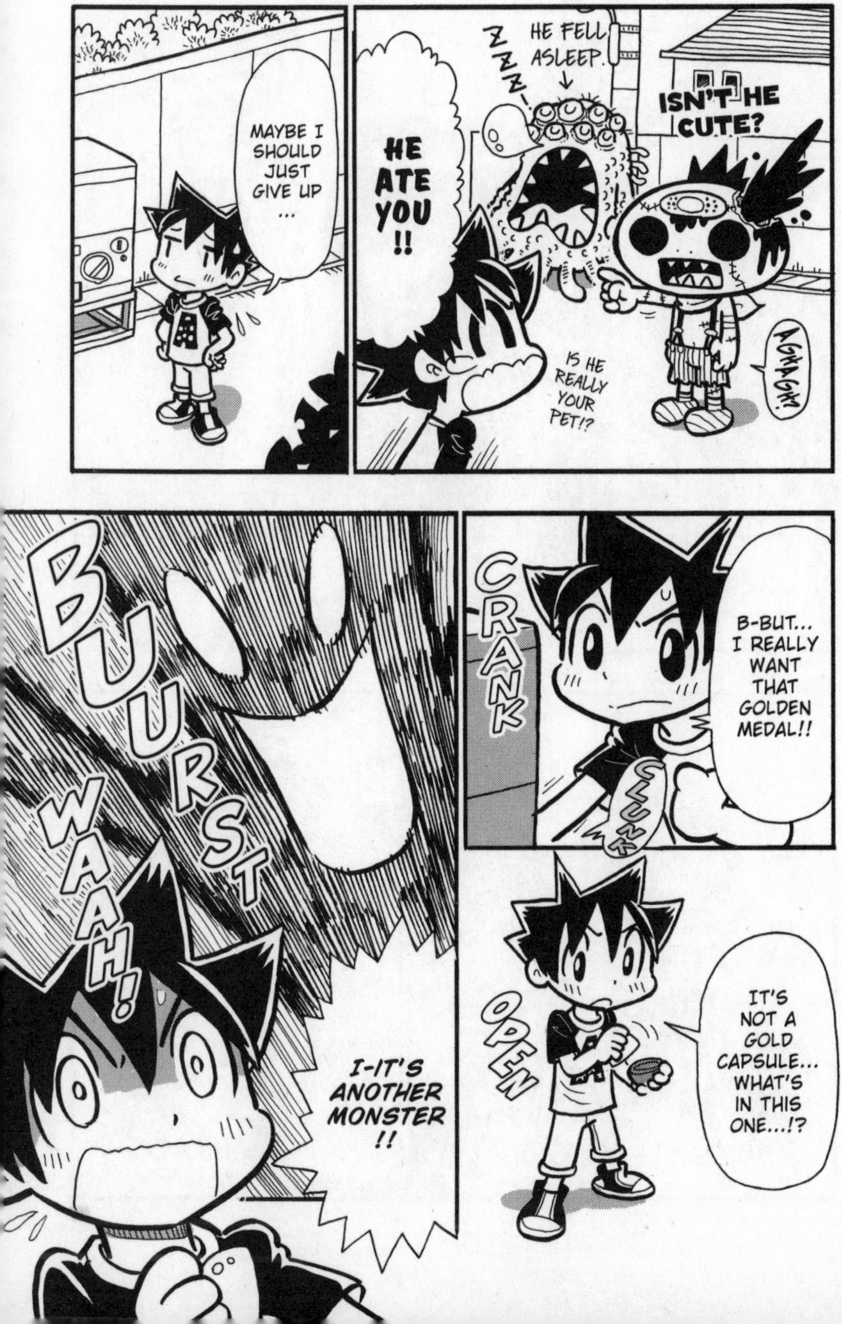
ISN'T HE CUTE?
AGHAGH!
HE FELL ASLEEP.
ZZZ
HE ATE YOU!!
IS HE REALLY YOUR PET!?
MAYBE I SHOULD JUST GIVE UP...
B-BUT... I REALLY WANT THAT GOLDEN MEDAL!!
CRANK
CLUNK
IT'S NOT A GOLD CAPSULE... WHAT'S IN THIS ONE...!?
OPEN
BUURST
WAAAH!
I-IT'S ANOTHER MONSTER!!

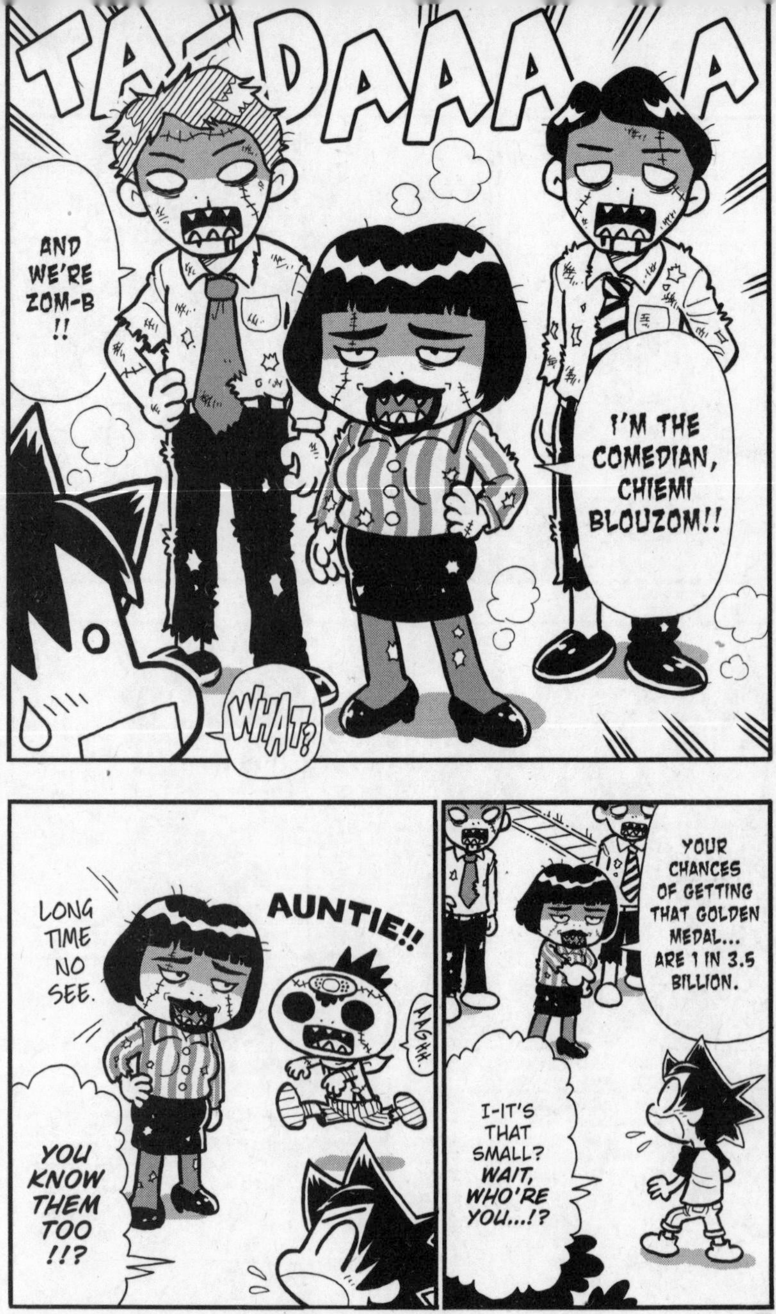
TA-DAAAA
I'M THE COMEDIAN, CHIEMI BLOUZOM!!
AND WE'RE ZOM-B!!
WHAT!?
YOUR CHANCES OF GETTING THAT GOLDEN MEDAL... ARE 1 IN 3.5 BILLION.
I-IT'S THAT SMALL? WAIT, WHO'RE YOU...!?
AUNTIE!!
AAGHH.
LONG TIME NO SEE.
YOU KNOW THEM TOO!!?

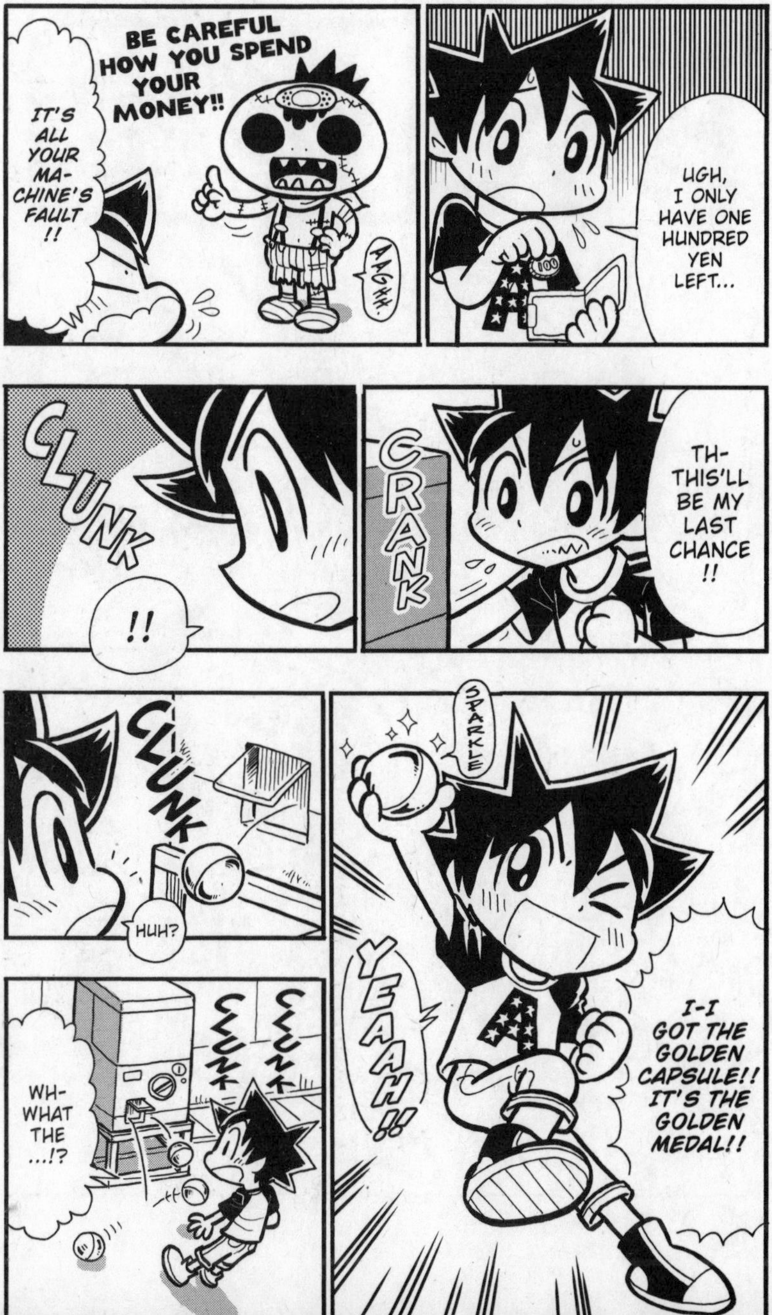
UGH, I ONLY HAVE ONE HUNDRED YEN LEFT...
100
BE CAREFUL HOW YOU SPEND YOUR MONEY!!
IT'S ALL YOUR MA-CHINE'S FAULT!!
AAGHH.
CRANK
TH-THIS'LL BE MY LAST CHANCE!!
CLUNK
!!
SPARKLE
I-I GOT THE GOLDEN CAPSULE!! IT'S THE GOLDEN MEDAL!!
YEAAAH!!
CLUNK
HUH?
CLUNK
CLUNK
WH-WHAT THE ...!?

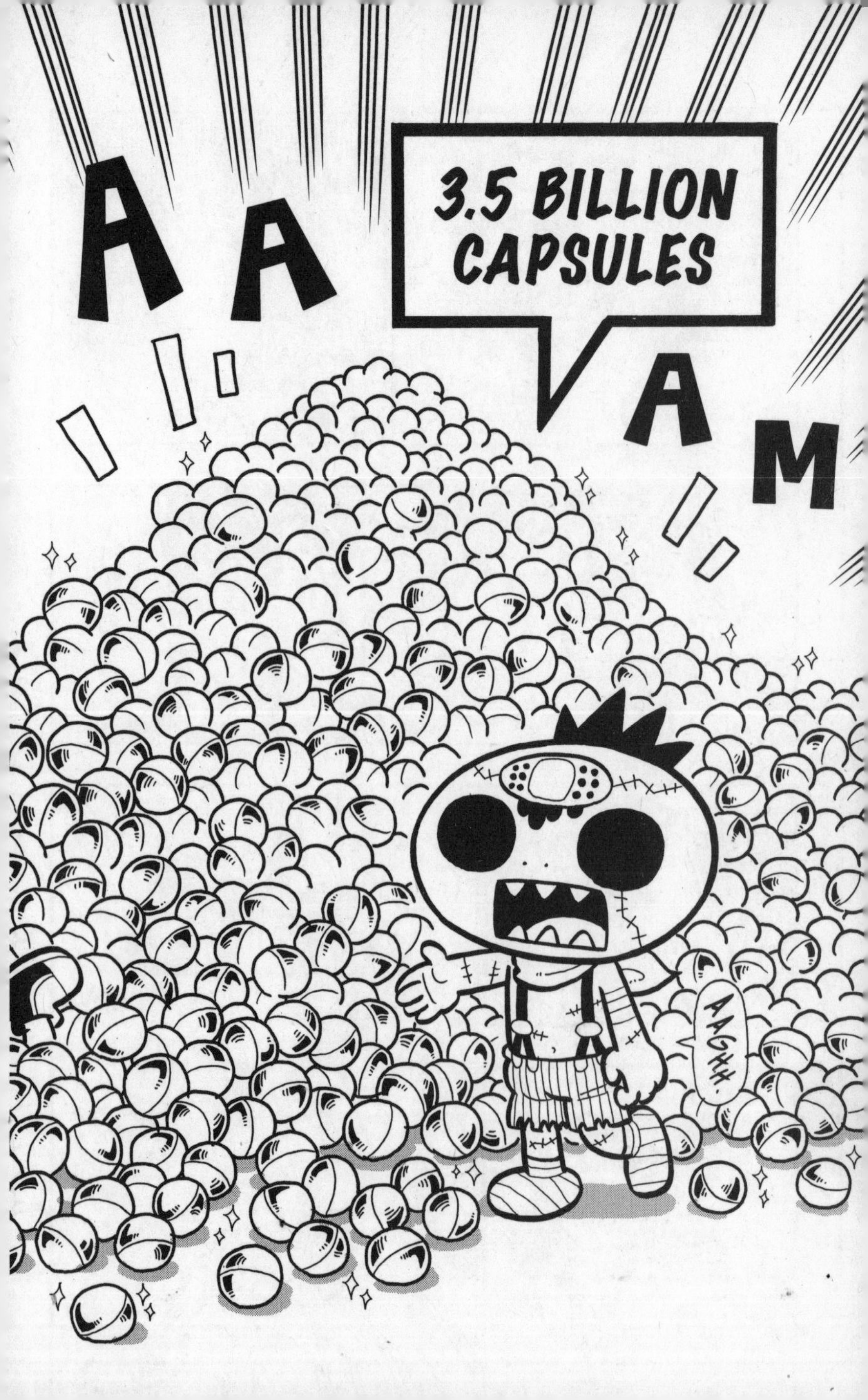
AAAAM
3.5 BILLION CAPSULES
AAGHH.

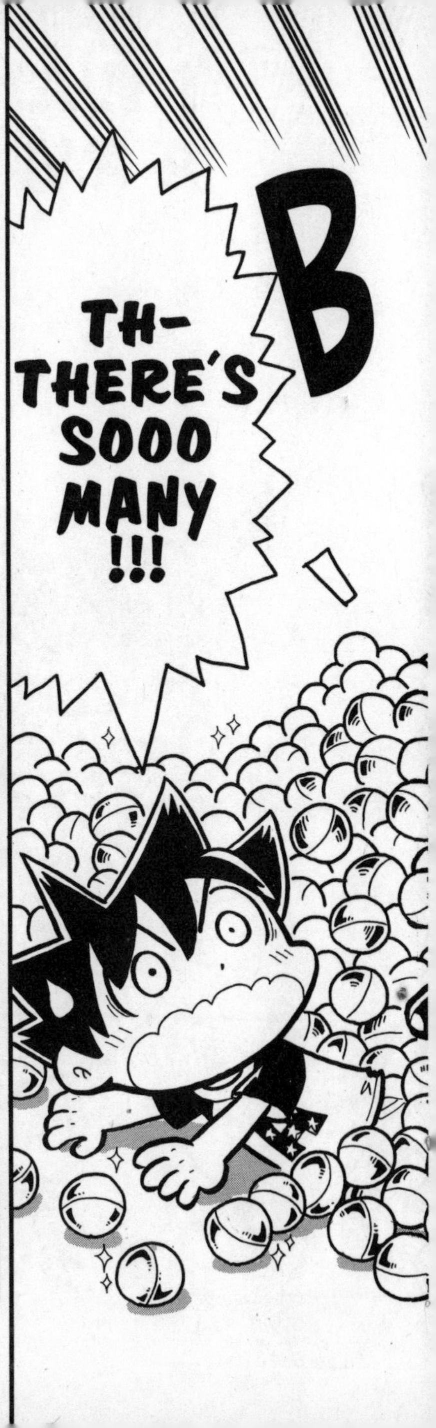
B
TH- THERE'S SOOO MANY!!!
!

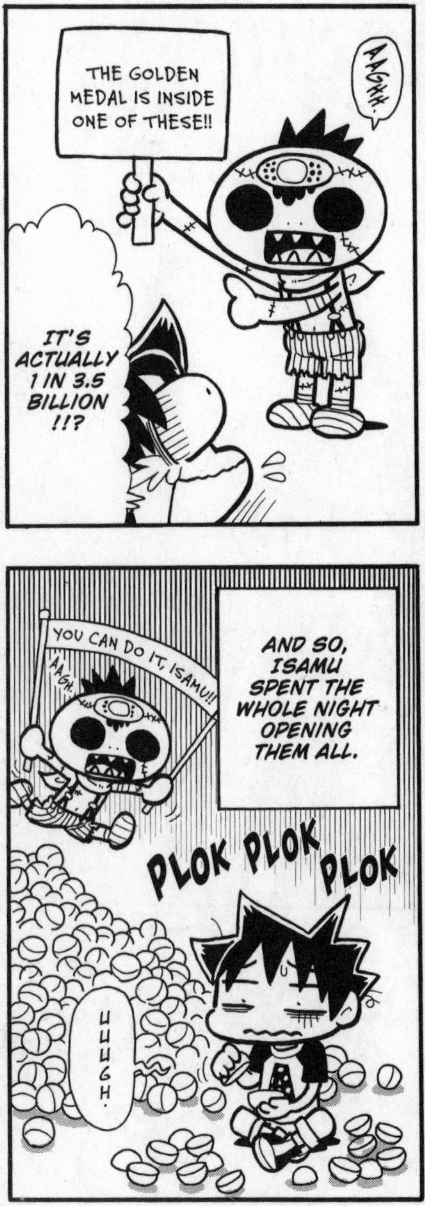
AAGHH.
THE GOLDEN MEDAL IS INSIDE ONE OF THESE!!
IT'S ACTUALLY 1 IN 3.5 BILLION!!?
AND SO, ISAMU SPENT THE WHOLE NIGHT OPENING THEM ALL.
YOU CAN DO IT, ISAMU!!
AAGH.
PLOK PLOK PLOK
UUUGH.

I WANNA GET A ZWITCH!

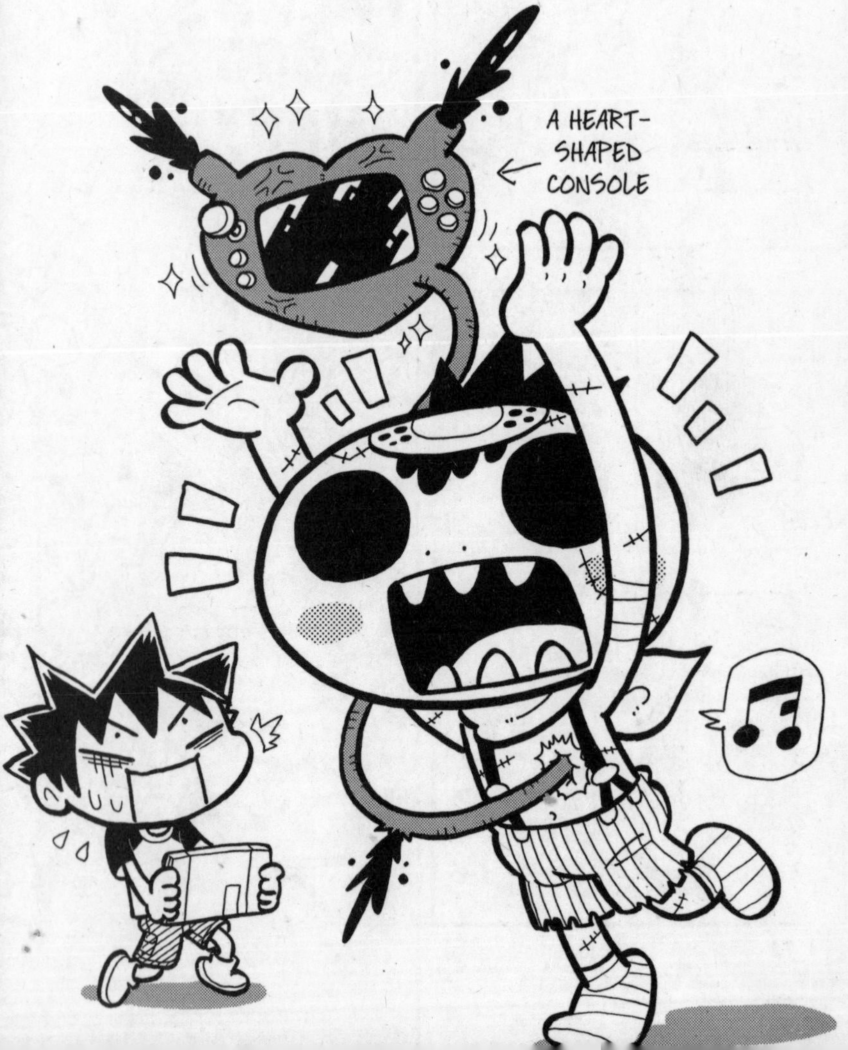
A HEART-SHAPED CONSOLE

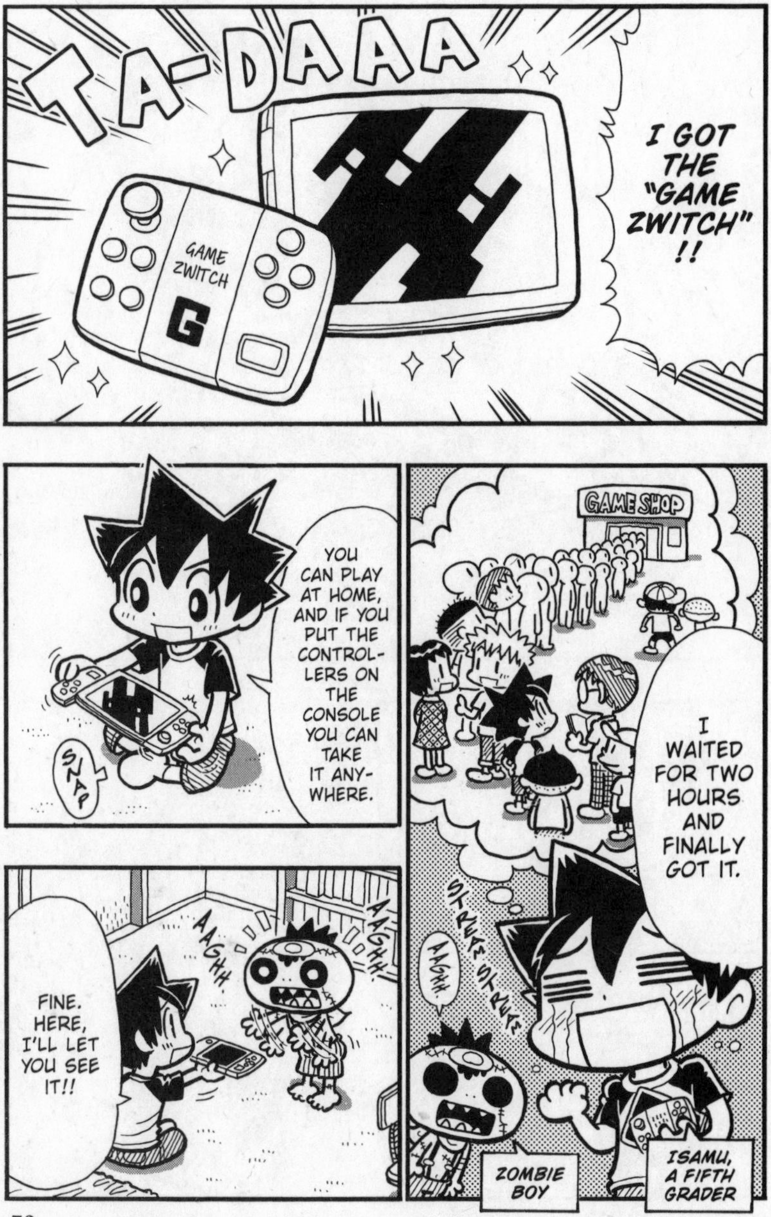
TA-DAAA
I GOT THE "GAME ZWITCH"!!
GAME ZWITCH
G
GAME SHOP
I WAITED FOR TWO HOURS AND FINALLY GOT IT.
STREAM STREAM
AAGHH
ISAMU, A FIFTH GRADER
ZOMBIE BOY
YOU CAN PLAY AT HOME, AND IF YOU PUT THE CONTROLLERS ON THE CONSOLE YOU CAN TAKE IT ANYWHERE.
SNAP
AAAGHH
AAGHH
FINE. HERE, I'LL LET YOU SEE IT!!

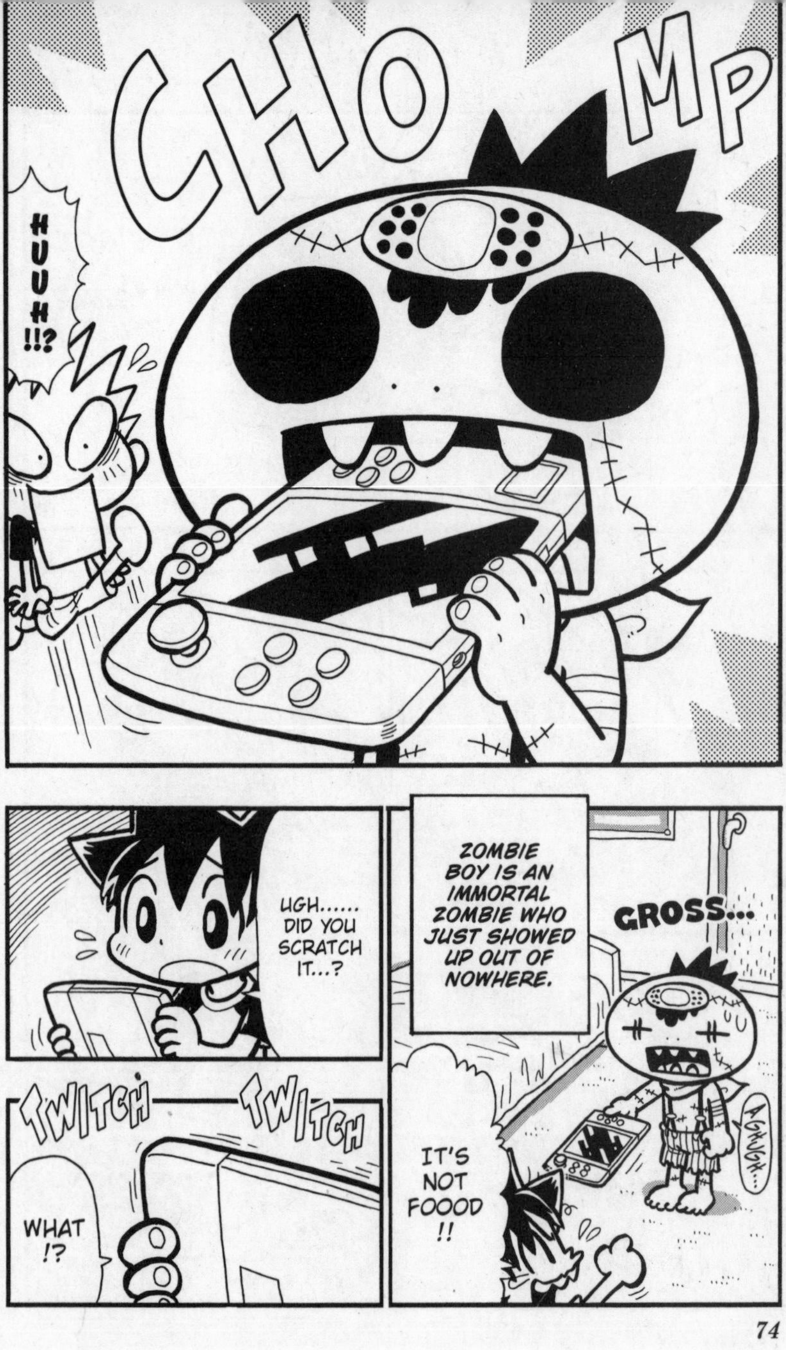
CHOMP
HUUUH!!?
ZOMBIE BOY IS AN IMMORTAL ZOMBIE WHO JUST SHOWED UP OUT OF NOWHERE.
GROSS...
AGHUGH...
IT'S NOT FOOOD!!
UGH...... DID YOU SCRATCH IT...?
TWITCH
TWITCH
WHAT!?

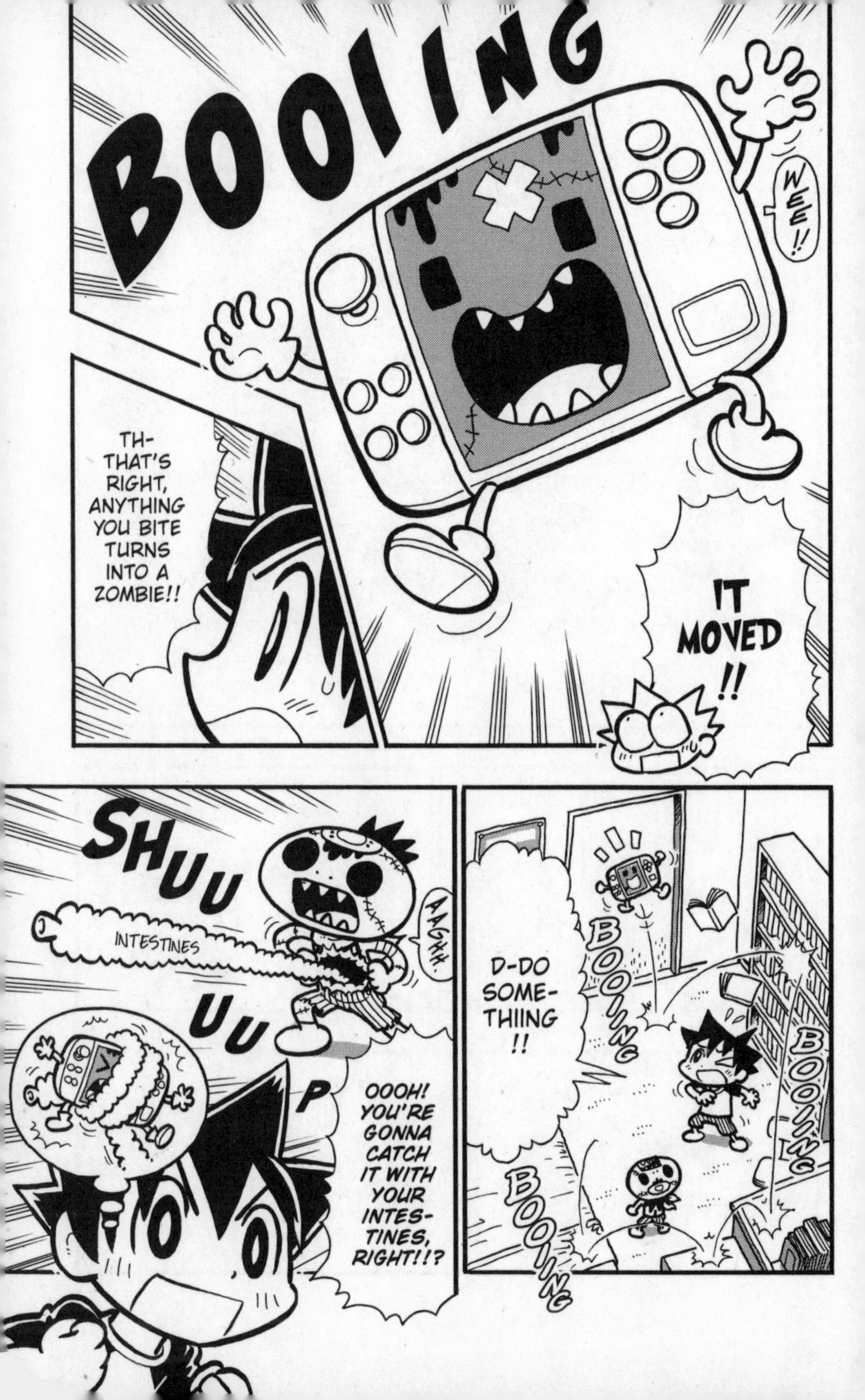
BOOIING
WEE!!
IT MOVED!!
TH-THAT'S RIGHT, ANYTHING YOU BITE TURNS INTO A ZOMBIE!!
BOOIING
D-DO SOMETHIING!!
BOOIING
BOOIING
SHUUUUP
AAGHH
INTESTINES
OOOH! YOU'RE GONNA CATCH IT WITH YOUR INTESTINES, RIGHT!!?

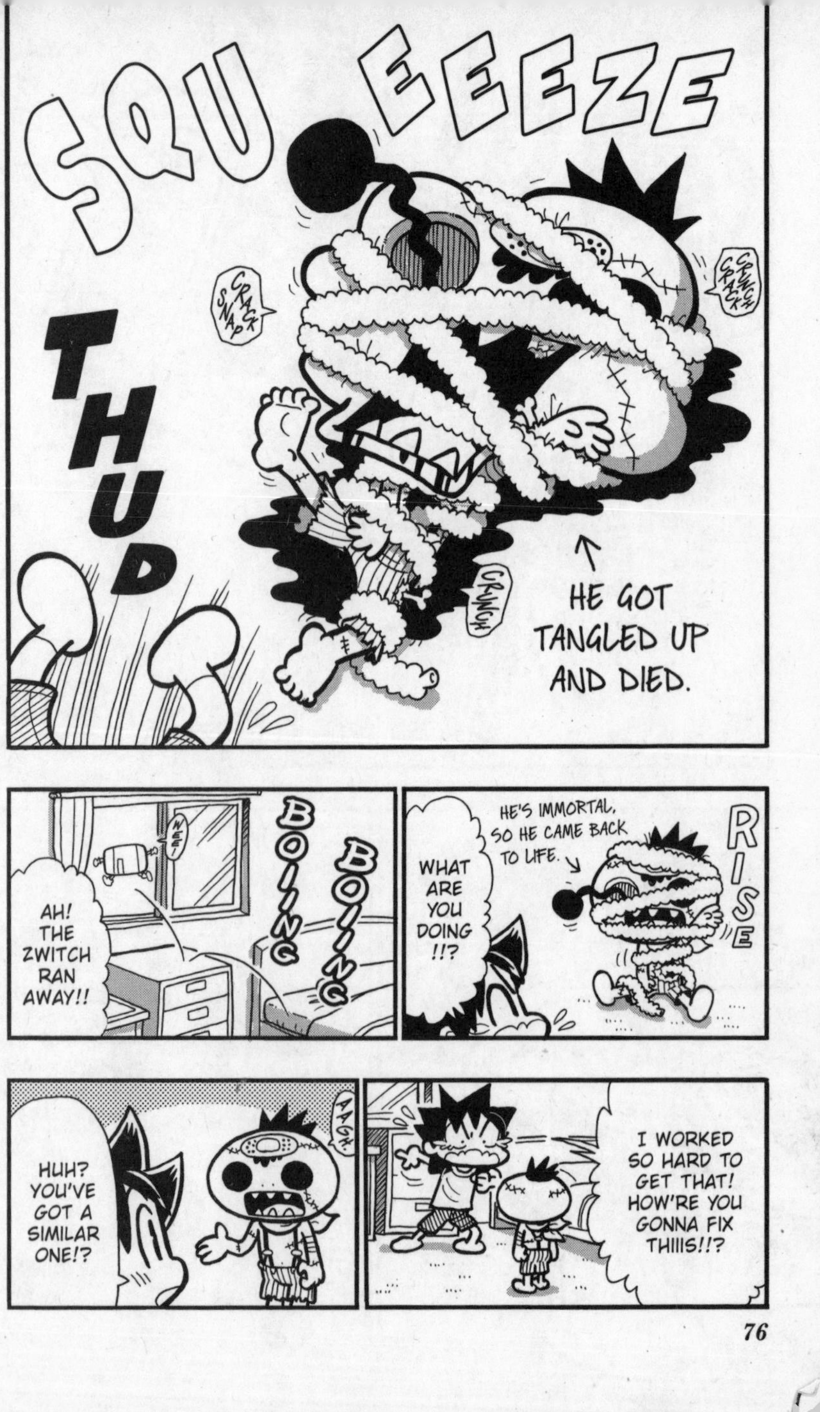
SQUEEEZE
CRUNCH CRACK
CRACK SNAP
THUD
HE GOT TANGLED UP AND DIED.
CRUNCH
RISE
HE'S IMMORTAL, SO HE CAME BACK TO LIFE.
WHAT ARE YOU DOING!!?
BOING
BOING
WEE!
AH! THE ZWITCH RAN AWAY!!
I WORKED SO HARD TO GET THAT! HOW'RE YOU GONNA FIX THIIIS!!?
AAGH.
HUH? YOU'VE GOT A SIMILAR ONE!?

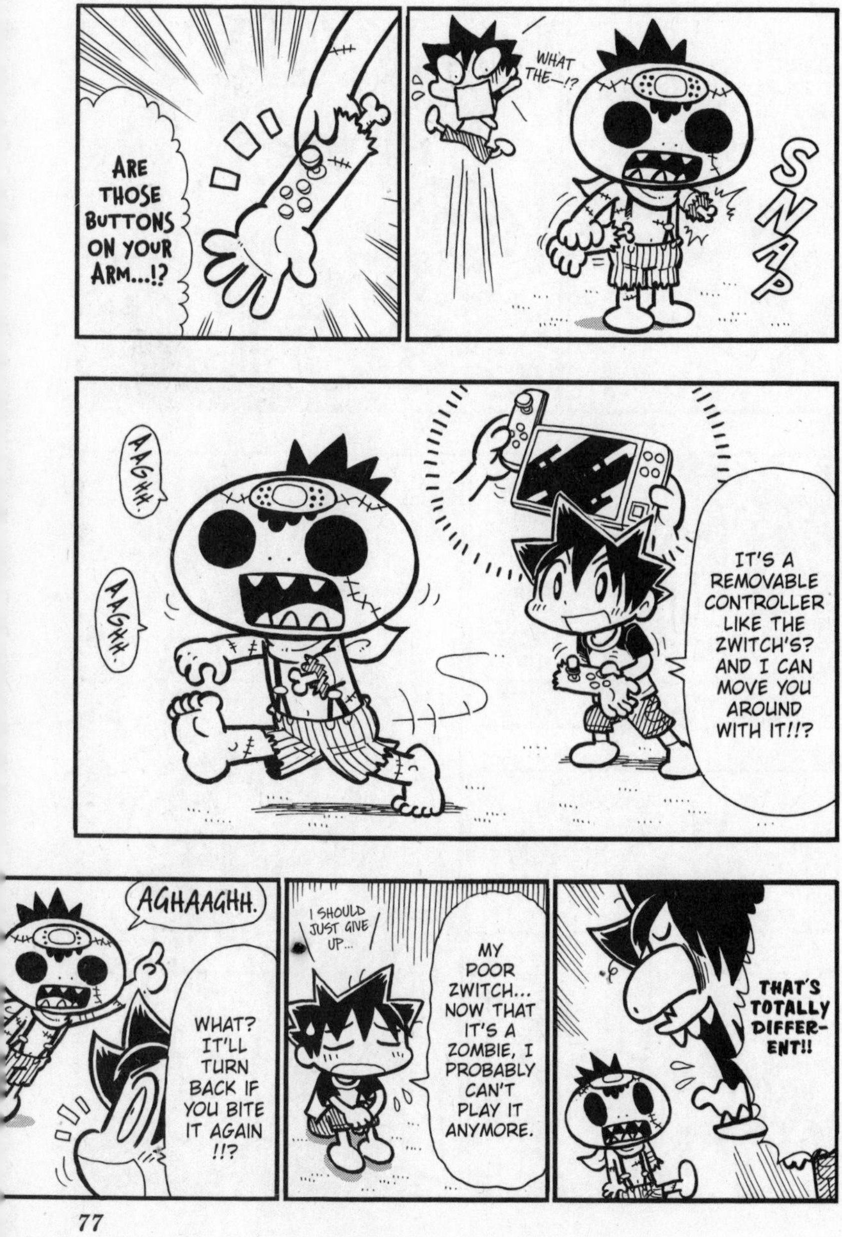
SNAP
WHAT THE—!?
ARE THOSE BUTTONS ON YOUR ARM...!?
IT'S A REMOVABLE CONTROLLER LIKE THE ZWITCH'S? AND I CAN MOVE YOU AROUND WITH IT!!?
AAGHH.
AAGHH.
THAT'S TOTALLY DIFFERENT!!
MY POOR ZWITCH... NOW THAT IT'S A ZOMBIE, I PROBABLY CAN'T PLAY IT ANYMORE.
I SHOULD JUST GIVE UP...
AGHAAGHH.
WHAT? IT'LL TURN BACK IF YOU BITE IT AGAIN!!?

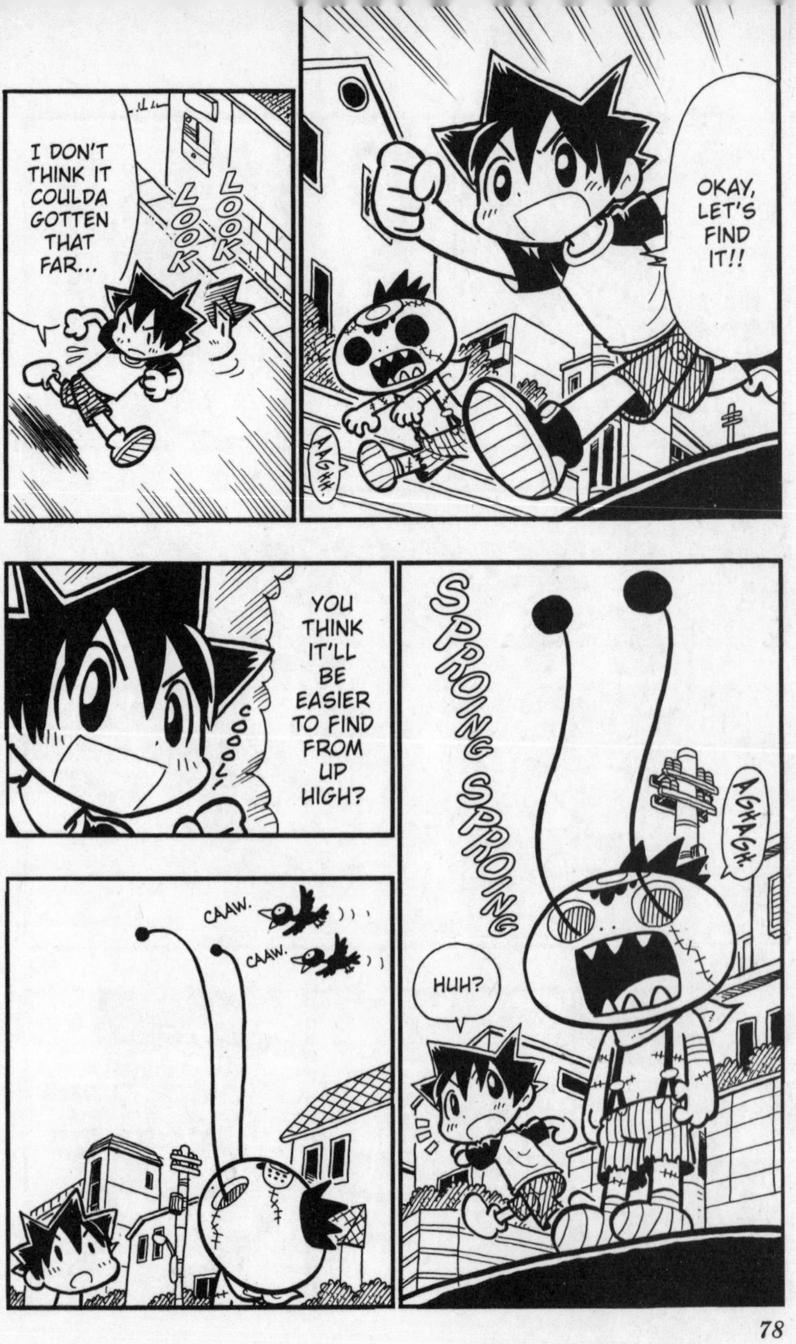
OKAY, LET'S FIND IT!!
AAGHH.
LOOK LOOK
I DON'T THINK IT COULDA GOTTEN THAT FAR...
SPROING SPROING
AGHAGH.
HUH?
YOU THINK IT'LL BE EASIER TO FIND FROM UP HIGH?
COOOL!
CAAW.
CAAW.

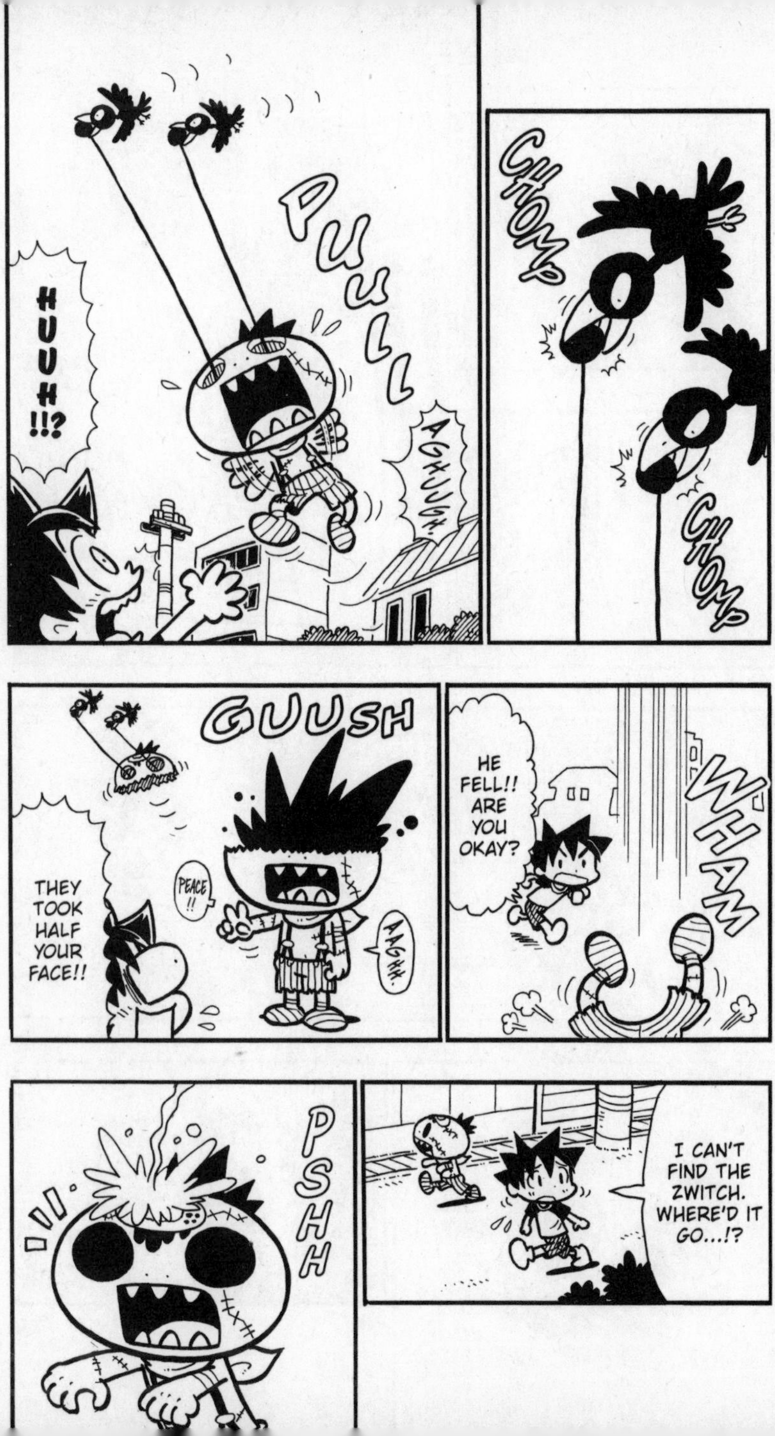
CHOMP
CHOMP
PUULL
AGHUUGH.
HUUUH!!?
WHAM
HE FELL!! ARE YOU OKAY?
GUUSH
AAGHH.
PEACE!!
THEY TOOK HALF YOUR FACE!!
I CAN'T FIND THE ZWITCH. WHERE'D IT GO...!?
PSHH

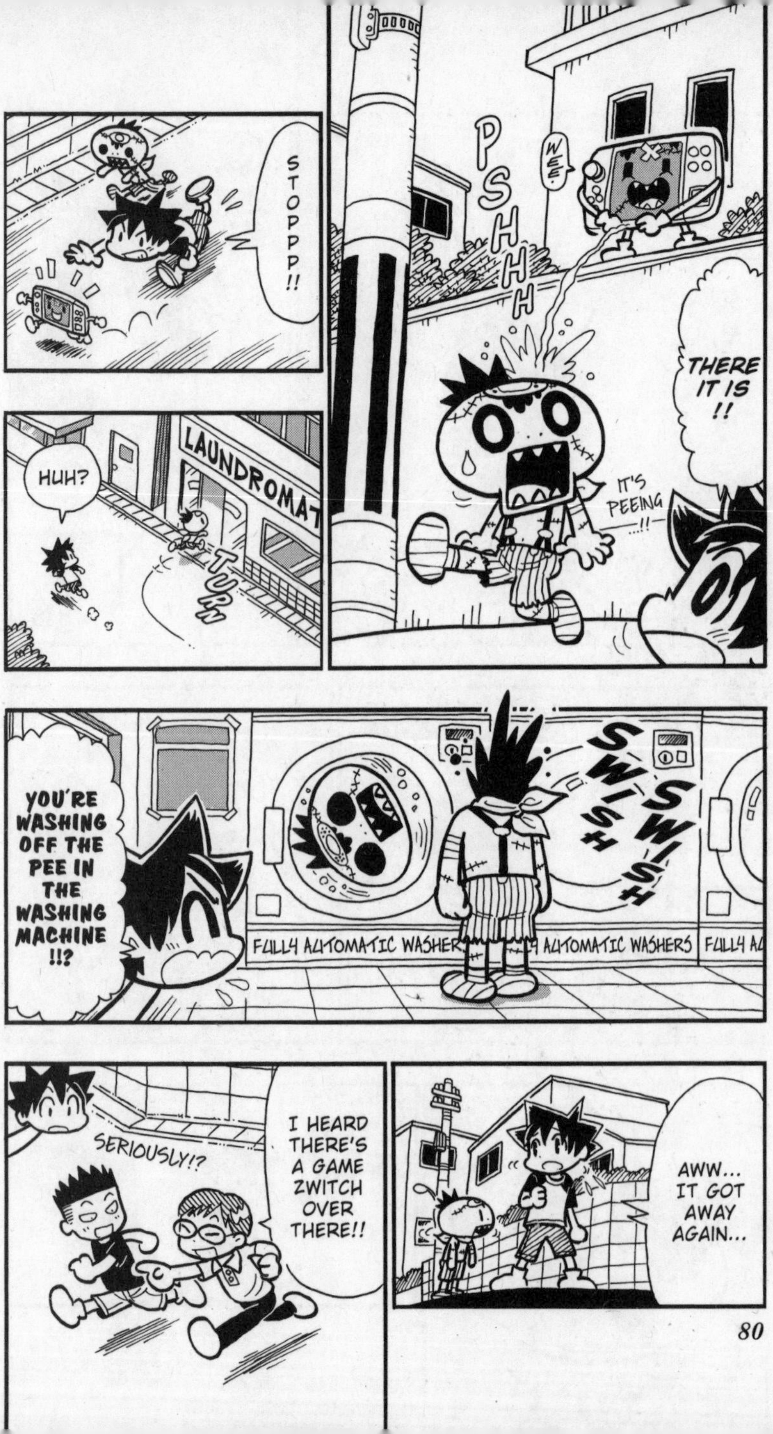
WEE.
PSHHHH
THERE IT IS!!
IT'S PEEING...!!
STOPPP!!
LAUNDROMAT
HUH?
TURN
SWISH
SWISH
YOU'RE WASHING OFF THE PEE IN THE WASHING MACHINE!!?
FULLY AUTOMATIC WASHERS
AUTOMATIC WASHERS
AWW... IT GOT AWAY AGAIN...
I HEARD THERE'S A GAME ZWITCH OVER THERE!!
SERIOUSLY!?

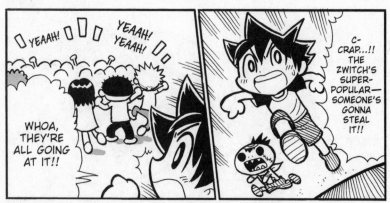

C-CRAP...!! THE ZWITCH'S SUPER-POPULAR—SOMEONE'S GONNA STEAL IT!!
YEAAH! YEAAH!
YEAAH!
WHOA, THEY'RE ALL GOING AT IT!!
GAME ZWITCH
AUTOGRAPH EVENT
SO CUTE!
YEEK! YEEK!
KYAAH!
WHOO-HOO!
SCRIBBLE
SKID
WHY'S A VIDEO GAME GIVING AUTO-GRAPHS!!?
AGHAGH!
ALL RIGHT, GET HIIIM!!

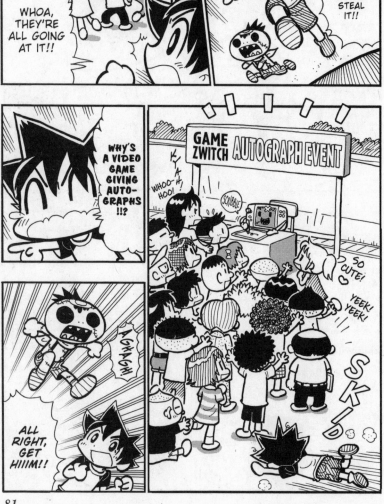

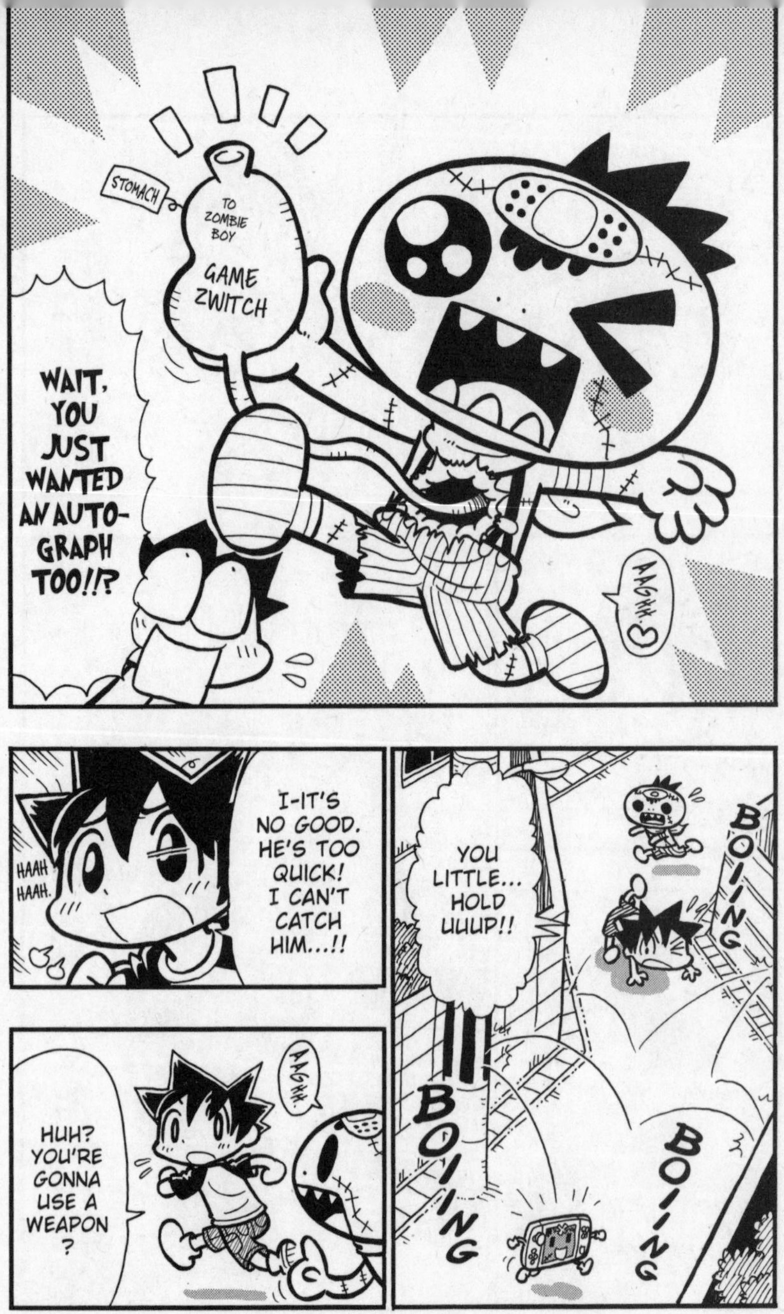
AAGHH.
STOMACH
TO ZOMBIE BOY
GAME ZWITCH
WAIT, YOU JUST WANTED AN AUTO-GRAPH TOO!!?
BOIIING
YOU LITTLE... HOLD UUUP!!
BOIIING
BOIIING
I-IT'S NO GOOD. HE'S TOO QUICK! I CAN'T CATCH HIM...!!
HAAH HAAH.
AAGHH.
HUH? YOU'RE GONNA USE A WEAPON?

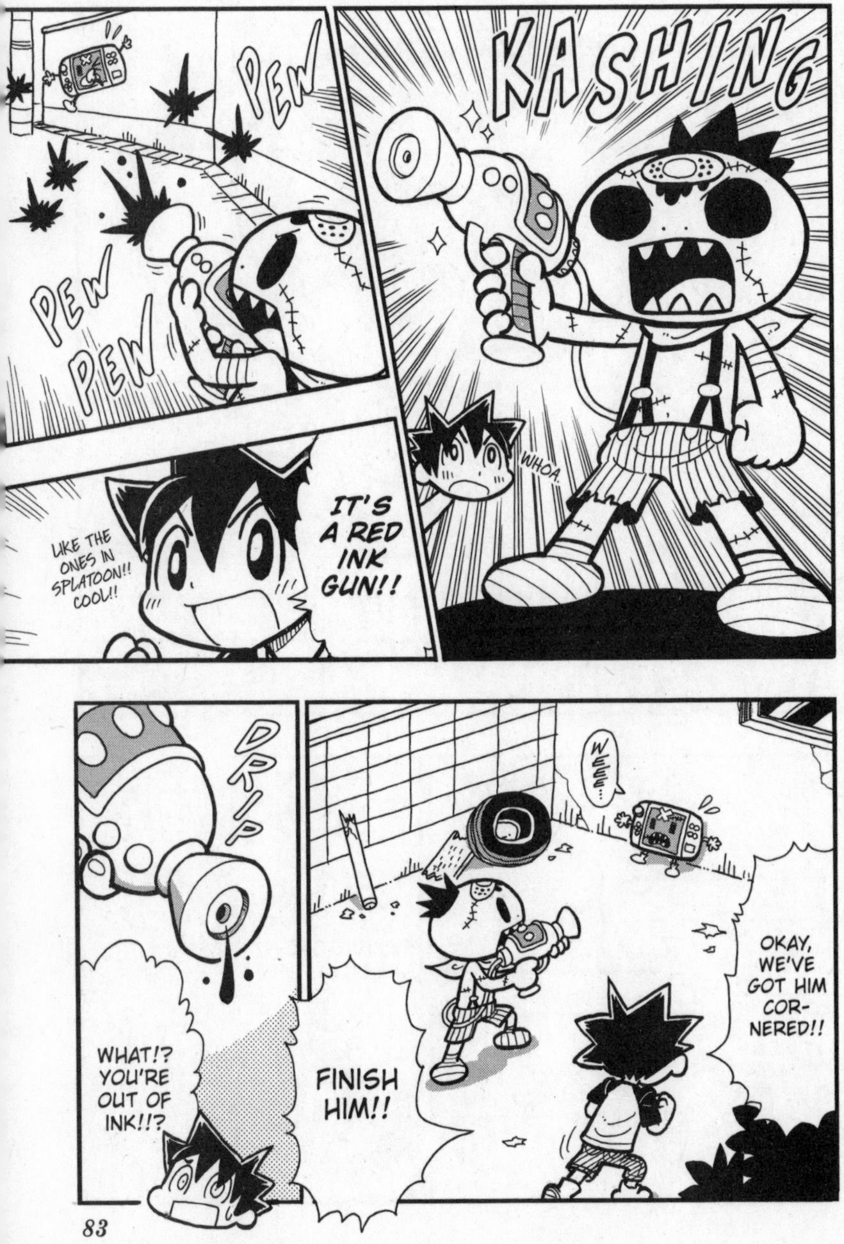
KASHING
WHOA.
PEW
PEW
PEW
IT'S A RED INK GUN!!
LIKE THE ONES IN SPLATOON!! COOL!!
WEEE...
OKAY, WE'VE GOT HIM COR-NERED!!
FINISH HIM!!
DRIP
WHAT!? YOU'RE OUT OF INK!!?

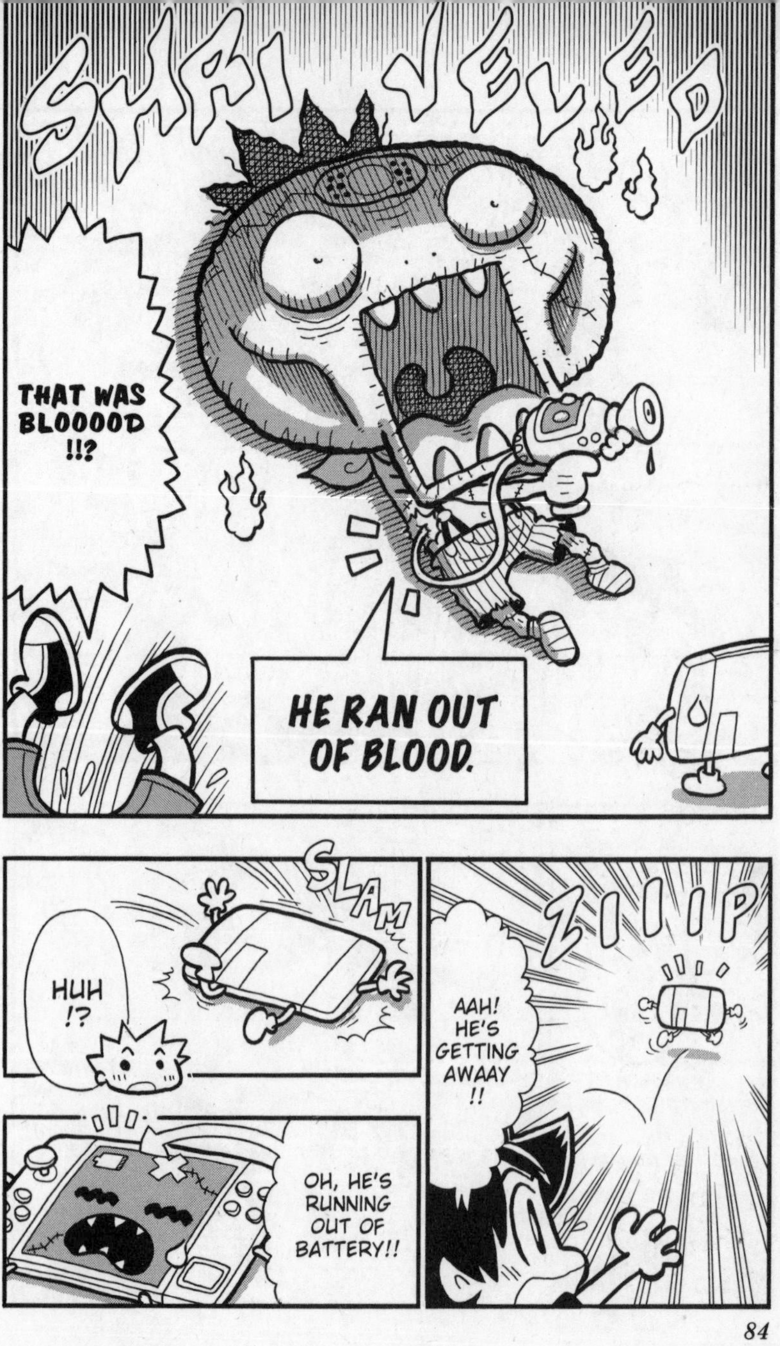
SHRIVELED
THAT WAS BLOOOOD !!?
HE RAN OUT OF BLOOD.
ZIIIP
AAH! HE'S GETTING AWAAY !!
SLAM
HUH !?
OH, HE'S RUNNING OUT OF BATTERY!!

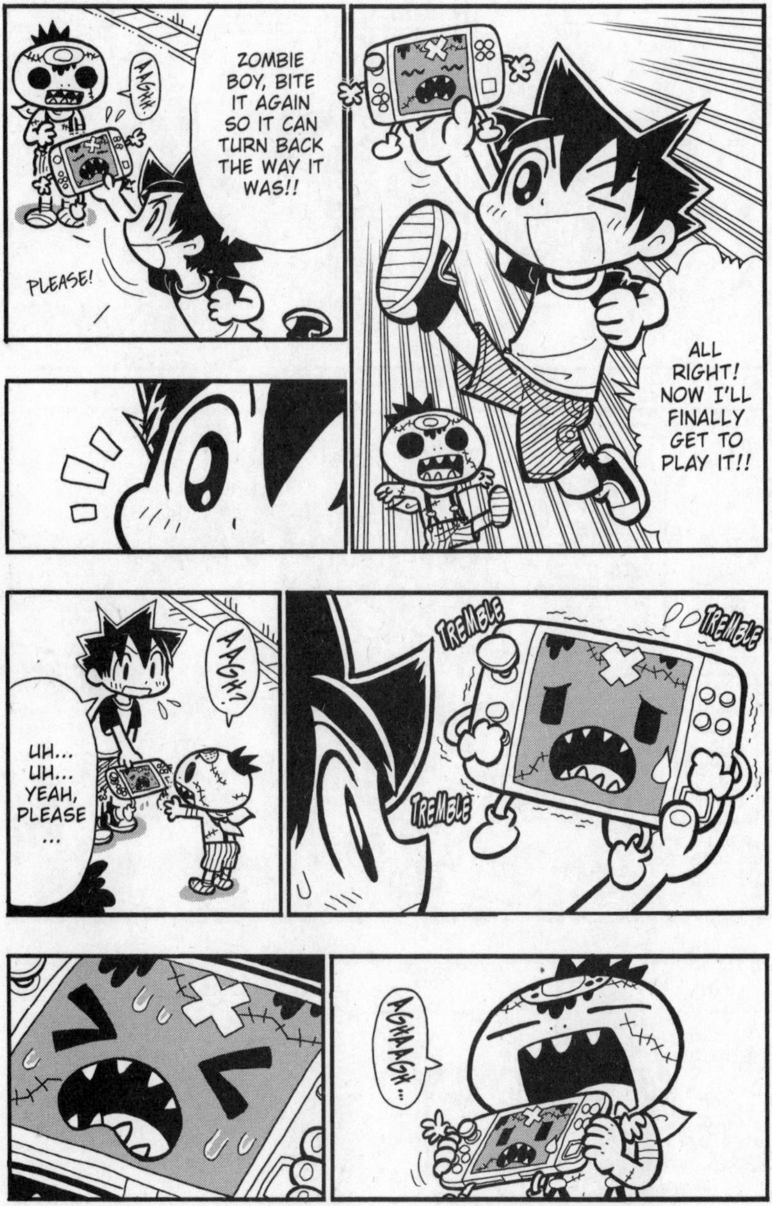
ALL RIGHT! NOW I'LL FINALLY GET TO PLAY IT!!
ZOMBIE BOY, BITE IT AGAIN SO IT CAN TURN BACK THE WAY IT WAS!!
AAGH.
PLEASE!
TREMBLE
TREMBLE
TREMBLE
AAGH?
UH... UH... YEAH, PLEASE ...
AGHAAGH...

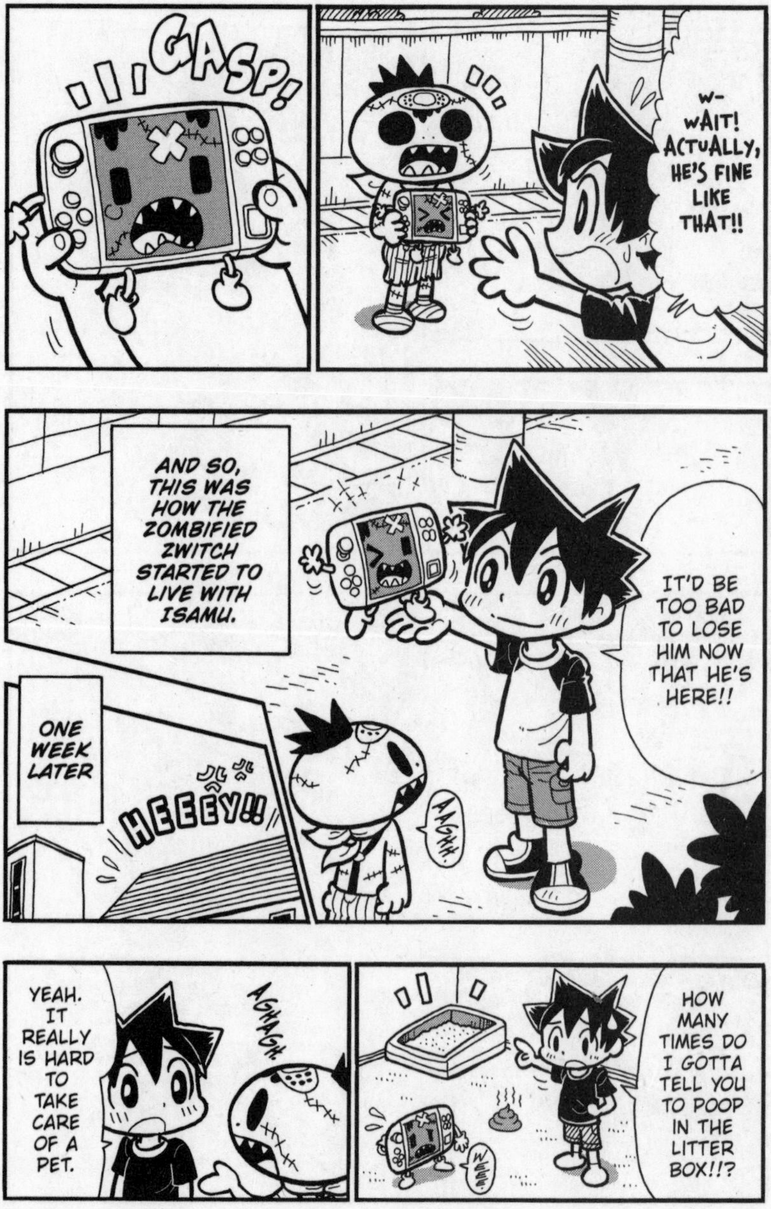
W- WAIT! ACTUALLY, HE'S FINE LIKE THAT!!
GASP!
IT'D BE TOO BAD TO LOSE HIM NOW THAT HE'S HERE!!
AND SO, THIS WAS HOW THE ZOMBIFIED ZWITCH STARTED TO LIVE WITH ISAMU.
ONE WEEK LATER
HEEEEY!!
AAGHH.
HOW MANY TIMES DO I GOTTA TELL YOU TO POOP IN THE LITTER BOX!!?
WEEE.
AGHAGH.
YEAH. IT REALLY IS HARD TO TAKE CARE OF A PET.

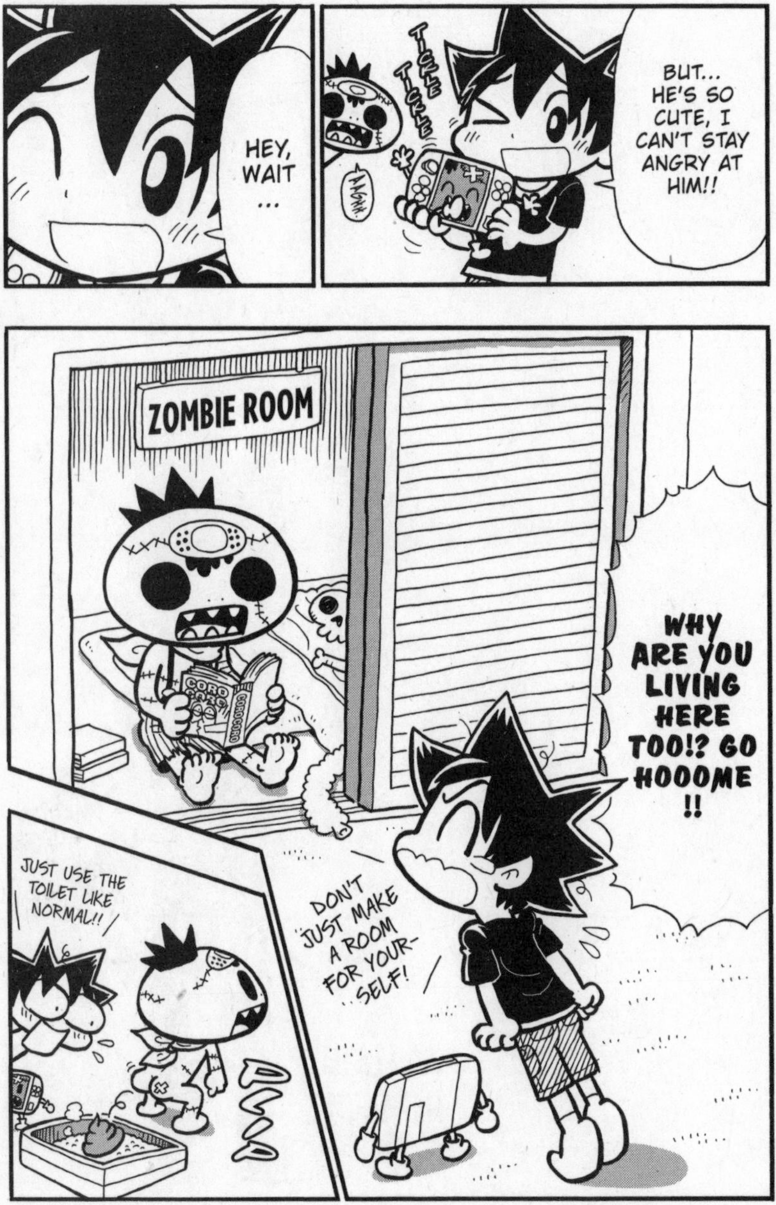
TICKLE TICKLE
BUT... HE'S SO CUTE, I CAN'T STAY ANGRY AT HIM!!
HEY, WAIT ...
ZOMBIE ROOM
WHY ARE YOU LIVING HERE TOO!? GO HOOOME !!
DON'T JUST MAKE A ROOM FOR YOURSELF!
JUST USE THE TOILET LIKE NORMAL!!

BYE!!

ZOMBIE
HUNTER
JOE

IMMORTAL ZUPERHEROEZ ZPOTTING!

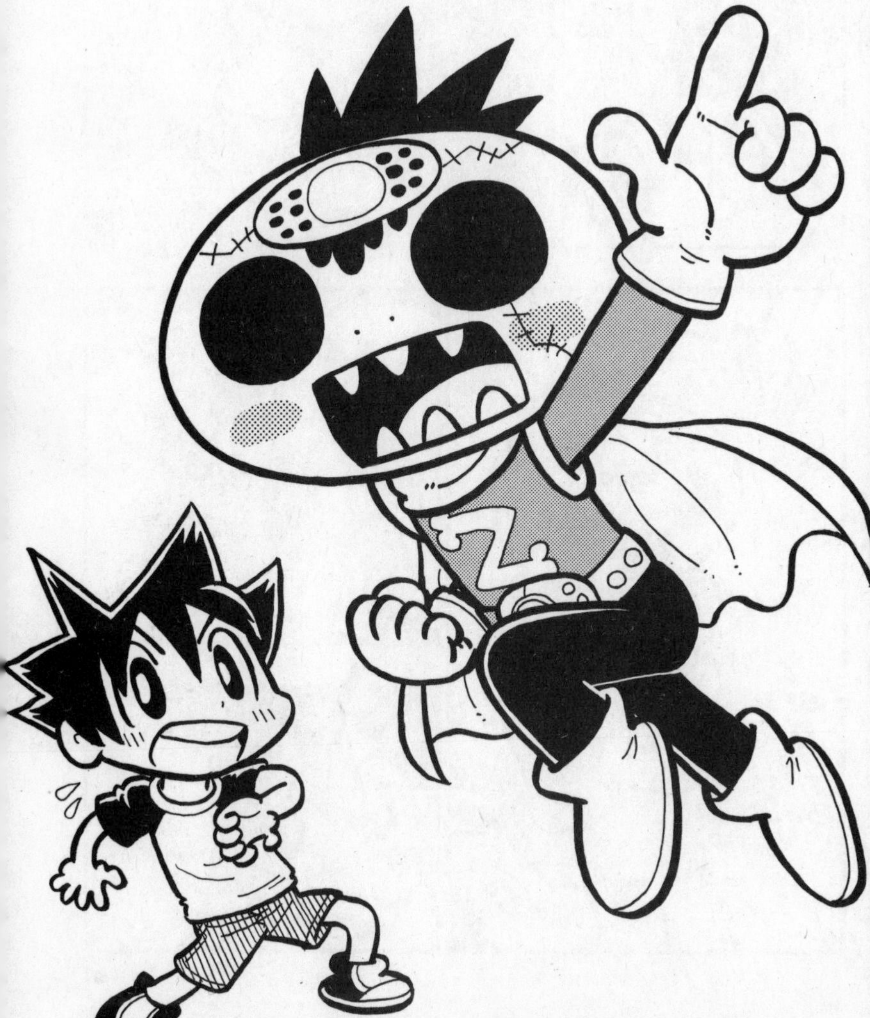

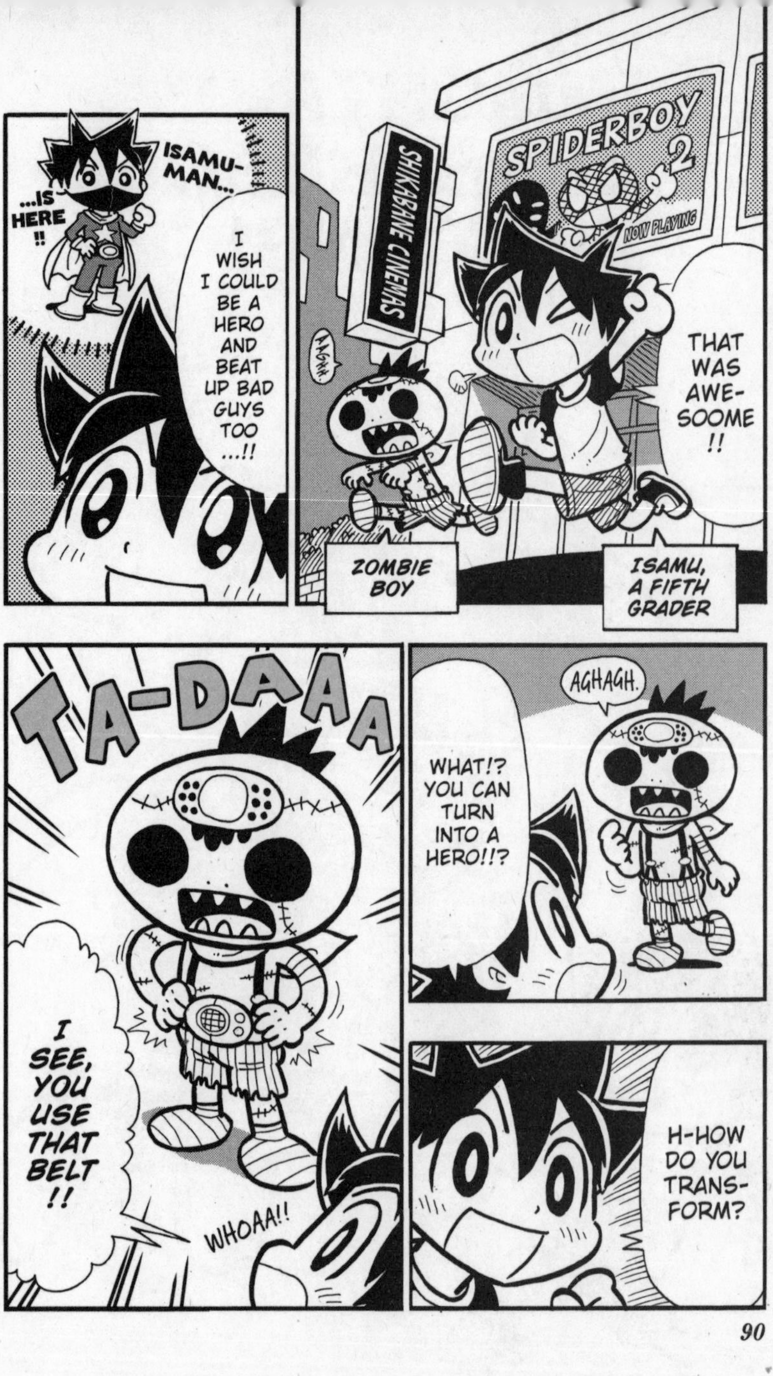
SPIDERBOY 2
NOW PLAYING
SHIKABANE CINEMAS
THAT WAS AWE-SOOME!!
AGHGH.
ISAMU, A FIFTH GRADER
ZOMBIE BOY
I WISH I COULD BE A HERO AND BEAT UP BAD GUYS TOO ...!!
ISAMU-MAN...
...IS HERE!!
AGHGH.
WHAT!? YOU CAN TURN INTO A HERO!!?
H-HOW DO YOU TRANS-FORM?
TA-DAAAA
I SEE, YOU USE THAT BELT!!
WHOAA!!

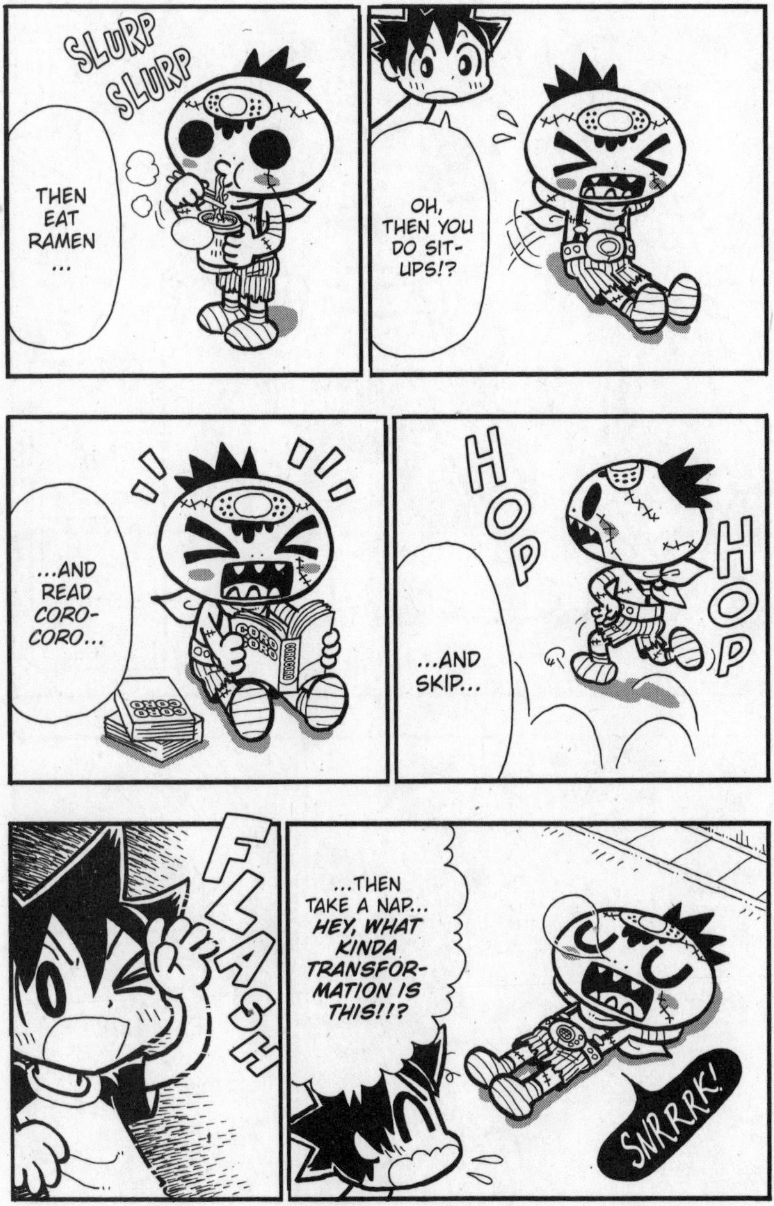
OH, THEN YOU DO SIT-UPS!?
SLURP SLURP
THEN EAT RAMEN ...
HOP HOP
...AND SKIP...
HOP HOP
...AND READ CORO-CORO...
CORO CORO
...THEN TAKE A NAP... HEY, WHAT KINDA TRANSFORMATION IS THIS!!?
SNRRRK!
FLASH

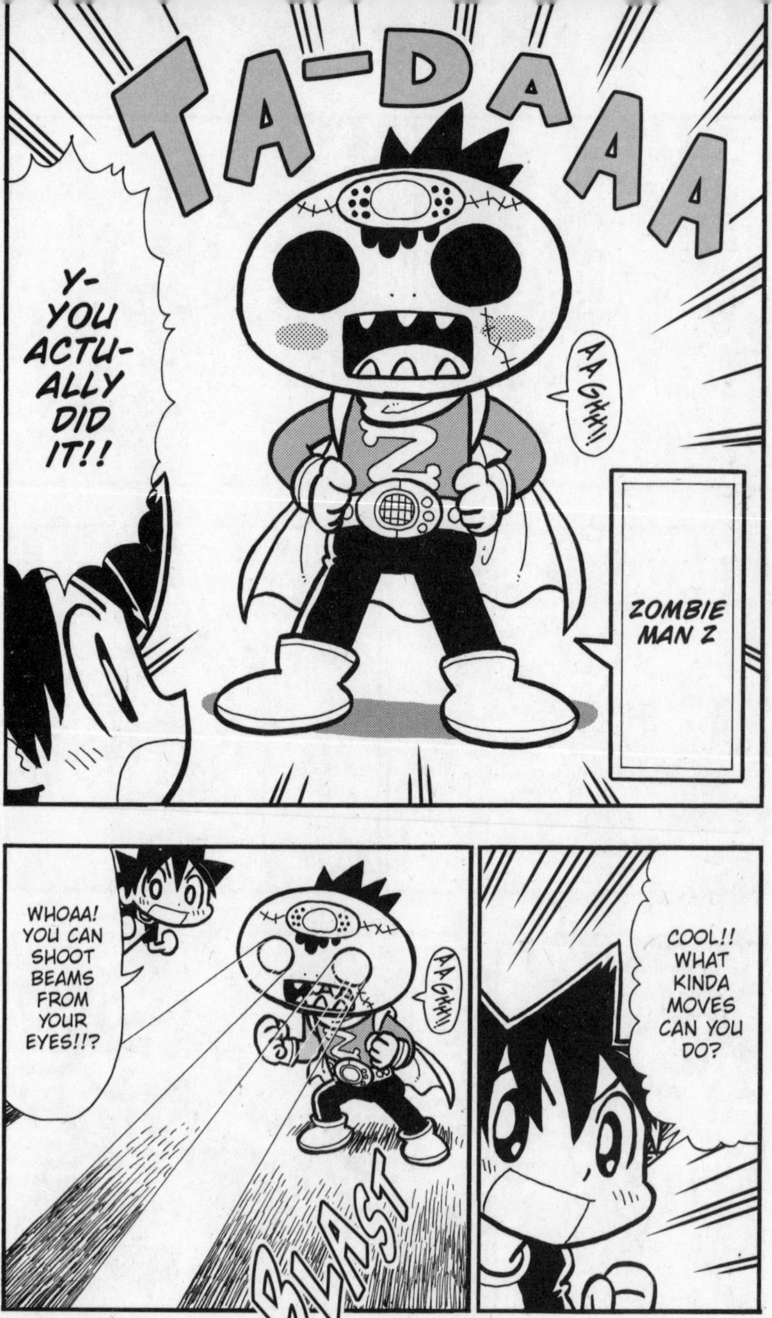
TA-DAAAA
AAGHH!!
ZOMBIE MAN Z
Y-YOU ACTU-ALLY DID IT!!
COOL!! WHAT KINDA MOVES CAN YOU DO?
AAGHH!!
WHOAA! YOU CAN SHOOT BEAMS FROM YOUR EYES!!?
BLAST

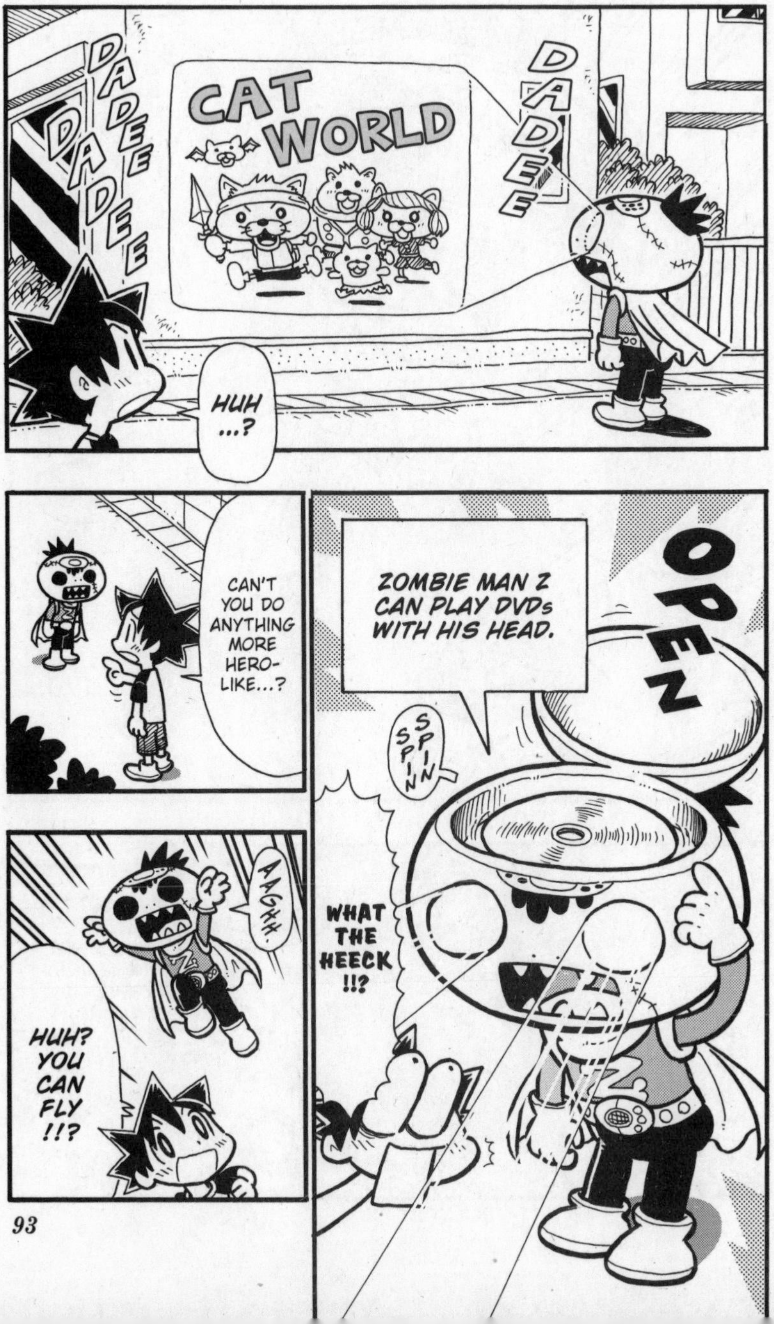

DADEE
CAT WORLD
DADADEE DEE
HUH ...?
OPEN
ZOMBIE MAN Z CAN PLAY DVDs WITH HIS HEAD.
SPIN SPIN
WHAT THE HEECK !!?
CAN'T YOU DO ANYTHING MORE HERO-LIKE...?
AAGHH
HUH? YOU CAN FLY !!?

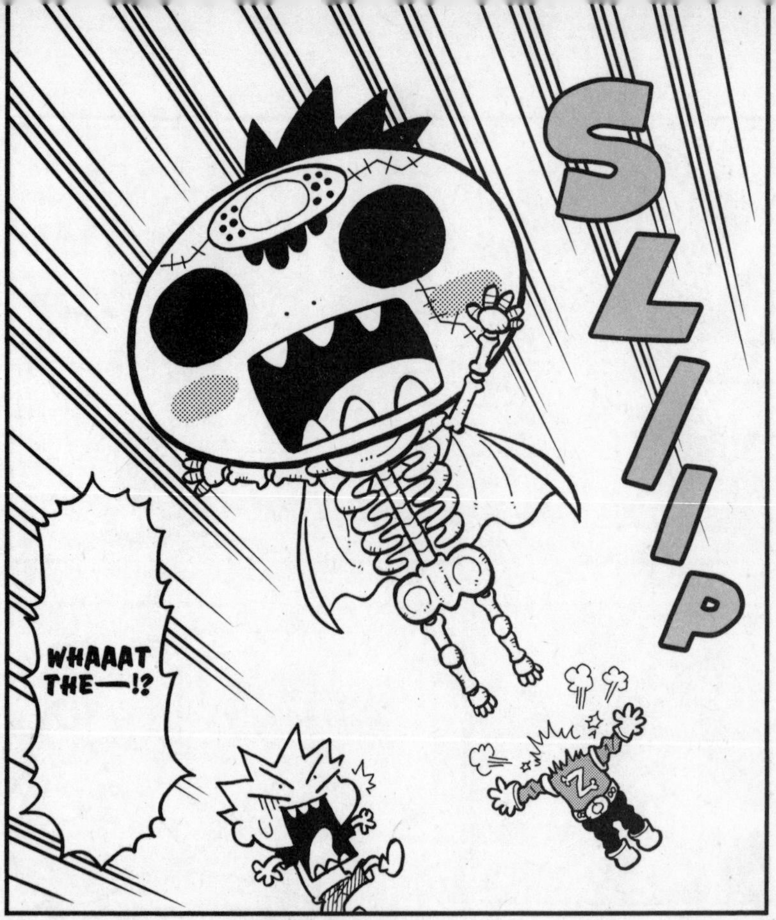
SLIIP
WHAAAT THE—!?

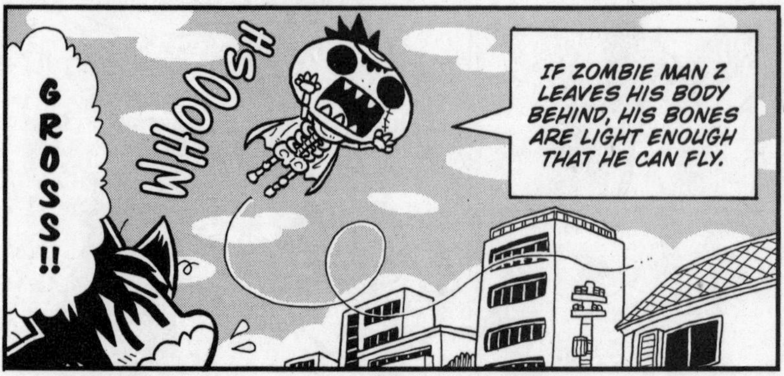
IF ZOMBIE MAN Z LEAVES HIS BODY BEHIND, HIS BONES ARE LIGHT ENOUGH THAT HE CAN FLY.
WHOOSH
GROSS!!

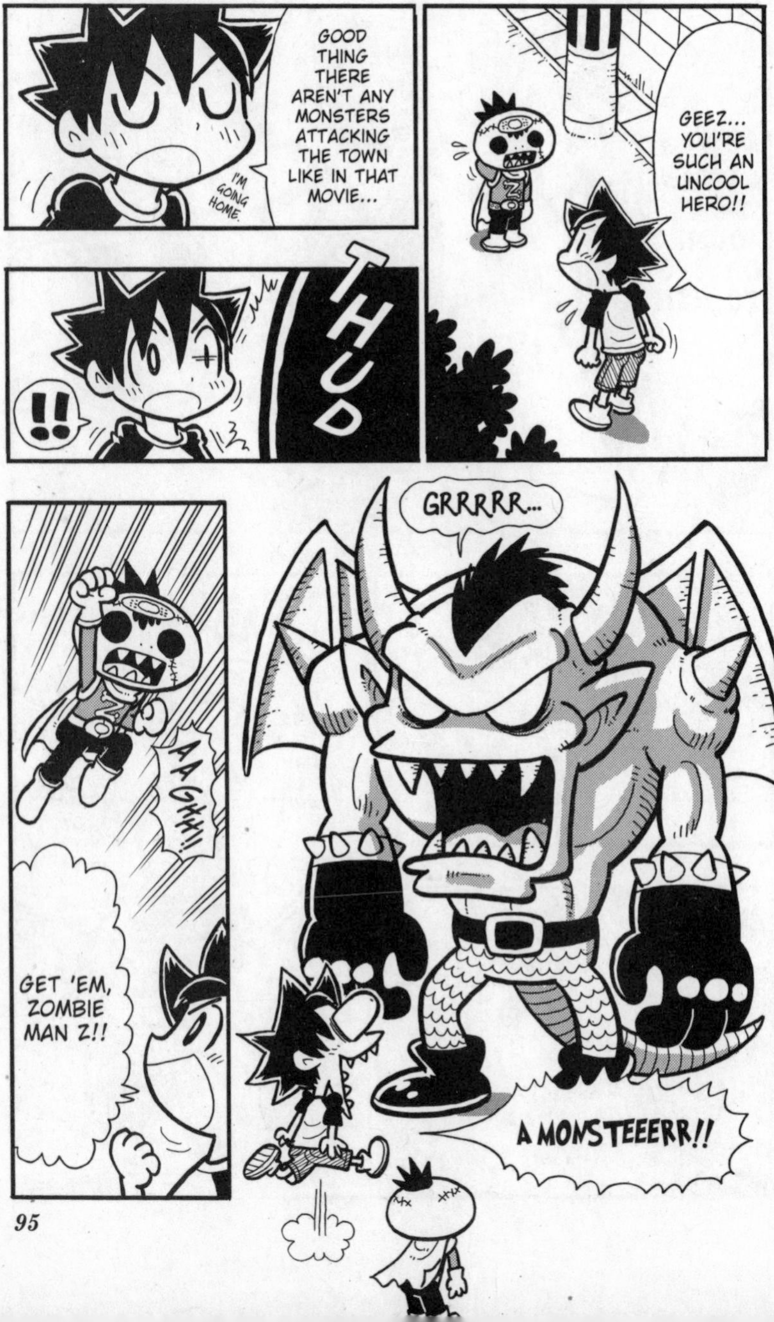
GEEZ... YOU'RE SUCH AN UNCOOL HERO!!
GOOD THING THERE AREN'T ANY MONSTERS ATTACKING THE TOWN LIKE IN THAT MOVIE...
I'M GOING HOME.
!!
THUD
GRRRRR...
A MONSTEEERR!!
AAGHH!!
GET 'EM, ZOMBIE MAN Z!!

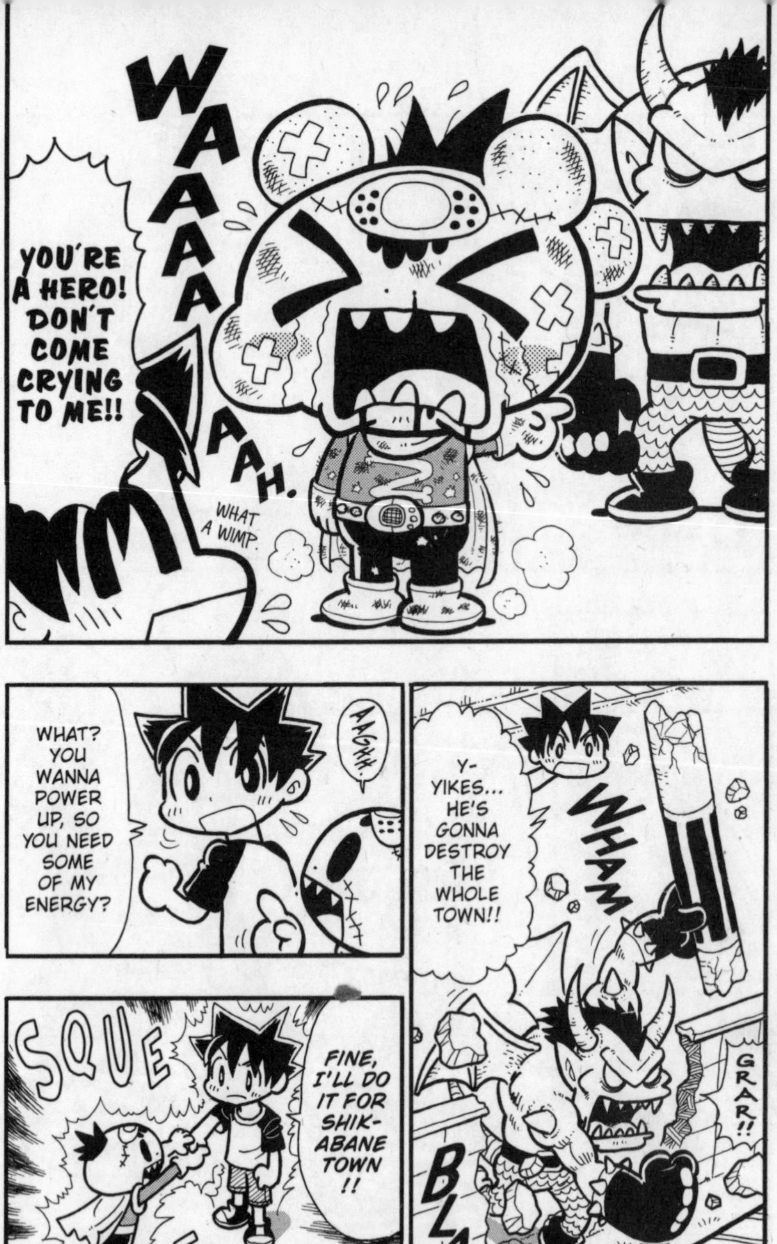
WAAAAAAH.
YOU'RE A HERO! DON'T COME CRYING TO ME!!
WHAT A WIMP.
Y-YIKES... HE'S GONNA DESTROY THE WHOLE TOWN!!
WHAM
GRAR!!
BLAM
AAGHH
WHAT? YOU WANNA POWER UP, SO YOU NEED SOME OF MY ENERGY?
FINE, I'LL DO IT FOR SHIKABANE TOWN!!
SQUEEEZE

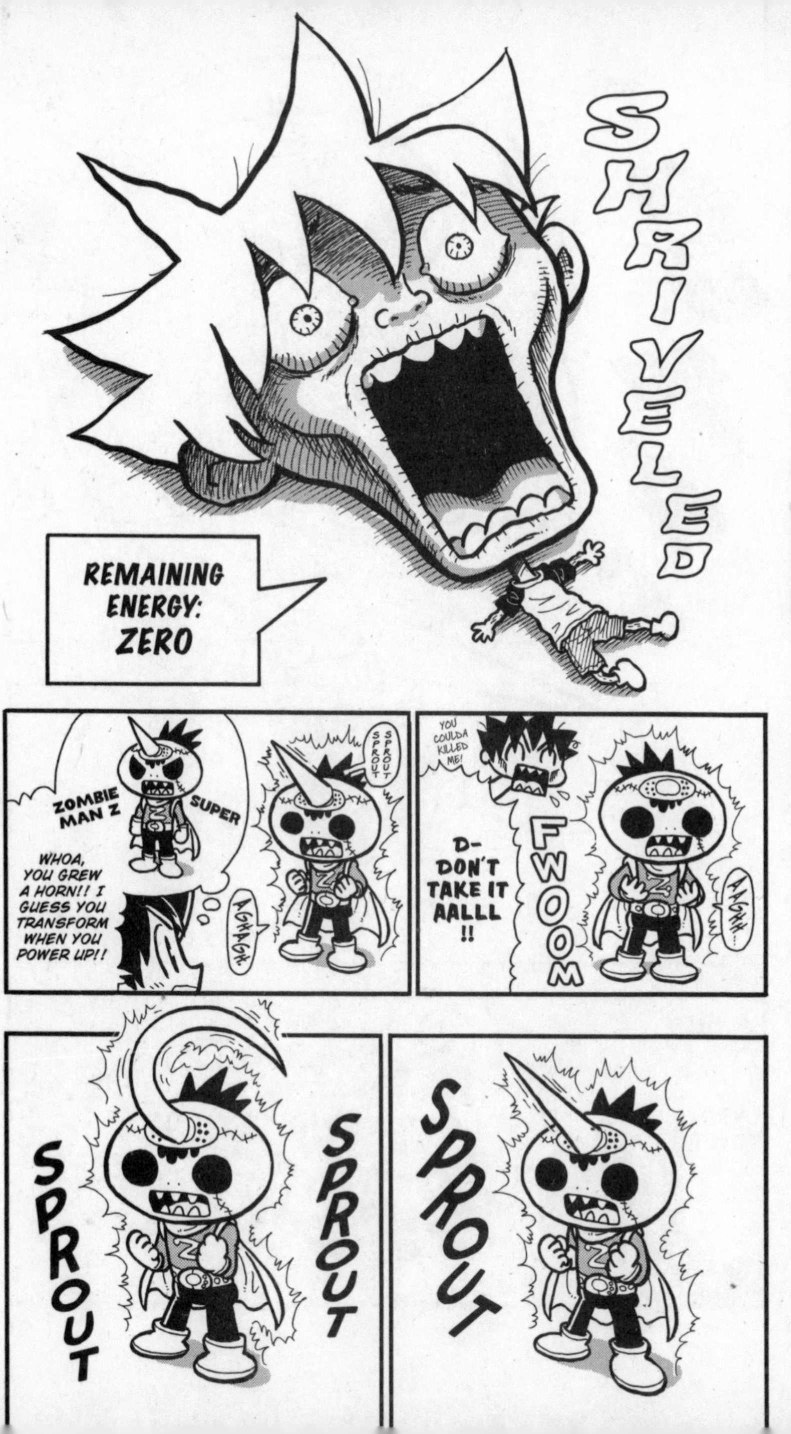
SHRIVELED
REMAINING ENERGY: ZERO
YOU COULDA KILLED ME!
D- DON'T TAKE IT AALLL !!
FWOOM
AAGHH...
SPROUT SPROUT
AGHAGH.
ZOMBIE MAN Z SUPER
WHOA, YOU GREW A HORN!! I GUESS YOU TRANSFORM WHEN YOU POWER UP!!
SPROUT
SPROUT
SPROUT

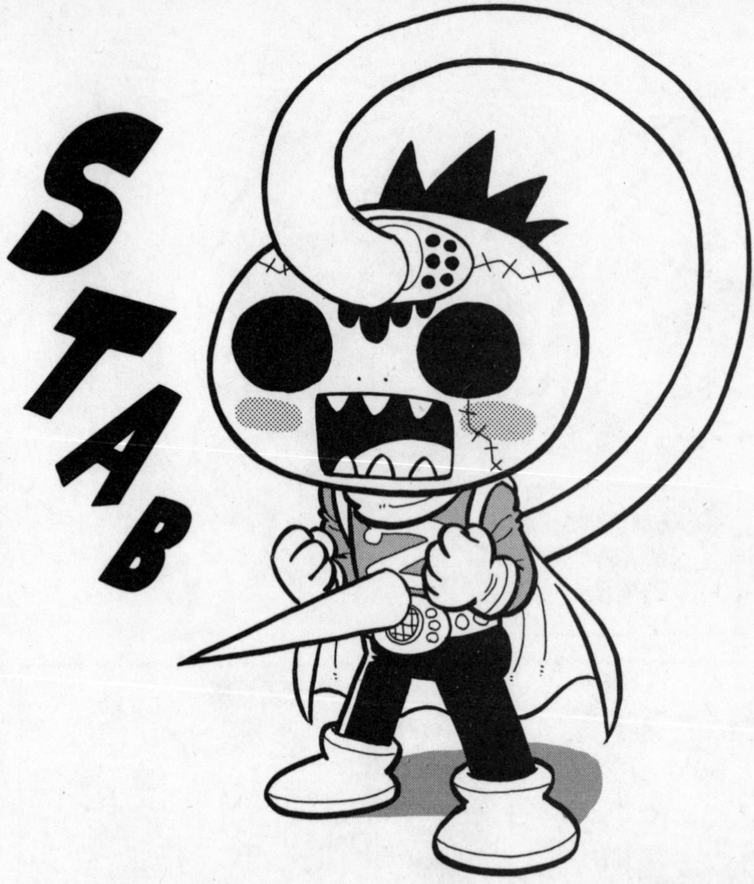
STAB

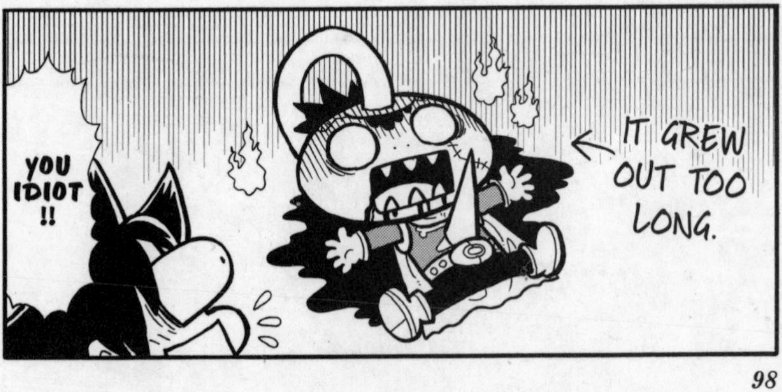
IT GREW OUT TOO LONG.
YOU IDIOT!!

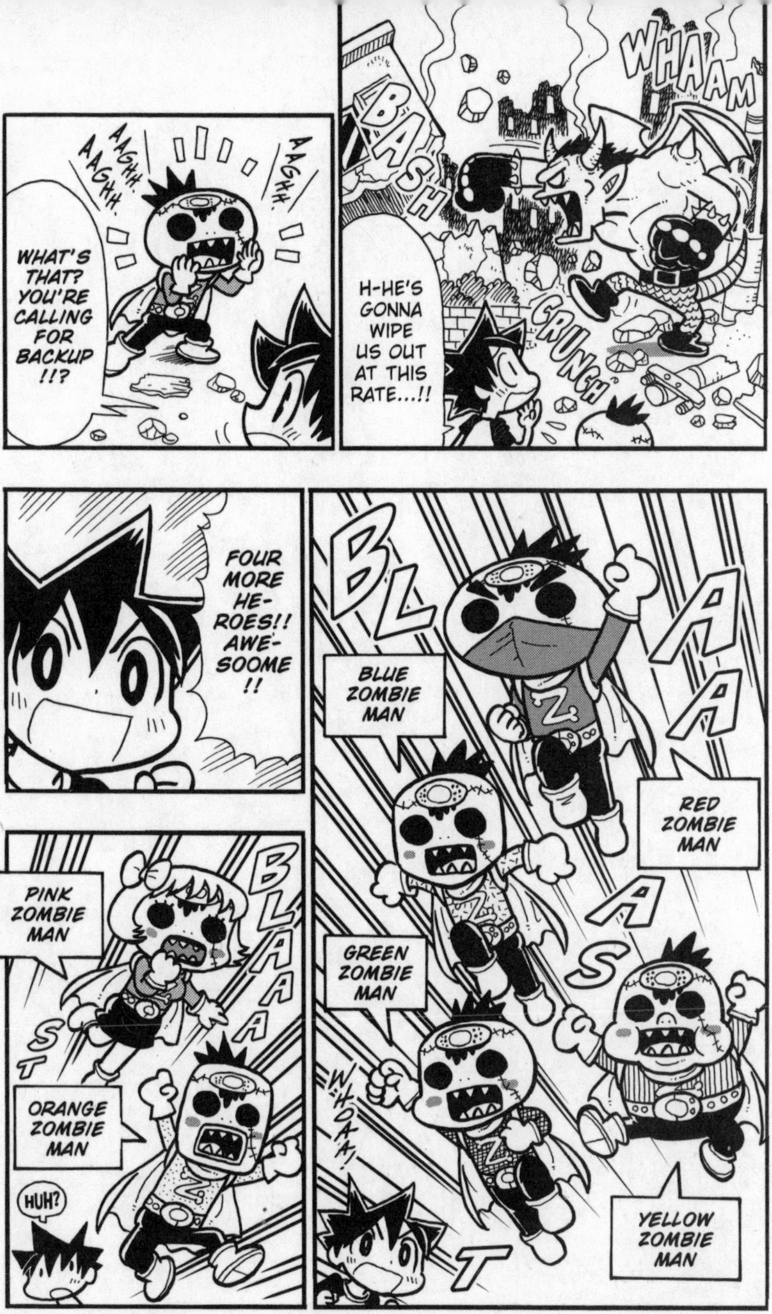
WHAAAM
BASH
H-HE'S GONNA WIPE US OUT AT THIS RATE...!!
CRUNCH
AAGHH
AAGHH
AAGHH
WHAT'S THAT? YOU'RE CALLING FOR BACKUP!!?
BLAAAASST
BLUE ZOMBIE MAN
RED ZOMBIE MAN
GREEN ZOMBIE MAN
WHOAA!
YELLOW ZOMBIE MAN
FOUR MORE HE-ROES!! AWE-SOOME!!
BLAAAAST
PINK ZOMBIE MAN
ORANGE ZOMBIE MAN
HUH?

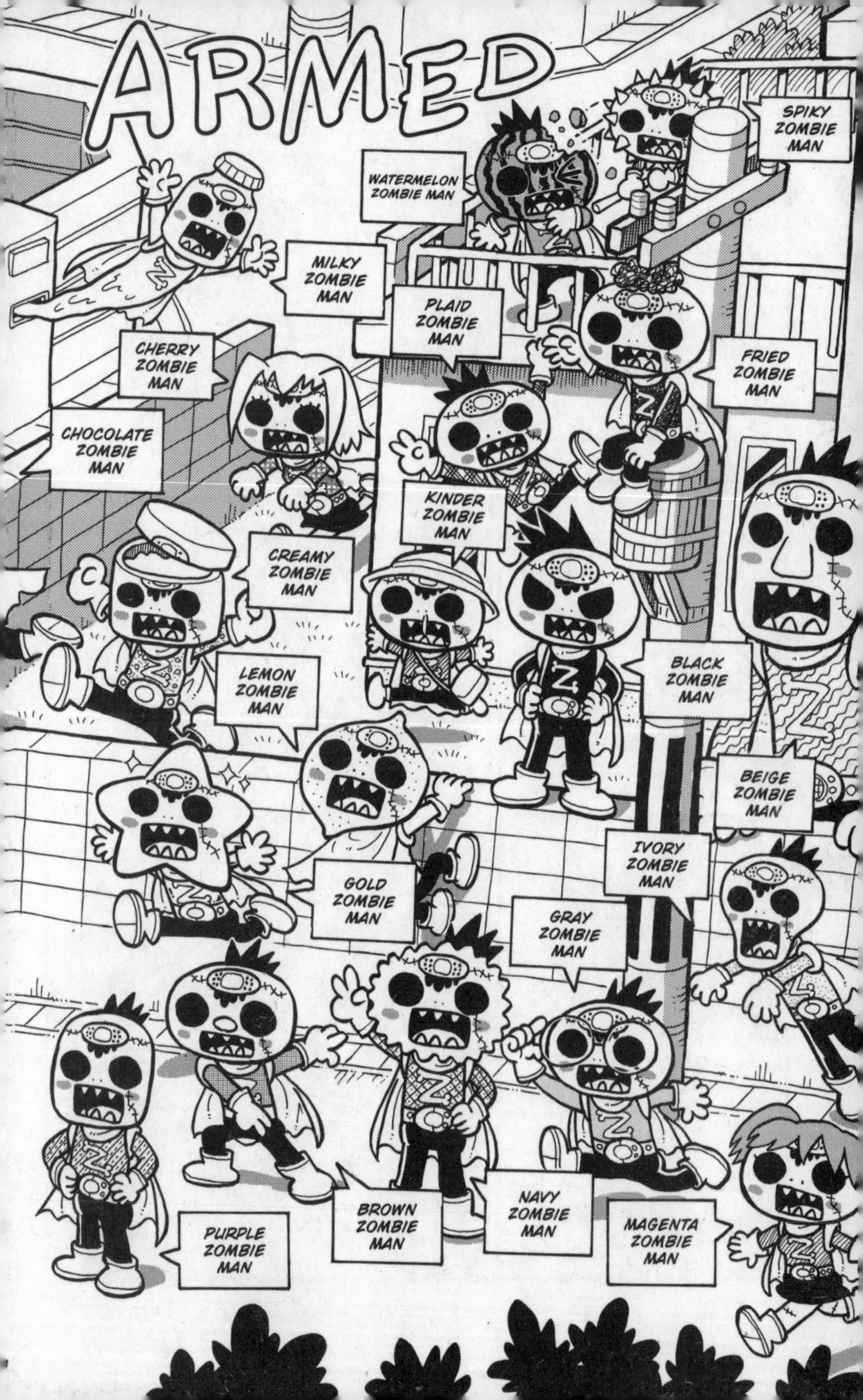
ARMED
SPIKY ZOMBIE MAN
WATERMELON ZOMBIE MAN
MILKY ZOMBIE MAN
FRIED ZOMBIE MAN
PLAID ZOMBIE MAN
CHERRY ZOMBIE MAN
CHOCOLATE ZOMBIE MAN
KINDER ZOMBIE MAN
CREAMY ZOMBIE MAN
BLACK ZOMBIE MAN
LEMON ZOMBIE MAN
BEIGE ZOMBIE MAN
IVORY ZOMBIE MAN
GOLD ZOMBIE MAN
GRAY ZOMBIE MAN
MAGENTA ZOMBIE MAN
NAVY ZOMBIE MAN
BROWN ZOMBIE MAN
PURPLE ZOMBIE MAN

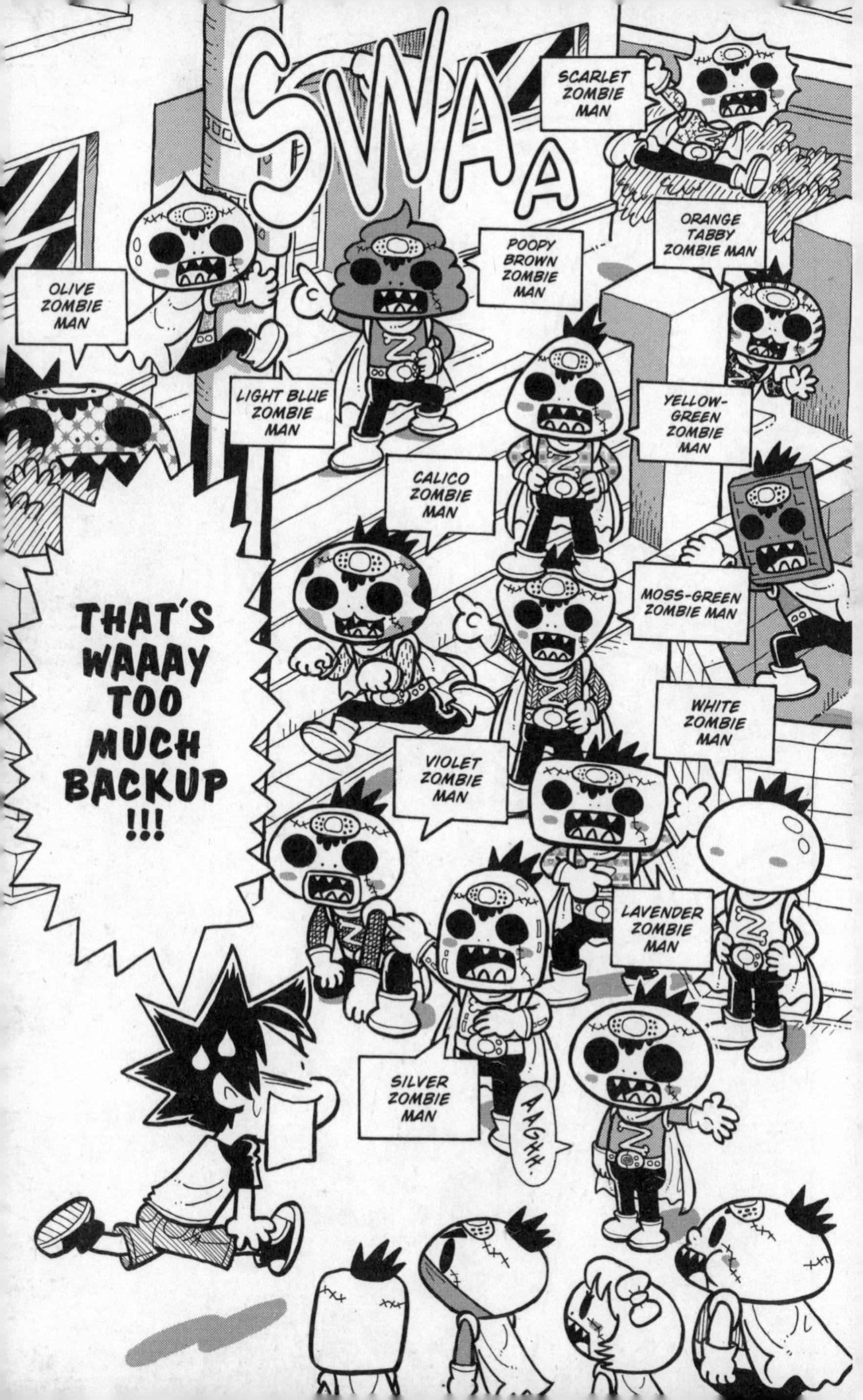
SWAAA
SCARLET ZOMBIE MAN
ORANGE TABBY ZOMBIE MAN
POOPY BROWN ZOMBIE MAN
OLIVE ZOMBIE MAN
YELLOW-GREEN ZOMBIE MAN
LIGHT BLUE ZOMBIE MAN
CALICO ZOMBIE MAN
MOSS-GREEN ZOMBIE MAN
WHITE ZOMBIE MAN
VIOLET ZOMBIE MAN
THAT'S WAAAY TOO MUCH BACKUP !!!
LAVENDER ZOMBIE MAN
SILVER ZOMBIE MAN
AAGHH.

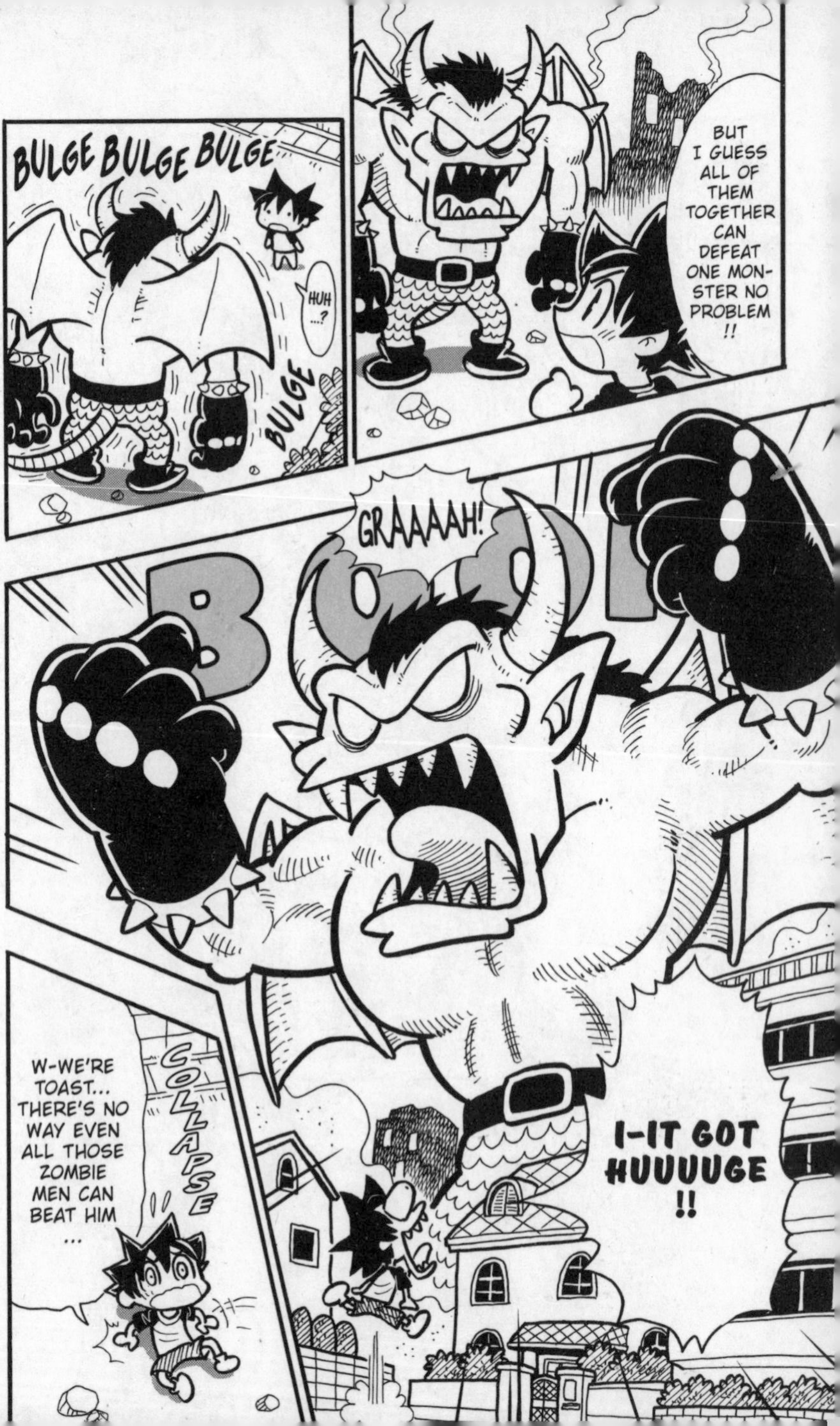

BUT I GUESS ALL OF THEM TOGETHER CAN DEFEAT ONE MONSTER NO PROBLEM !!
BULGE BULGE BULGE
HUH ...?
BULGE
GRAAAAH!
I-IT GOT HUUUUGE !!
W-WE'RE TOAST... THERE'S NO WAY EVEN ALL THOSE ZOMBIE MEN CAN BEAT HIM ...
COLLAPSE

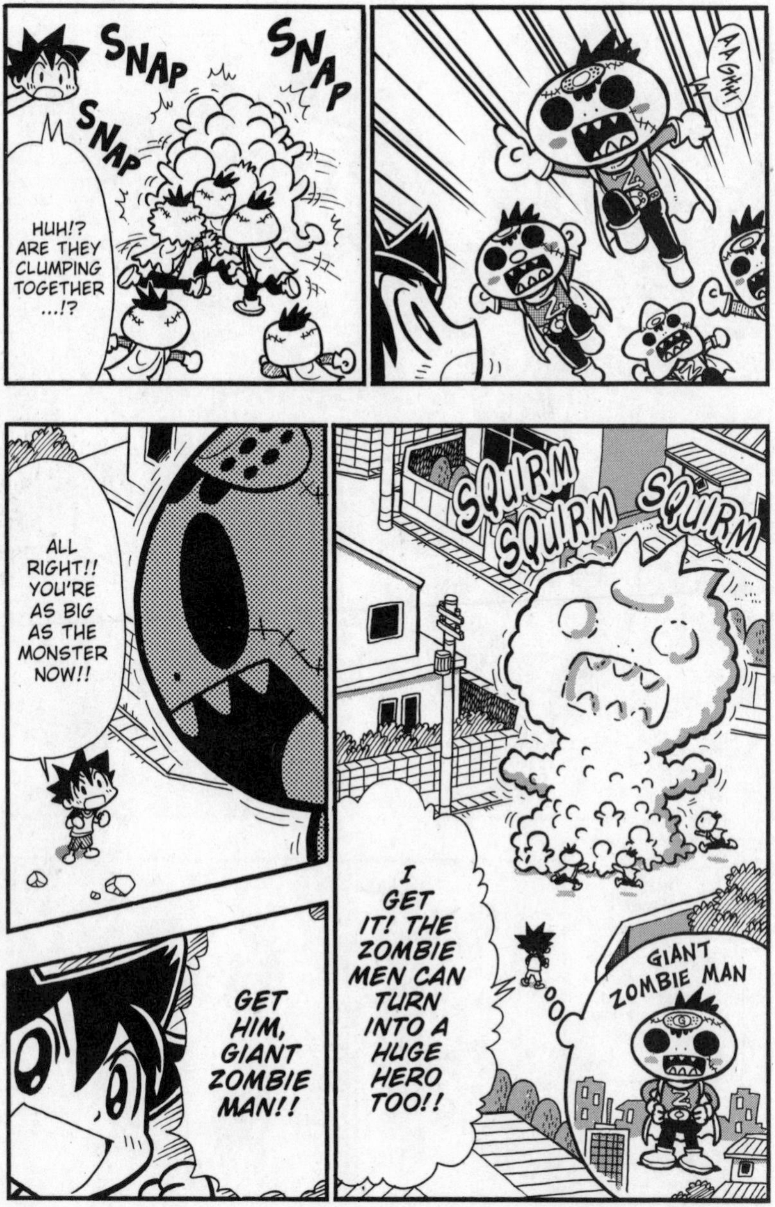
AAGHH!
SNAP
SNAP
SNAP
HUH!? ARE THEY CLUMPING TOGETHER ...!?
SQUIRM
SQUIRM
SQUIRM
I GET IT! THE ZOMBIE MEN CAN TURN INTO A HUGE HERO TOO!!
GIANT ZOMBIE MAN
ALL RIGHT!! YOU'RE AS BIG AS THE MONSTER NOW!!
GET HIM, GIANT ZOMBIE MAN!!

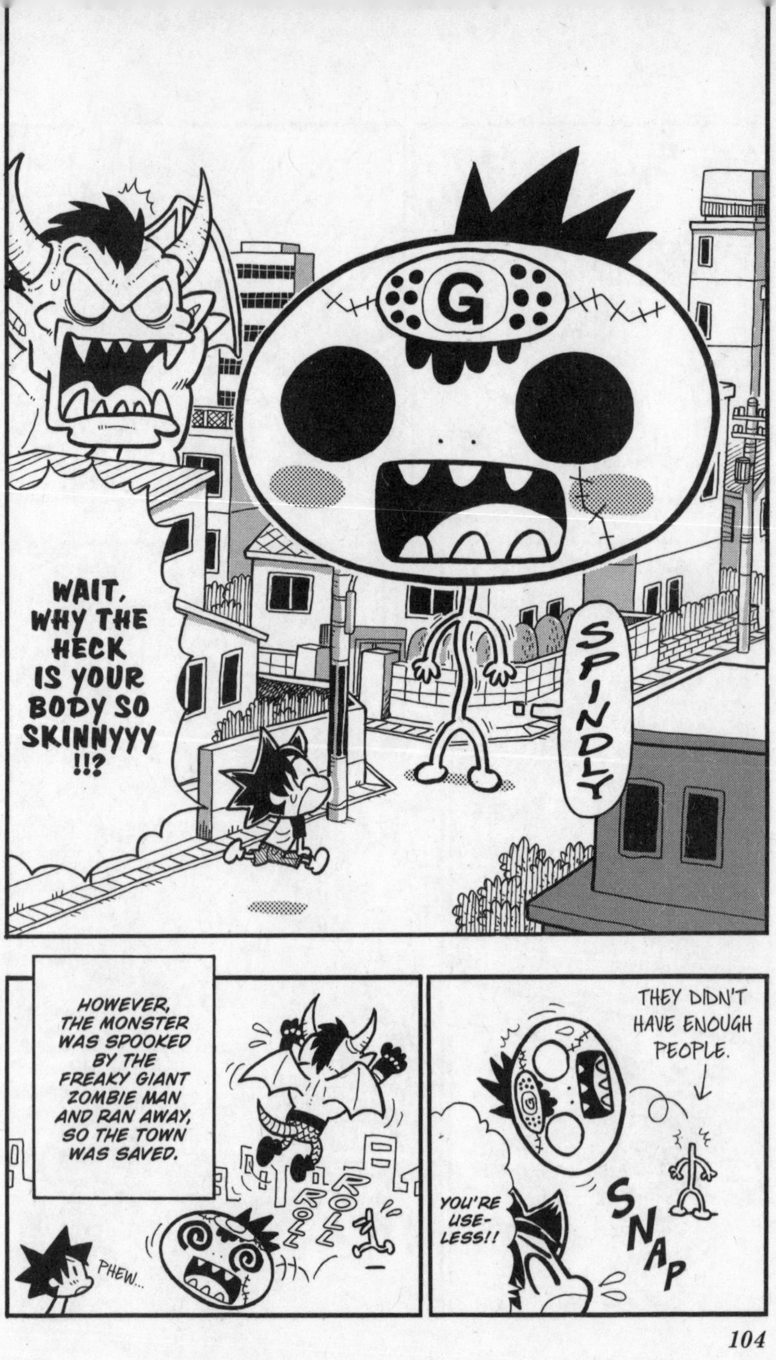
SPINDLY
WAIT, WHY THE HECK IS YOUR BODY SO SKINNYYY!!?
THEY DIDN'T HAVE ENOUGH PEOPLE.
SNAP
YOU'RE USE-LESS!!
HOWEVER, THE MONSTER WAS SPOOKED BY THE FREAKY GIANT ZOMBIE MAN AND RAN AWAY, SO THE TOWN WAS SAVED.
ROLL ROLL
PHEW...

PEACH BOY, THE DEMON DEZTROYER!

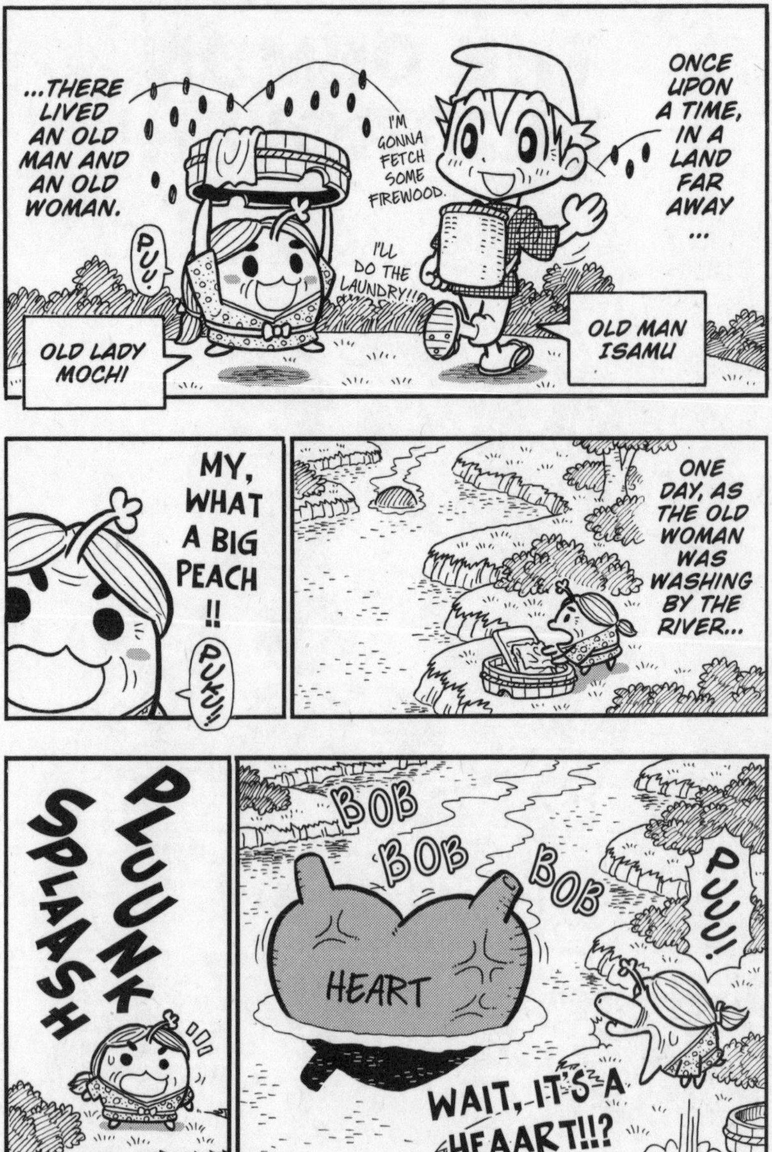
ONCE UPON A TIME, IN A LAND FAR AWAY ...
OLD MAN ISAMU
I'M GONNA FETCH SOME FIREWOOD.
I'LL DO THE LAUNDRY!!
...THERE LIVED AN OLD MAN AND AN OLD WOMAN.
PUU.
OLD LADY MOCHI
ONE DAY, AS THE OLD WOMAN WAS WASHING BY THE RIVER...
MY, WHAT A BIG PEACH !!
PUKU!!
PUUU!
BOB
BOB
BOB
HEART
WAIT, IT'S A HEAART!!?
PLUUNK
SPLAASH

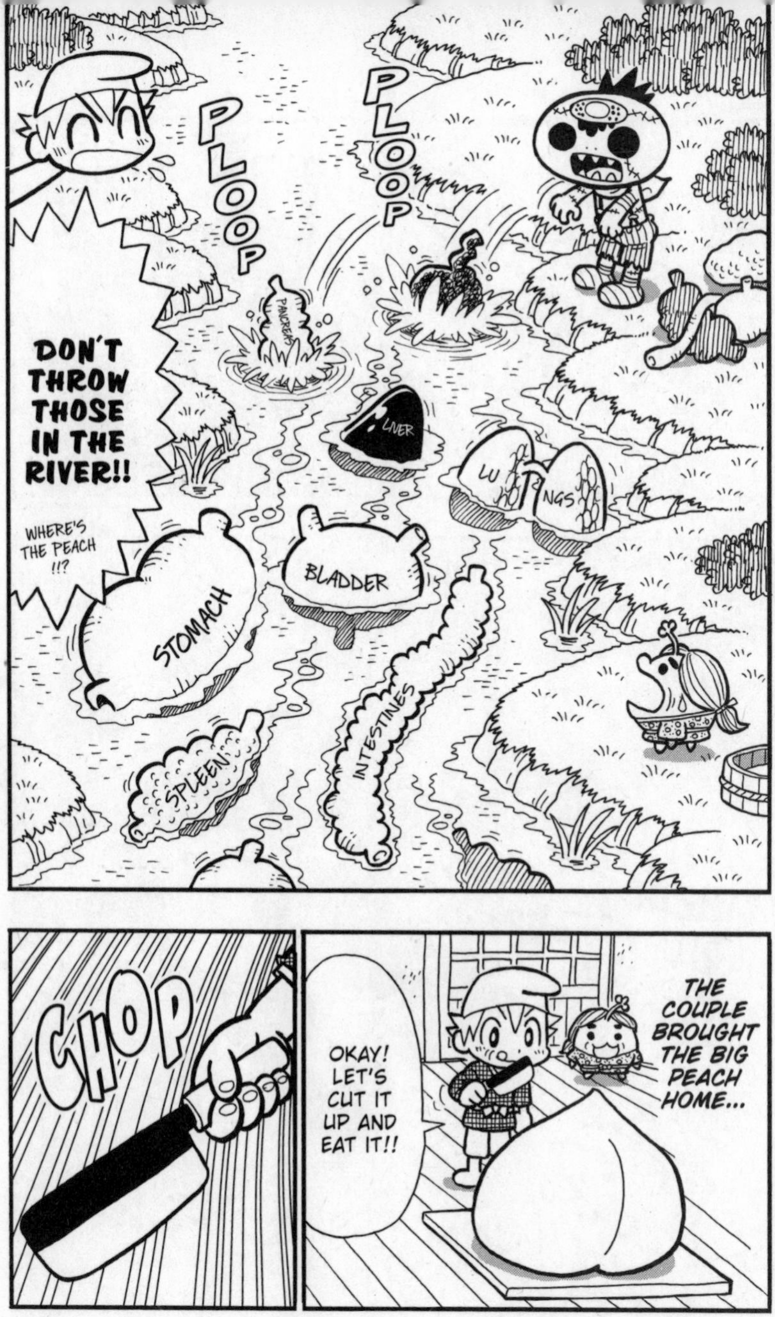
PLOOP
PLOOP
DON'T THROW THOSE IN THE RIVER!!
WHERE'S THE PEACH !!?
PANCREAS
LIVER
LU
NGS
BLADDER
STOMACH
INTESTINES
SPLEEN
THE COUPLE BROUGHT THE BIG PEACH HOME...
OKAY! LET'S CUT IT UP AND EAT IT!!
CHOP

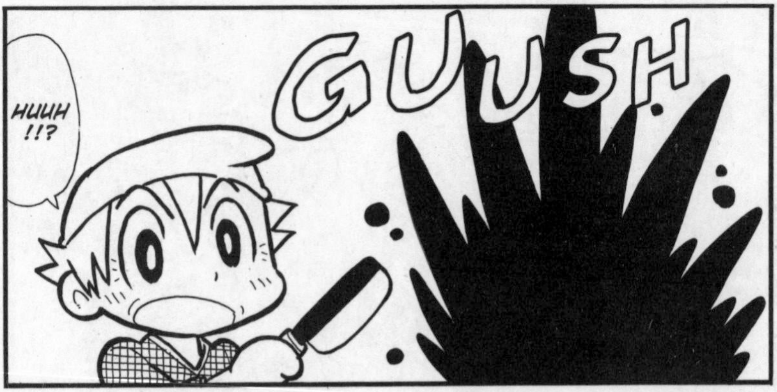
GUUSH
HUUH !!?
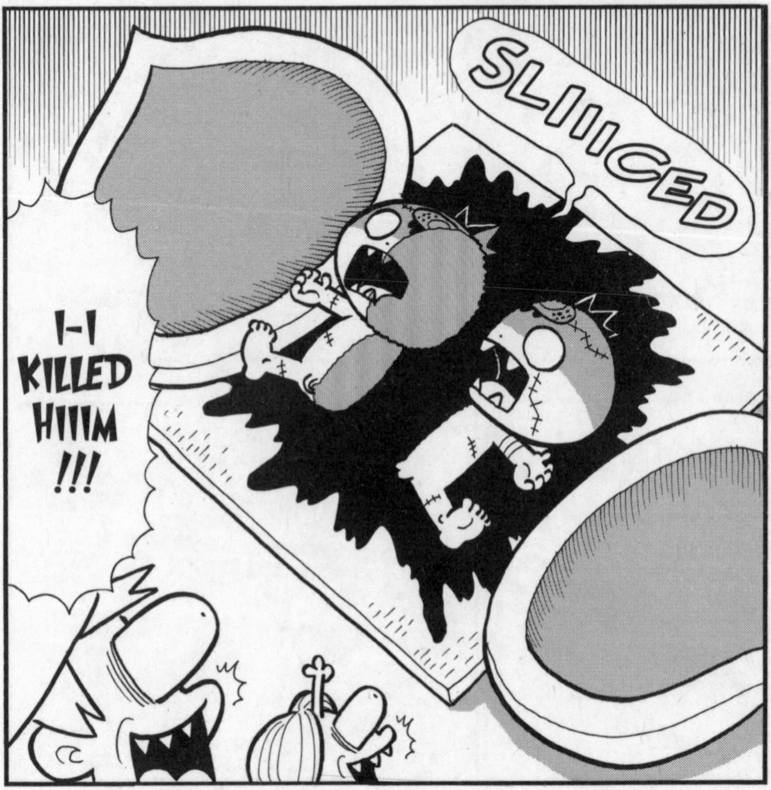
SLIIICED
I-I KILLED HIIIM !!!

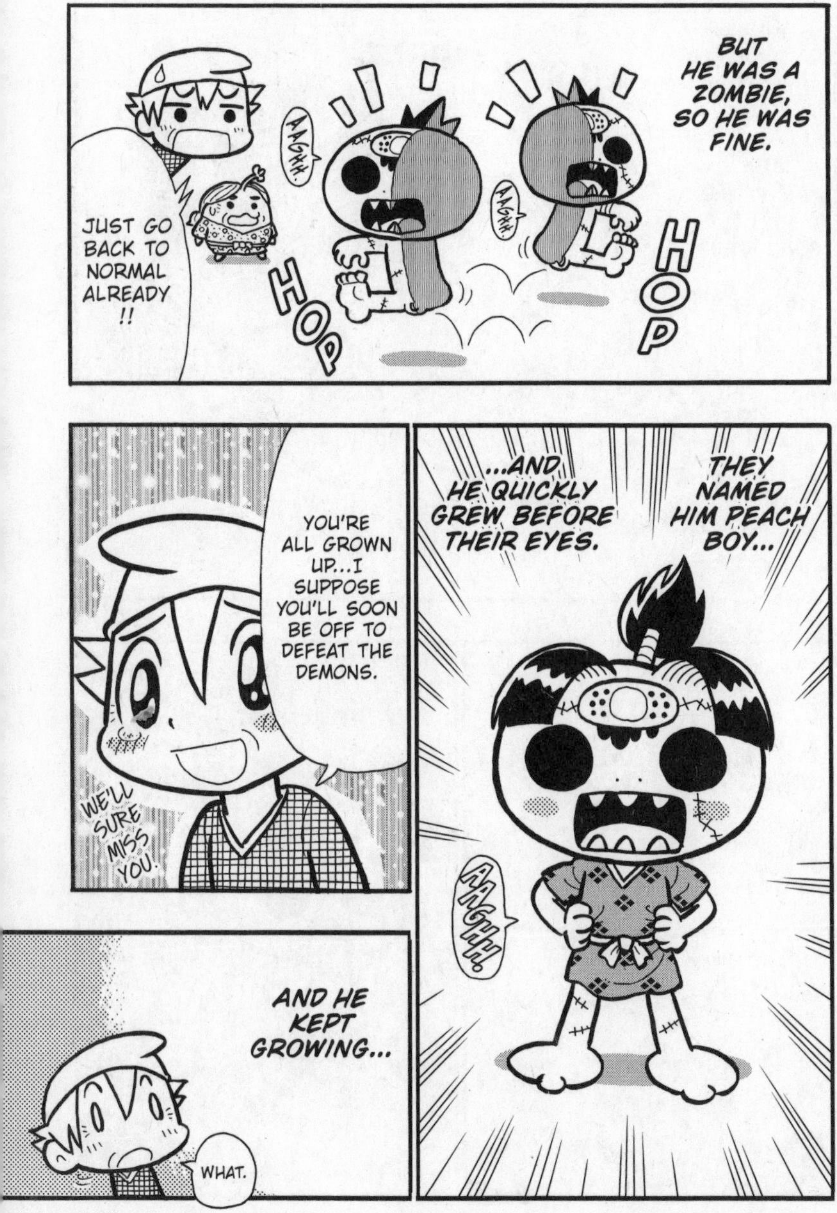
BUT HE WAS A ZOMBIE, SO HE WAS FINE.
AAGHH.
HOP
AAGHH.
HOP
JUST GO BACK TO NORMAL ALREADY !!
THEY NAMED HIM PEACH BOY...
...AND HE QUICKLY GREW BEFORE THEIR EYES.
AAGHH!
YOU'RE ALL GROWN UP...I SUPPOSE YOU'LL SOON BE OFF TO DEFEAT THE DEMONS.
WE'LL SURE MISS YOU.
AND HE KEPT GROWING...
WHAT.

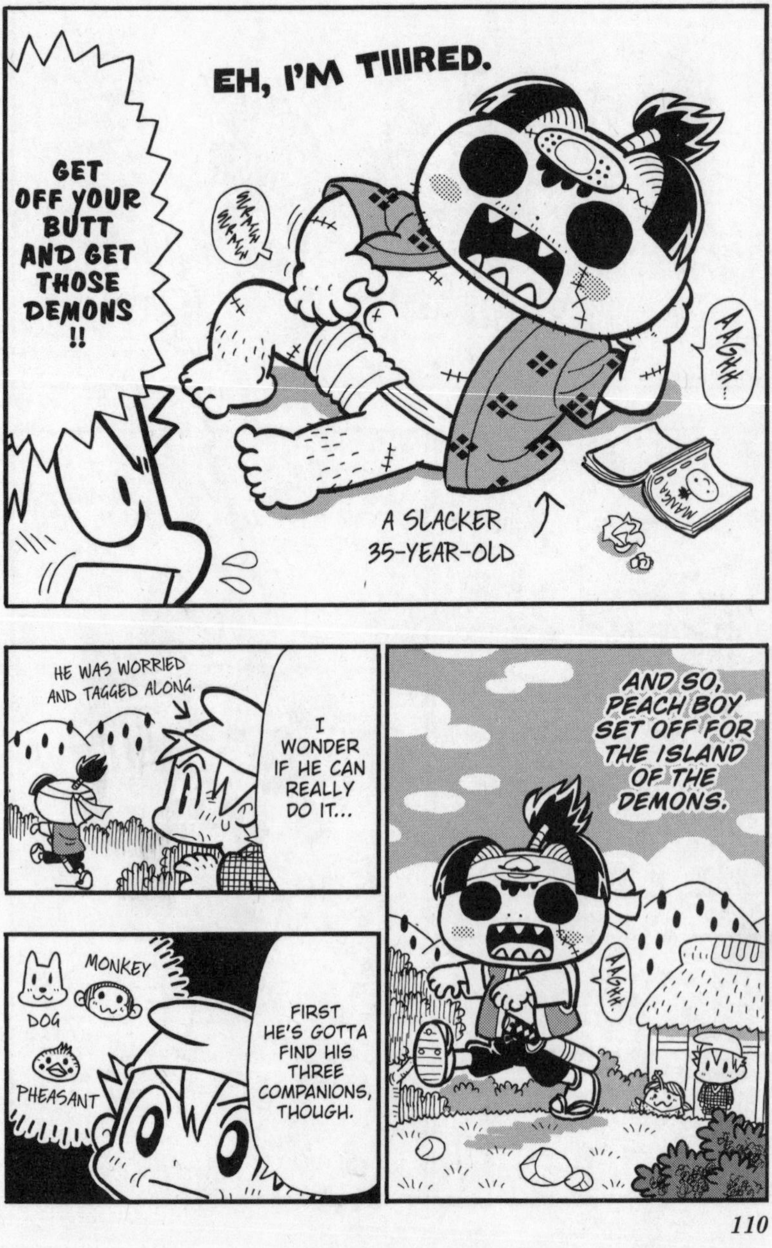
EH, I'M TIIIRED.
SCRATCH SCRATCH
AAGHH...
GET OFF YOUR BUTT AND GET THOSE DEMONS!!
A SLACKER 35-YEAR-OLD
MANGA
AND SO, PEACH BOY SET OFF FOR THE ISLAND OF THE DEMONS.
AAGHH.
I WONDER IF HE CAN REALLY DO IT...
HE WAS WORRIED AND TAGGED ALONG.
FIRST HE'S GOTTA FIND HIS THREE COMPANIONS, THOUGH.
MONKEY
DOG
PHEASANT

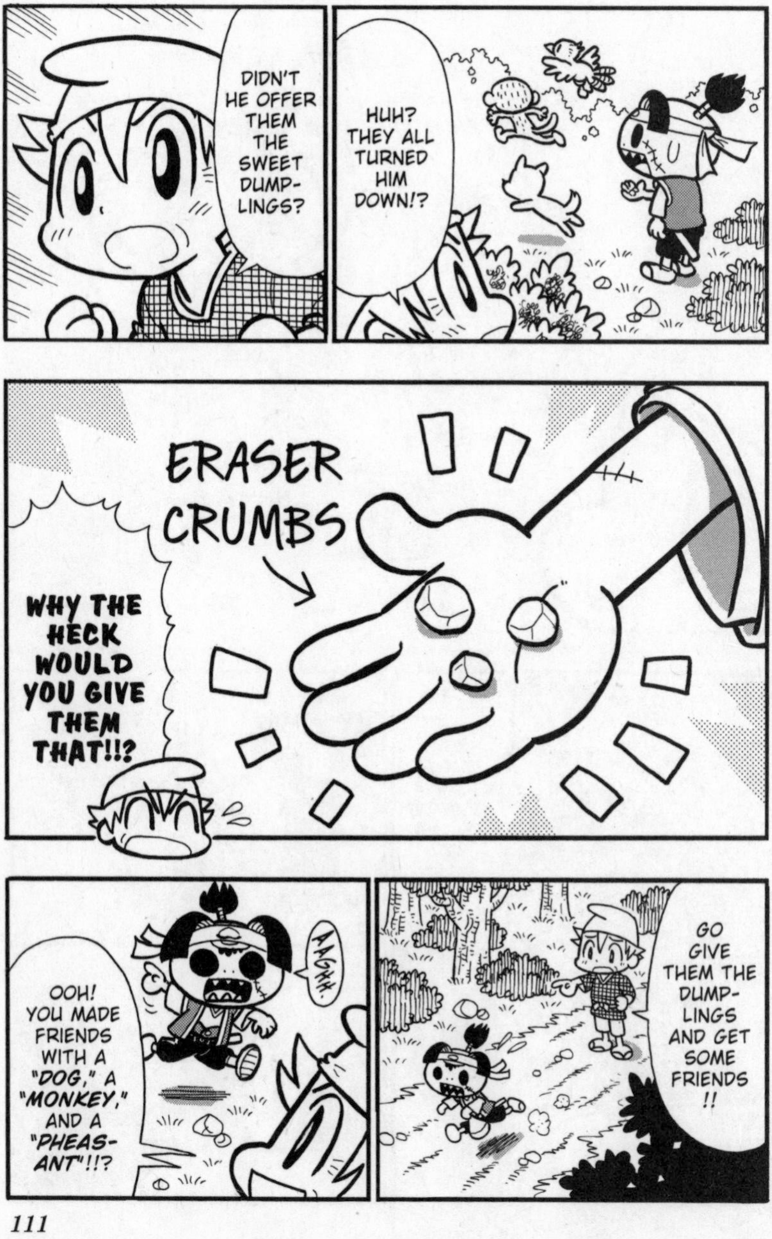
HUH? THEY ALL TURNED HIM DOWN!?
DIDN'T HE OFFER THEM THE SWEET DUMP-LINGS?
ERASER CRUMBS
WHY THE HECK WOULD YOU GIVE THEM THAT!!?
GO GIVE THEM THE DUMP-LINGS AND GET SOME FRIENDS !!
AAGHH.
OOH! YOU MADE FRIENDS WITH A *"DOG,"* A *"MONKEY,"* AND A *"PHEAS-ANT"*!!?

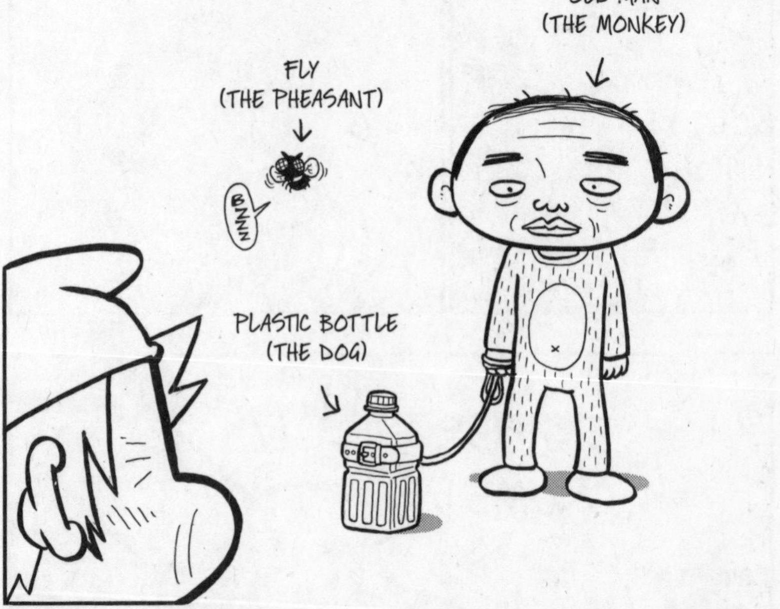
OLD MAN (THE MONKEY)
FLY (THE PHEASANT)
BZZZ
PLASTIC BOTTLE (THE DOG)

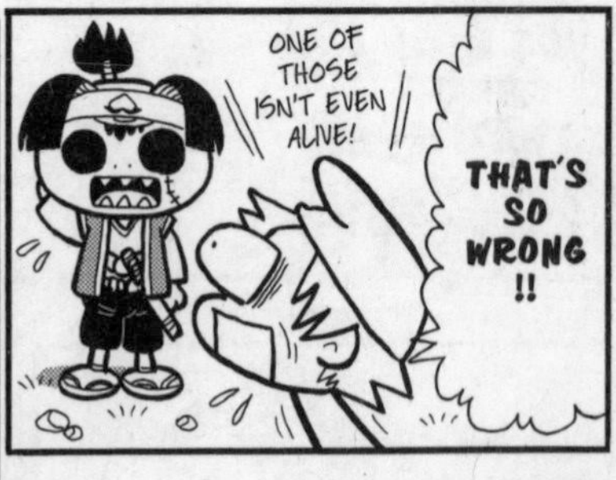
ONE OF THOSE ISN'T EVEN ALIVE!
THAT'S SO WRONG !!

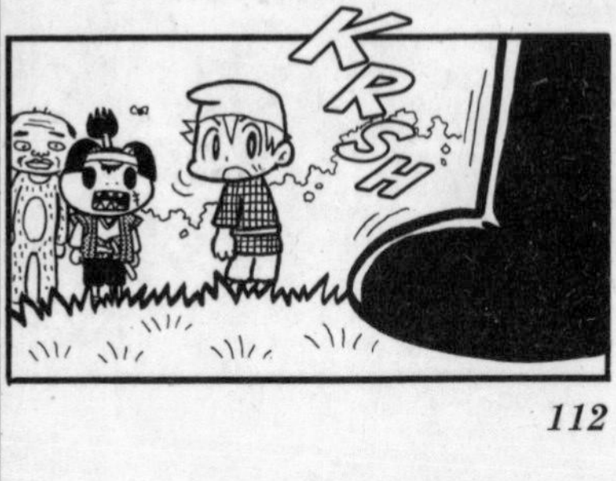
KRSH

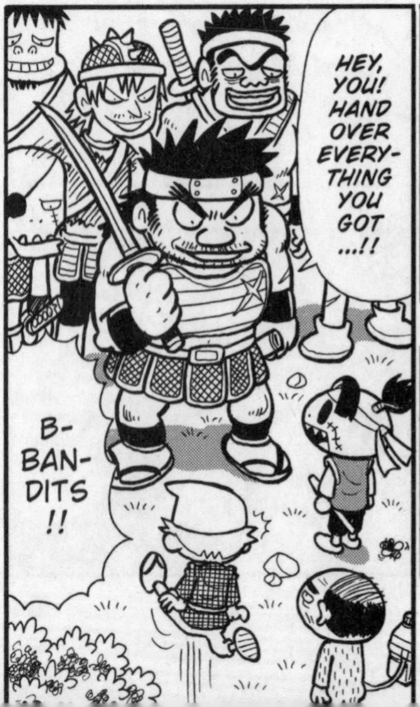
HEY, YOU! HAND OVER EVERY-THING YOU GOT ...!!
B-BAN-DITS !!

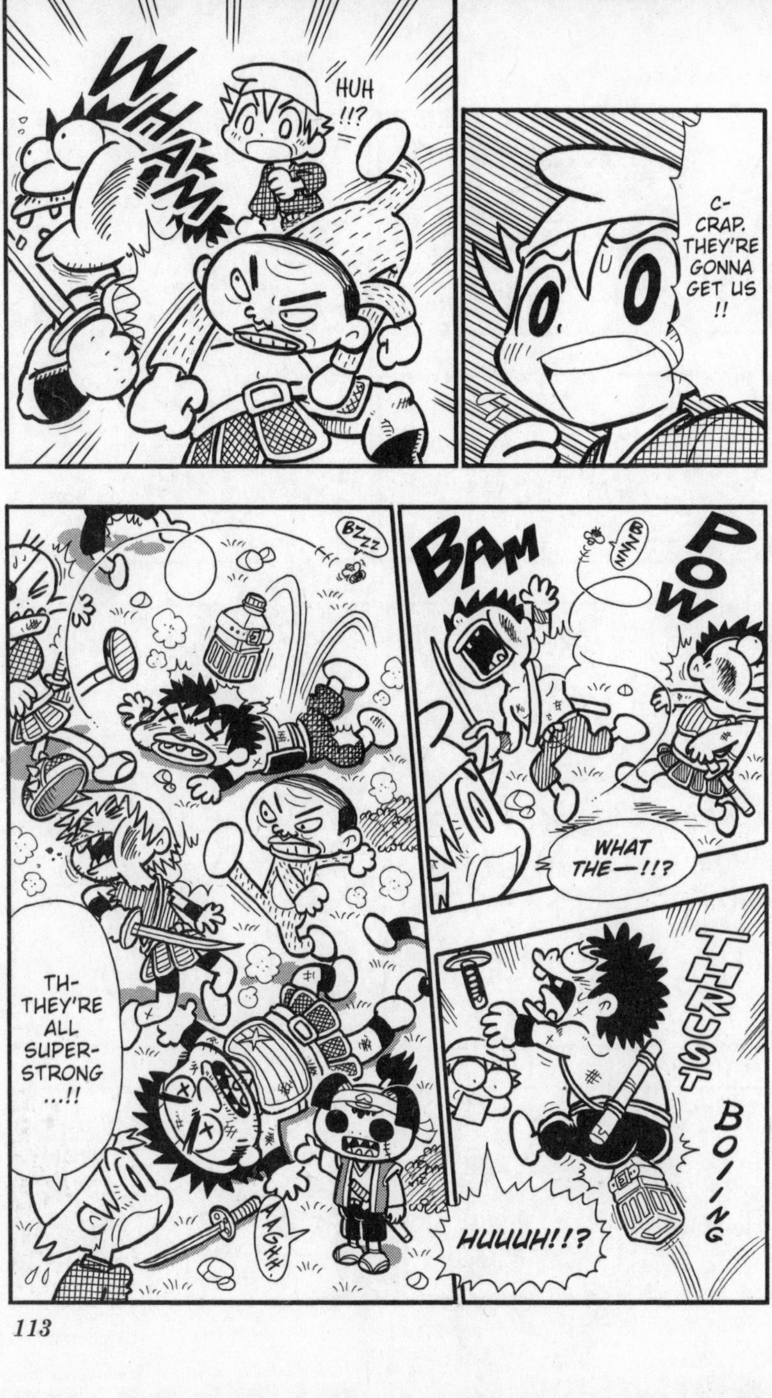
C-CRAP. THEY'RE GONNA GET US!!
WHAM
HUH!!?
POW
BNNN
BAM
WHAT THE—!!?
THRUST
BOING
HUUUH!!?
BZZZ
TH-THEY'RE ALL SUPER-STRONG...!!
AAGHH

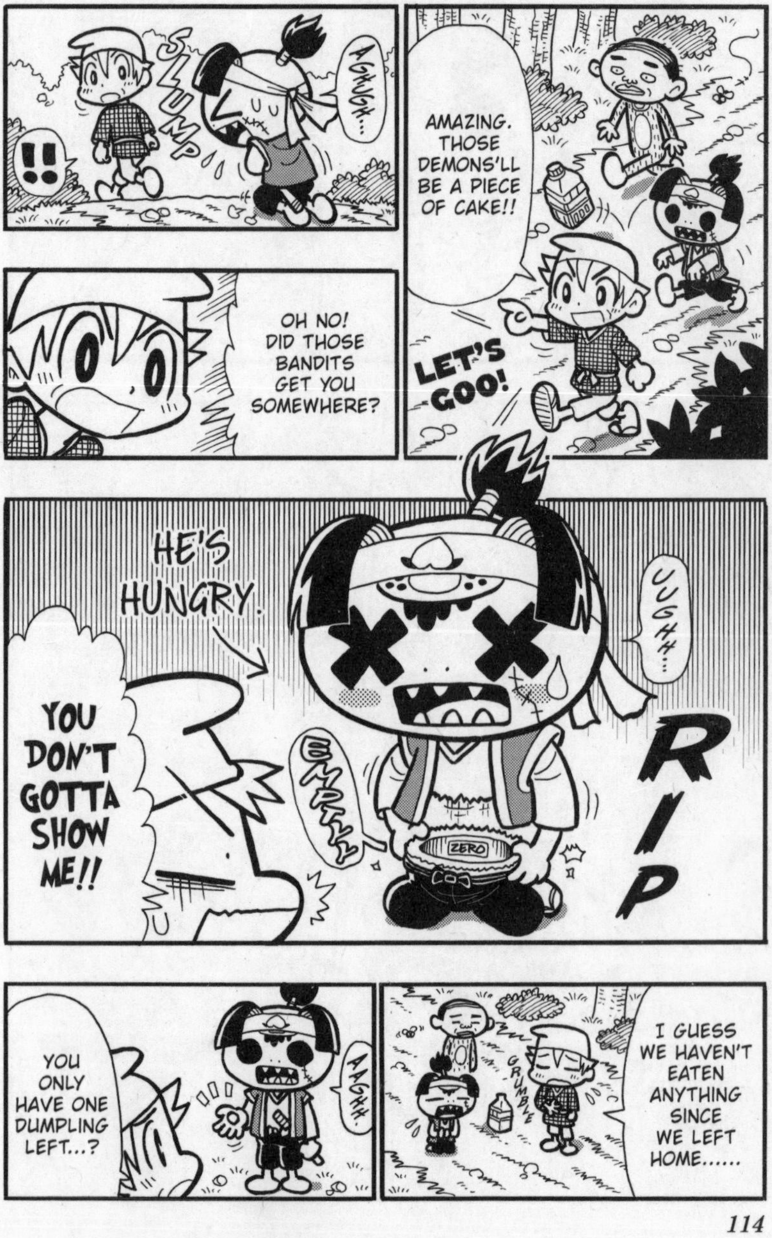
AMAZING. THOSE DEMONS'LL BE A PIECE OF CAKE!!
LET'S GOO!
AGHUGH...
SLUMP
!!
OH NO! DID THOSE BANDITS GET YOU SOMEWHERE?
UUGHH...
RIP
HE'S HUNGRY.
EMPTY
ZERO
YOU DON'T GOTTA SHOW ME!!
I GUESS WE HAVEN'T EATEN ANYTHING SINCE WE LEFT HOME......
GRUMBLE
AAGHH.
YOU ONLY HAVE ONE DUMPLING LEFT...?

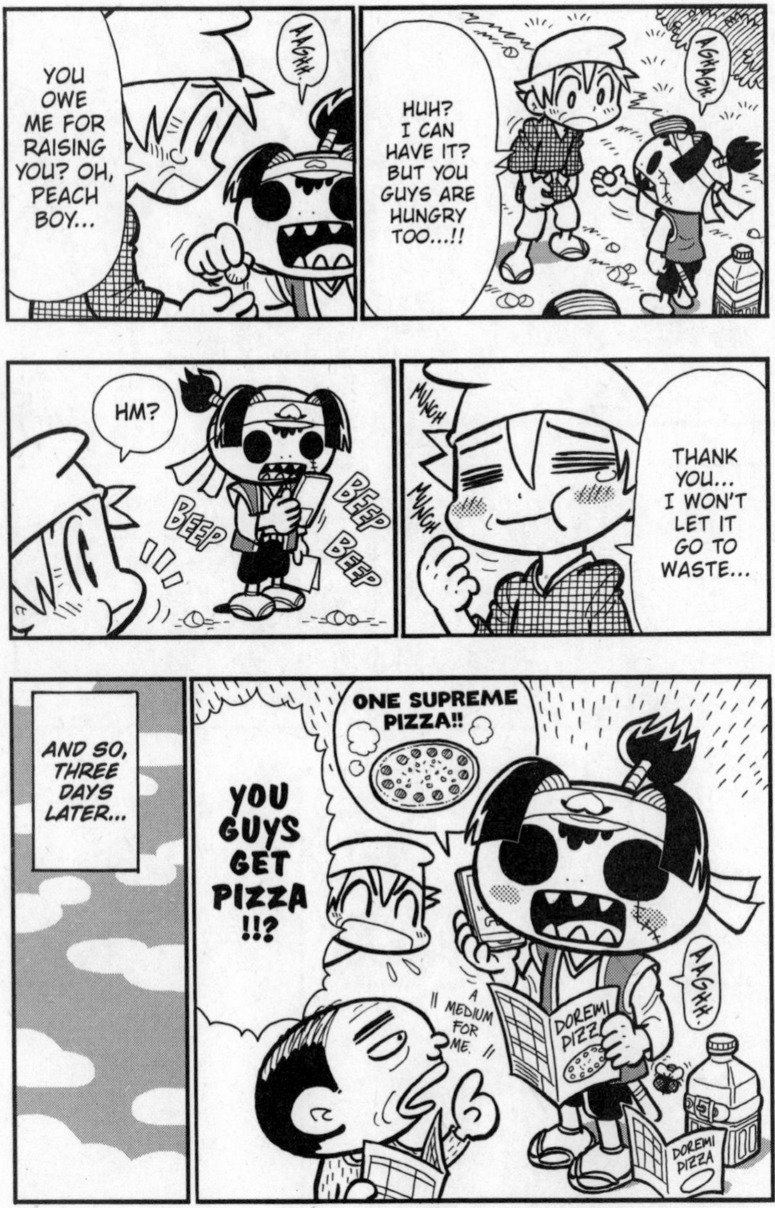
AGHAGH.
HUH? I CAN HAVE IT? BUT YOU GUYS ARE HUNGRY TOO...!!
AAGHH.
YOU OWE ME FOR RAISING YOU? OH, PEACH BOY...
MUNCH
MUNCH
THANK YOU... I WON'T LET IT GO TO WASTE...
HM?
BEEP
BEEP
BEEP
!!!
ONE SUPREME PIZZA!!
YOU GUYS GET PIZZA!!?
A MEDIUM FOR ME.
AAGHH.
DOREMI PIZZ
DOREMI PIZZA
AND SO, THREE DAYS LATER...

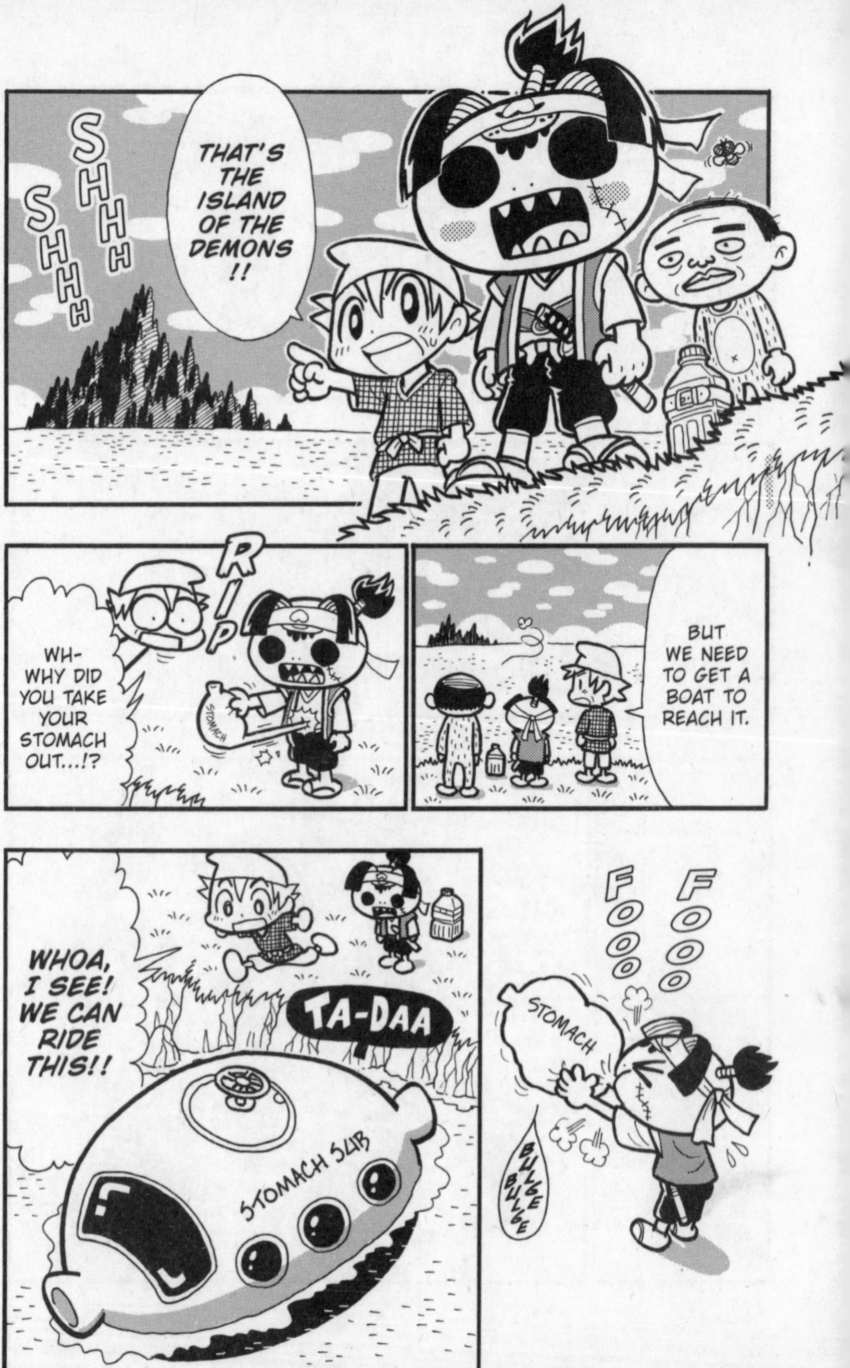

THAT'S THE ISLAND OF THE DEMONS!!
SHHHH
SHHHH
BUT WE NEED TO GET A BOAT TO REACH IT.
RIP
STOMACH
WH- WHY DID YOU TAKE YOUR STOMACH OUT...!?
FOOOO
FOOOO
STOMACH
BULGE BULGE
TA-DAA
STOMACH SUB
WHOA, I SEE! WE CAN RIDE THIS!!

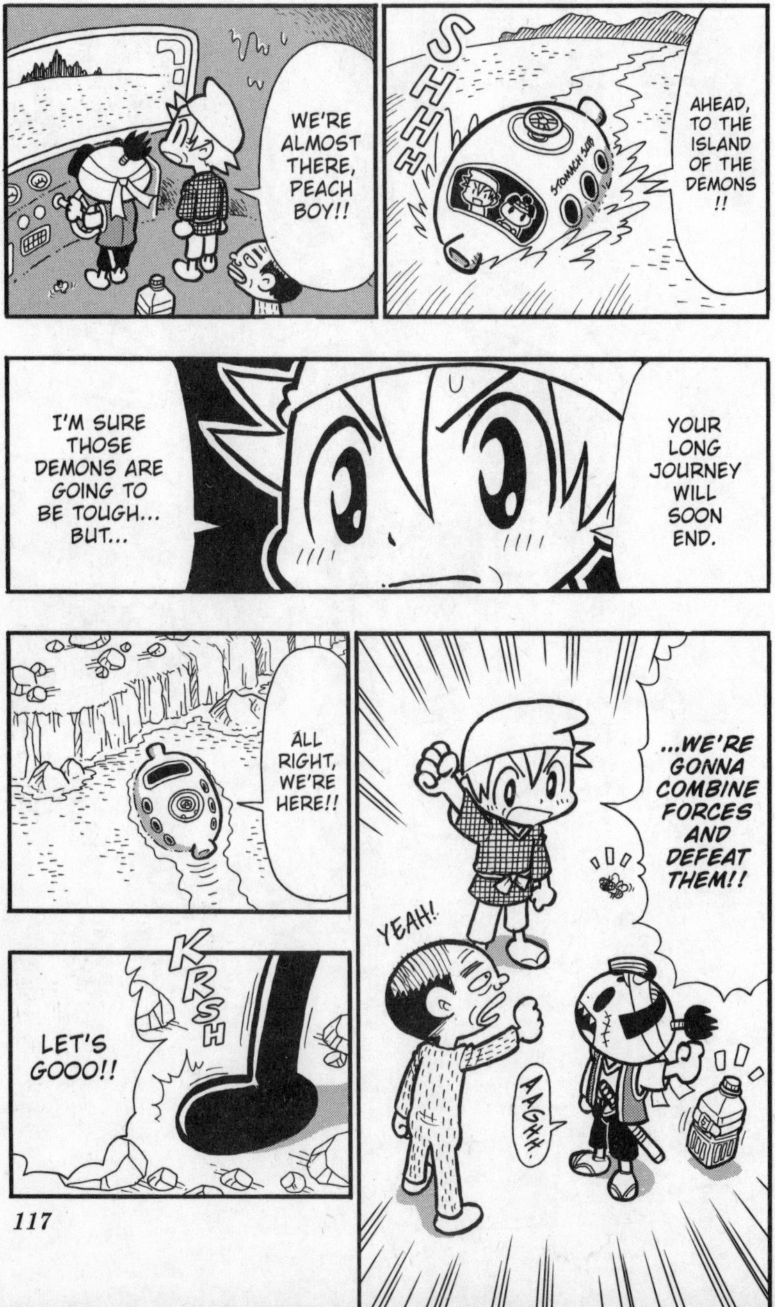
SHHHH
STOMACH SUB
AHEAD, TO THE ISLAND OF THE DEMONS!!
WE'RE ALMOST THERE, PEACH BOY!!
YOUR LONG JOURNEY WILL SOON END.
I'M SURE THOSE DEMONS ARE GOING TO BE TOUGH... BUT...
...WE'RE GONNA COMBINE FORCES AND DEFEAT THEM!!
YEAH!
AAGHH.
ALL RIGHT, WE'RE HERE!!
KRSH
LET'S GOOO!!

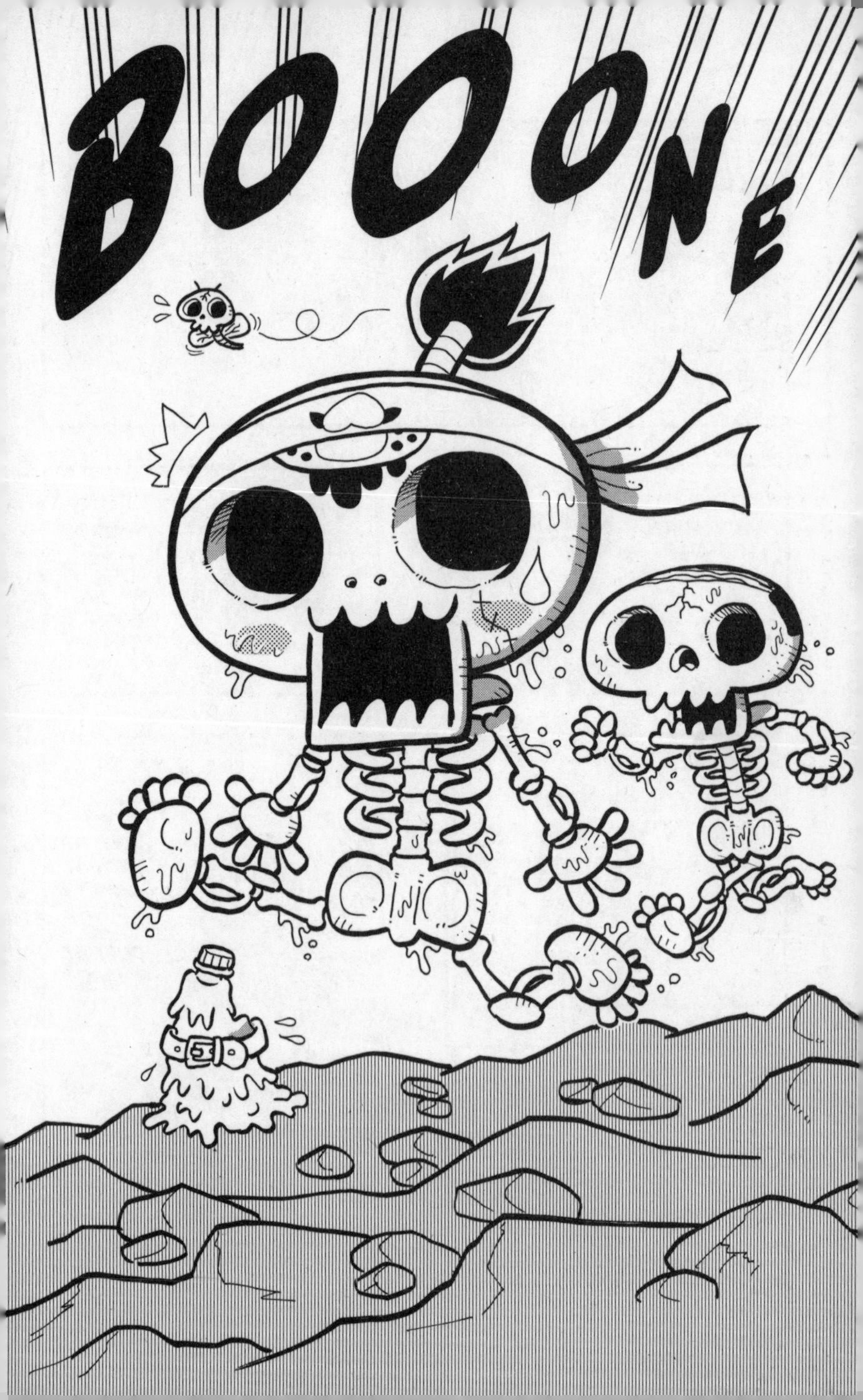
BOOONE

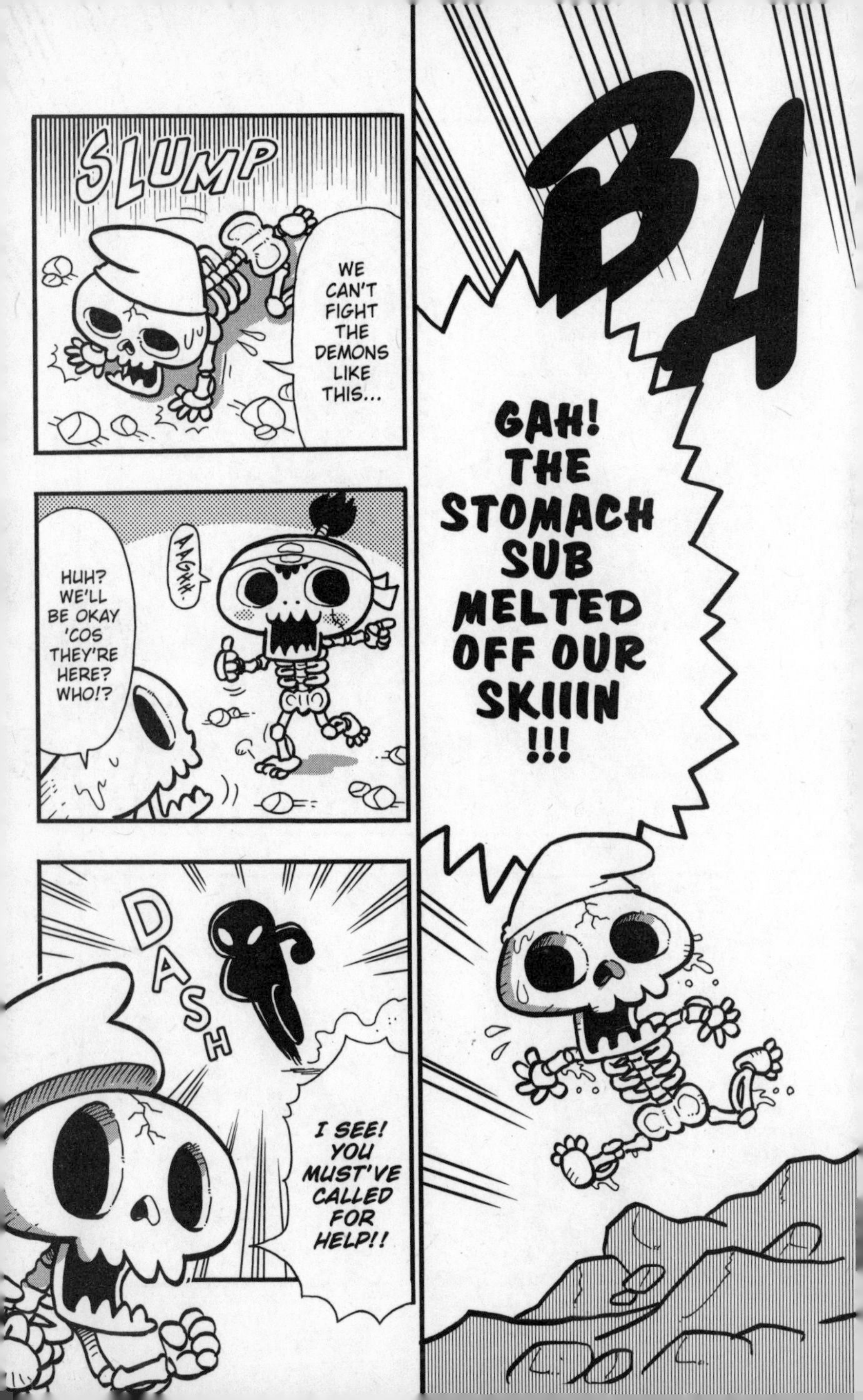
BA
GAH! THE STOMACH SUB MELTED OFF OUR SKIIIN!!!
SLUMP
WE CAN'T FIGHT THE DEMONS LIKE THIS...
AAGHH.
HUH? WE'LL BE OKAY 'COS THEY'RE HERE? WHO!?
DASH
I SEE! YOU MUST'VE CALLED FOR HELP!!

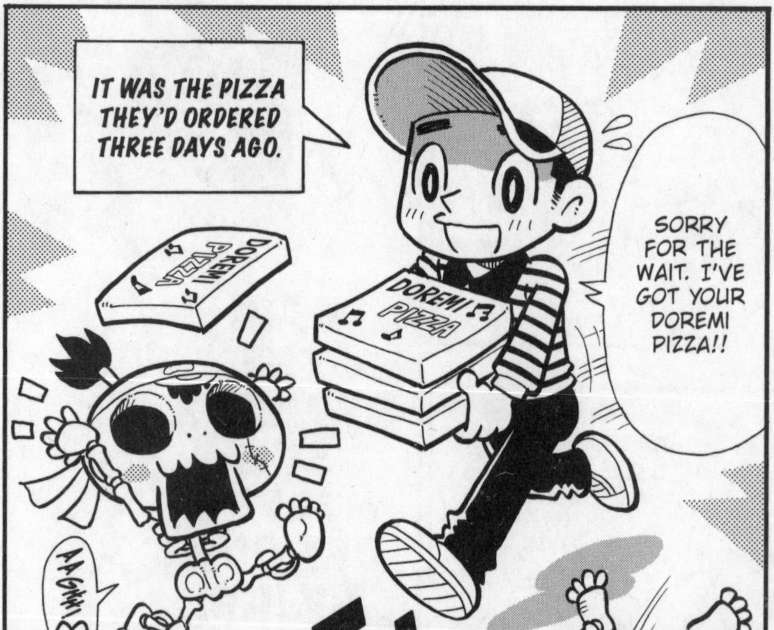
SORRY FOR THE WAIT. I'VE GOT YOUR DOREMI PIZZA!!
IT WAS THE PIZZA THEY'D ORDERED THREE DAYS AGO.
DOREMI PIZZA
DOREMI PIZZA
AAGHH!!
THUD

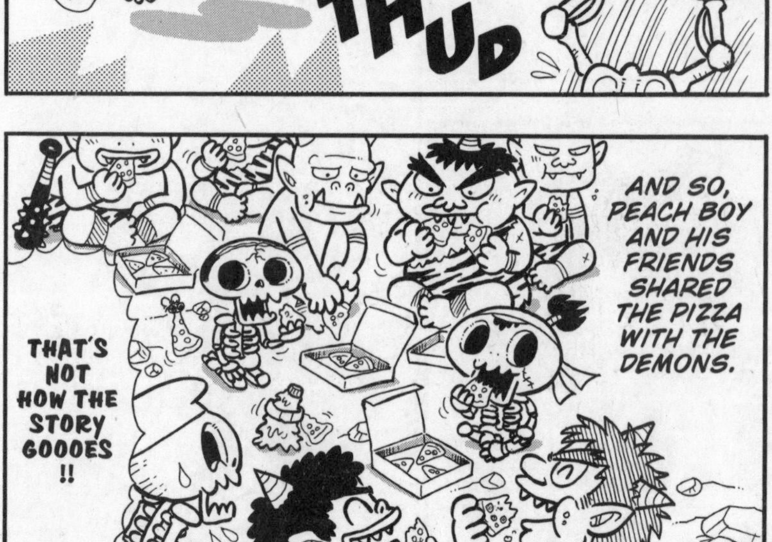
AND SO, PEACH BOY AND HIS FRIENDS SHARED THE PIZZA WITH THE DEMONS.
THAT'S NOT HOW THE STORY GOOOES!!

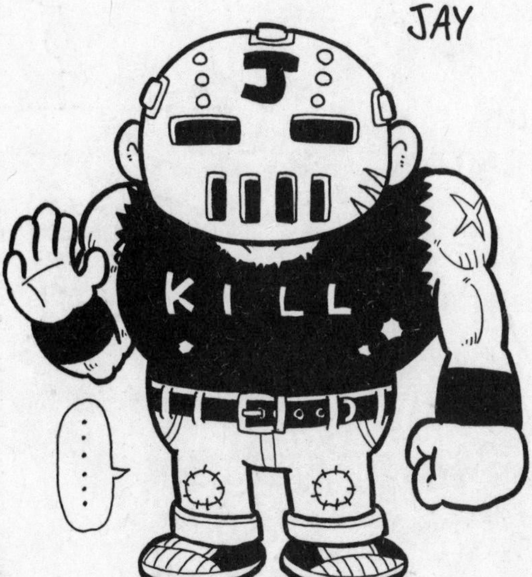
JAY
J
KILL
......

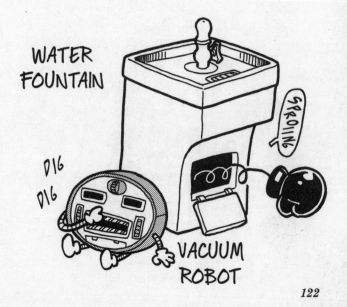

WATER
FOUNTAIN

DIG
DIG

SPROIING

VACUUM
ROBOT

122

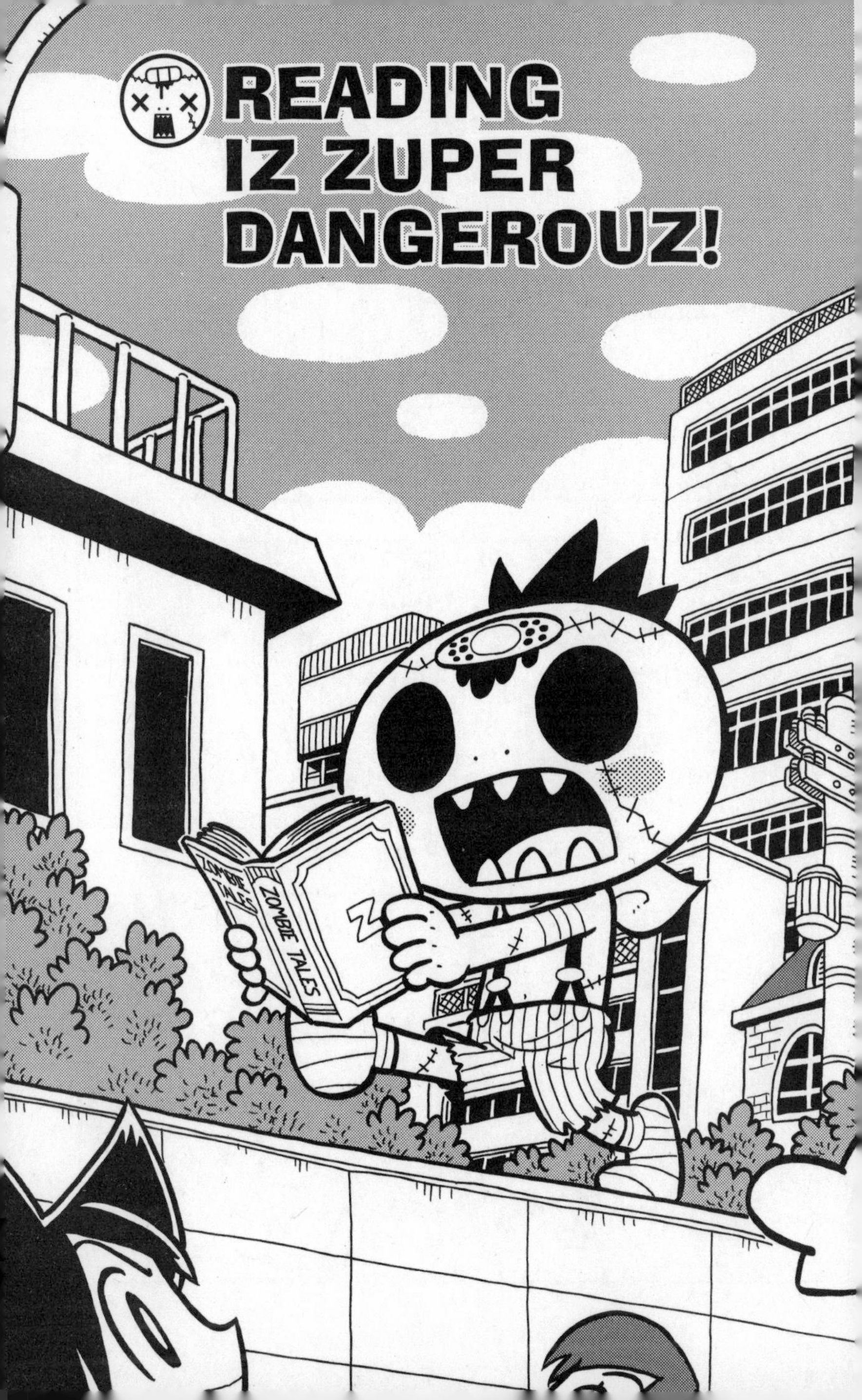
READING IZ ZUPER DANGEROUZ!
ZOMBIE TALES
ZOMBIE TALES

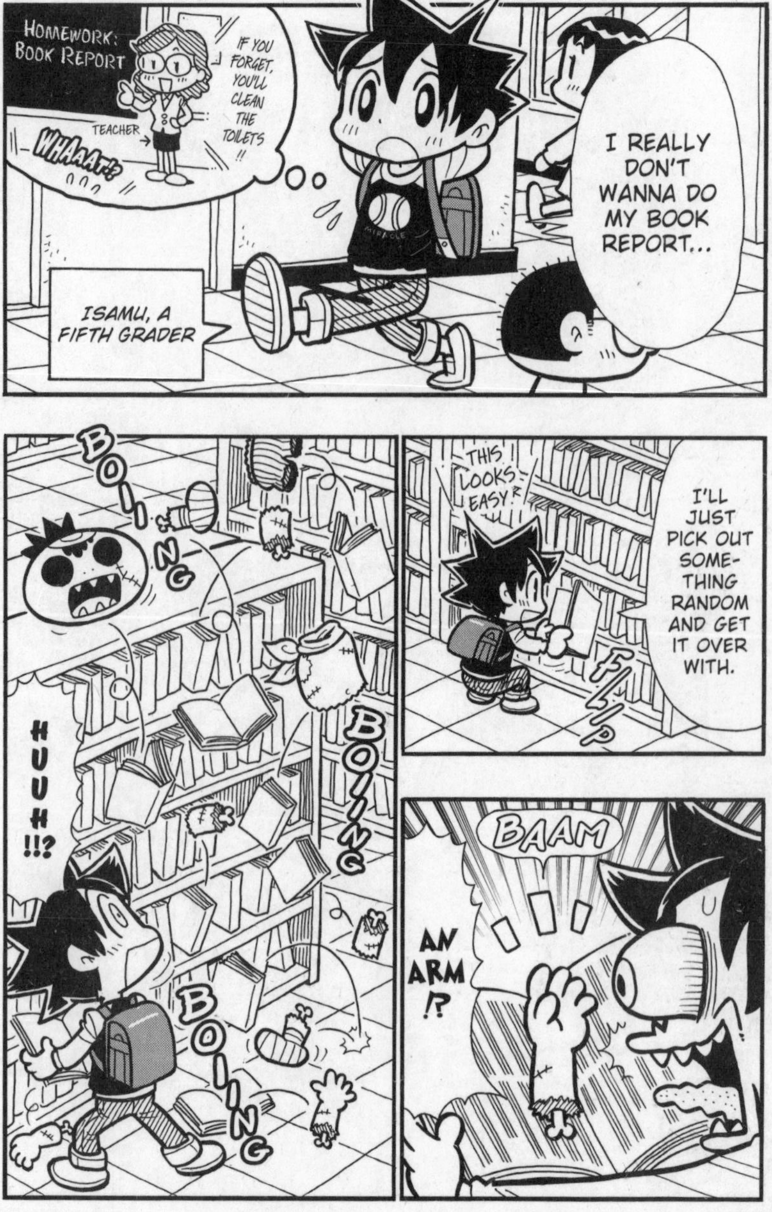
I REALLY DON'T WANNA DO MY BOOK REPORT...
HOMEWORK: BOOK REPORT
IF YOU FORGET, YOU'LL CLEAN THE TOILETS!!
TEACHER
WHAAAT!?
ISAMU, A FIFTH GRADER
I'LL JUST PICK OUT SOME-THING RANDOM AND GET IT OVER WITH.
THIS LOOKS EASY
FLIP
BAAM
AN ARM!?
BOIIING
BOIING
HUUUH!!?
BOIING

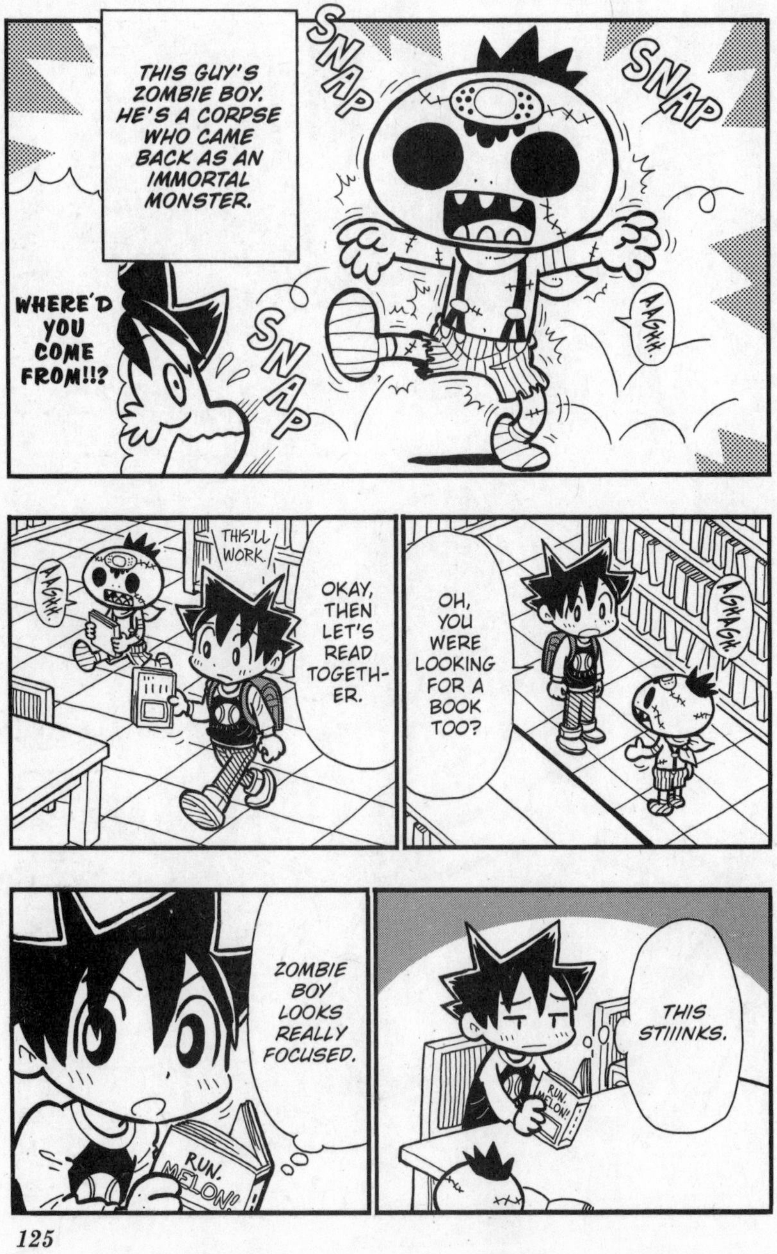
SNAP
SNAP
THIS GUY'S ZOMBIE BOY. HE'S A CORPSE WHO CAME BACK AS AN IMMORTAL MONSTER.
AAGHH.
SNAP
WHERE'D YOU COME FROM!!?
AAGHAGH.
OH, YOU WERE LOOKING FOR A BOOK TOO?
OKAY, THEN LET'S READ TOGETH-ER.
THIS'LL WORK.
AAGHH.
THIS STIIINKS.
RUN, MELON!
ZOMBIE BOY LOOKS REALLY FOCUSED.
RUN, MELON!

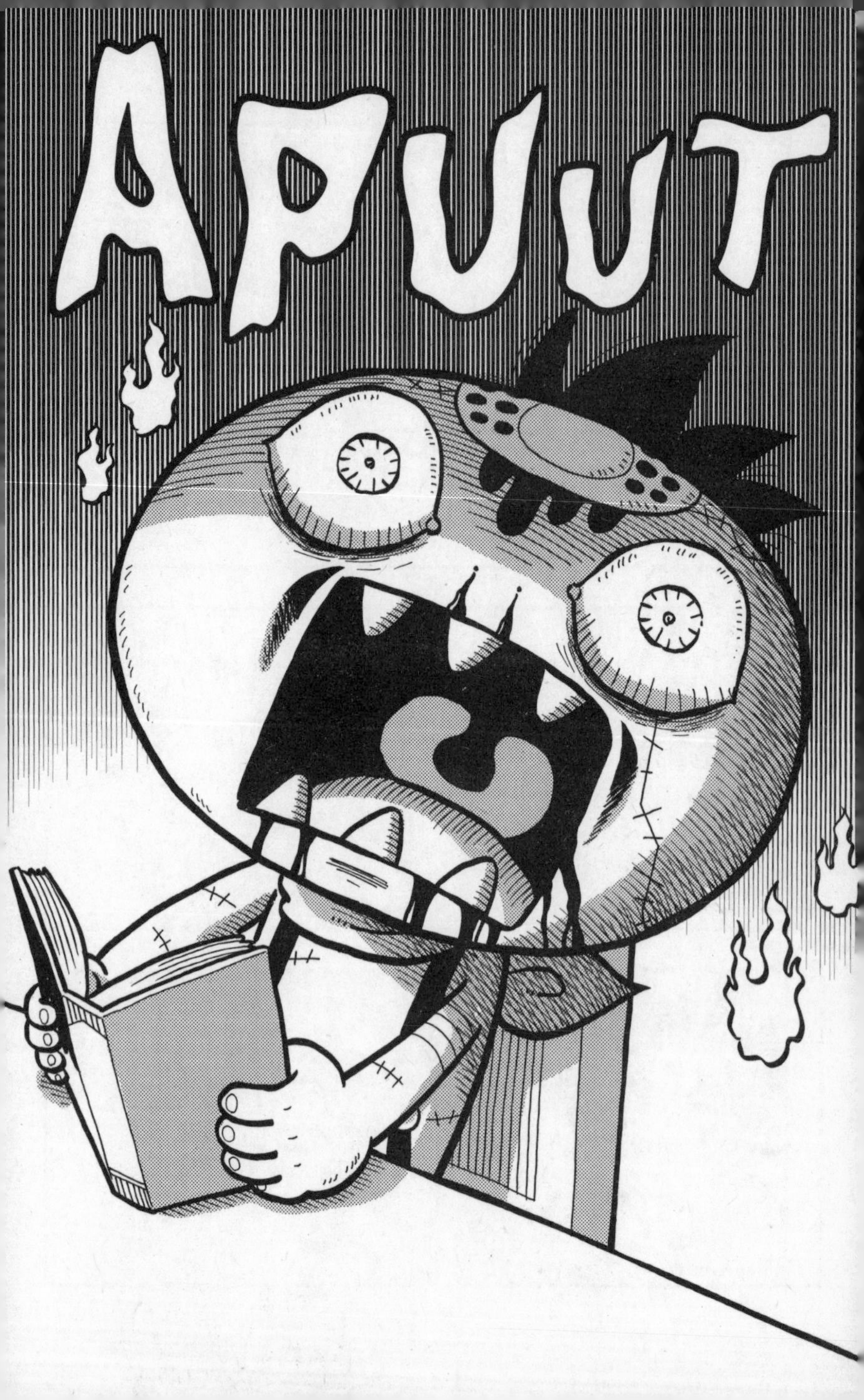
APUUT

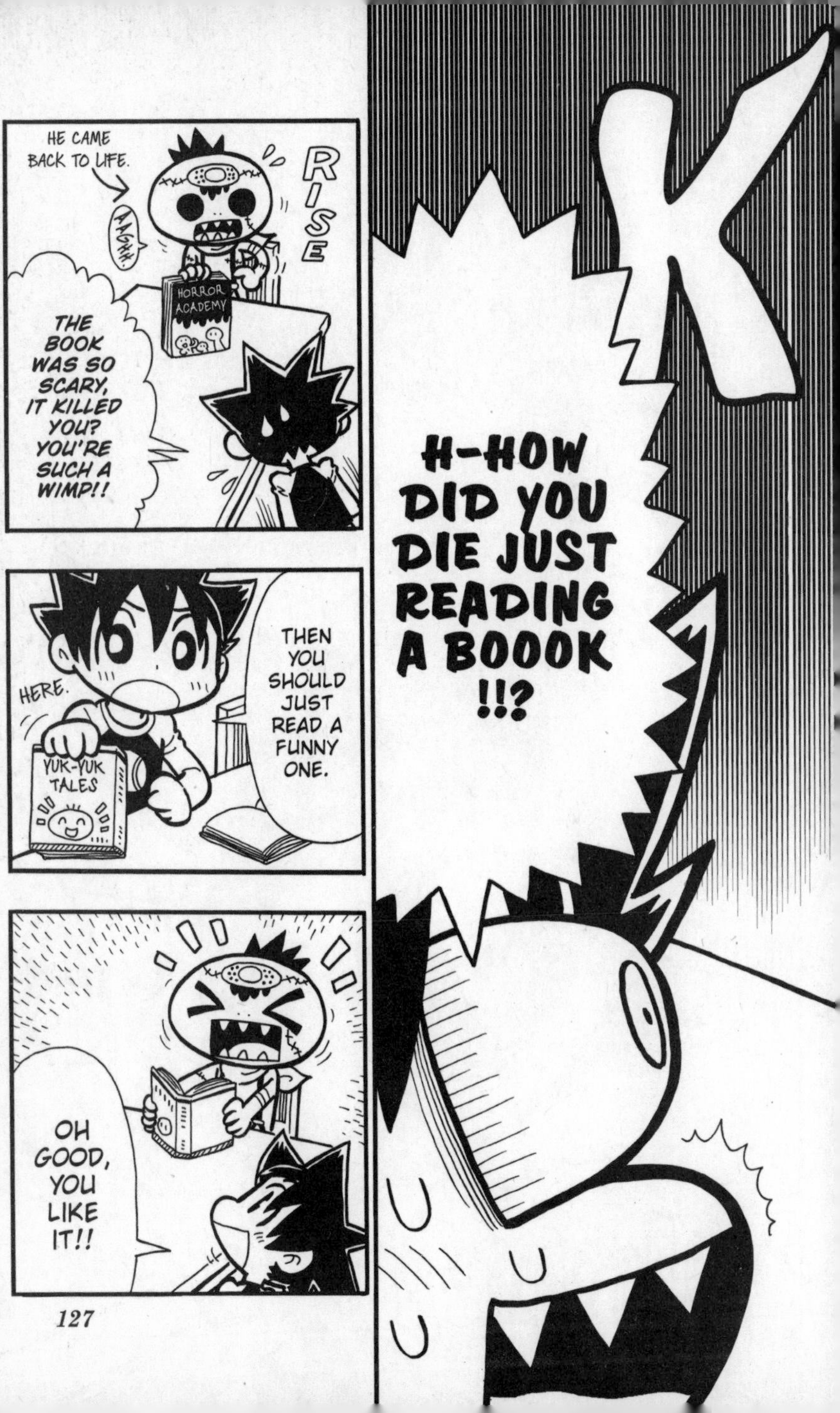
H-HOW DID YOU DIE JUST READING A BOOOK !!?
RISE
HE CAME BACK TO LIFE.
AAGHH.
HORROR ACADEMY
THE BOOK WAS SO SCARY, IT KILLED YOU? YOU'RE SUCH A WIMP!!
THEN YOU SHOULD JUST READ A FUNNY ONE.
HERE.
YUK-YUK TALES
OH GOOD, YOU LIKE IT!!

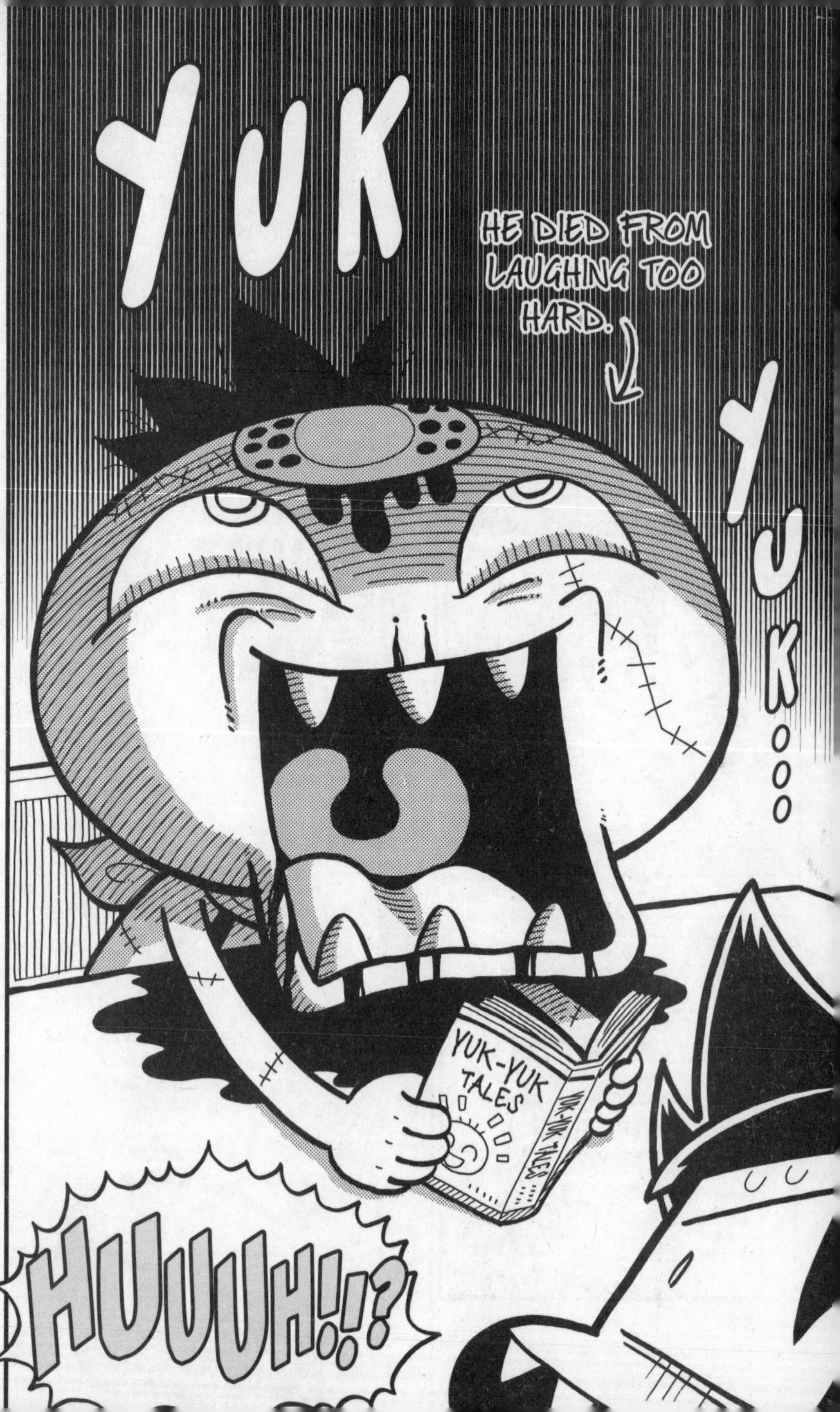
YUK
HE DIED FROM LAUGHING TOO HARD.
YUKOOO
YUK-YUK TALES
YUK-YUK TALES
HUUUH!!?

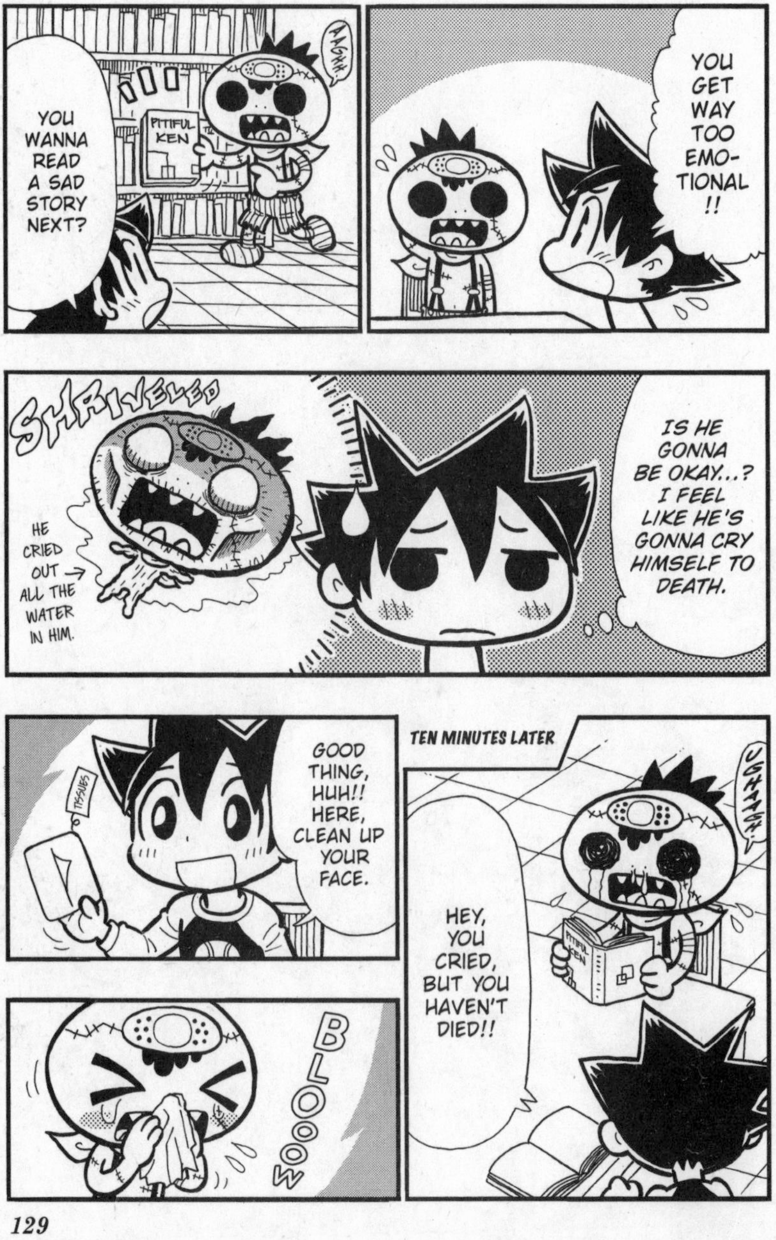
YOU GET WAY TOO EMO-TIONAL!!
AAGHH.
PITIFUL KEN
YOU WANNA READ A SAD STORY NEXT?
IS HE GONNA BE OKAY...? I FEEL LIKE HE'S GONNA CRY HIMSELF TO DEATH.
SHRIVELED
HE CRIED OUT ALL THE WATER IN HIM.
TEN MINUTES LATER
UGHAAGH.
PITIFUL KEN
HEY, YOU CRIED, BUT YOU HAVEN'T DIED!!
GOOD THING, HUH!! HERE, CLEAN UP YOUR FACE.
TISSUES
BLOOOOW

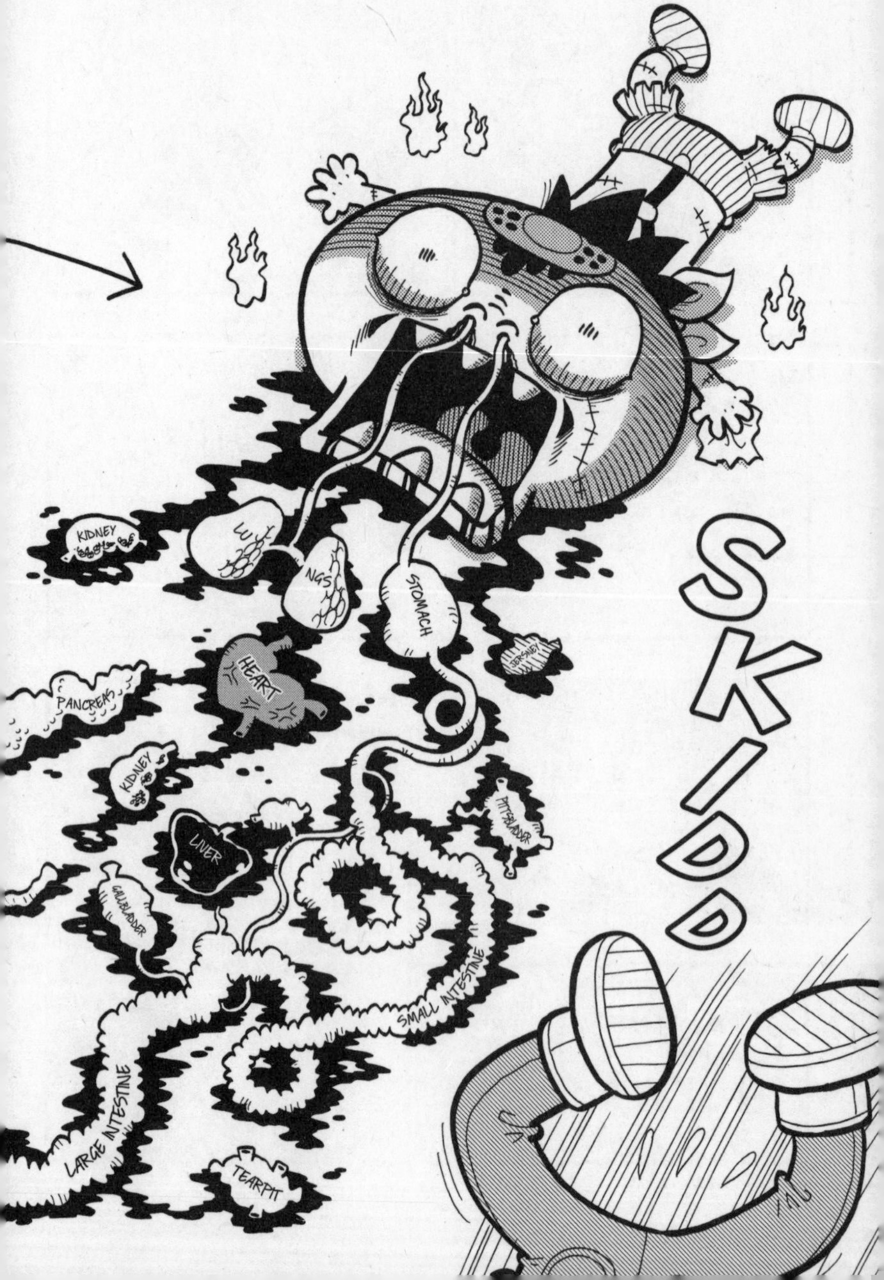

SKIDD
LU
NGS
STOMACH
JERSNEY
KIDNEY
HEART
PANCREAS
KIDNEY
PITTSBLADDER
LIVER
GALLBLADDER
SMALL INTESTINE
LARGE INTESTINE
TEARPIT

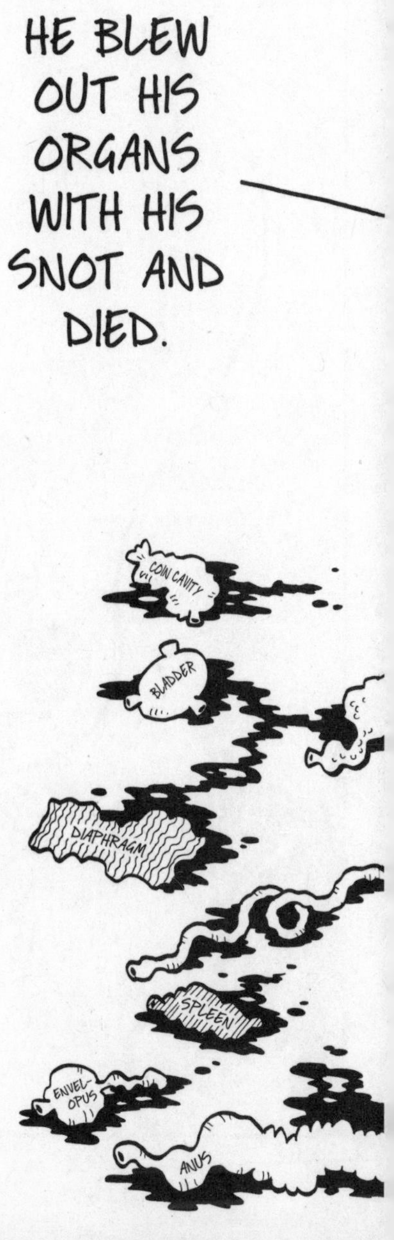
HE BLEW OUT HIS ORGANS WITH HIS SNOT AND DIED.
COIN CAVITY
BLADDER
DIAPHRAGM
SPLEEN
ENVEL-OPUS
ANUS

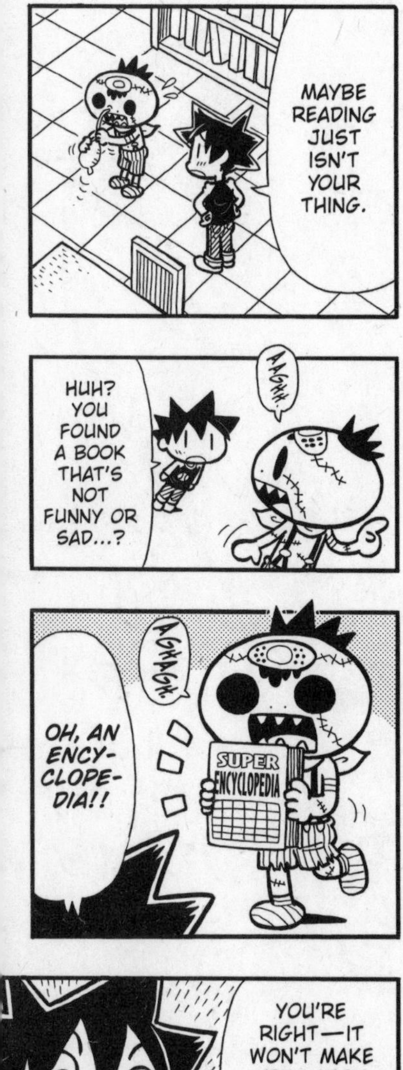
MAYBE READING JUST ISN'T YOUR THING.
HUH? YOU FOUND A BOOK THAT'S NOT FUNNY OR SAD...?
OH, AN ENCY-CLOPE-DIA!!
SUPER ENCYCLOPEDIA
YOU'RE RIGHT—IT WON'T MAKE YOU LAUGH OR CRY, BUT YOU CAN LEARN A LOT!!

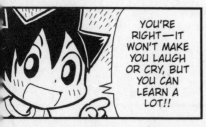

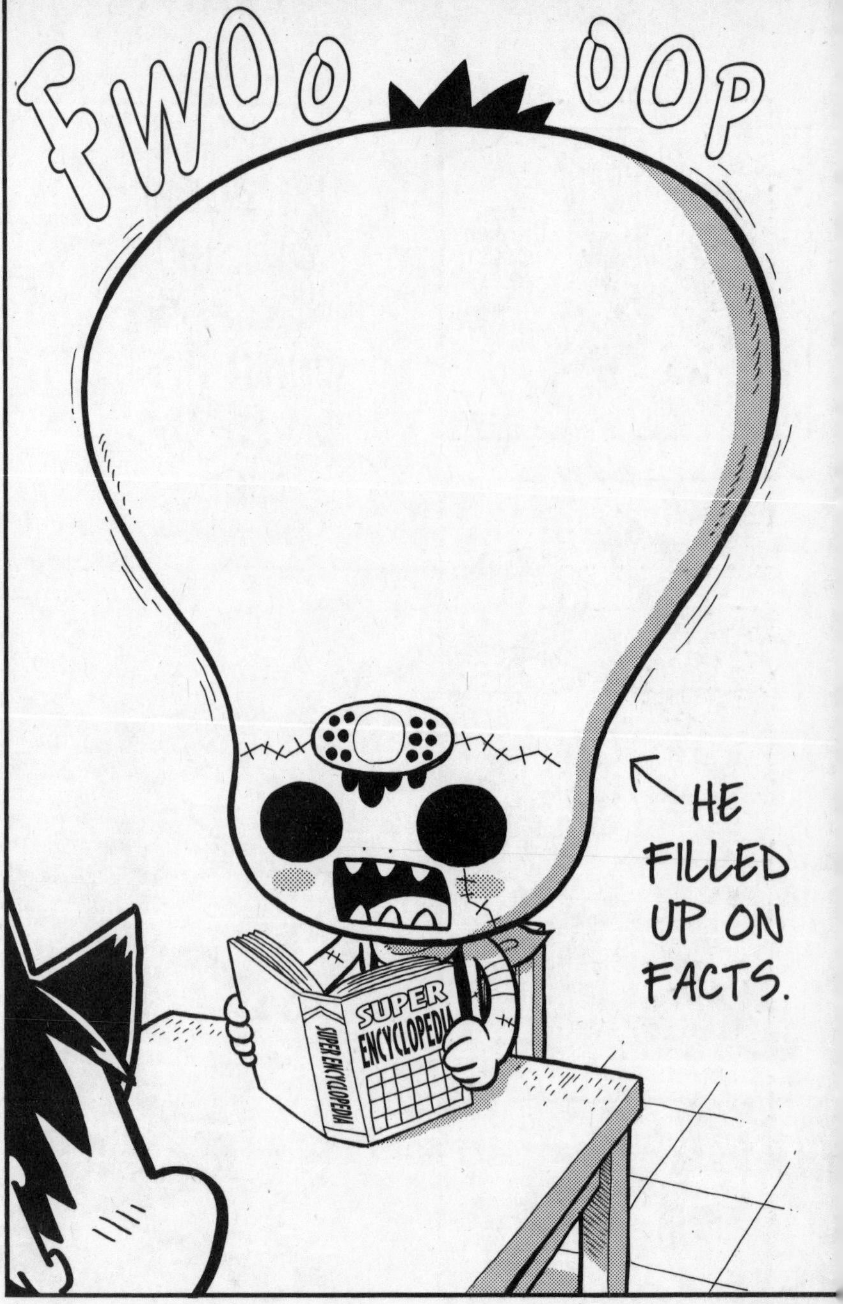
FWOo OOP
HE FILLED UP ON FACTS.
SUPER ENCYCLOPEDIA
SUPER ENCYCLOPEDIA

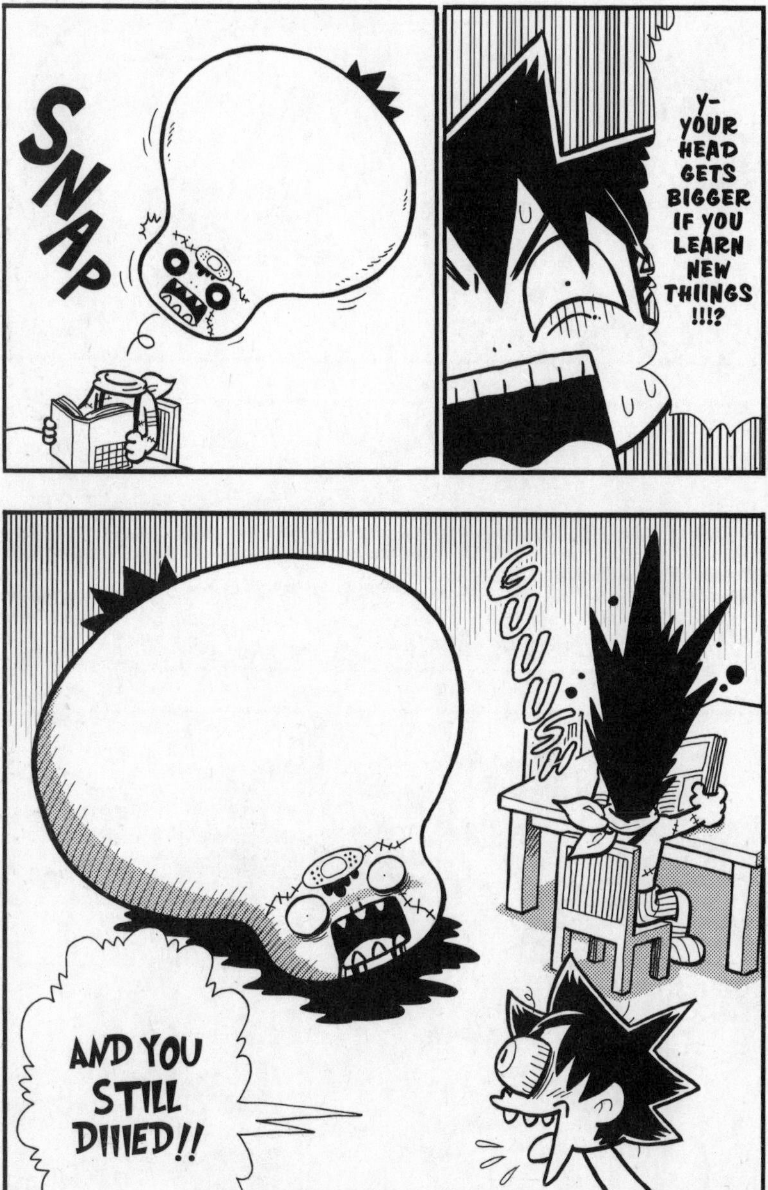
Y-YOUR HEAD GETS BIGGER IF YOU LEARN NEW THIINGS!!!?
SNAP
GUUUSH
AND YOU STILL DIIIED!!

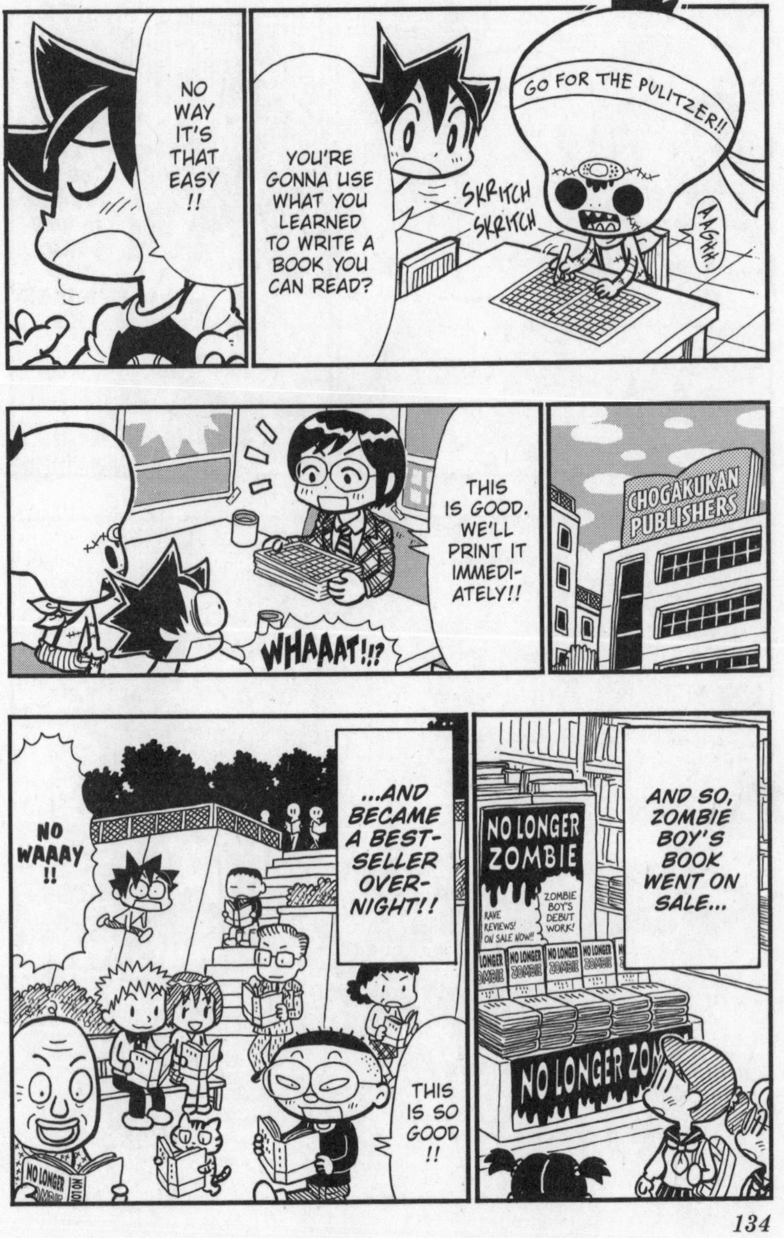
GO FOR THE PULITZER!!
AAGHH
SKRITCH SKRITCH
YOU'RE GONNA USE WHAT YOU LEARNED TO WRITE A BOOK YOU CAN READ?
NO WAY IT'S THAT EASY!!
CHOGAKUKAN PUBLISHERS
THIS IS GOOD. WE'LL PRINT IT IMMEDIATELY!!
WHAAAT!!?
AND SO, ZOMBIE BOY'S BOOK WENT ON SALE...
NO LONGER ZOMBIE
ZOMBIE BOY'S DEBUT WORK!
RAVE REVIEWS! ON SALE NOW!!
NO LONGER ZOMBIE
NO LONGER ZO
...AND BECAME A BEST-SELLER OVERNIGHT!!
NO WAAAY!!
THIS IS SO GOOD!!
NO LONGER ZOMBIE

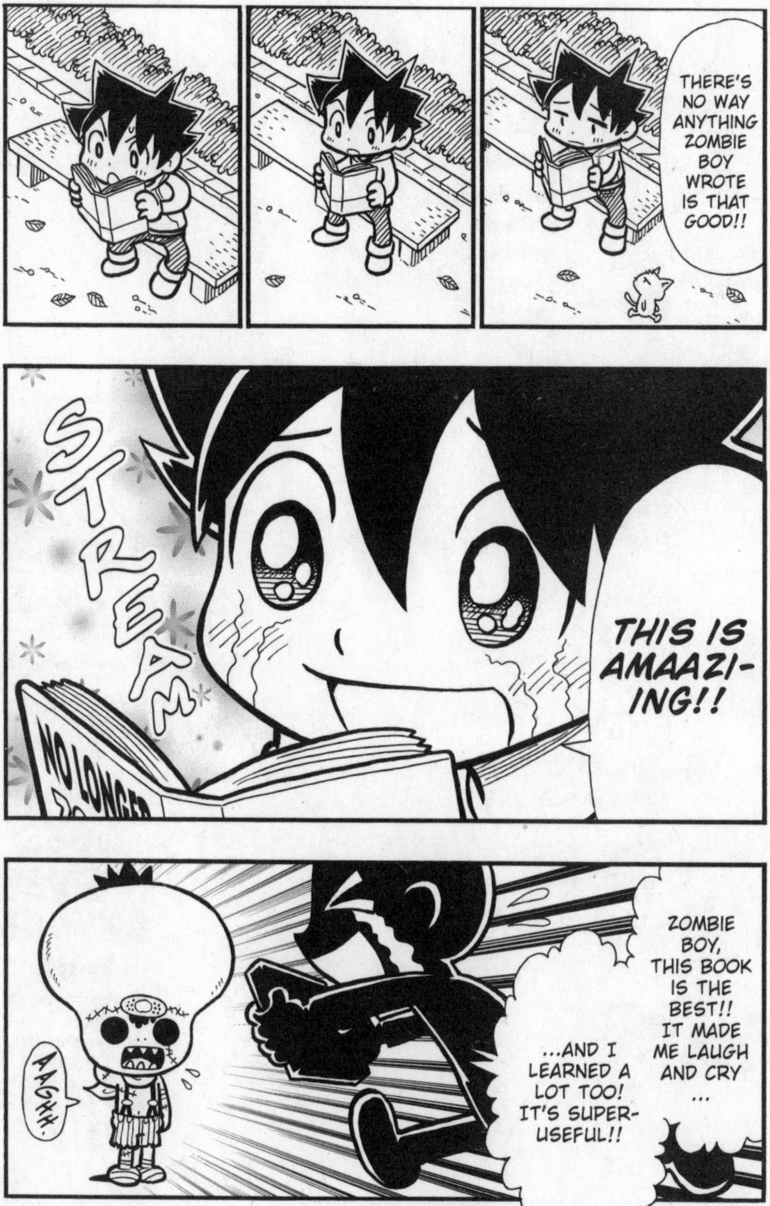
THERE'S NO WAY ANYTHING ZOMBIE BOY WROTE IS THAT GOOD!!
THIS IS AMAAZI-ING!!
STREAM
NO LONGER
ZOMBIE BOY, THIS BOOK IS THE BEST!! IT MADE ME LAUGH AND CRY ...
...AND I LEARNED A LOT TOO! IT'S SUPER-USEFUL!!
AAGHH.

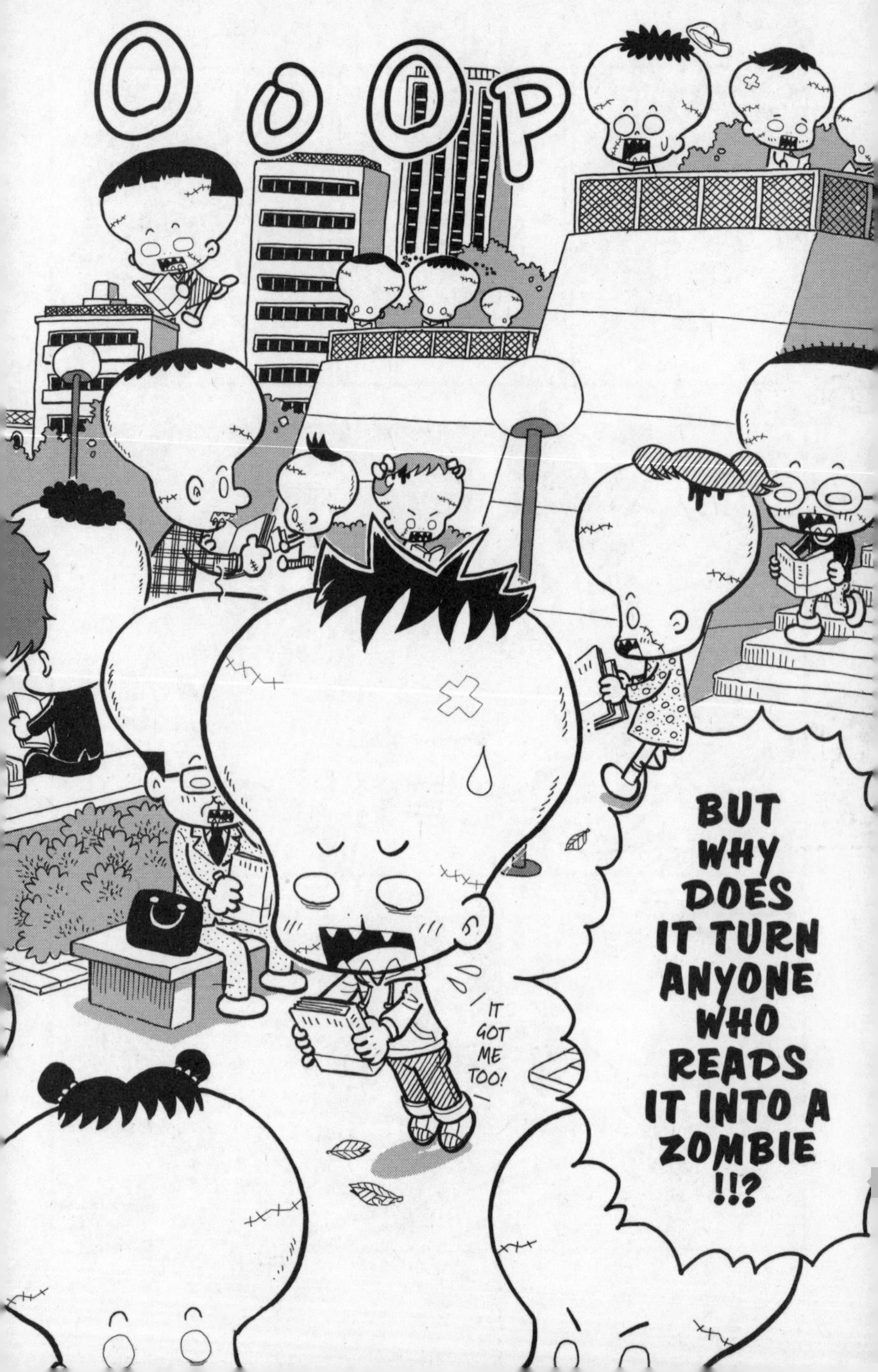
OOOP
BUT WHY DOES IT TURN ANYONE WHO READS IT INTO A ZOMBIE !!?
IT GOT ME TOO!

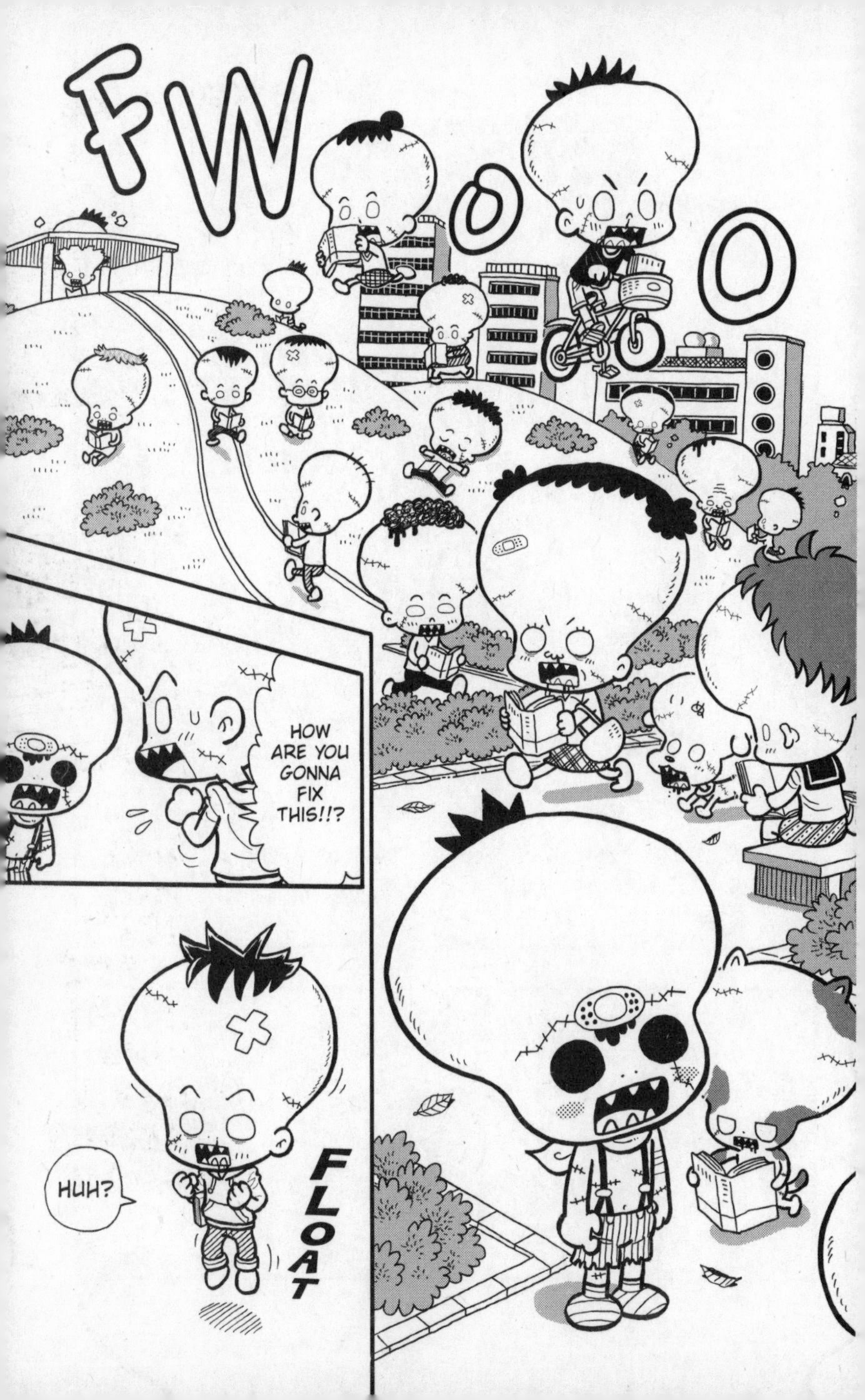
FWOOO
HOW ARE YOU GONNA FIX THIS!!?
HUH?
FLOAT

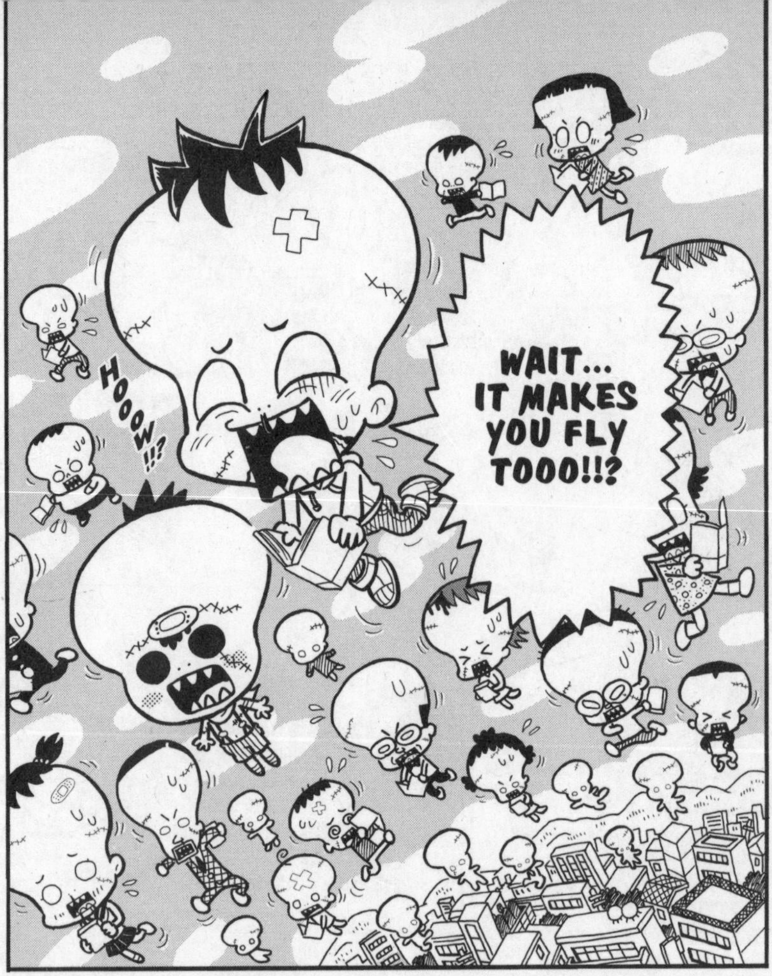
WAIT... IT MAKES YOU FLY TOOO!!?
HOOOW!!?

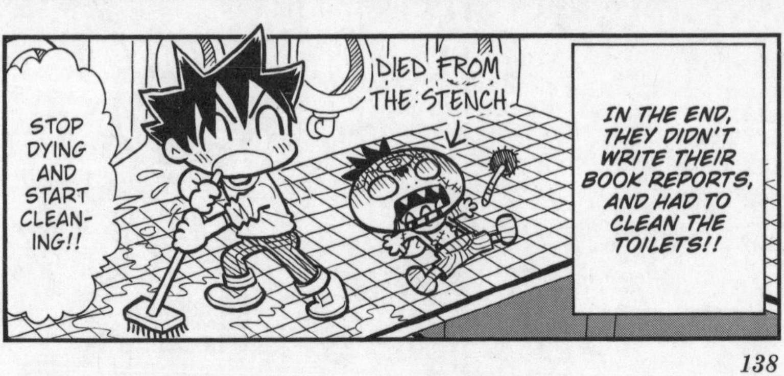
IN THE END, THEY DIDN'T WRITE THEIR BOOK REPORTS, AND HAD TO CLEAN THE TOILETS!!
DIED FROM THE STENCH
STOP DYING AND START CLEANING!!

NO CURZE IZ GONNA GET ME!

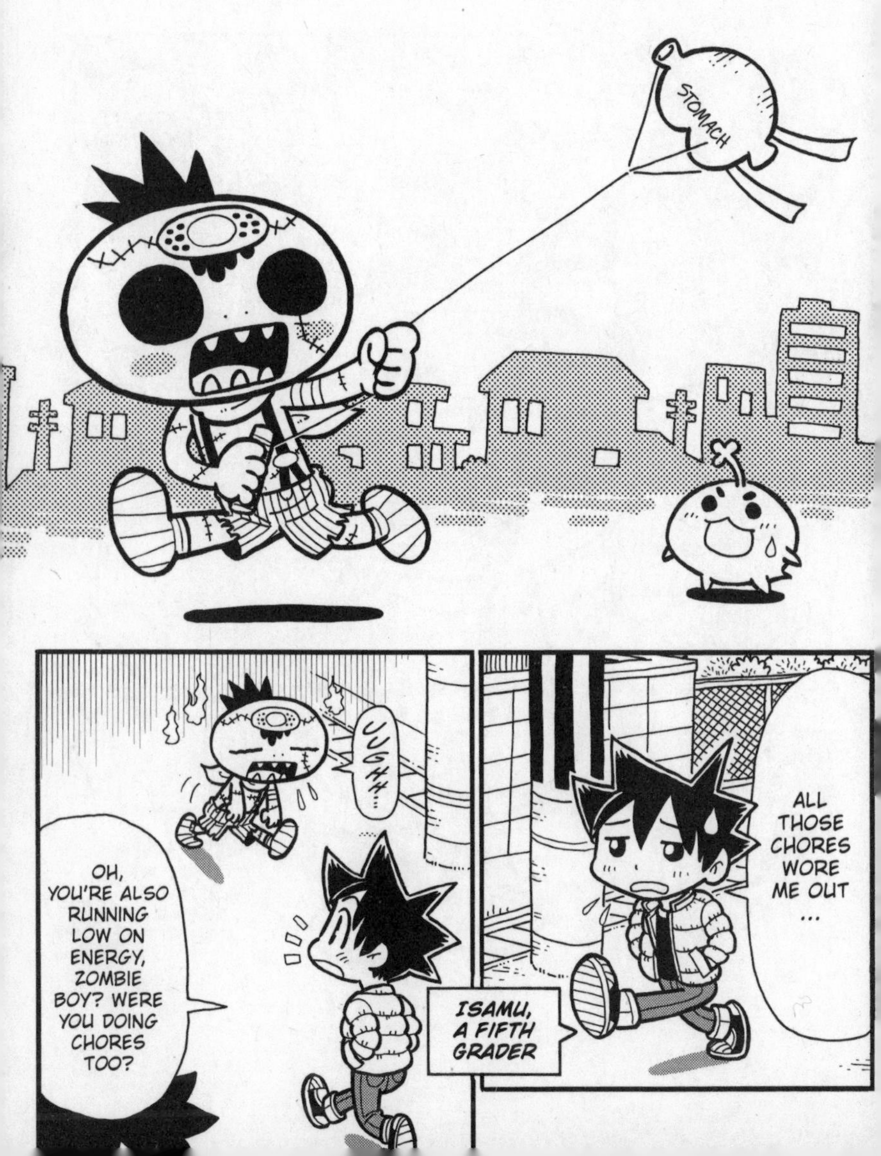
STOMACH
ALL THOSE CHORES WORE ME OUT...
ISAMU, A FIFTH GRADER
UUGHH...
OH, YOU'RE ALSO RUNNING LOW ON ENERGY, ZOMBIE BOY? WERE YOU DOING CHORES TOO?

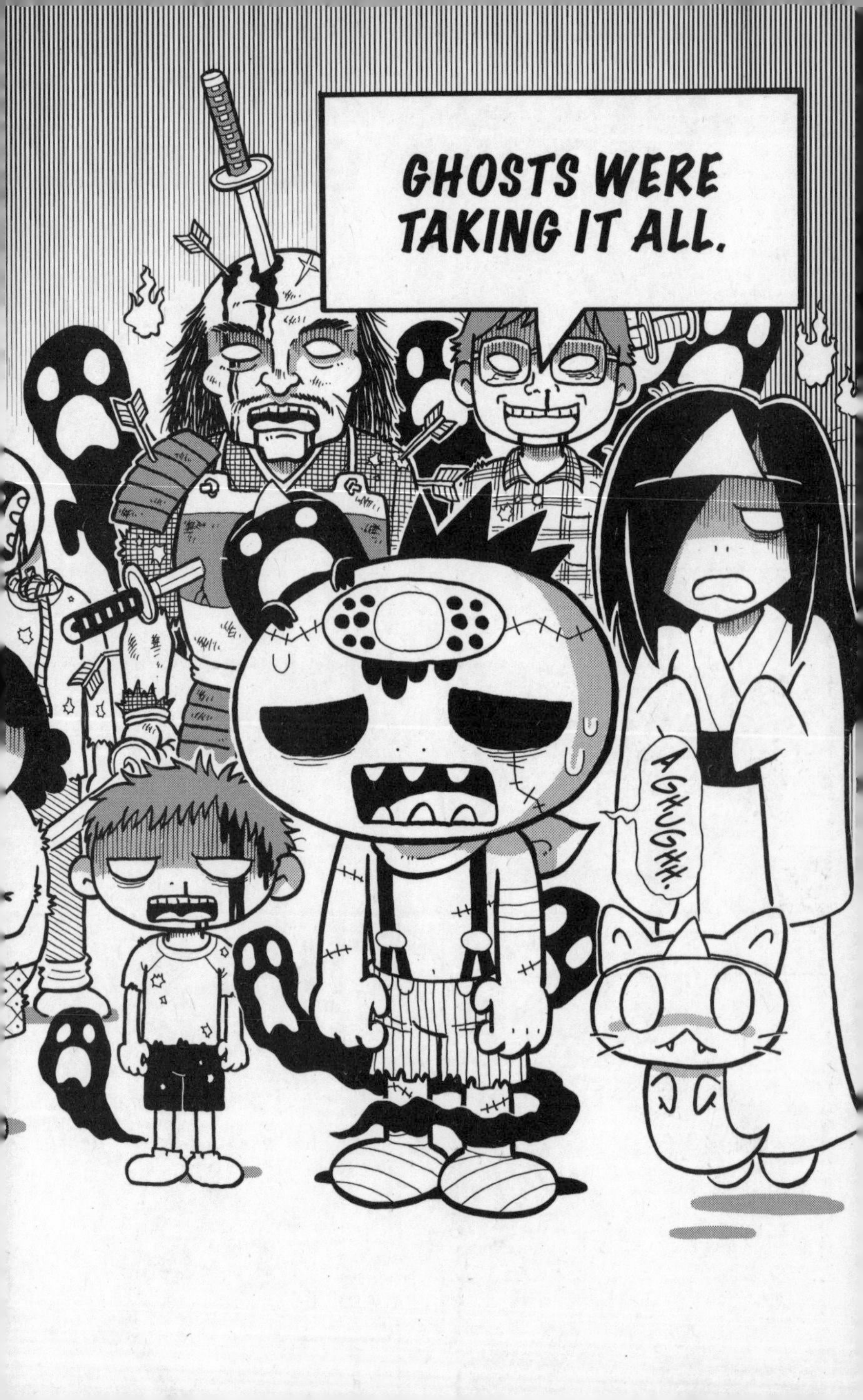
GHOSTS WERE TAKING IT ALL.
AGHUGHH.

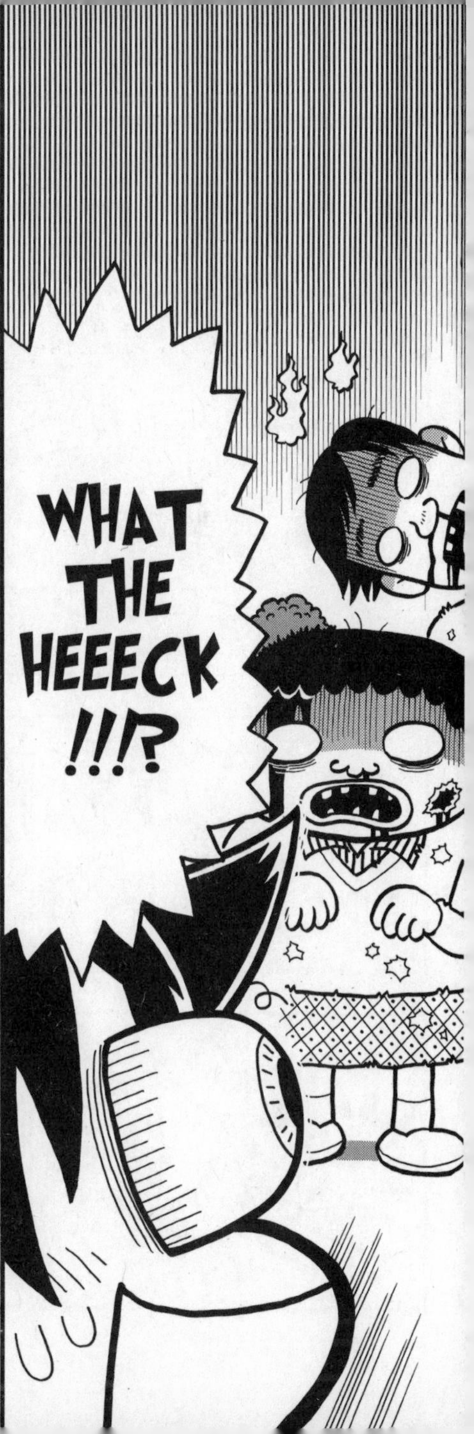
WHAT THE HEEECK !!!?

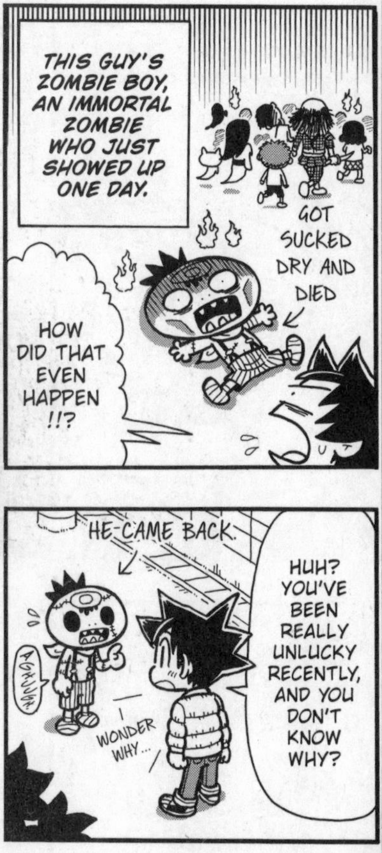
THIS GUY'S ZOMBIE BOY, AN IMMORTAL ZOMBIE WHO JUST SHOWED UP ONE DAY.
GOT SUCKED DRY AND DIED
HOW DID THAT EVEN HAPPEN !!?
HE CAME BACK.
HUH? YOU'VE BEEN REALLY UNLUCKY RECENTLY, AND YOU DON'T KNOW WHY?
I WONDER WHY...
HEY, WHAT'S THAT IN YOUR POCKET?

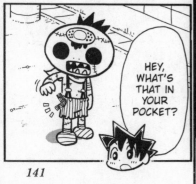

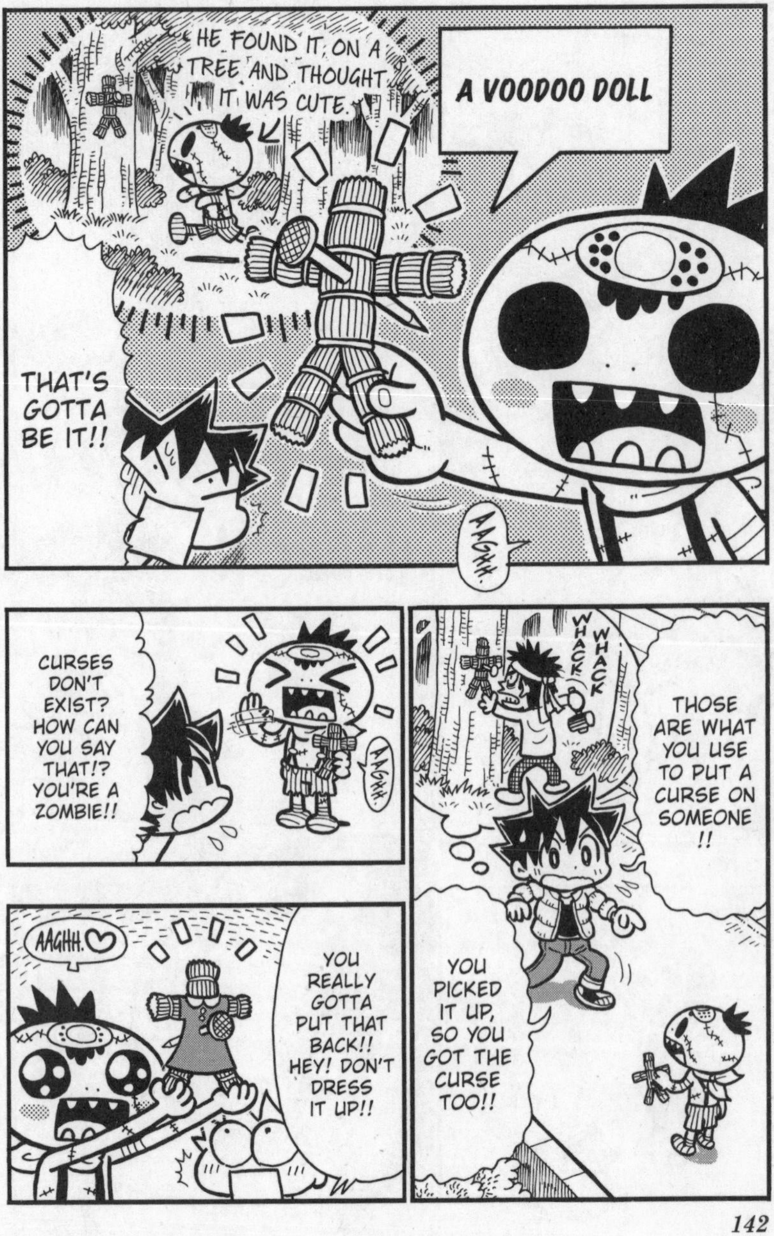
A VOODOO DOLL
HE FOUND IT ON A TREE AND THOUGHT IT WAS CUTE.
AAGHH.
THAT'S GOTTA BE IT!!
WHACK WHACK
THOSE ARE WHAT YOU USE TO PUT A CURSE ON SOMEONE !!
YOU PICKED IT UP, SO YOU GOT THE CURSE TOO!!
AAGHH.
CURSES DON'T EXIST? HOW CAN YOU SAY THAT!? YOU'RE A ZOMBIE!!
YOU REALLY GOTTA PUT THAT BACK!! HEY! DON'T DRESS IT UP!!
AAGHH.♡

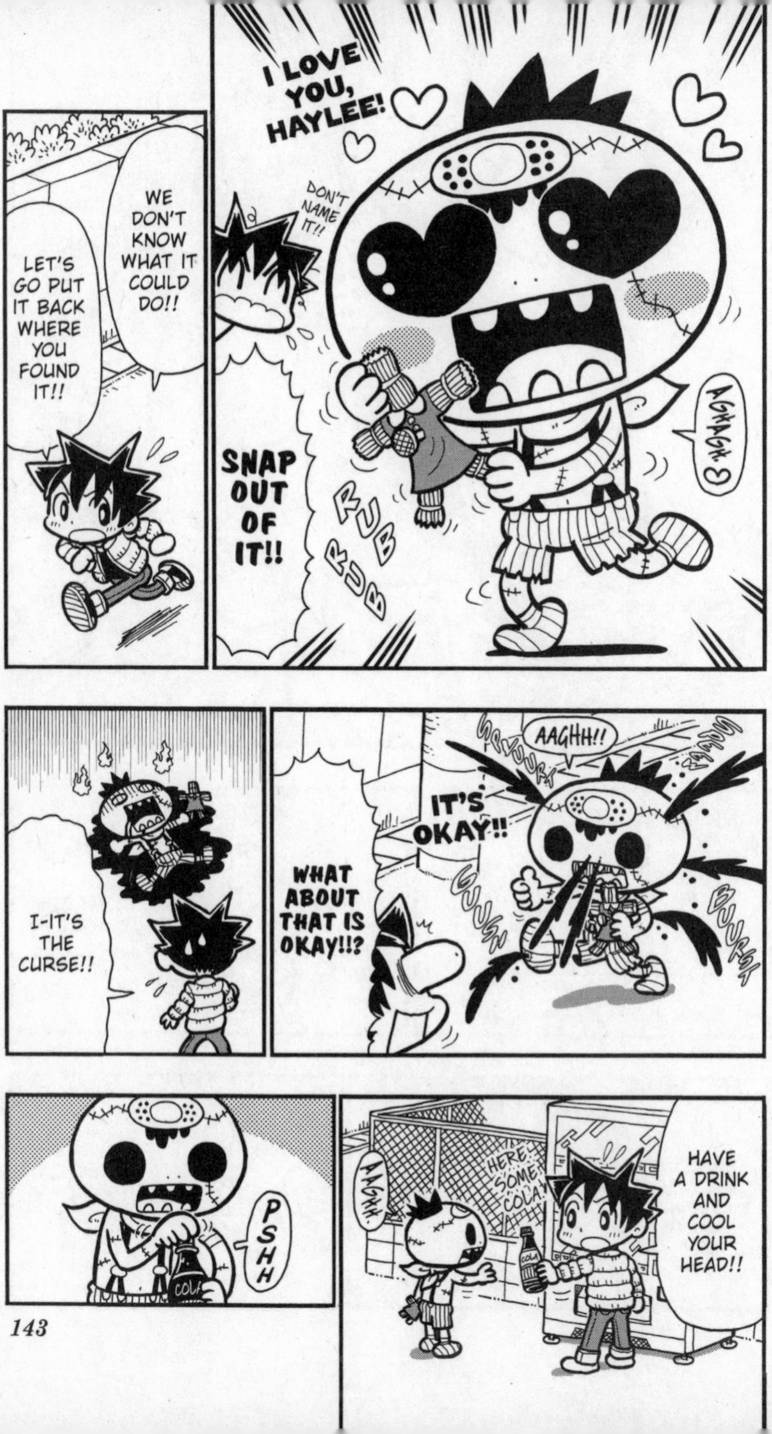
I LOVE YOU, HAYLEE!
DON'T NAME IT!!
SNAP OUT OF IT!!
RUB RUB
WE DON'T KNOW WHAT IT COULD DO!!
LET'S GO PUT IT BACK WHERE YOU FOUND IT!!
AAGHH!!
IT'S OKAY!!
WHAT ABOUT THAT IS OKAY!!?
I-IT'S THE CURSE!!
HAVE A DRINK AND COOL YOUR HEAD!!
HERE, SOME COLA.
PSHH

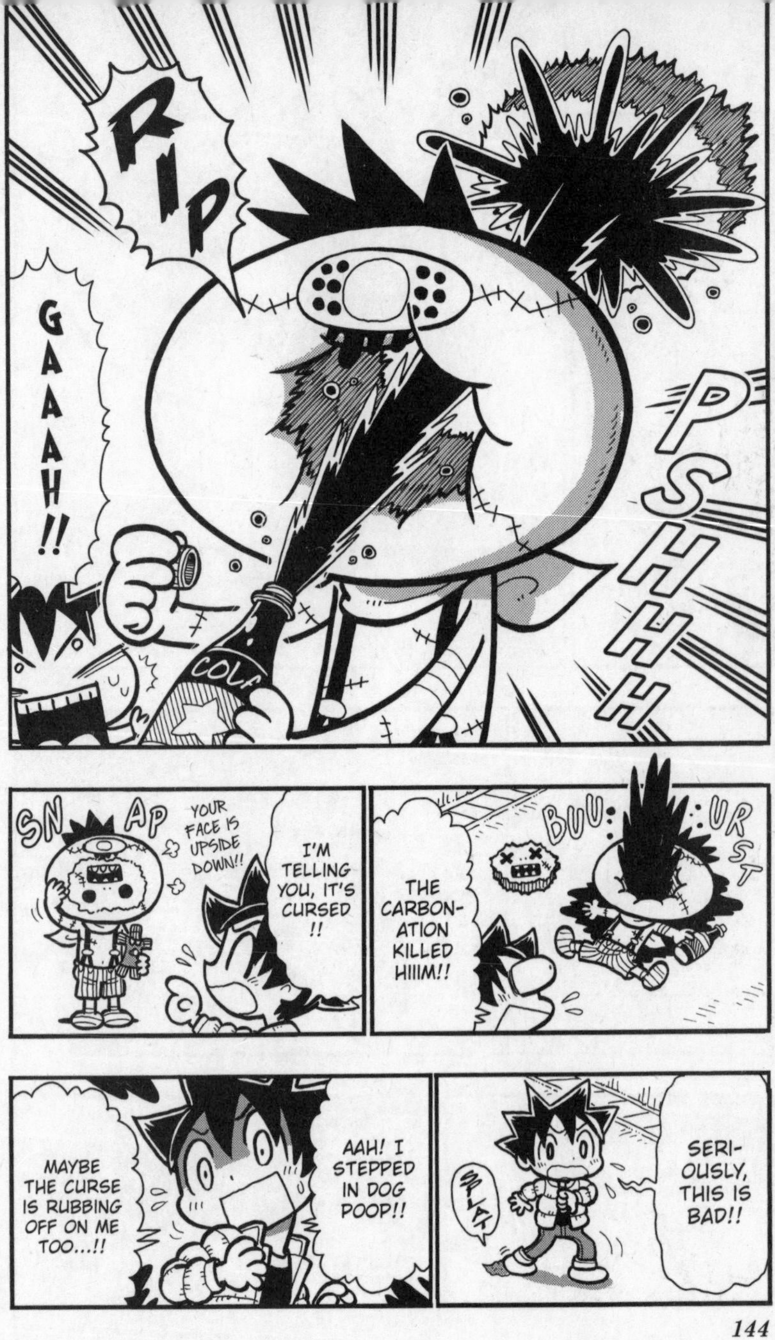
RIP
PSHHHHH
GAAAAH!!
BUU: :URST
THE CARBON-ATION KILLED HIIIM!!
I'M TELLING YOU, IT'S CURSED!!
YOUR FACE IS UPSIDE DOWN!!
SNAP
SERI-OUSLY, THIS IS BAD!!
SPLAT
AAH! I STEPPED IN DOG POOP!!
MAYBE THE CURSE IS RUBBING OFF ON ME TOO...!!

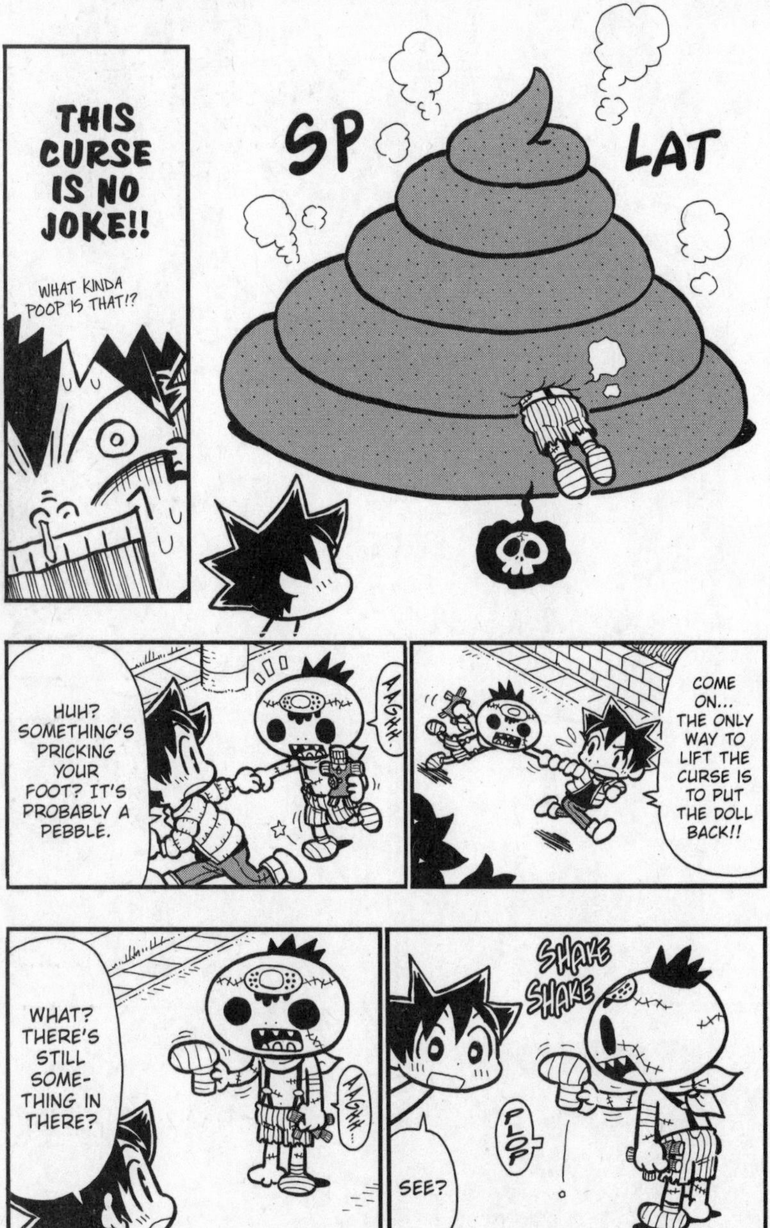
SP LAT
THIS CURSE IS NO JOKE!!
WHAT KINDA POOP IS THAT!?
COME ON... THE ONLY WAY TO LIFT THE CURSE IS TO PUT THE DOLL BACK!!
AAGHH...
HUH? SOMETHING'S PRICKING YOUR FOOT? IT'S PROBABLY A PEBBLE.
SHAKE SHAKE
PLOP
SEE?
AAGHH...
WHAT? THERE'S STILL SOME-THING IN THERE?

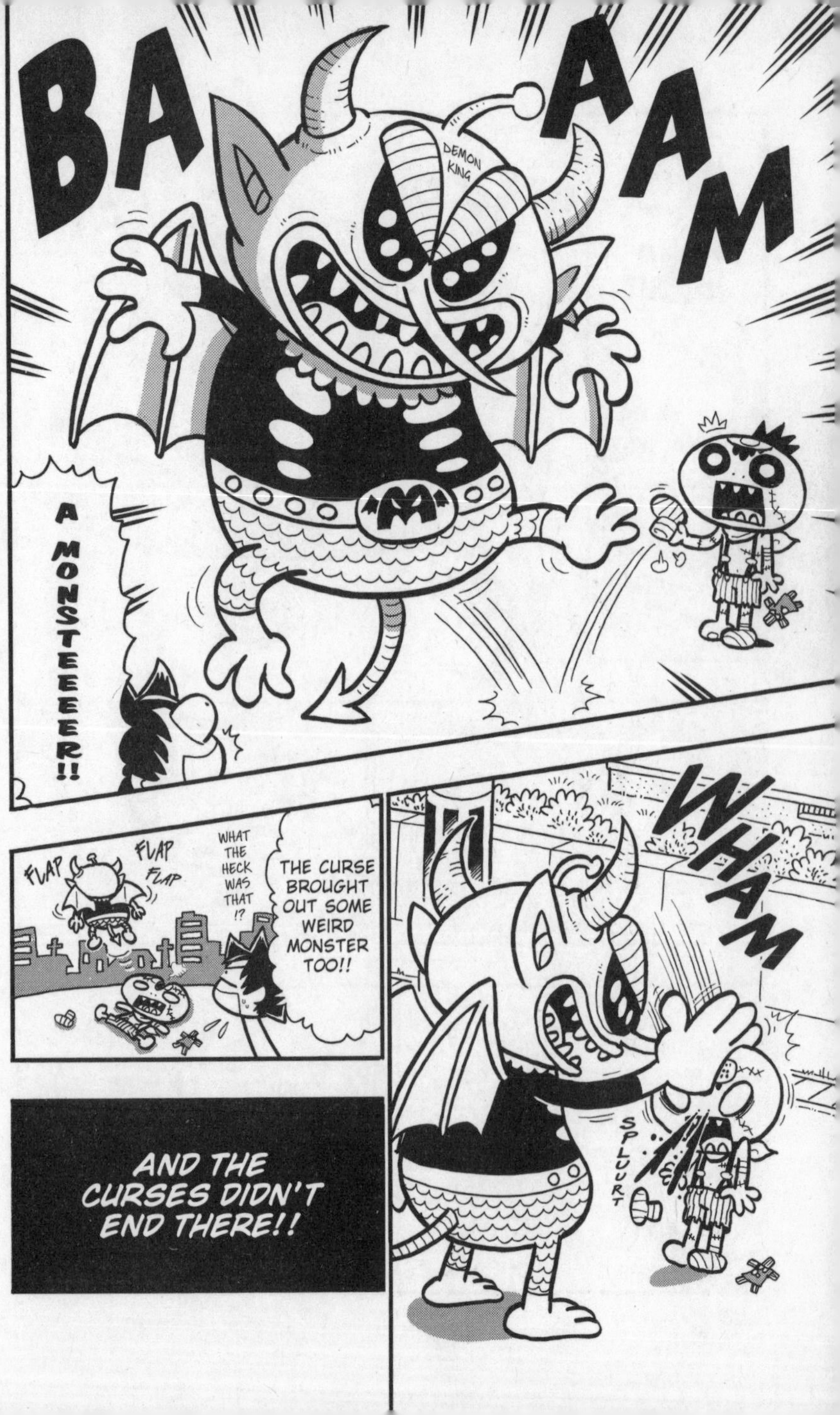
BAAAM
DEMON KING
A MONSTEEEEER!!
WHAM
SPLUURT
THE CURSE BROUGHT OUT SOME WEIRD MONSTER TOO!!
WHAT THE HECK WAS THAT!?
FLAP FLAP FLAP
AND THE CURSES DIDN'T END THERE!!

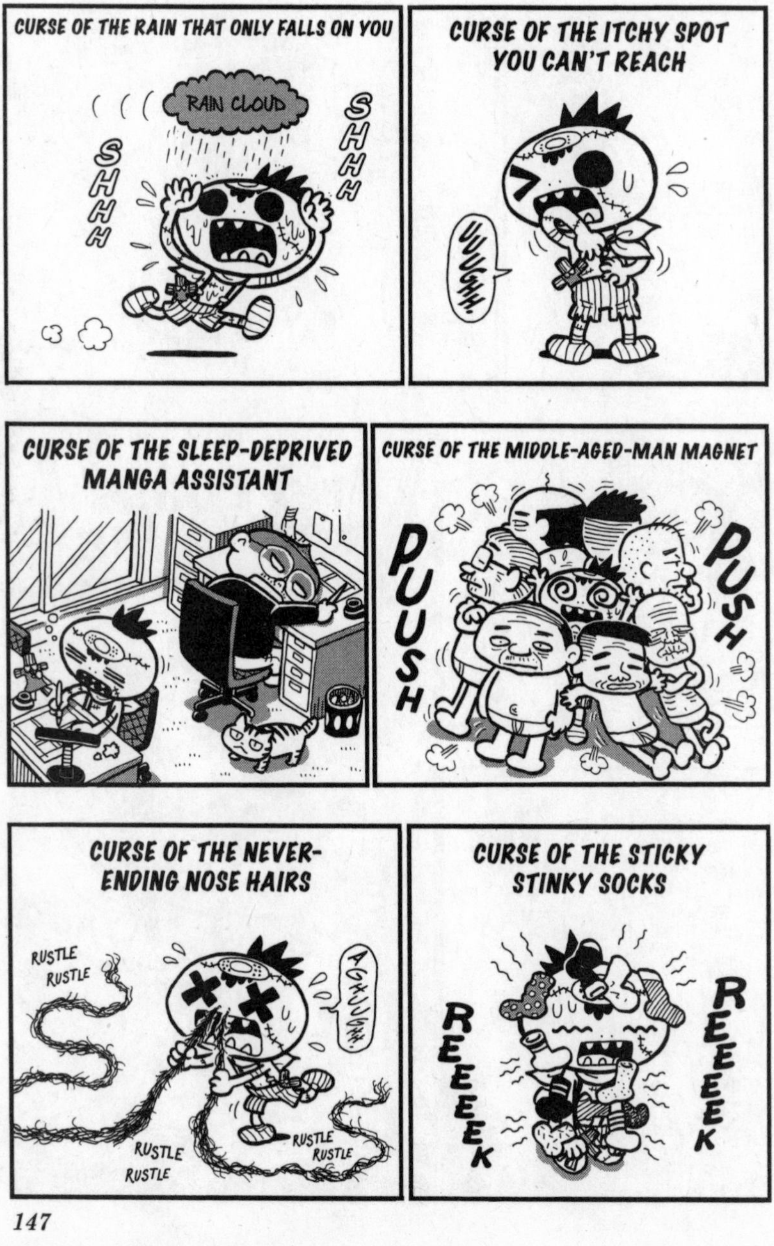
CURSE OF THE ITCHY SPOT YOU CAN'T REACH
UUUGHH.
CURSE OF THE RAIN THAT ONLY FALLS ON YOU
RAIN CLOUD
SHHHH
SHHHH
CURSE OF THE MIDDLE-AGED-MAN MAGNET
PUSH
PUUSH
CURSE OF THE SLEEP-DEPRIVED MANGA ASSISTANT
CURSE OF THE STICKY STINKY SOCKS
REEEEK
REEEEK
CURSE OF THE NEVER-ENDING NOSE HAIRS
AGHUUGHH.
RUSTLE RUSTLE
RUSTLE RUSTLE
RUSTLE RUSTLE

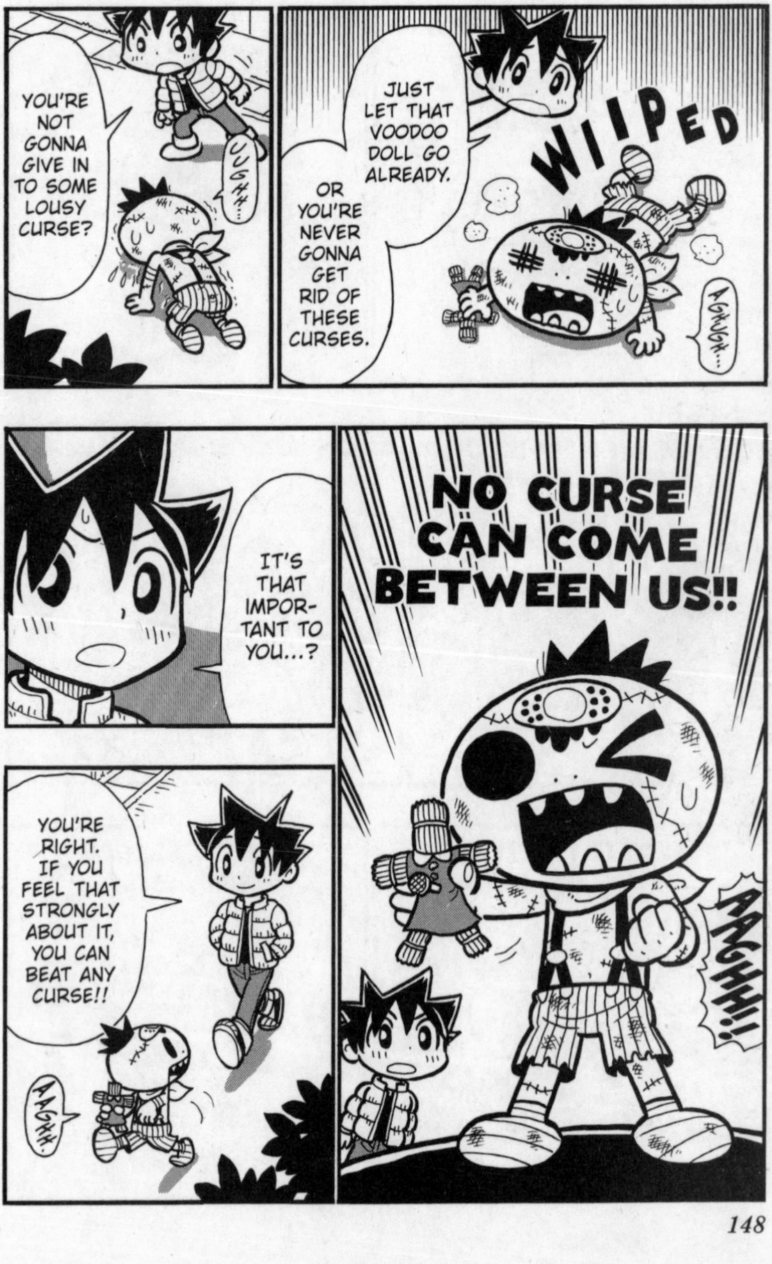
JUST LET THAT VOODOO DOLL GO ALREADY.
OR YOU'RE NEVER GONNA GET RID OF THESE CURSES.
WIIPED
AGHUGH...
YOU'RE NOT GONNA GIVE IN TO SOME LOUSY CURSE?
UGHHH...
NO CURSE CAN COME BETWEEN US!!
AAGHHH!!
IT'S THAT IMPOR-TANT TO YOU...?
YOU'RE RIGHT. IF YOU FEEL THAT STRONGLY ABOUT IT, YOU CAN BEAT ANY CURSE!!
AAGHH.

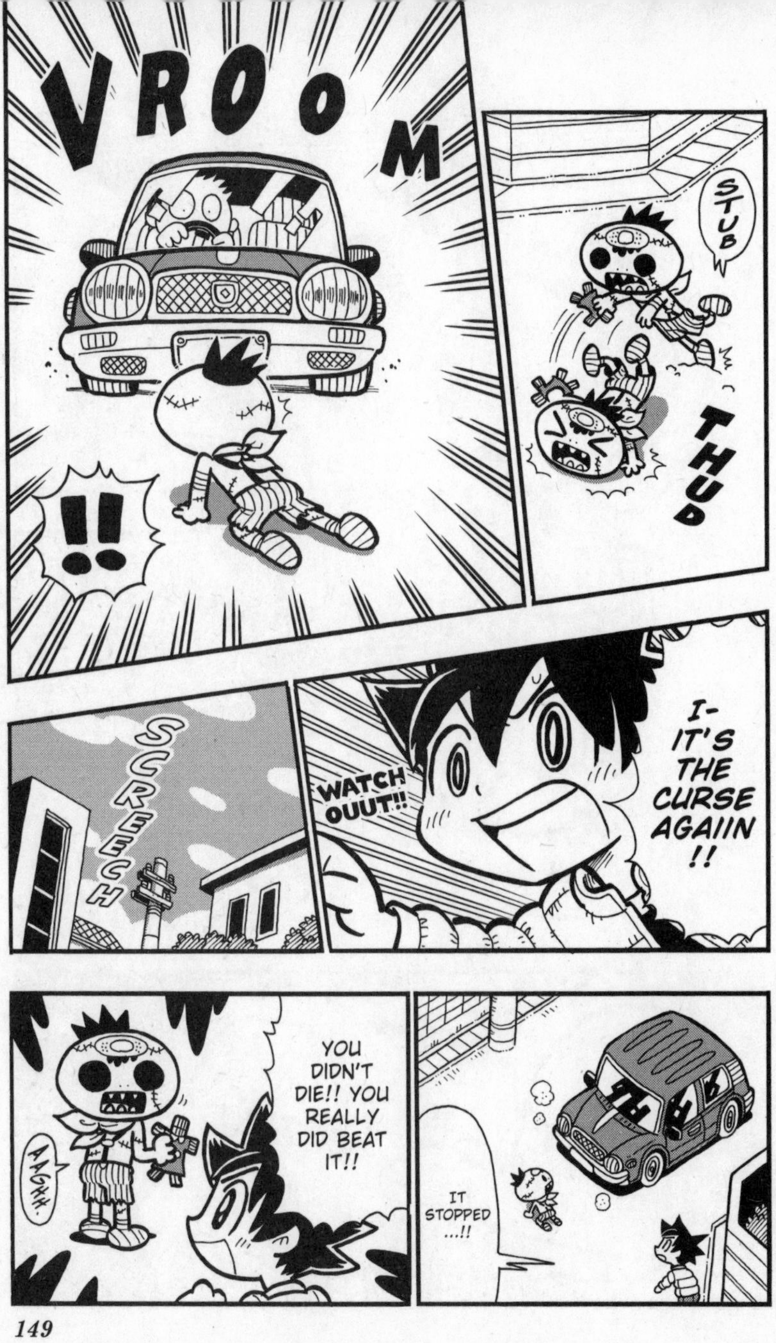
STUB
THUD
VROOM
!!
I- IT'S THE CURSE AGAIIN!!
WATCH OUUT!!
SCREECH
IT STOPPED ...!!
YOU DIDN'T DIE!! YOU REALLY DID BEAT IT!!
AAGHH.

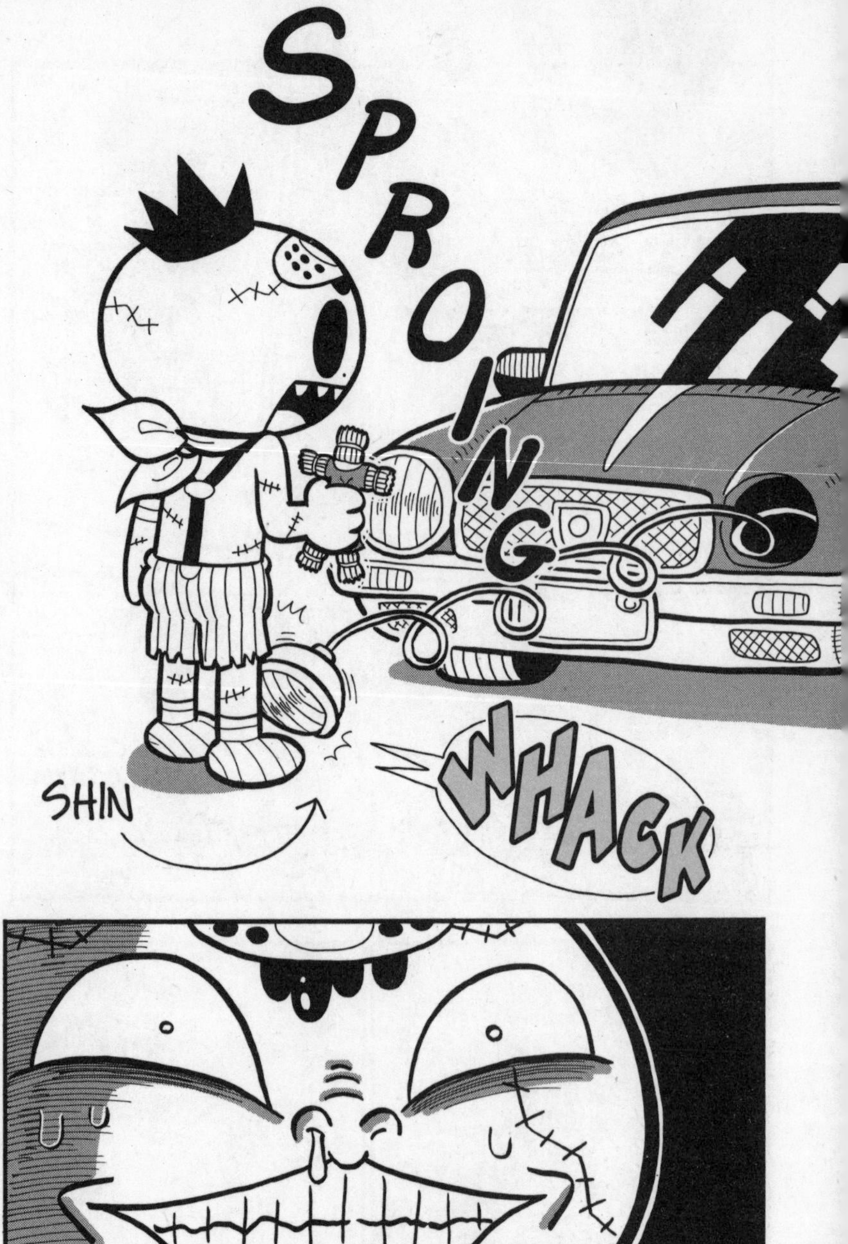
SPROING
SHIN
WHACK

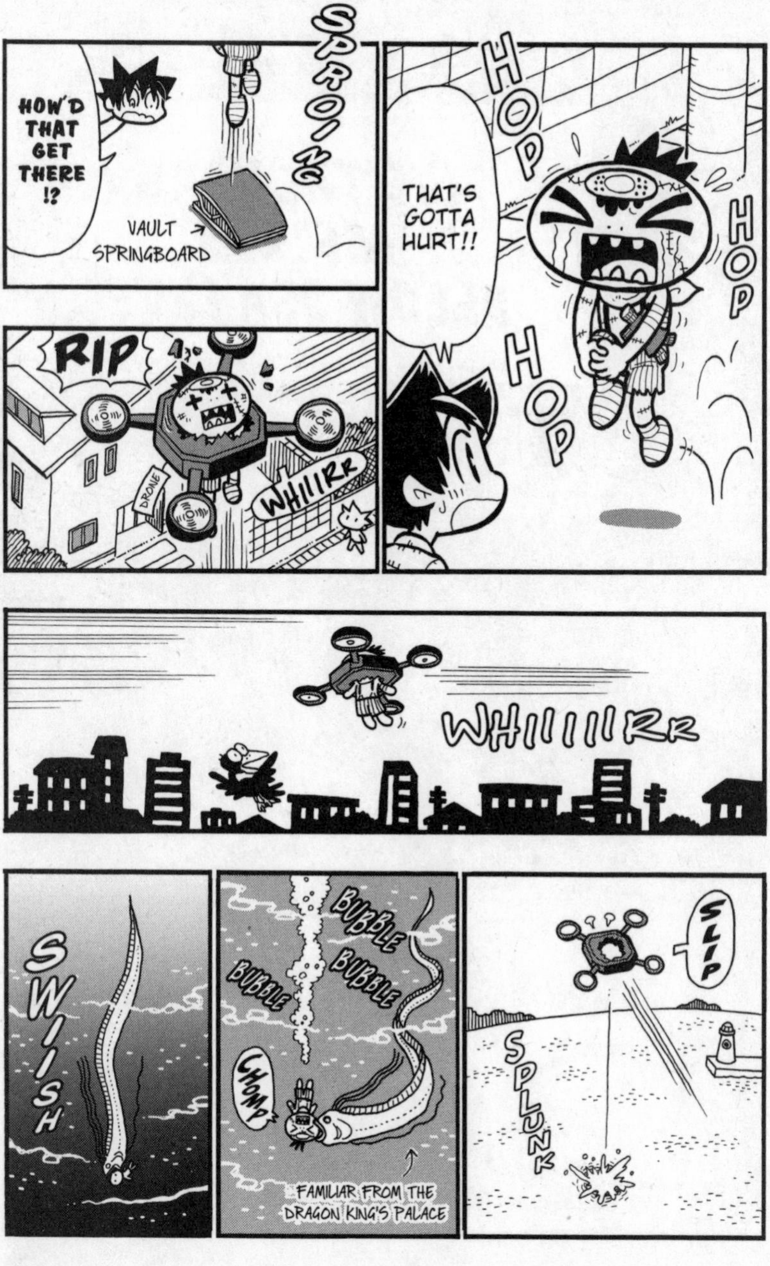
HOP
HOP
THAT'S GOTTA HURT!!
HOP
HOP
HOP
HOP
SPROING
HOW'D THAT GET THERE!?
VAULT SPRINGBOARD
RIP
DRONE
WHIIIRR
WHIIIIIIRR
SLIP
SPLUNK
BUBBLE
BUBBLE
BUBBLE
CHOMP
FAMILIAR FROM THE DRAGON KING'S PALACE
SWISH

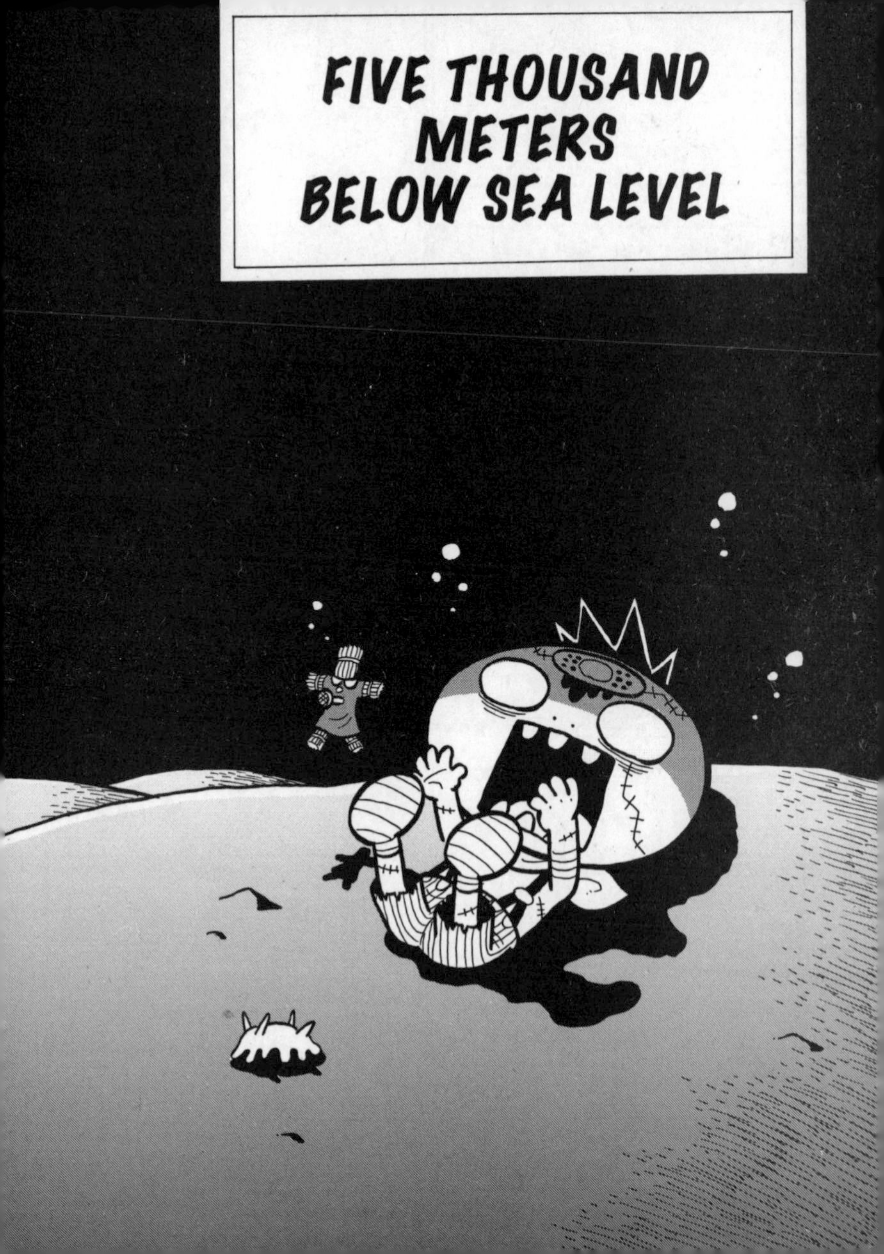
FIVE THOUSAND METERS BELOW SEA LEVEL

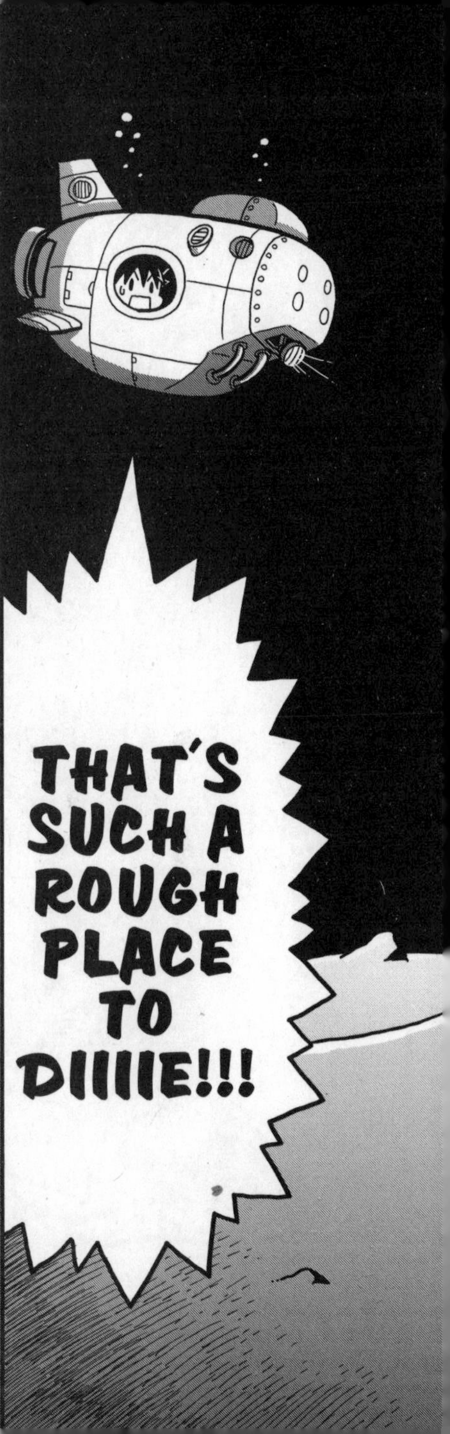
THAT'S SUCH A ROUGH PLACE TO DIIIIE!!!
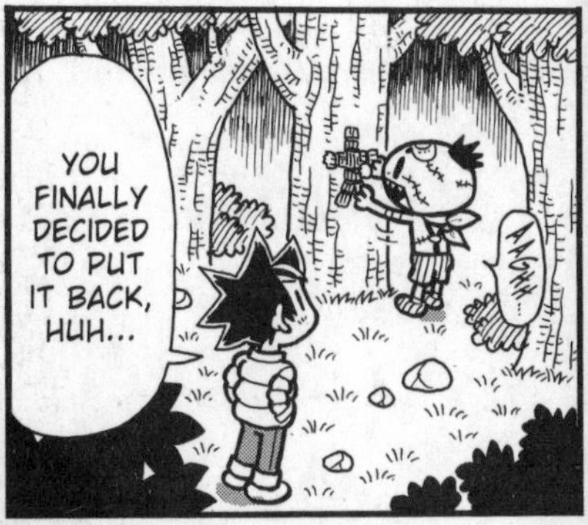
YOU FINALLY DECIDED TO PUT IT BACK, HUH...
AAGHH...
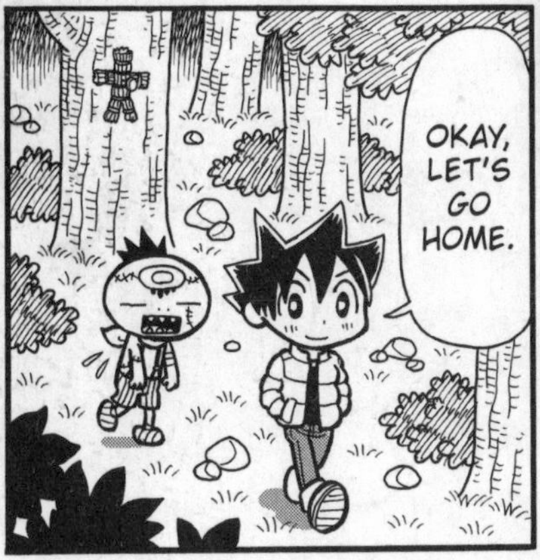
OKAY, LET'S GO HOME.
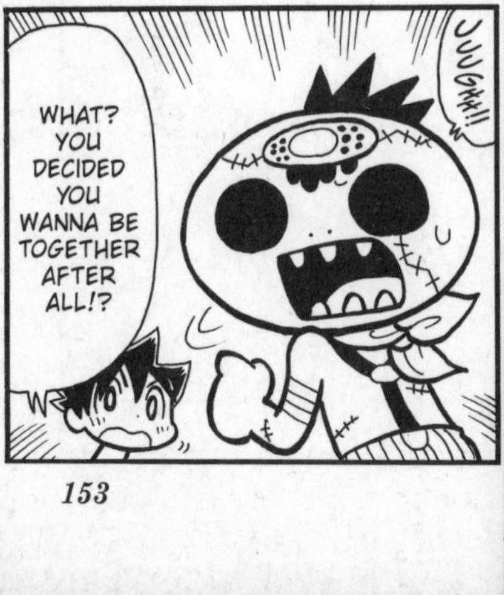
JUUGHH!!!
WHAT? YOU DECIDED YOU WANNA BE TOGETHER AFTER ALL!?

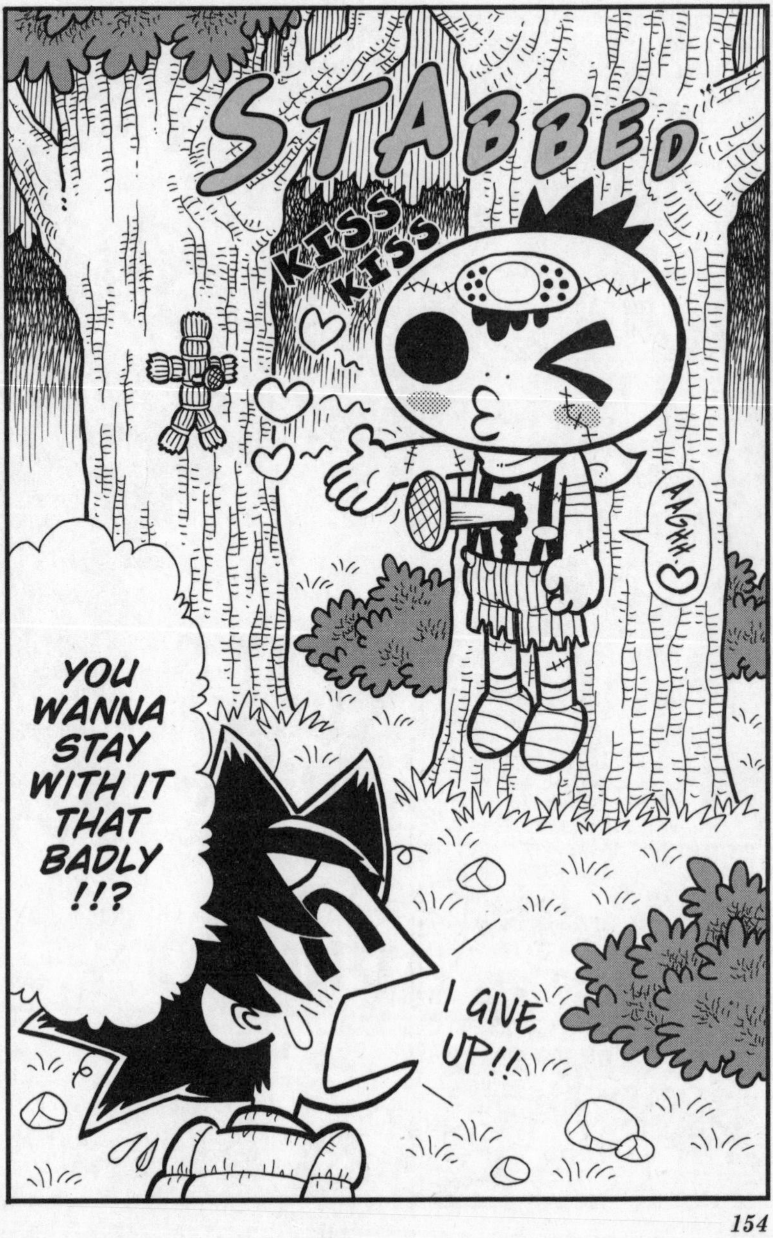
STABBED
KISS KISS
AAGHH.♡
YOU WANNA STAY WITH IT THAT BADLY!!?
I GIVE UP!!

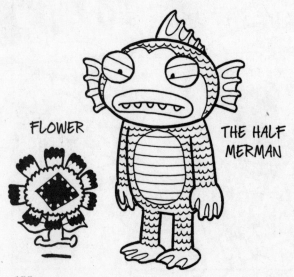

FLOWER

THE HALF
MERMAN

THE IMMORTAL ZOMBIE'Z BIRTHDAY!

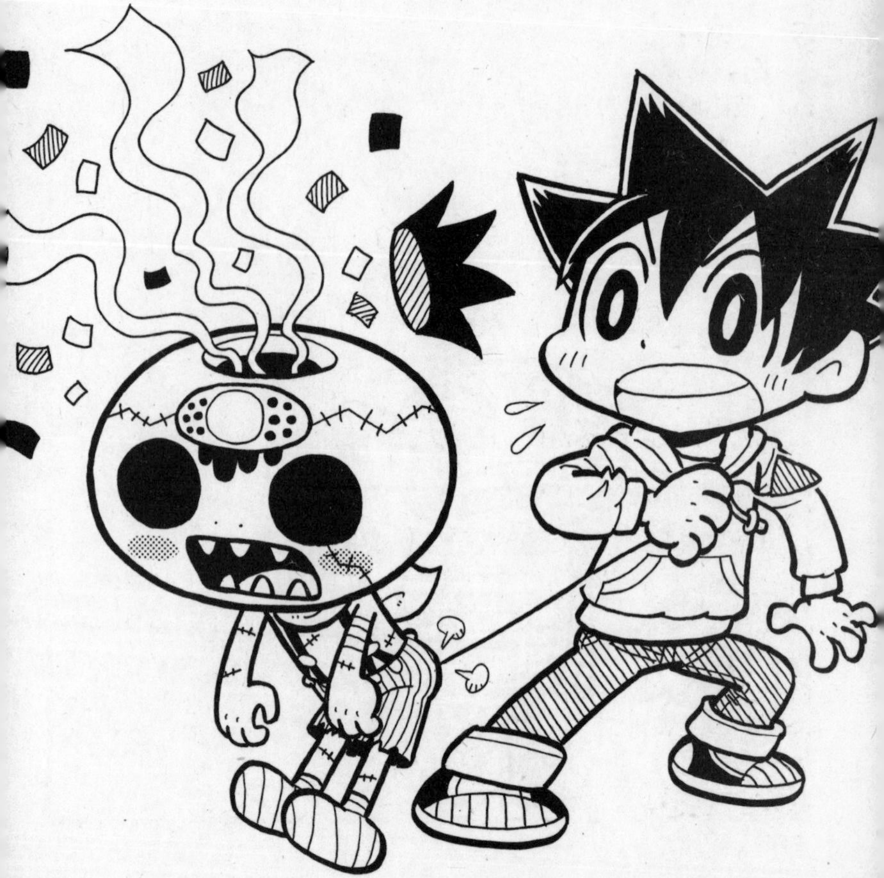

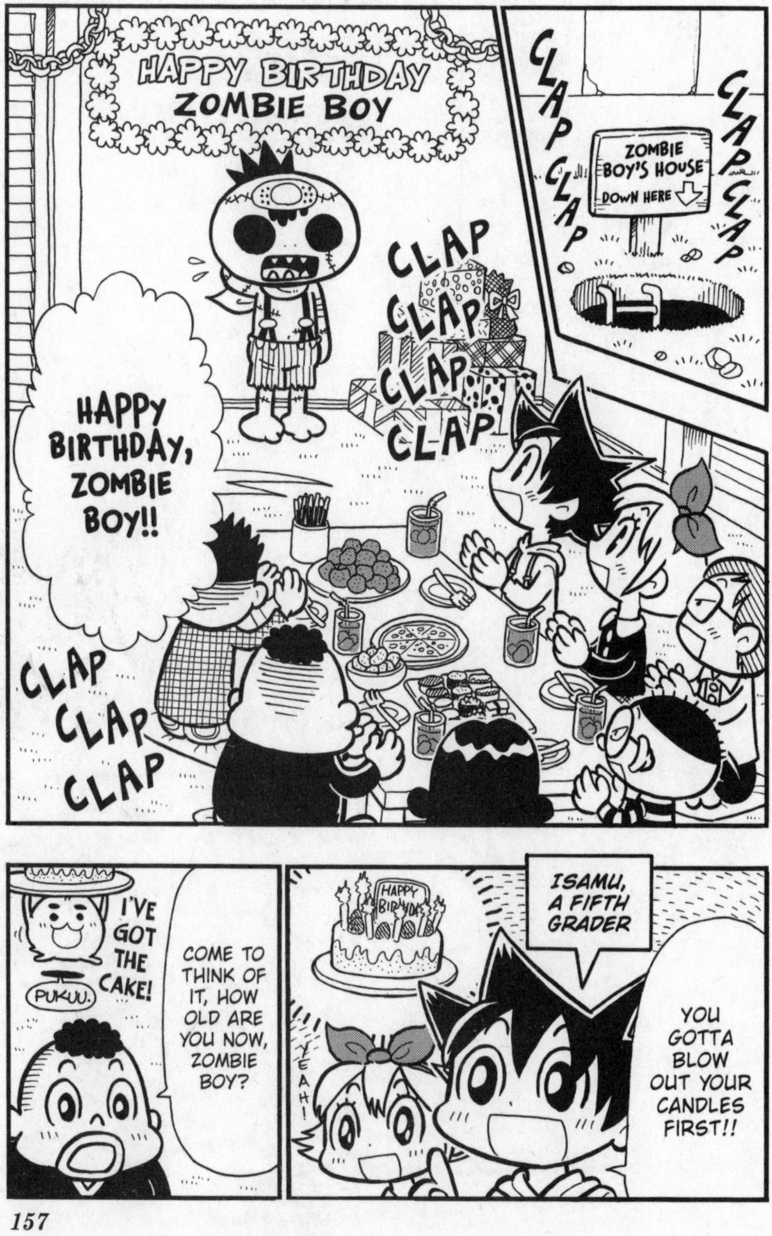
CLAP CLAP
ZOMBIE BOY'S HOUSE
DOWN HERE
CLAP CLAP
HAPPY BIRTHDAY
ZOMBIE BOY
CLAP CLAP CLAP CLAP
HAPPY BIRTHDAY, ZOMBIE BOY!!
CLAP CLAP CLAP
YOU GOTTA BLOW OUT YOUR CANDLES FIRST!!
ISAMU, A FIFTH GRADER
YEAH!
COME TO THINK OF IT, HOW OLD ARE YOU NOW, ZOMBIE BOY?
I'VE GOT THE CAKE!
PUKUU.

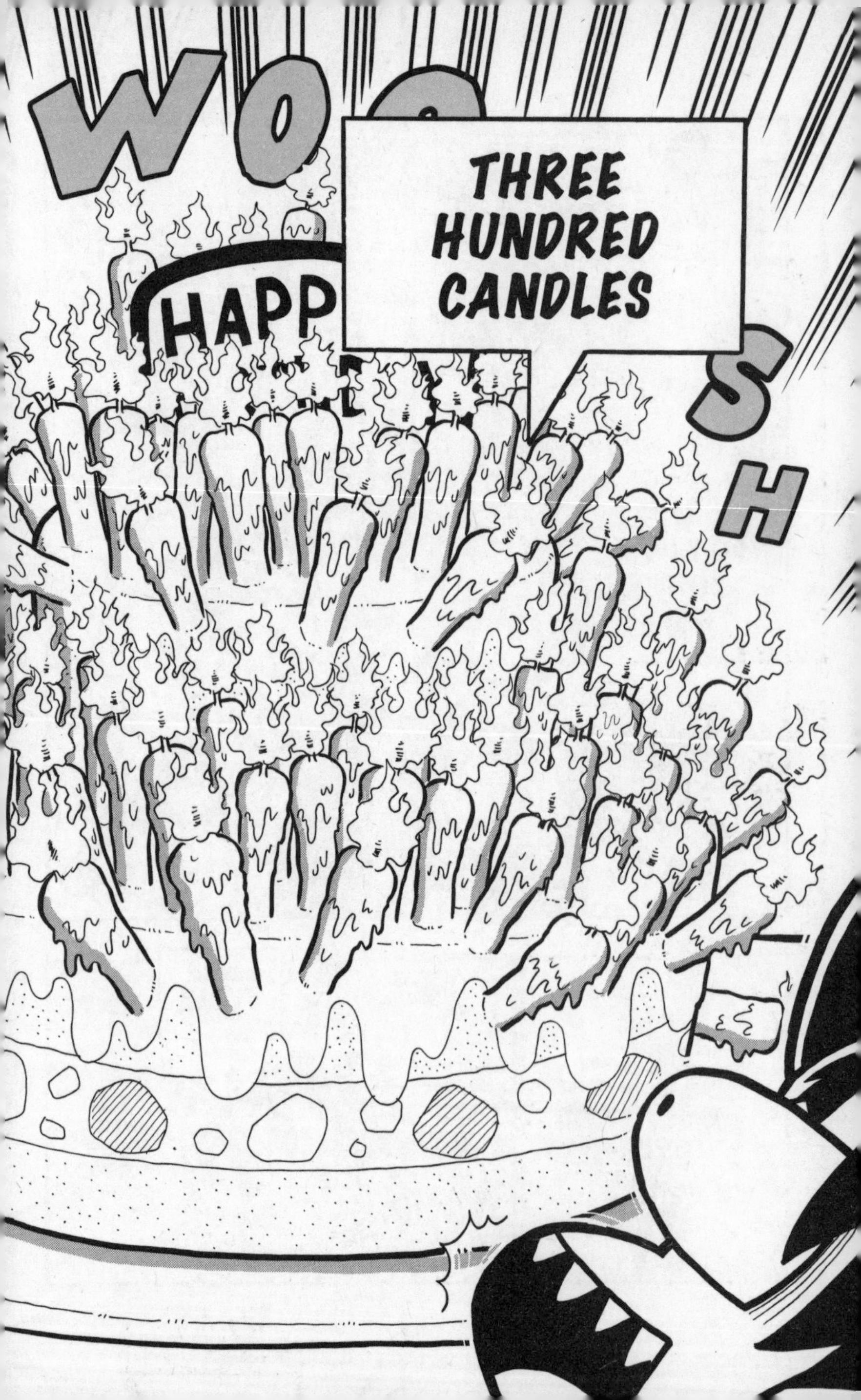
THREE HUNDRED CANDLES
WO SH
HAPP

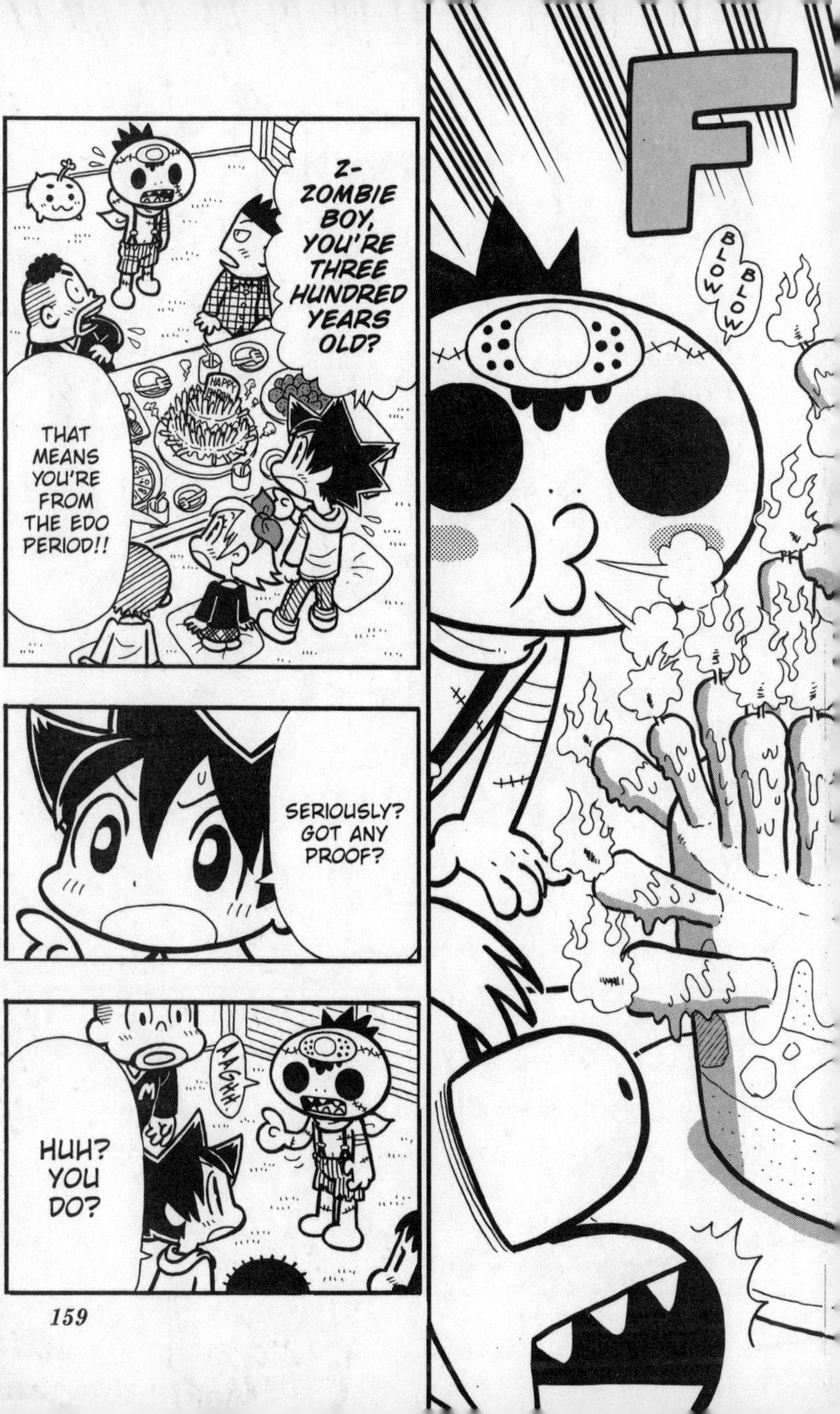
F
BLOW BLOW
Z-ZOMBIE BOY, YOU'RE THREE HUNDRED YEARS OLD?
THAT MEANS YOU'RE FROM THE EDO PERIOD!!
SERIOUSLY? GOT ANY PROOF?
AAGHH
HUH? YOU DO?

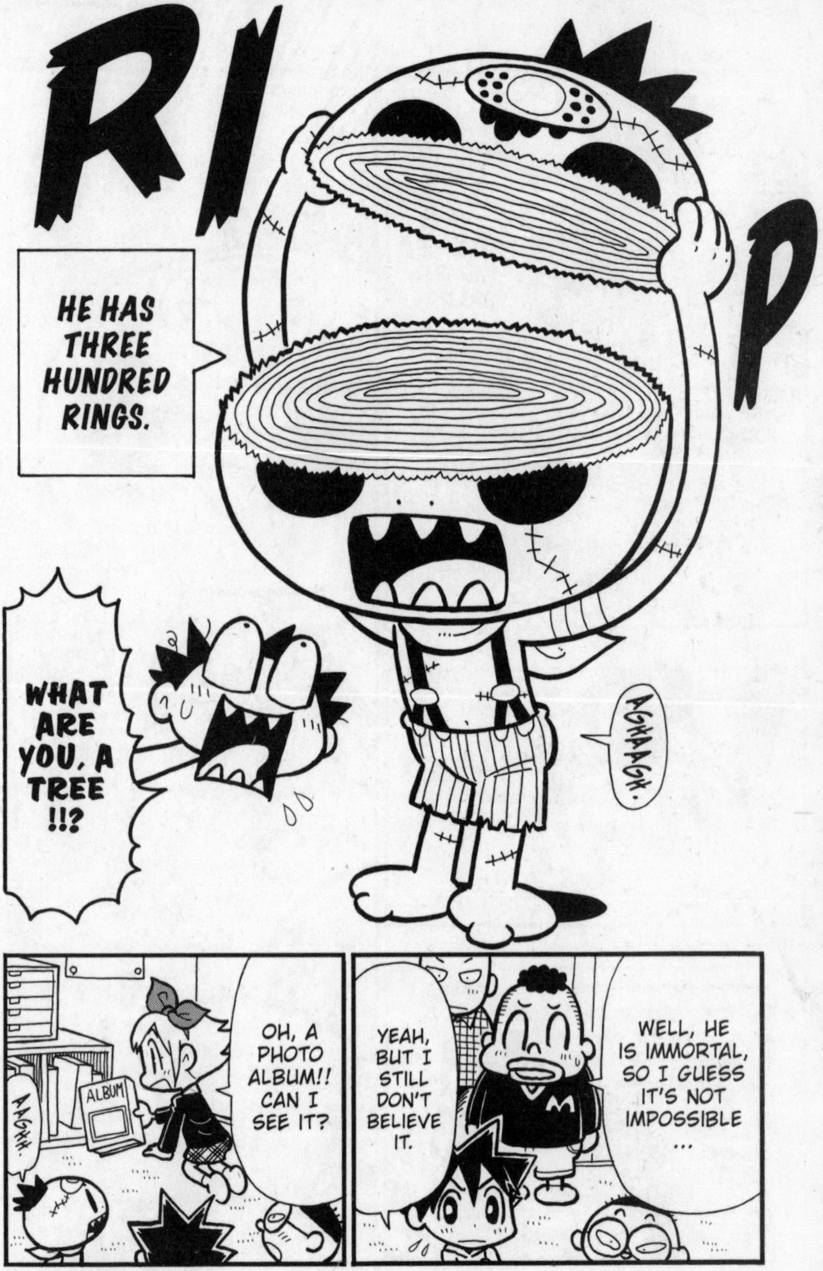
RIP
HE HAS THREE HUNDRED RINGS.
AGHAAGH.
WHAT ARE YOU, A TREE!!?
WELL, HE IS IMMORTAL, SO I GUESS IT'S NOT IMPOSSIBLE ...
YEAH, BUT I STILL DON'T BELIEVE IT.
OH, A PHOTO ALBUM!! CAN I SEE IT?
ALBUM
AAGHH.

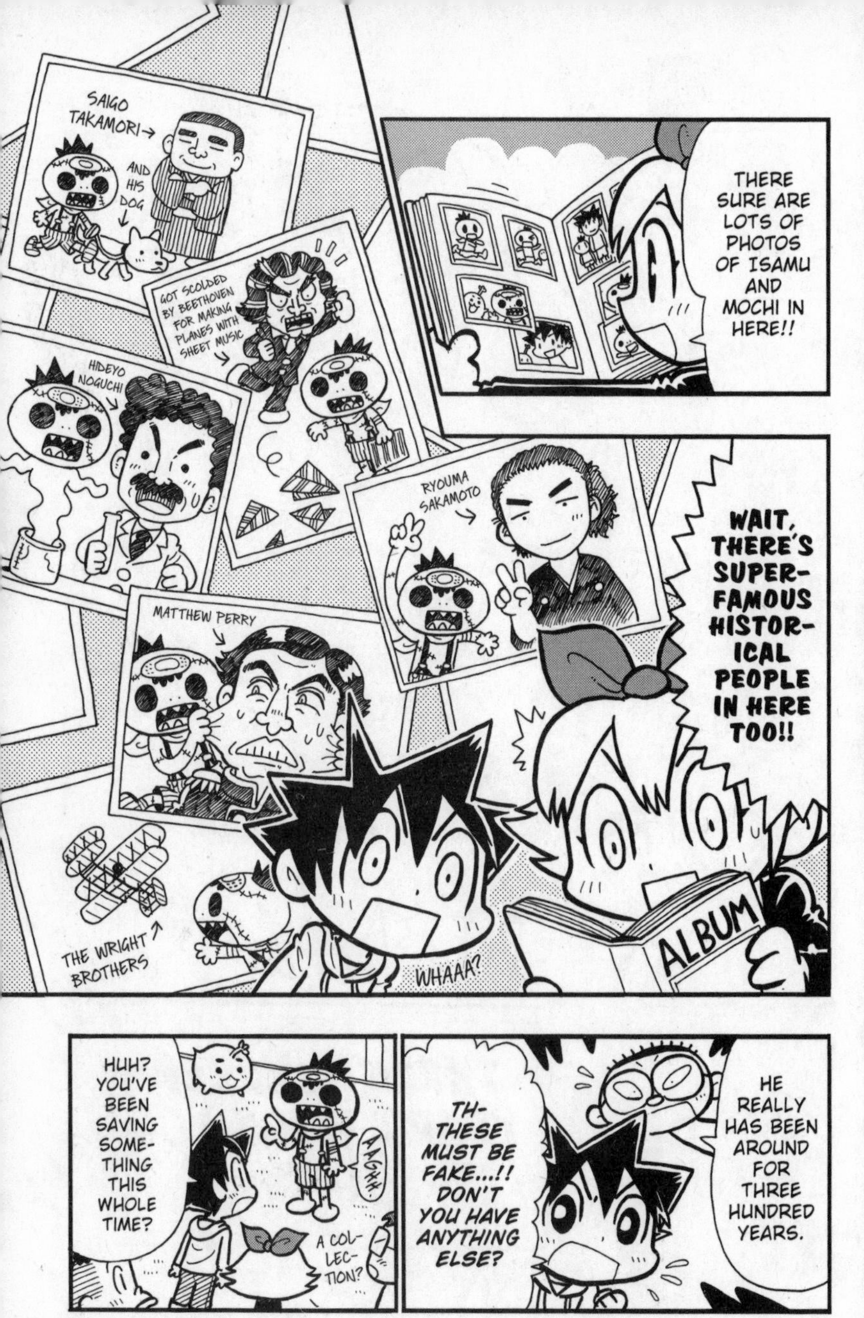
THERE SURE ARE LOTS OF PHOTOS OF ISAMU AND MOCHI IN HERE!!
WAIT, THERE'S SUPER-FAMOUS HISTORICAL PEOPLE IN HERE TOO!!
SAIGO TAKAMORI →
AND HIS DOG
GOT SCOLDED BY BEETHOVEN FOR MAKING PLANES WITH SHEET MUSIC
HIDEYO NOGUCHI
RYOUMA SAKAMOTO
MATTHEW PERRY
THE WRIGHT BROTHERS
ALBUM
WHAAA?
HE REALLY HAS BEEN AROUND FOR THREE HUNDRED YEARS.
TH-THESE MUST BE FAKE...!! DON'T YOU HAVE ANYTHING ELSE?
HUH? YOU'VE BEEN SAVING SOMETHING THIS WHOLE TIME?
A COLLECTION?

THREE HUNDRED
YEARS' WORTH OF
FARTS

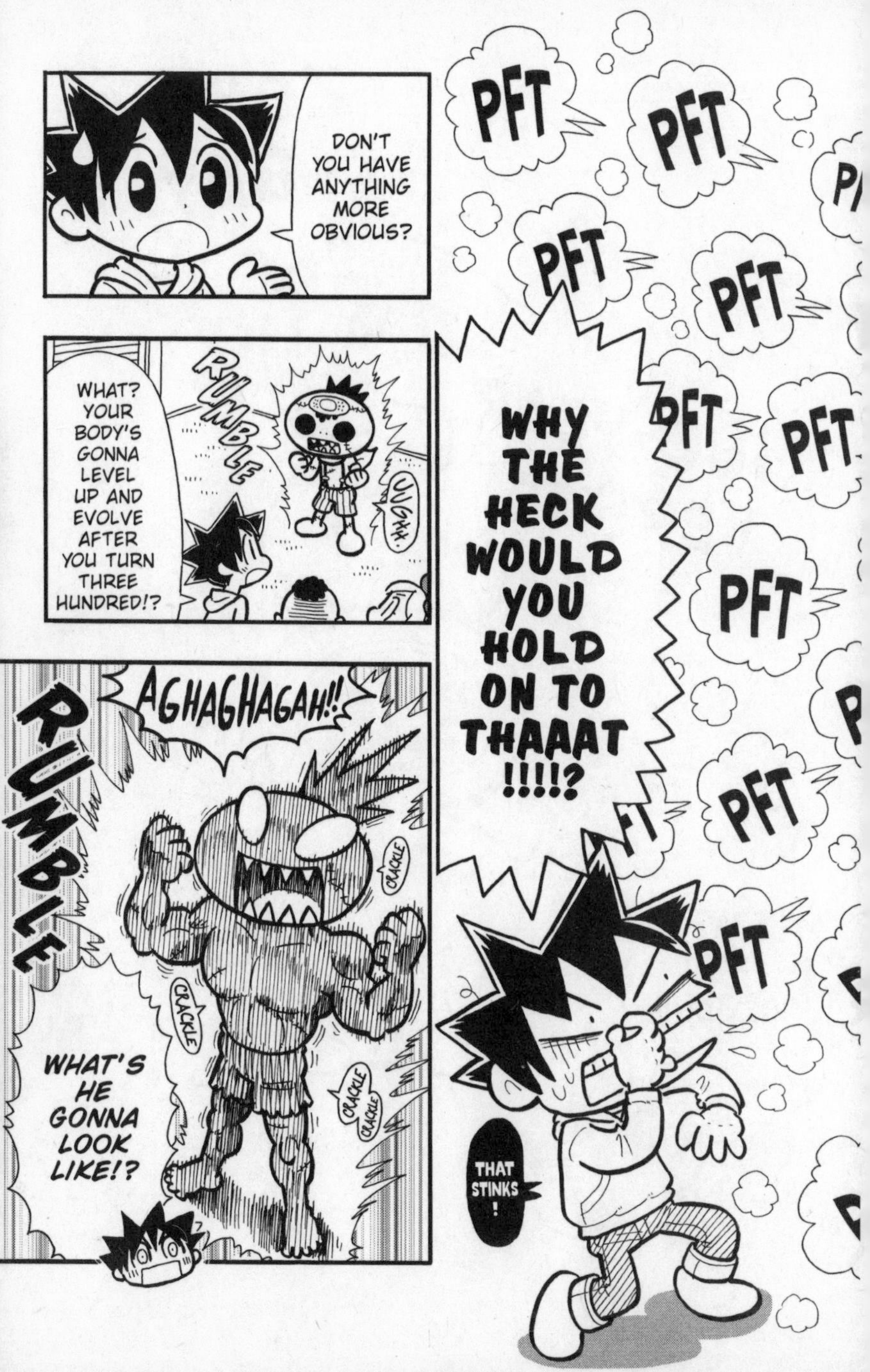
PFT
PFT
PFT
PFT
PFT
PFT
PFT
PFT
PFT
WHY THE HECK WOULD YOU HOLD ON TO THAAAT!!!!?
THAT STINKS!
DON'T YOU HAVE ANYTHING MORE OBVIOUS?
RUMBLE
UGHXX...
WHAT? YOUR BODY'S GONNA LEVEL UP AND EVOLVE AFTER YOU TURN THREE HUNDRED!?
AGHAGHAGAH!!
RUMBLE
CRACKLE
CRACKLE
CRACKLE CRACKLE
WHAT'S HE GONNA LOOK LIKE!?

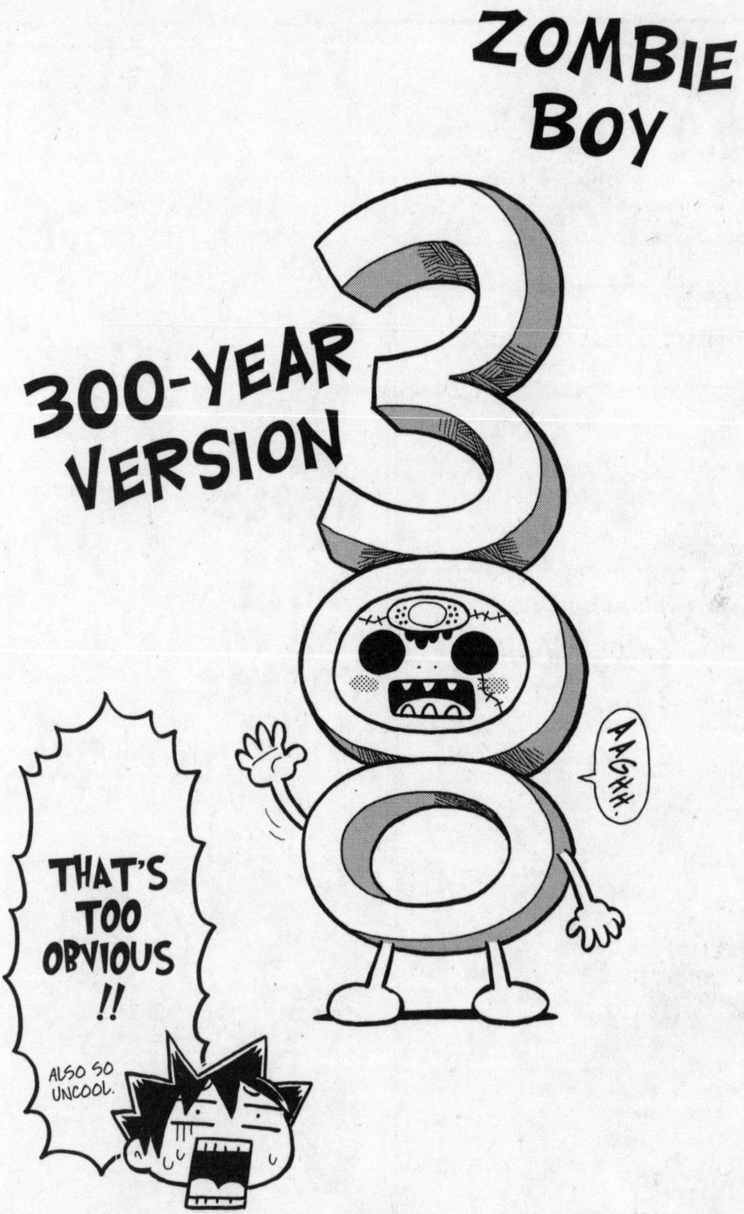
ZOMBIE BOY
300-YEAR VERSION
AAGHH.
THAT'S TOO OBVIOUS!!
ALSO SO UNCOOL.

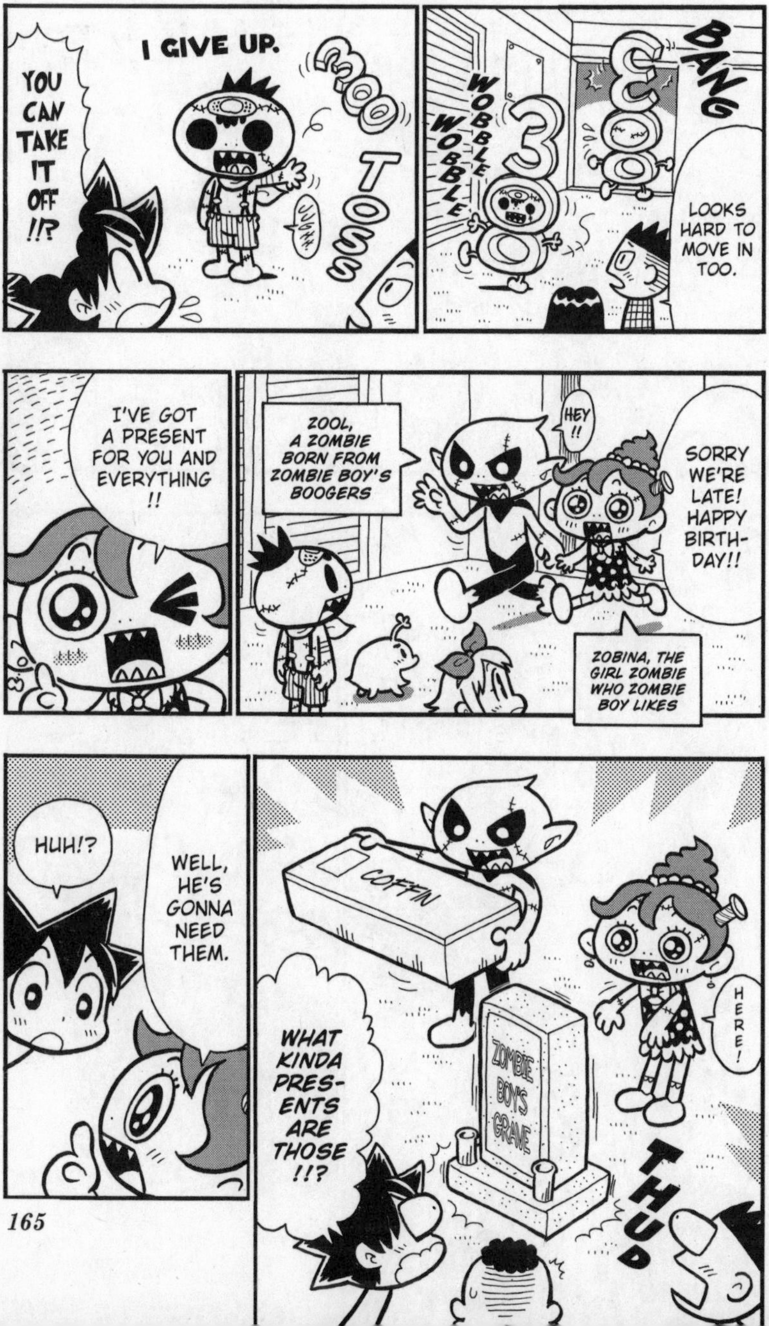
BANG
WOBBLE WOBBLE
LOOKS HARD TO MOVE IN TOO.
I GIVE UP.
YOU CAN TAKE IT OFF!!?
TOSS
UGH.
SORRY WE'RE LATE! HAPPY BIRTH-DAY!!
HEY!!
ZOOL, A ZOMBIE BORN FROM ZOMBIE BOY'S BOOGERS
ZOBINA, THE GIRL ZOMBIE WHO ZOMBIE BOY LIKES
I'VE GOT A PRESENT FOR YOU AND EVERYTHING!!
HERE!
COFFIN
ZOMBIE BOY'S GRAVE
THUD
WHAT KINDA PRES-ENTS ARE THOSE!!?
WELL, HE'S GONNA NEED THEM.
HUH!?

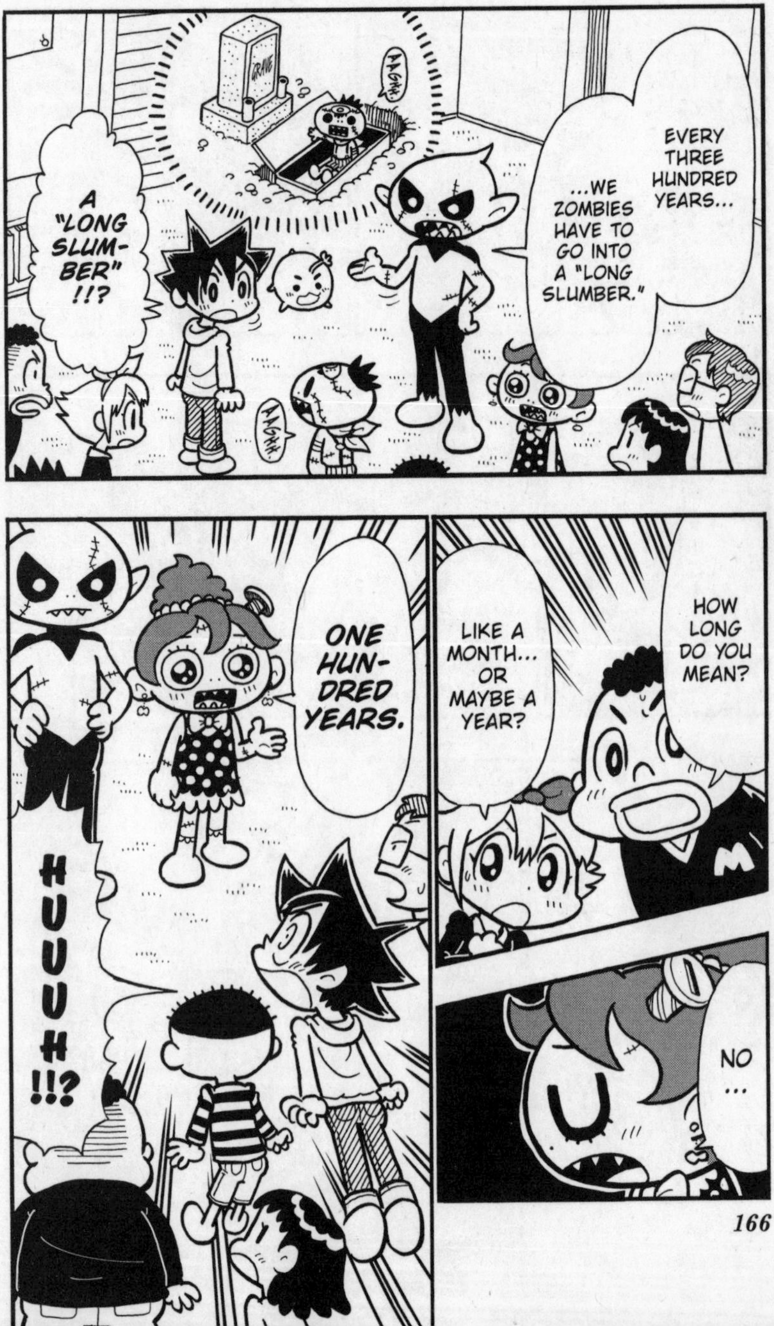

AAGHH.
GRAVE
EVERY THREE HUNDRED YEARS...
...WE ZOMBIES HAVE TO GO INTO A "LONG SLUMBER."
A "LONG SLUM-BER" !!?
AAGHH.
HOW LONG DO YOU MEAN?
LIKE A MONTH... OR MAYBE A YEAR?
NO...
ONE HUN-DRED YEARS.
HUUUUH!!?

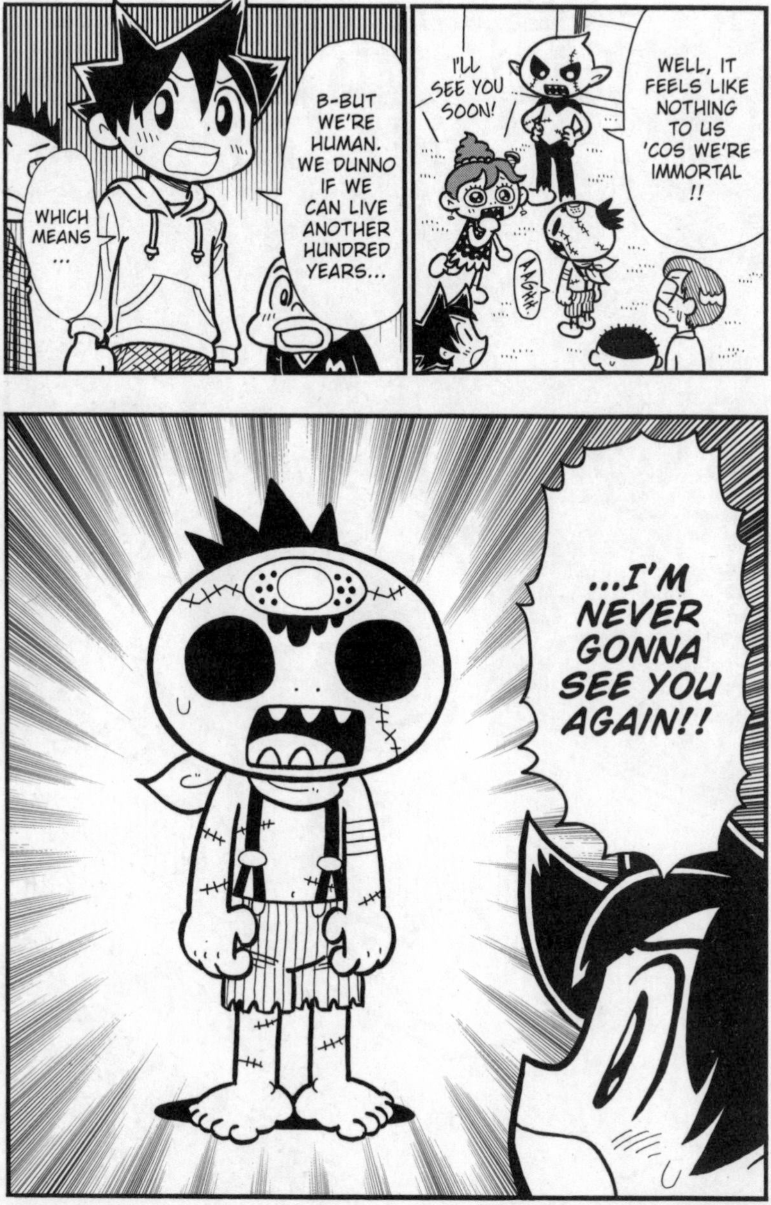
WELL, IT FEELS LIKE NOTHING TO US 'COS WE'RE IMMORTAL !!
I'LL SEE YOU SOON!
AAGHH.
B-BUT WE'RE HUMAN. WE DUNNO IF WE CAN LIVE ANOTHER HUNDRED YEARS...
WHICH MEANS ...
...I'M NEVER GONNA SEE YOU AGAIN!!

FINALLY, THE ZTIRRING LAZT CHAPTER!

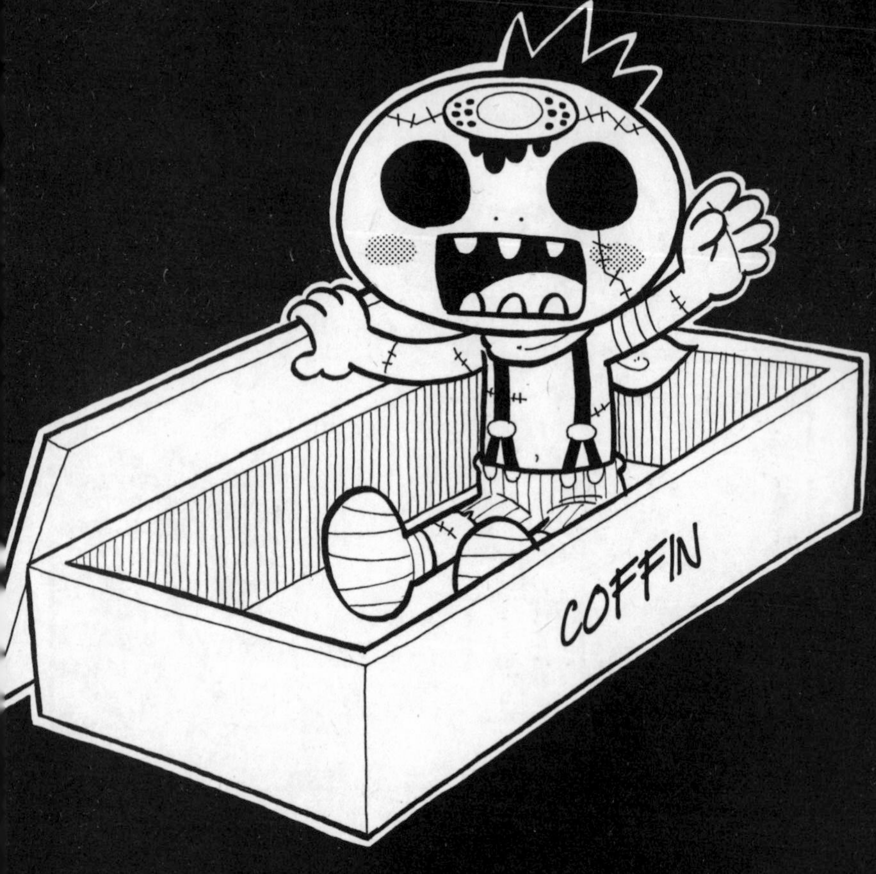
COFFIN

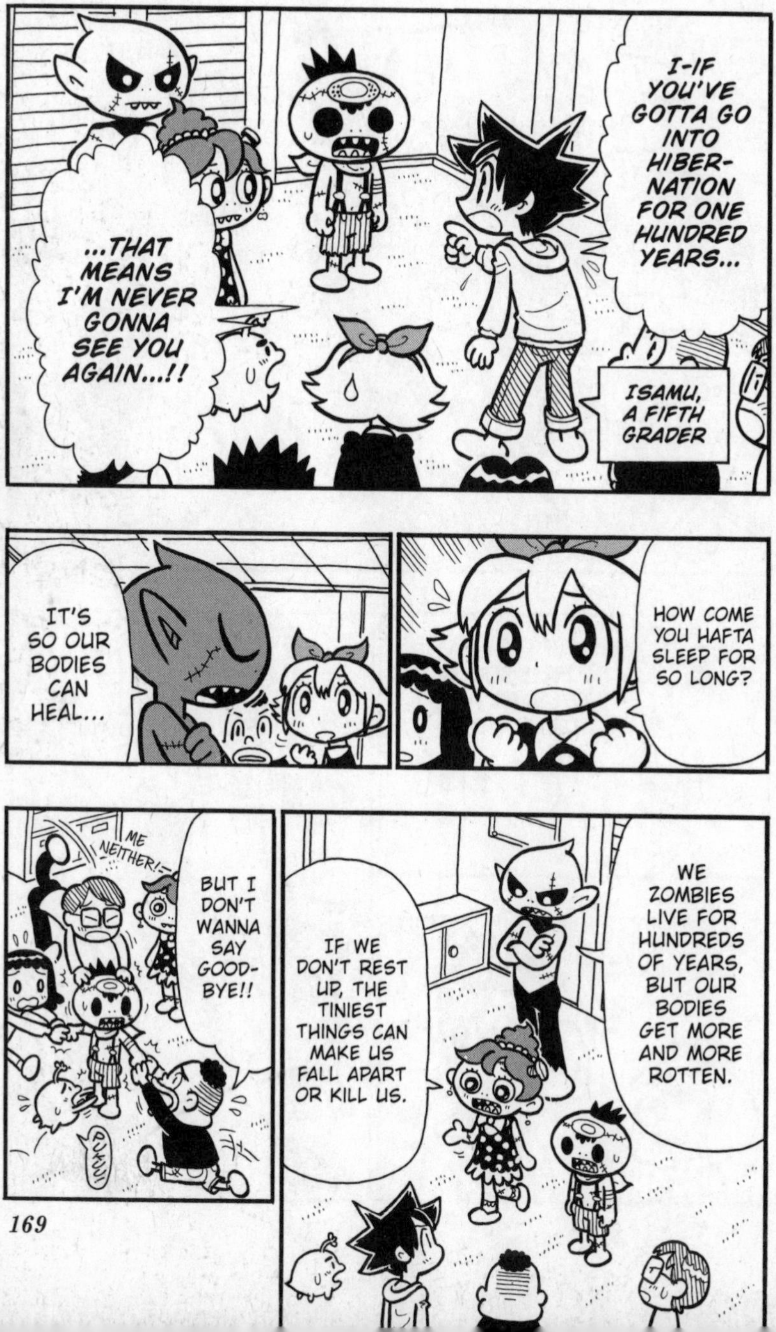
I-IF YOU'VE GOTTA GO INTO HIBER-NATION FOR ONE HUNDRED YEARS...
ISAMU, A FIFTH GRADER
...THAT MEANS I'M NEVER GONNA SEE YOU AGAIN...!!
HOW COME YOU HAFTA SLEEP FOR SO LONG?
IT'S SO OUR BODIES CAN HEAL...
WE ZOMBIES LIVE FOR HUNDREDS OF YEARS, BUT OUR BODIES GET MORE AND MORE ROTTEN.
IF WE DON'T REST UP, THE TINIEST THINGS CAN MAKE US FALL APART OR KILL US.
BUT I DON'T WANNA SAY GOOD-BYE!!
ME NEITHER!

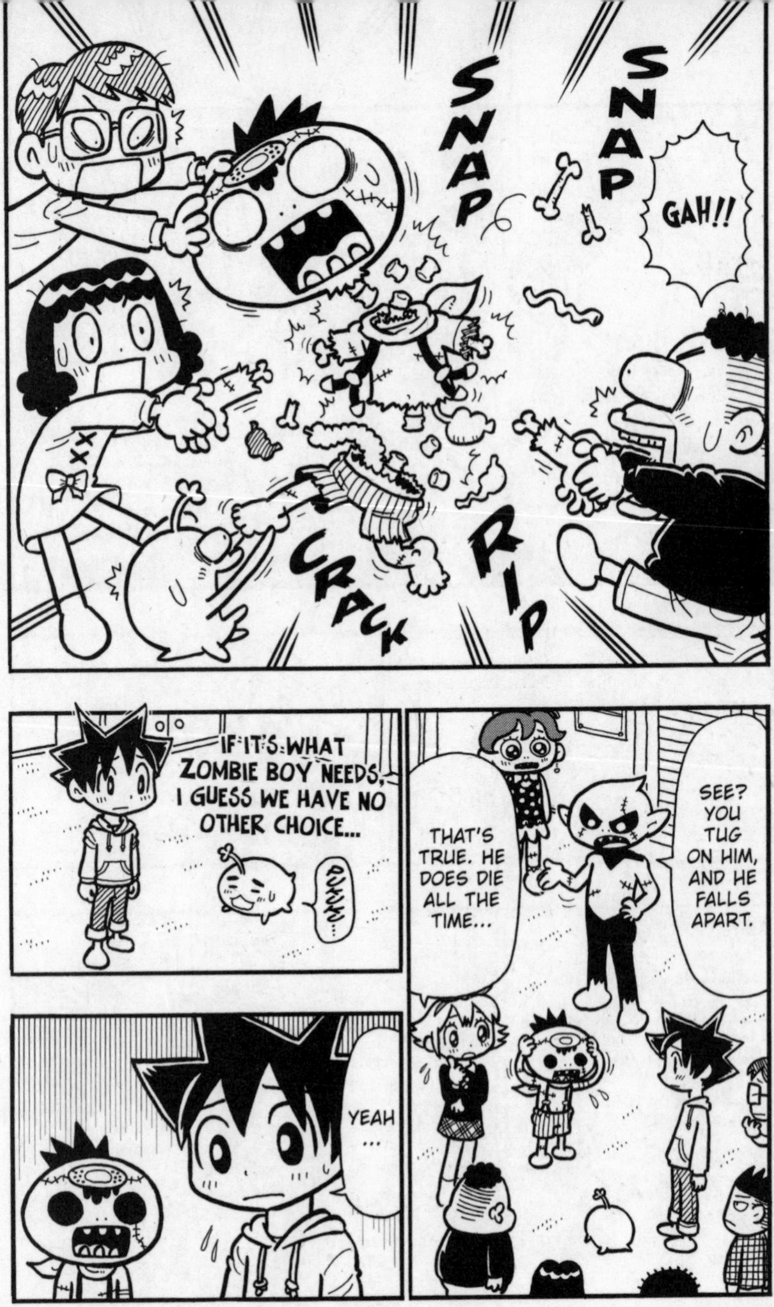
SNAP
SNAP
GAH!!
RIP
CRACK
SEE? YOU TUG ON HIM, AND HE FALLS APART.
THAT'S TRUE. HE DOES DIE ALL THE TIME...
IF IT'S WHAT ZOMBIE BOY NEEDS, I GUESS WE HAVE NO OTHER CHOICE...
YEAH...

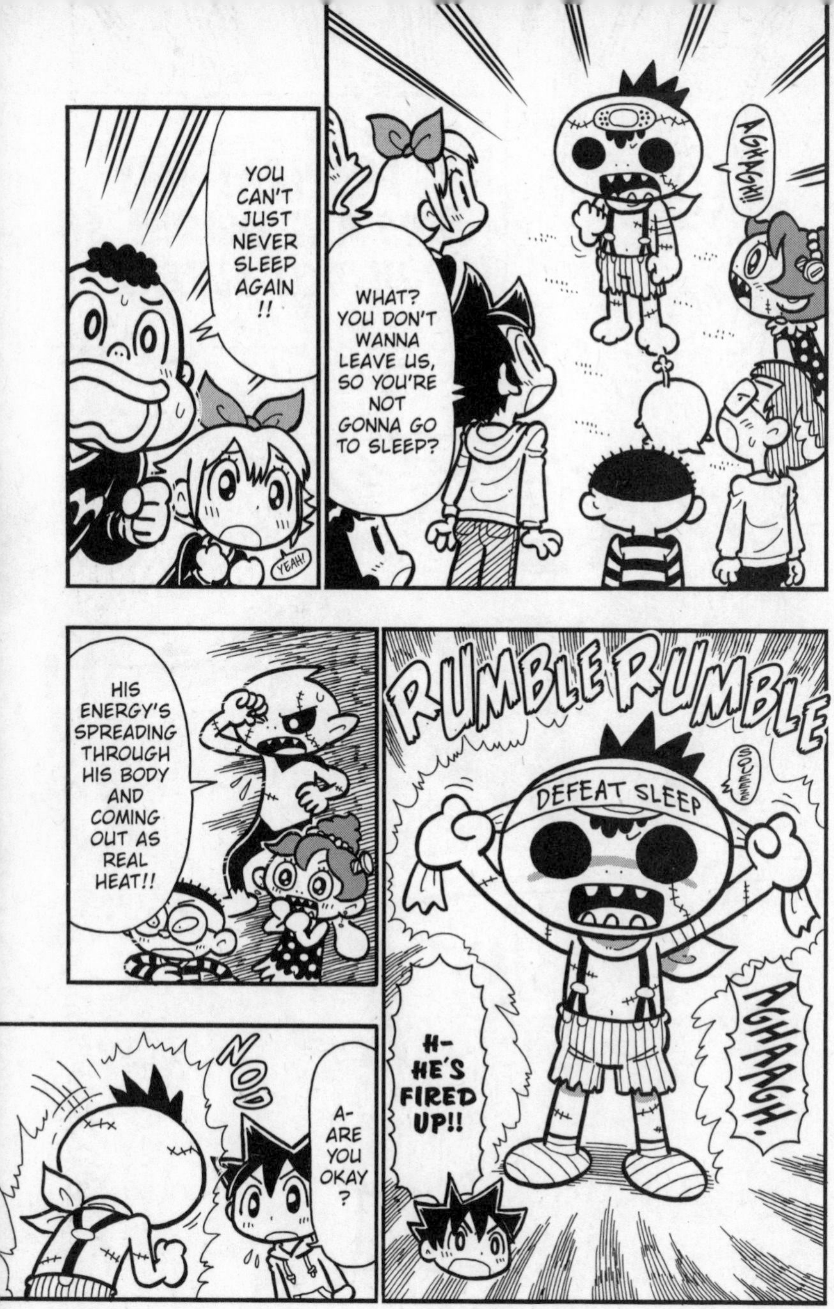
AGHAGH!!
WHAT? YOU DON'T WANNA LEAVE US, SO YOU'RE NOT GONNA GO TO SLEEP?
YOU CAN'T JUST NEVER SLEEP AGAIN!!
YEAH!
RUMBLE RUMBLE
SQUEEZE
DEFEAT SLEEP
AGHAAGH.
H- HE'S FIRED UP!!
HIS ENERGY'S SPREADING THROUGH HIS BODY AND COMING OUT AS REAL HEAT!!
NOD
A- ARE YOU OKAY?

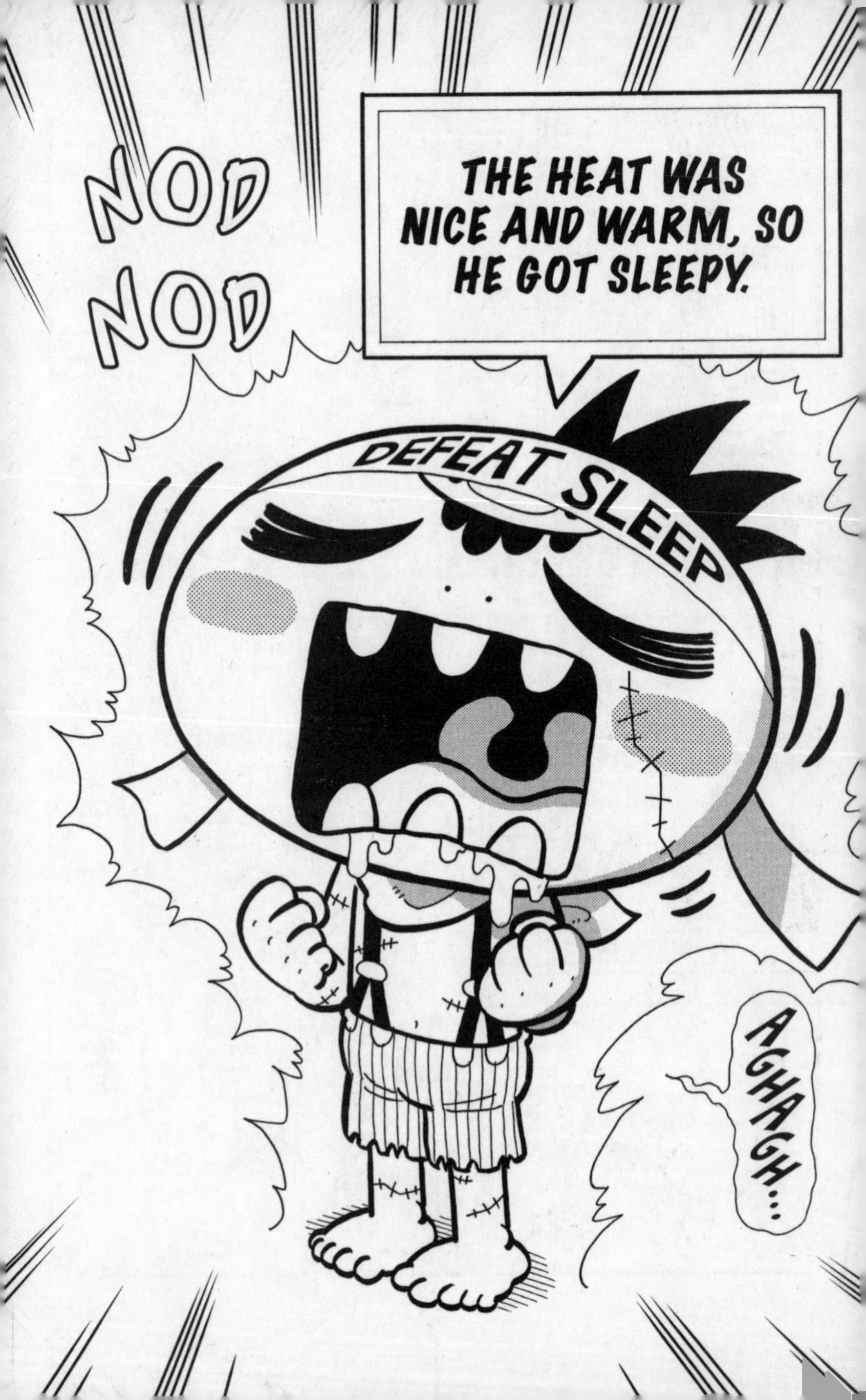
THE HEAT WAS NICE AND WARM, SO HE GOT SLEEPY.
NOD NOD
DEFEAT SLEEP
AGHAGH...

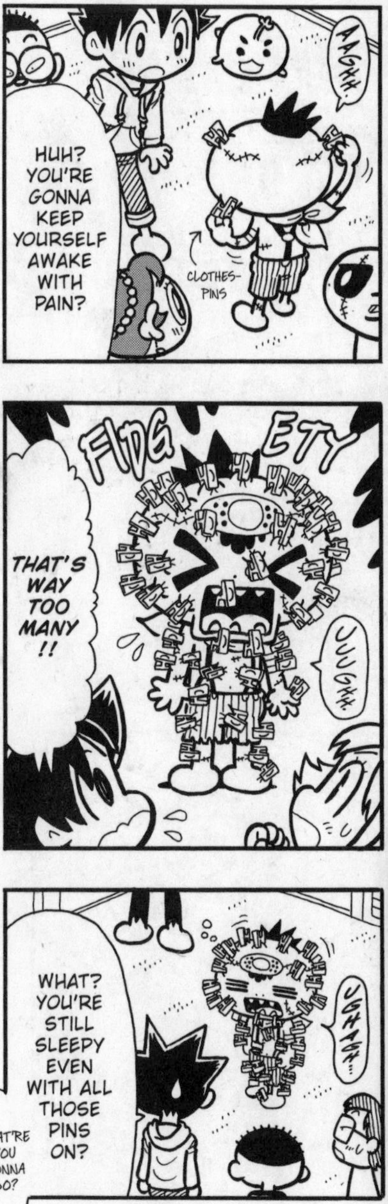
AAGHH
HUH? YOU'RE GONNA KEEP YOURSELF AWAKE WITH PAIN?
CLOTHES-PINS
FIDGETY
JUUGHH
THAT'S WAY TOO MANY!!
UGHHGH...
WHAT? YOU'RE STILL SLEEPY EVEN WITH ALL THOSE PINS ON?
WHAT'RE YOU GONNA DO?

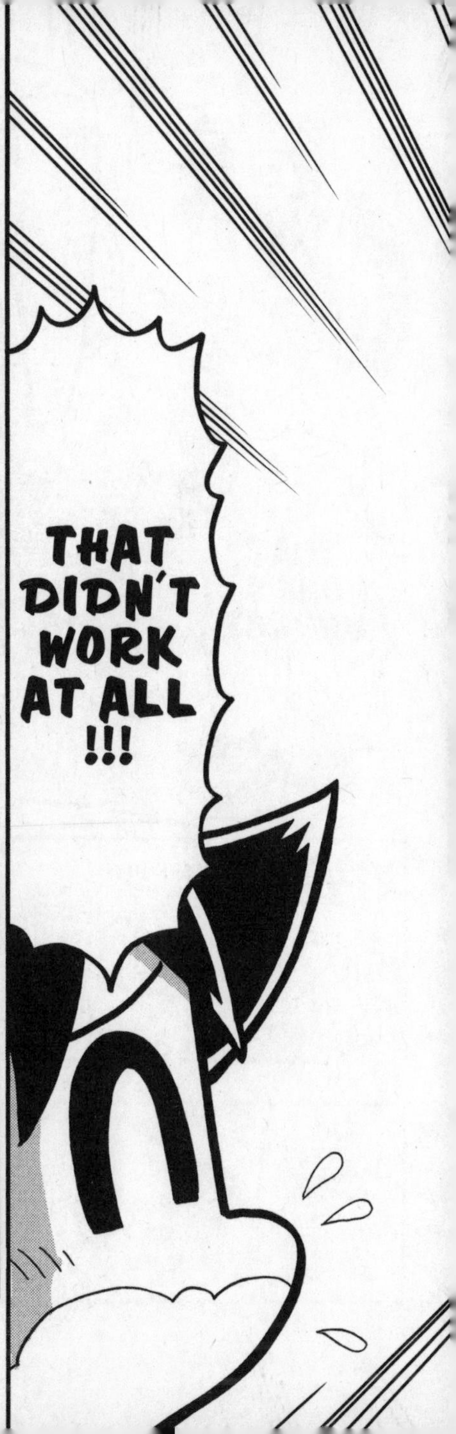
THAT DIDN'T WORK AT ALL!!!

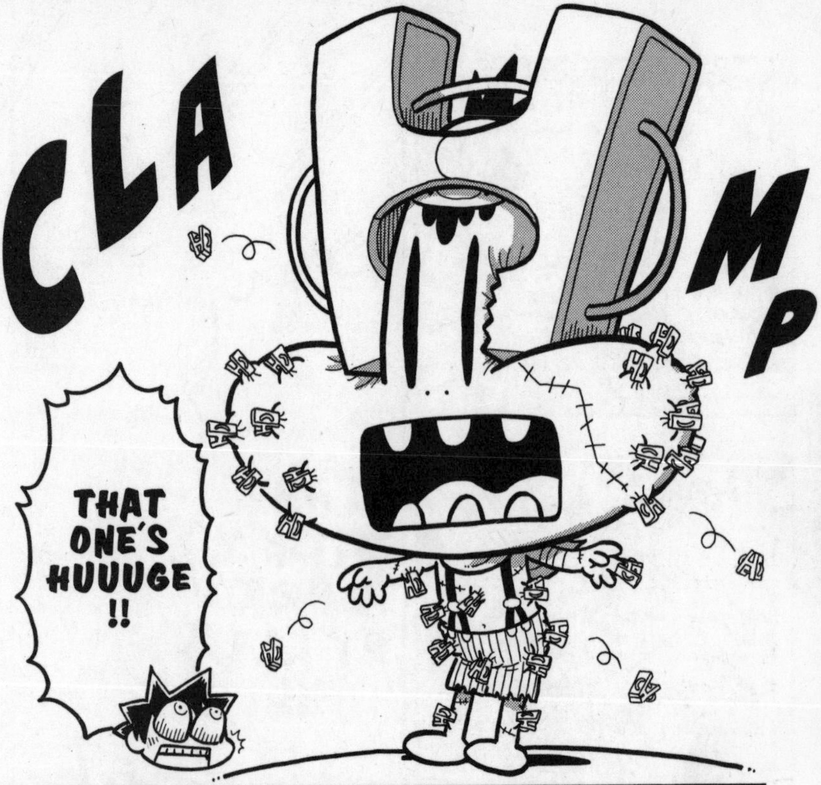
CLAMP
THAT ONE'S HUUUGE !!

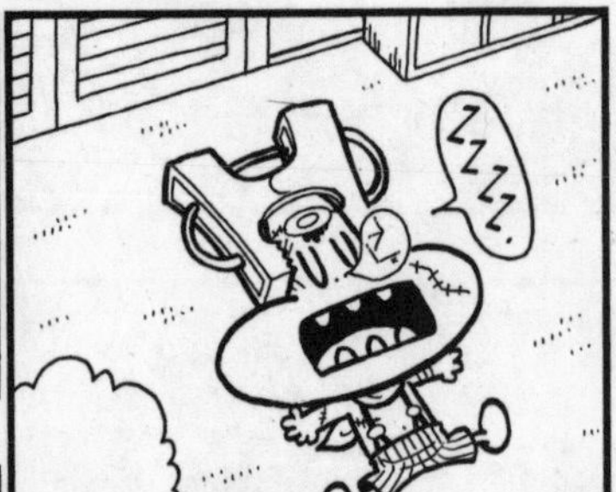
ZZZZ.
BUT YOU STILL FELL ASLEEP !!

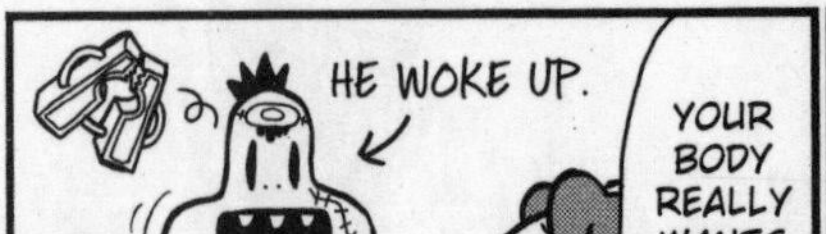
YOUR BODY REALLY WANTS TO SLEEP.
HE WOKE UP.
AGH.

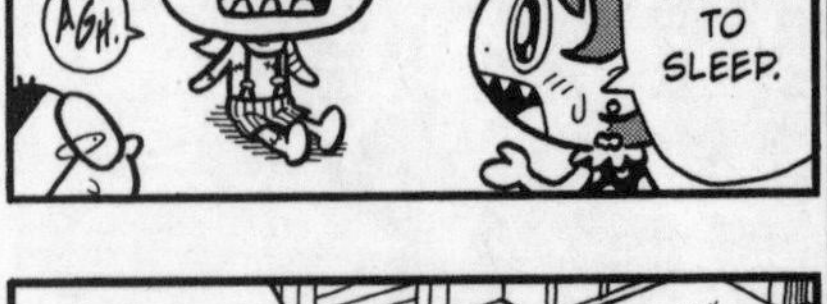
AAGHH.
HUH? YOU WANNA PLAY TAG? YOU THINK YOU'LL WAKE UP IF YOU MOVE AROUND?

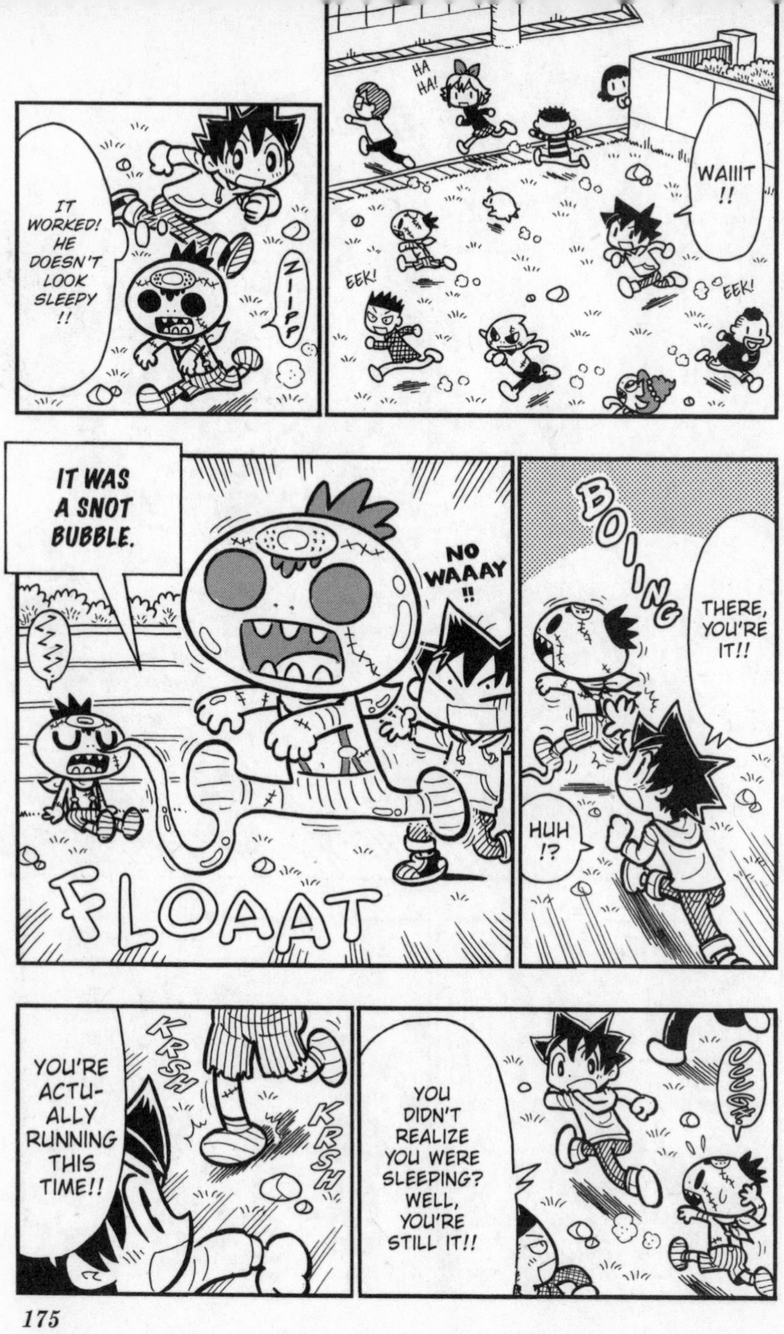

WAIIIT!!
HA HA!
EEK!
EEK!
IT WORKED! HE DOESN'T LOOK SLEEPY!!
ZIIPP
BOING
THERE, YOU'RE IT!!
HUH!?
IT WAS A SNOT BUBBLE.
NO WAAAY!!
ZZZZ
FLOAAT
YOU DIDN'T REALIZE YOU WERE SLEEPING? WELL, YOU'RE STILL IT!!
UUGH.
YOU'RE ACTU-ALLY RUNNING THIS TIME!!
KRSH
KRSH

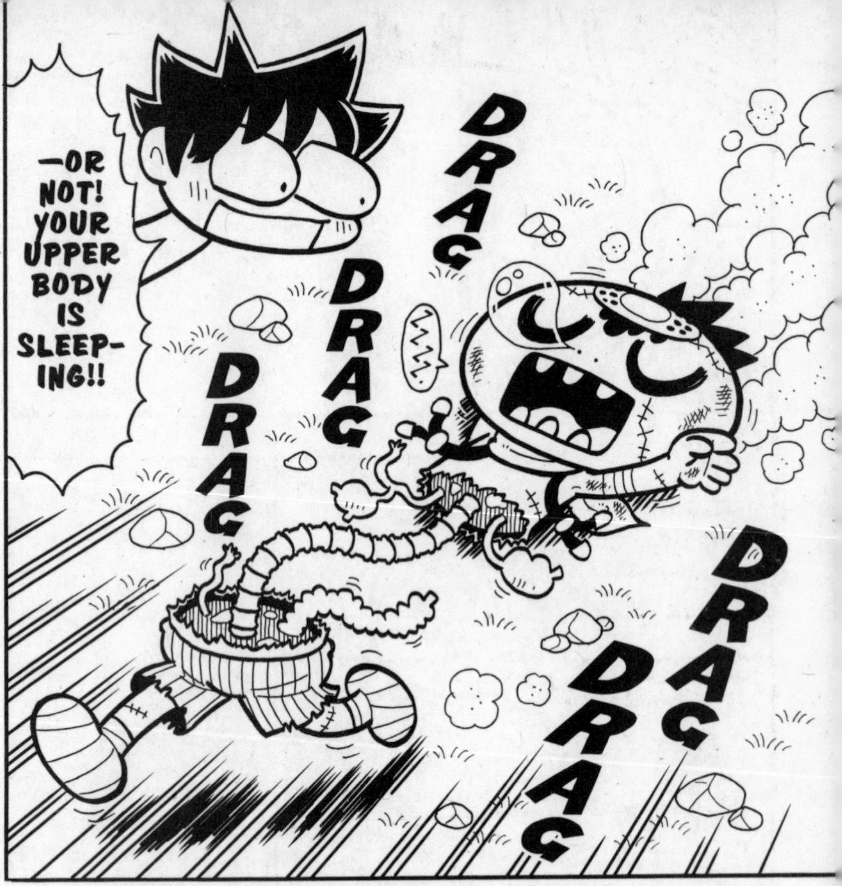
—OR NOT! YOUR UPPER BODY IS SLEEPING!!
DRAG DRAG DRAG
ZZZ...
DRAG DRAG

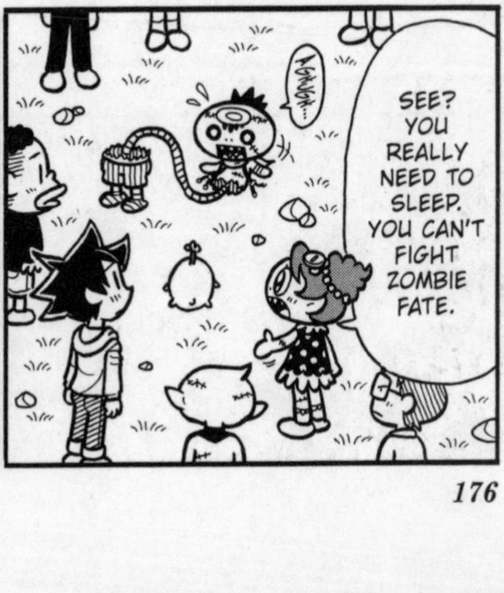
AGHUGH...
SEE? YOU REALLY NEED TO SLEEP. YOU CAN'T FIGHT ZOMBIE FATE.

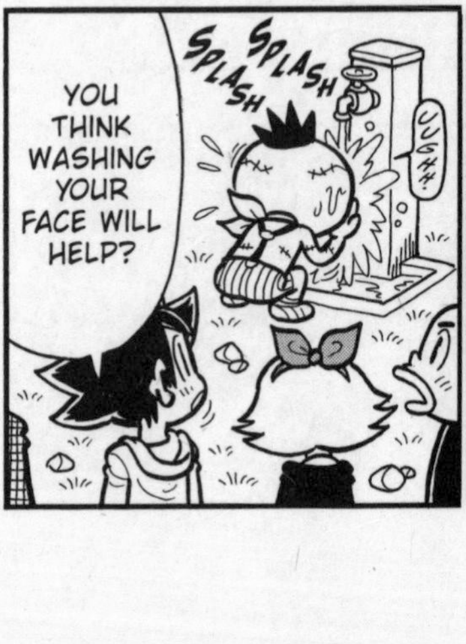
SPLASH SPLASH
UUGHH!
YOU THINK WASHING YOUR FACE WILL HELP?

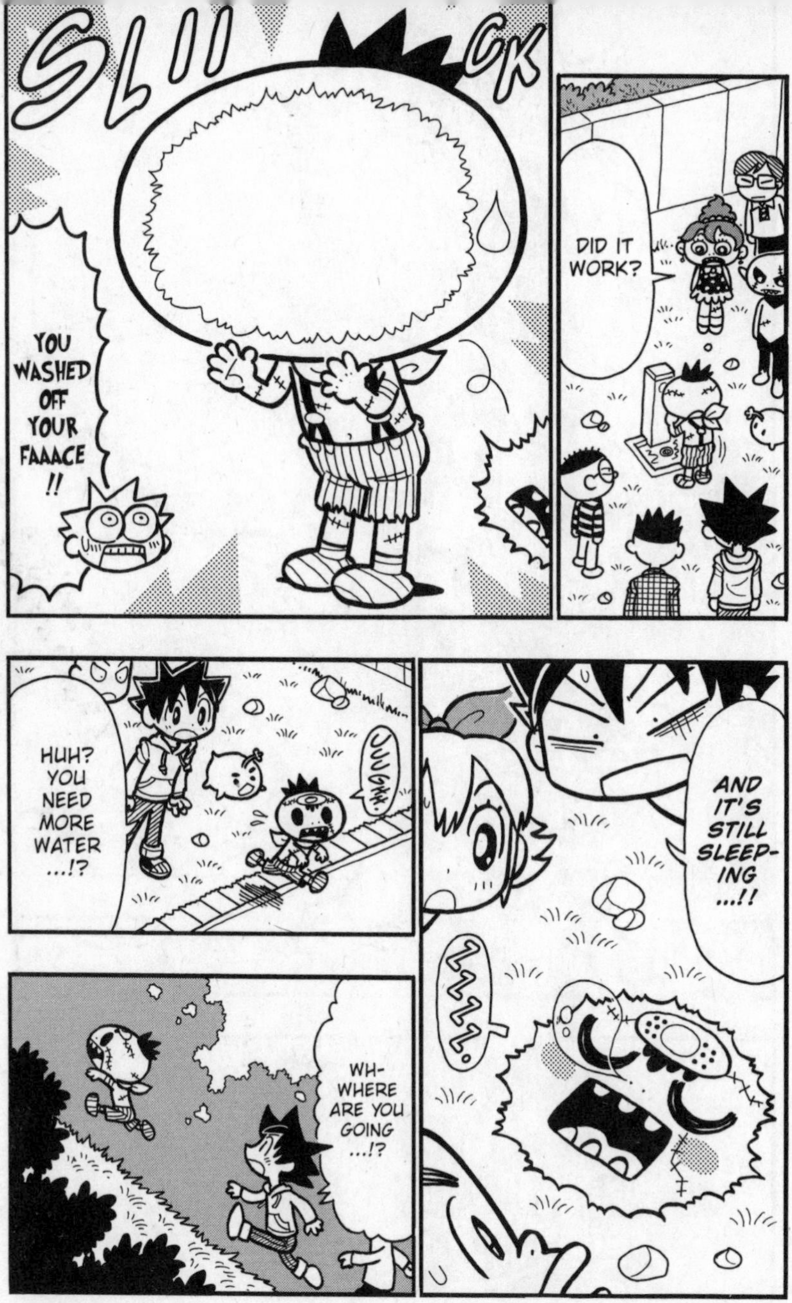
DID IT WORK?
SLIIICK
YOU WASHED OFF YOUR FAAACE!!
AND IT'S STILL SLEEPING...!!
ZZZZ.
HUH? YOU NEED MORE WATER...!?
JUUGKK.
WH-WHERE ARE YOU GOING...!?

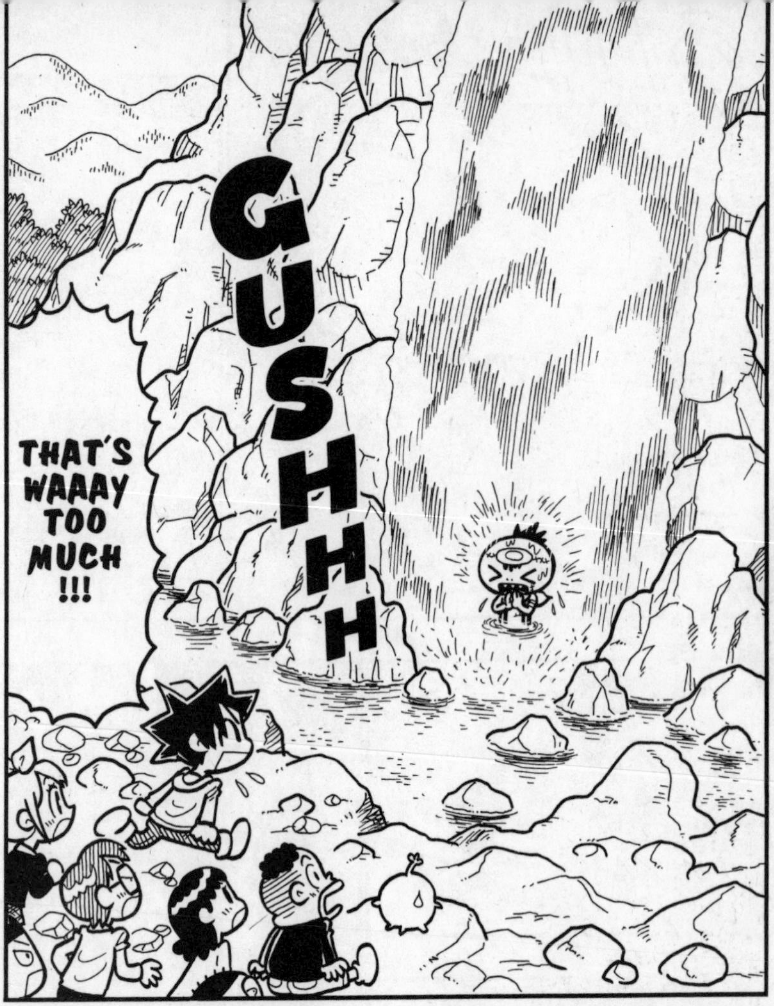
GUSHHH
THAT'S WAAAY TOO MUCH!!!

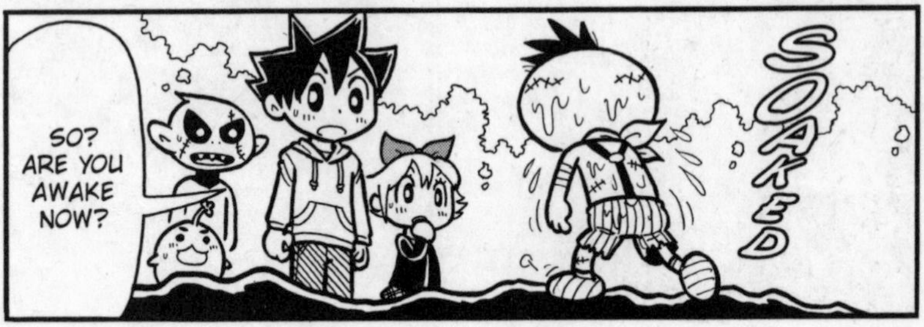
SOAKED
SO? ARE YOU AWAKE NOW?

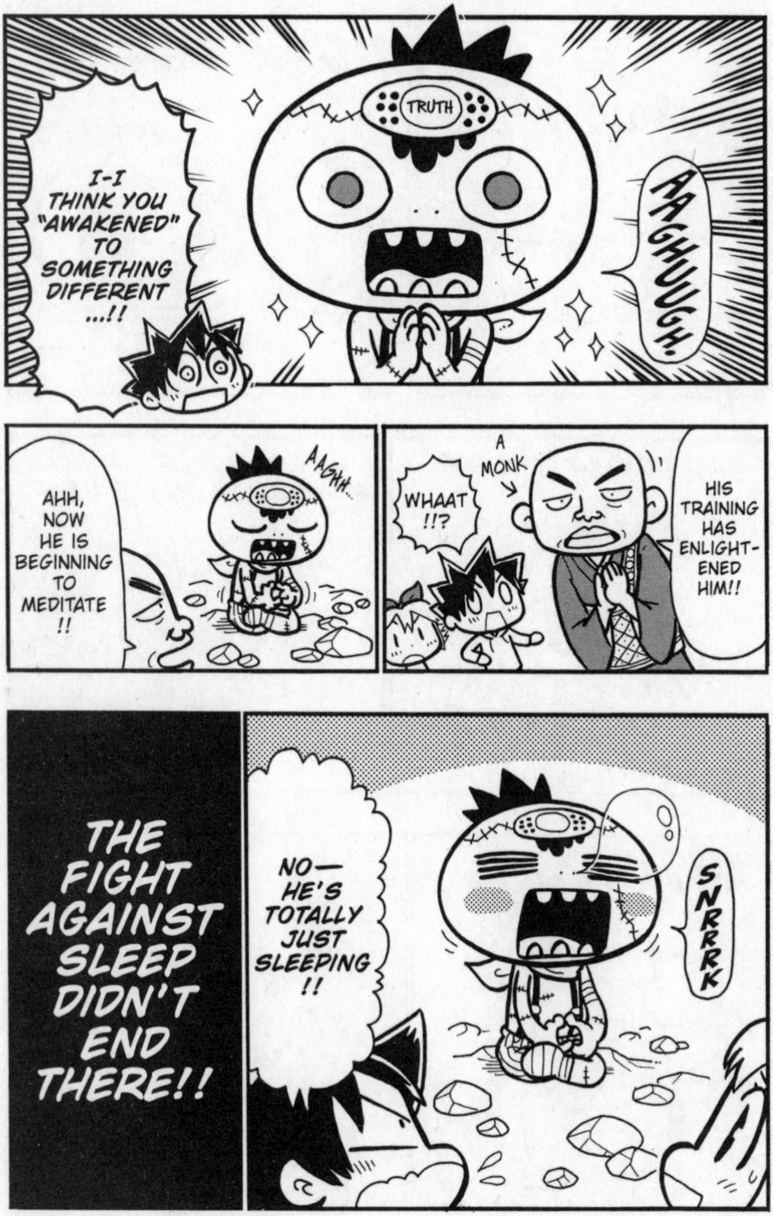
TRUTH
AAGHUUGH.
I-I THINK YOU "AWAKENED" TO SOMETHING DIFFERENT ...!!
HIS TRAINING HAS ENLIGHT-ENED HIM!!
A MONK
WHAAT!!?
AAGHH...
AHH, NOW HE IS BEGINNING TO MEDITATE!!
SNRRRK
NO— HE'S TOTALLY JUST SLEEPING!!
THE FIGHT AGAINST SLEEP DIDN'T END THERE!!

HE STITCHED HIS EYES OPEN SO HE COULDN'T CLOSE THEM.
THAT'S FREAKY— CUT IT OUT!!
HE ATE ULTRA-SPICY RAMEN.
UUGHH!
SWELLL
HE PUT SUPER-STINKY UNDERWEAR ON HIS HEAD.
UUGHH.
AGHUGH.
HE TICKLED HIMSELF.
COOCHEE
COOCHEE
STOMACH
INTESTINES
PANCREAS
COOCHEE
HE BLASTED MUSIC AT MAX VOLUME.
HE GOT POUNDED INTO STICKY RICE CAKE.
WHAAAAM
WHA
AAM

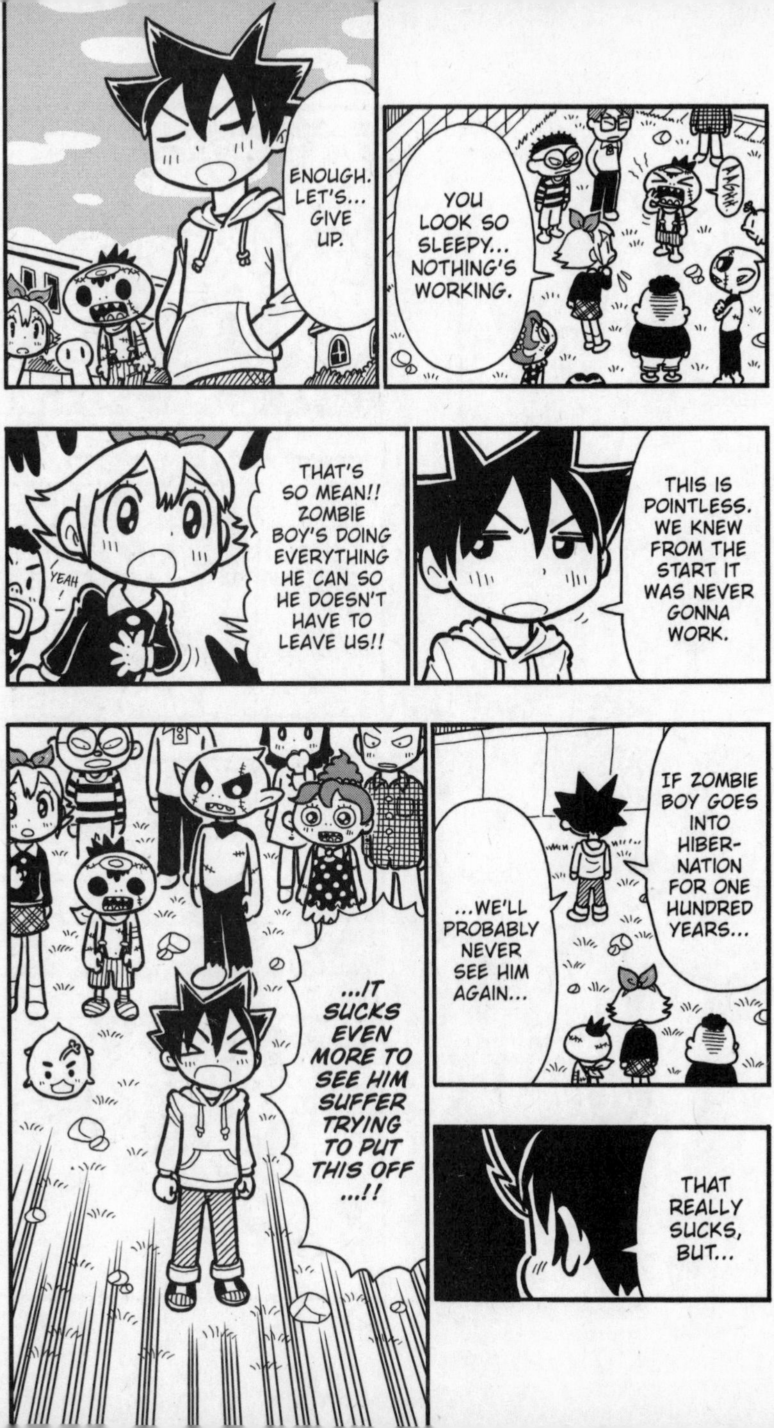
YOU LOOK SO SLEEPY... NOTHING'S WORKING.
ENOUGH. LET'S... GIVE UP.
THIS IS POINTLESS. WE KNEW FROM THE START IT WAS NEVER GONNA WORK.
THAT'S SO MEAN!! ZOMBIE BOY'S DOING EVERYTHING HE CAN SO HE DOESN'T HAVE TO LEAVE US!!
YEAH!
IF ZOMBIE BOY GOES INTO HIBER-NATION FOR ONE HUNDRED YEARS...
...WE'LL PROBABLY NEVER SEE HIM AGAIN...
THAT REALLY SUCKS, BUT...
...IT SUCKS EVEN MORE TO SEE HIM SUFFER TRYING TO PUT THIS OFF ...!!

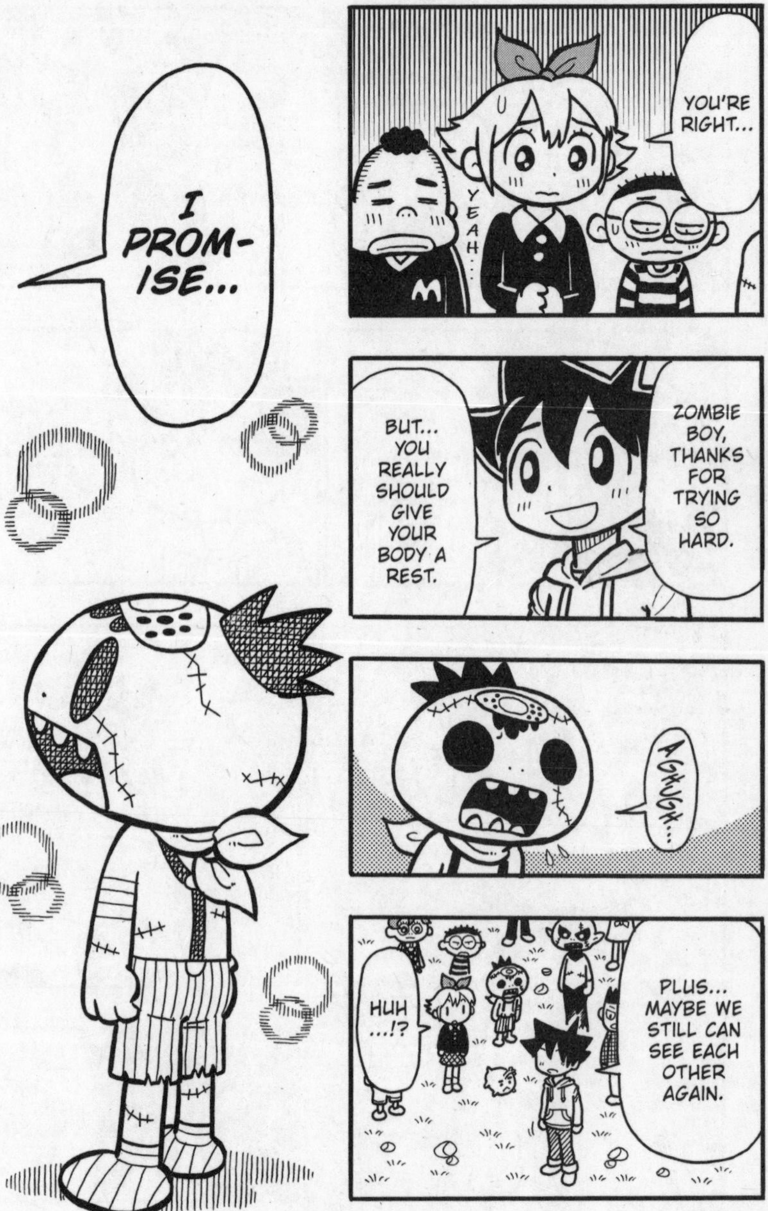
YOU'RE RIGHT...
YEAH...
ZOMBIE BOY, THANKS FOR TRYING SO HARD.
BUT... YOU REALLY SHOULD GIVE YOUR BODY A REST.
AGHUGH...
PLUS... MAYBE WE STILL CAN SEE EACH OTHER AGAIN.
HUH ...!?
I PROM-ISE...

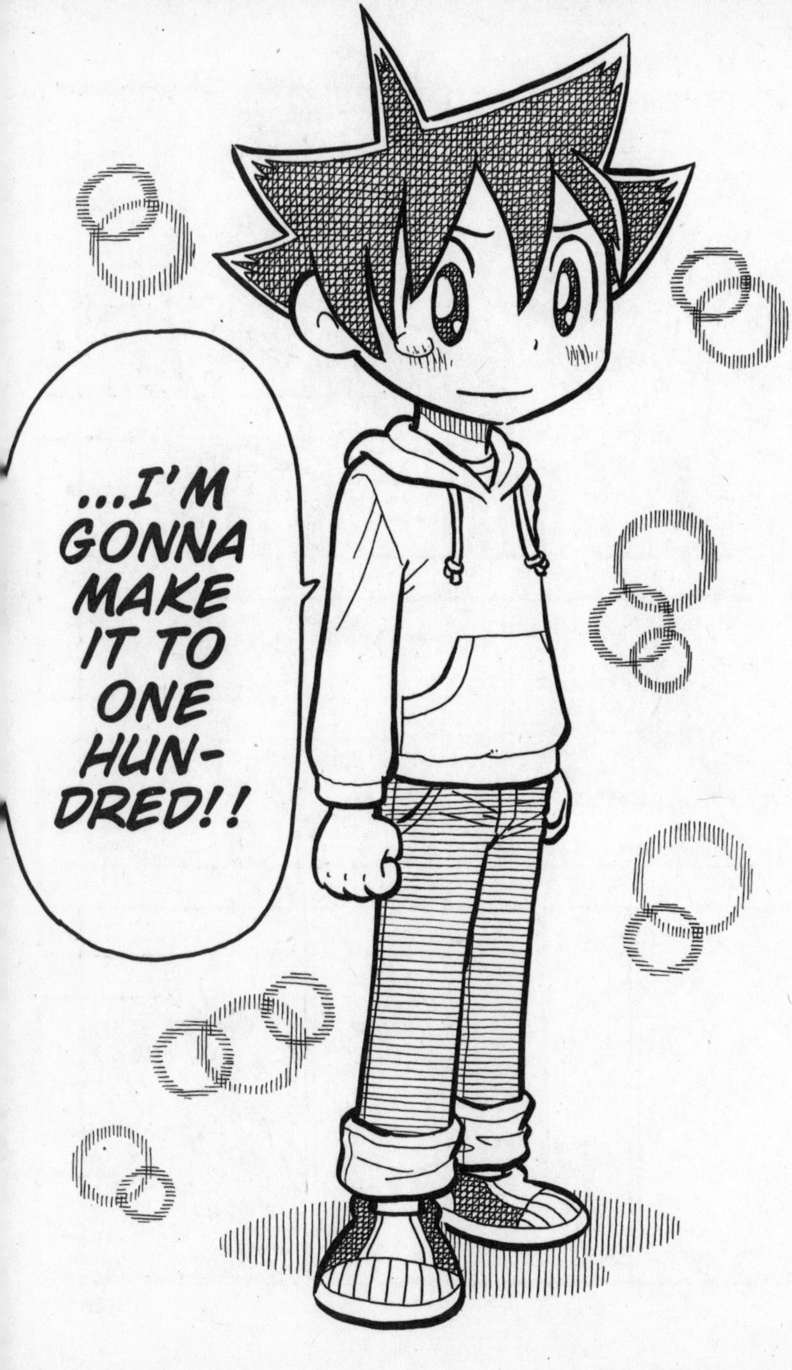
...I'M GONNA MAKE IT TO ONE HUN-DRED!!

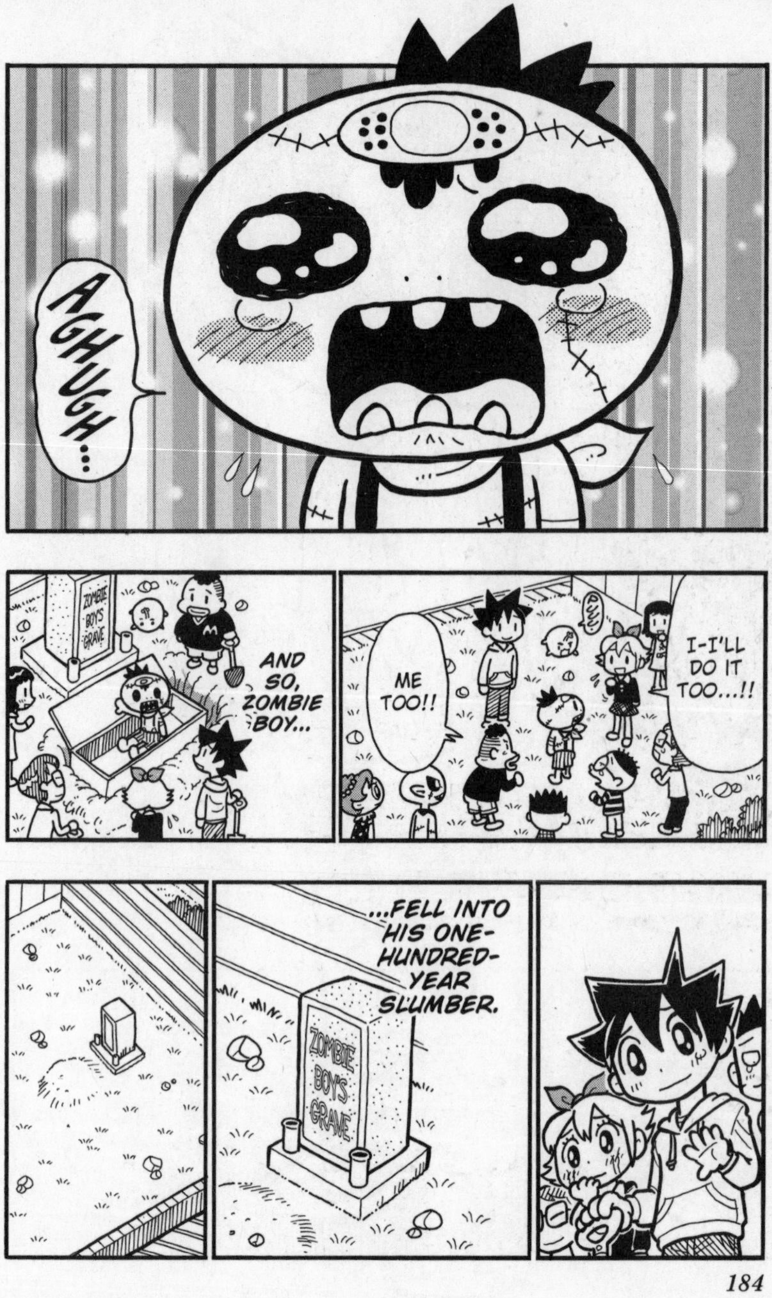
AGHUGH...
I-I'LL DO IT TOO...!!
PUU.
ME TOO!!
ZOMBIE BOY'S GRAVE
AND SO, ZOMBIE BOY...
...FELL INTO HIS ONE-HUNDRED-YEAR SLUMBER.
ZOMBIE BOY'S GRAVE

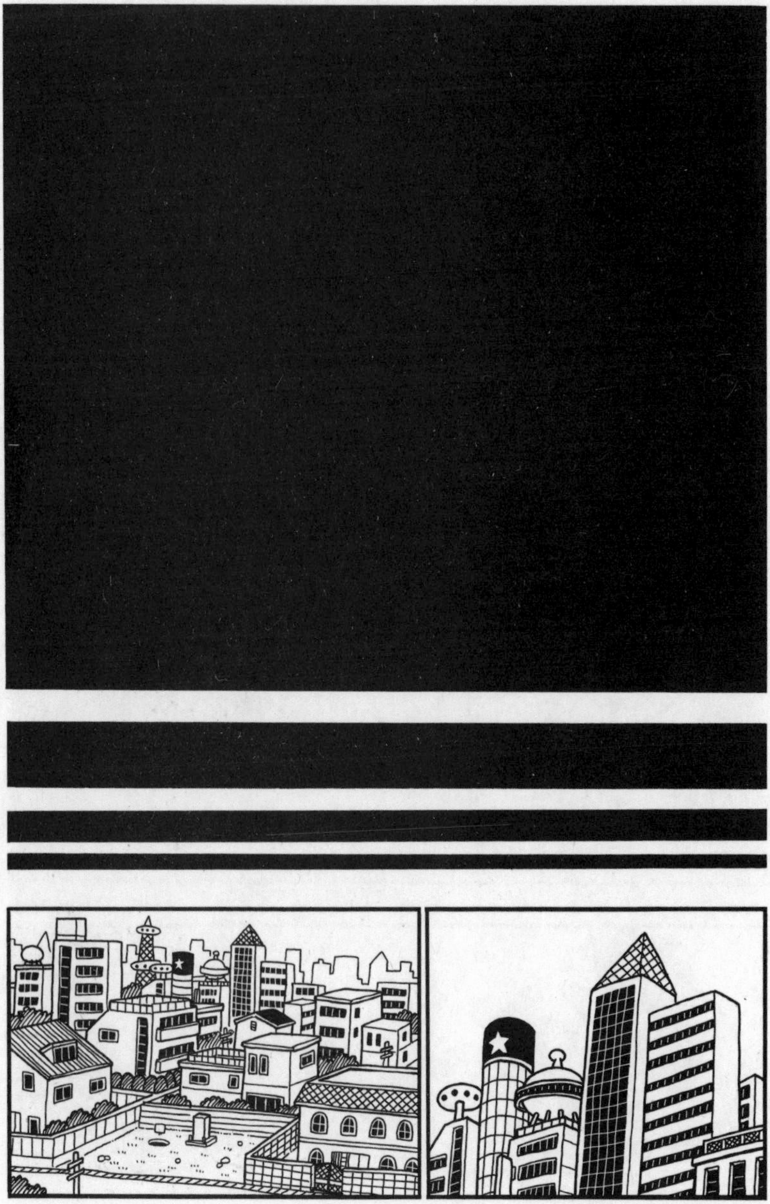

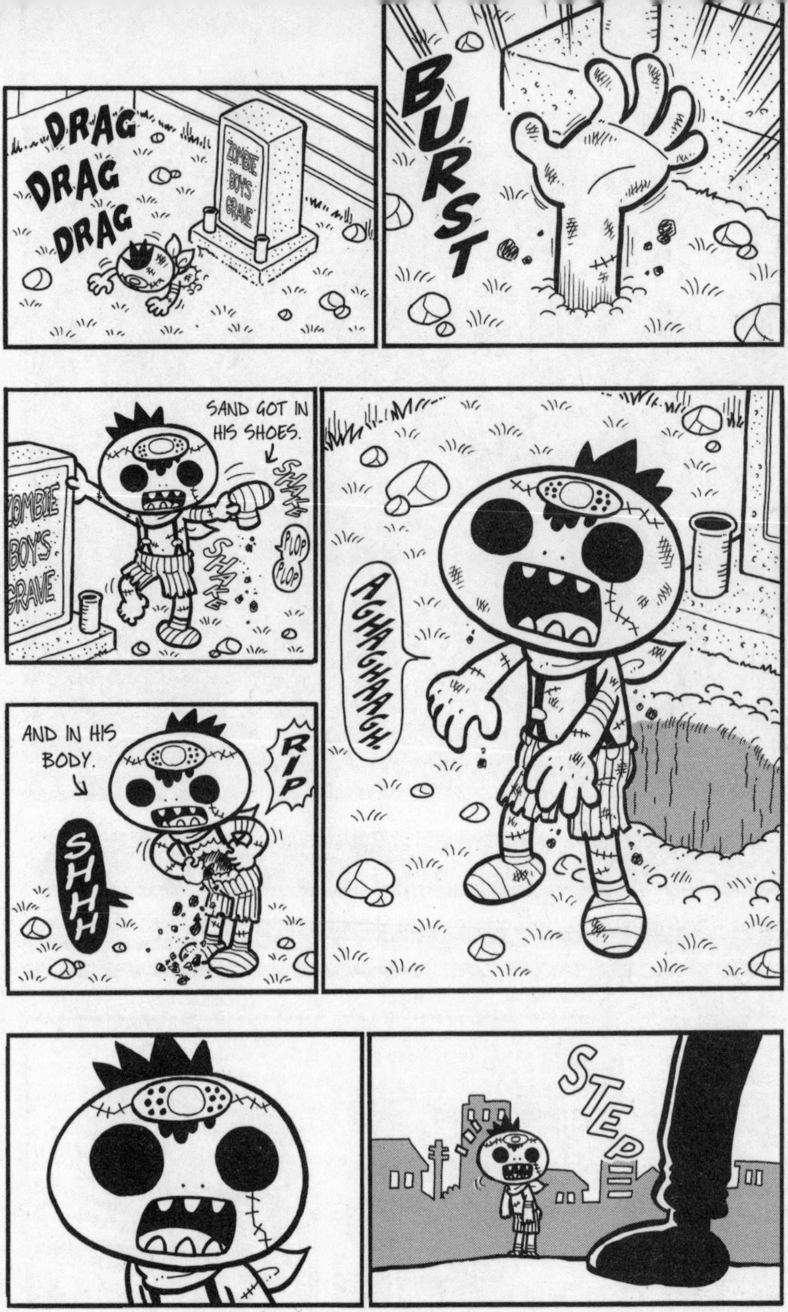
BURST
DRAG DRAG DRAG
ZOMBIE BOY'S GRAVE
AGHAGHAAGH
ZOMBIE BOY'S GRAVE
SAND GOT IN HIS SHOES.
SHAKE SHAKE
PLOP PLOP
AND IN HIS BODY.
RIP
SHHH
STEP

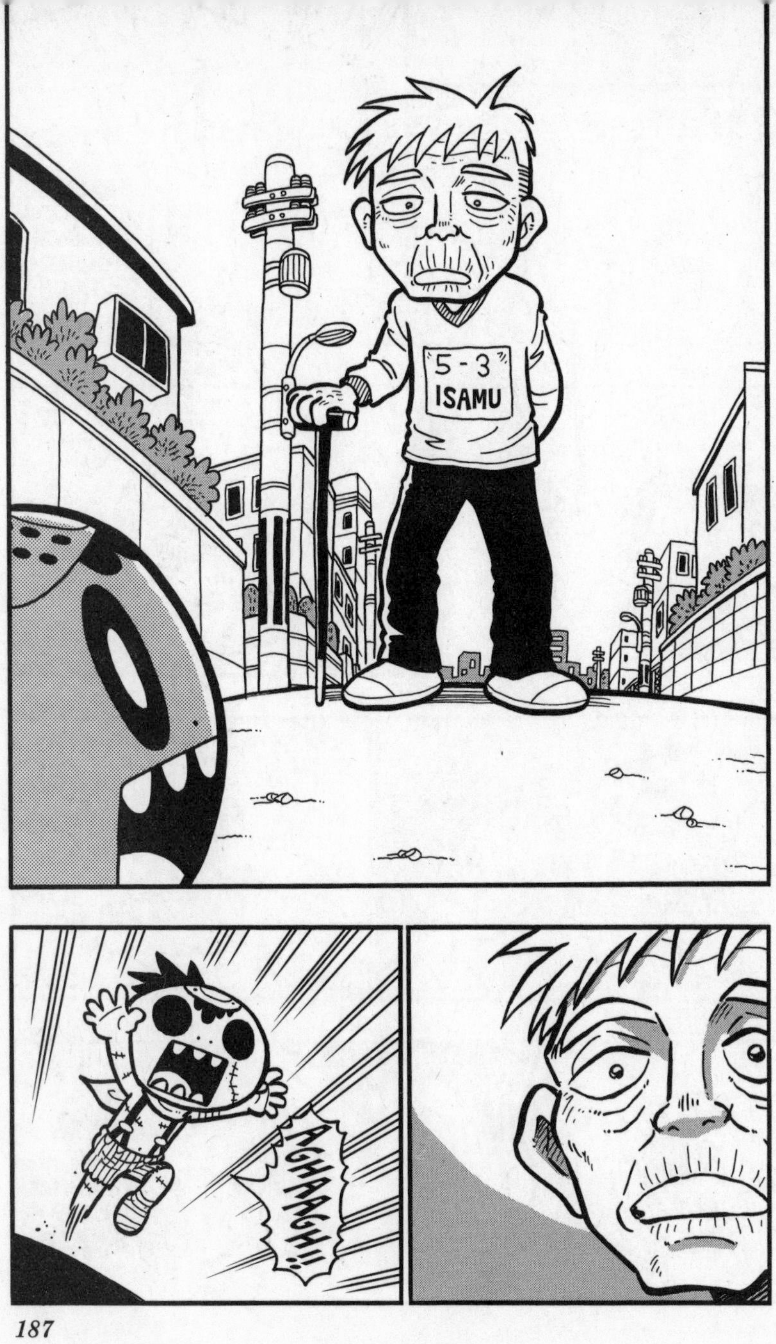
5-3
ISAMU
AGHAAGH!!

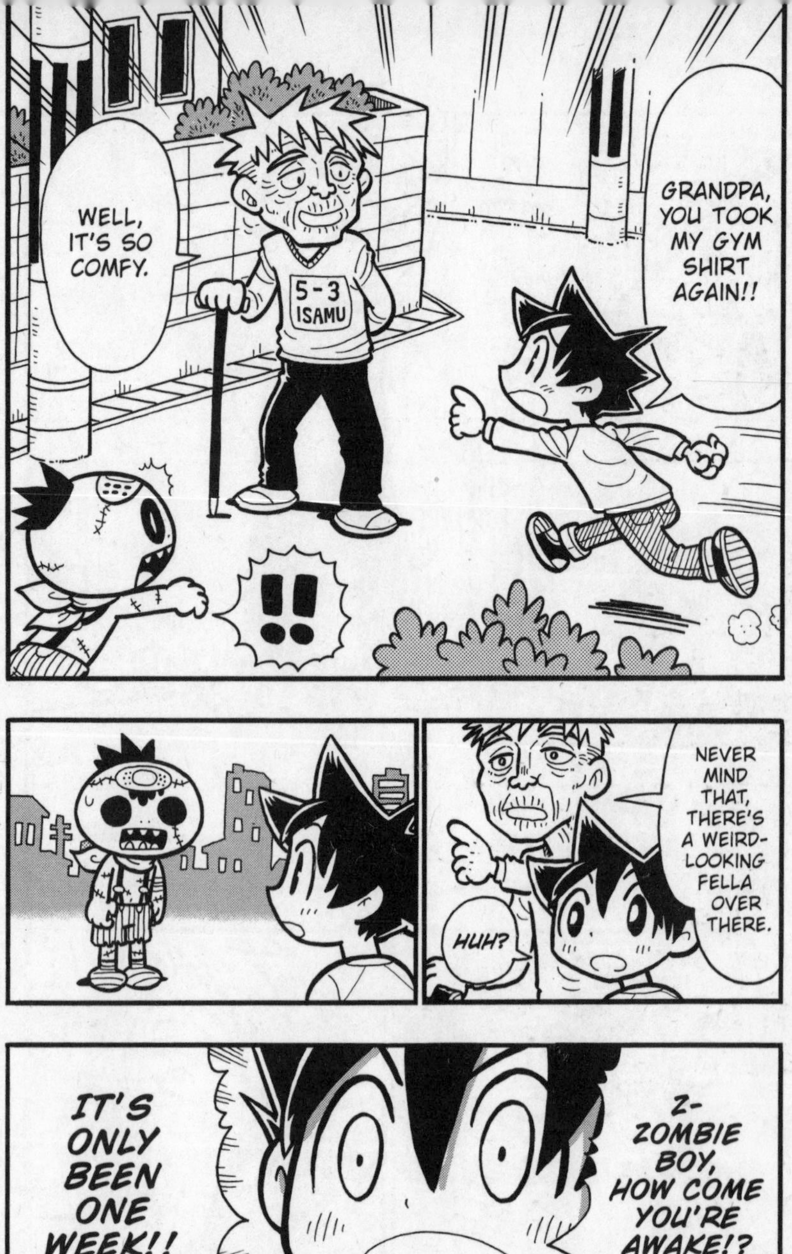
GRANDPA, YOU TOOK MY GYM SHIRT AGAIN!!
5-3 ISAMU
WELL, IT'S SO COMFY.
!!
NEVER MIND THAT, THERE'S A WEIRD-LOOKING FELLA OVER THERE.
HUH?
Z-ZOMBIE BOY, HOW COME YOU'RE AWAKE!?
IT'S ONLY BEEN ONE WEEK!!

ZOMBIE BOY WOKE UP IN A WEEK?
HOW !?
BUT DON'T YOU HAFTA SLEEP ONE HUNDRED YEARS TO HEAL YOUR BODY?
ARE YOU OKAY?
I DID THINK IT WAS KINDA WEIRD. USUALLY, THREE-HUNDRED-YEAR-OLD ZOMBIES ARE IN MUCH WORSE SHAPE.
I'M TURNING 300.
PLOP
PLOP
ZOMBIE BOY IS STILL LIVELY FOR THAT AGE...
COULD IT...HAVE SOMETHING TO DO WITH HOW LONG ZOMBIE BOY SLEEPS EVERY DAY......?
HUH? HOW MUCH DOES HE NORMALLY SLEEP?
FIFTEEN HOURS...
PUU...
THAT'S WAY TOO MUCH!!
IF HE GETS THAT MUCH SLEEP REGULARLY, MAYBE HE ONLY NEEDS TO HIBERNATE FOR ONE WEEK, NOT ONE HUNDRED YEARS.
THAT MEANS...

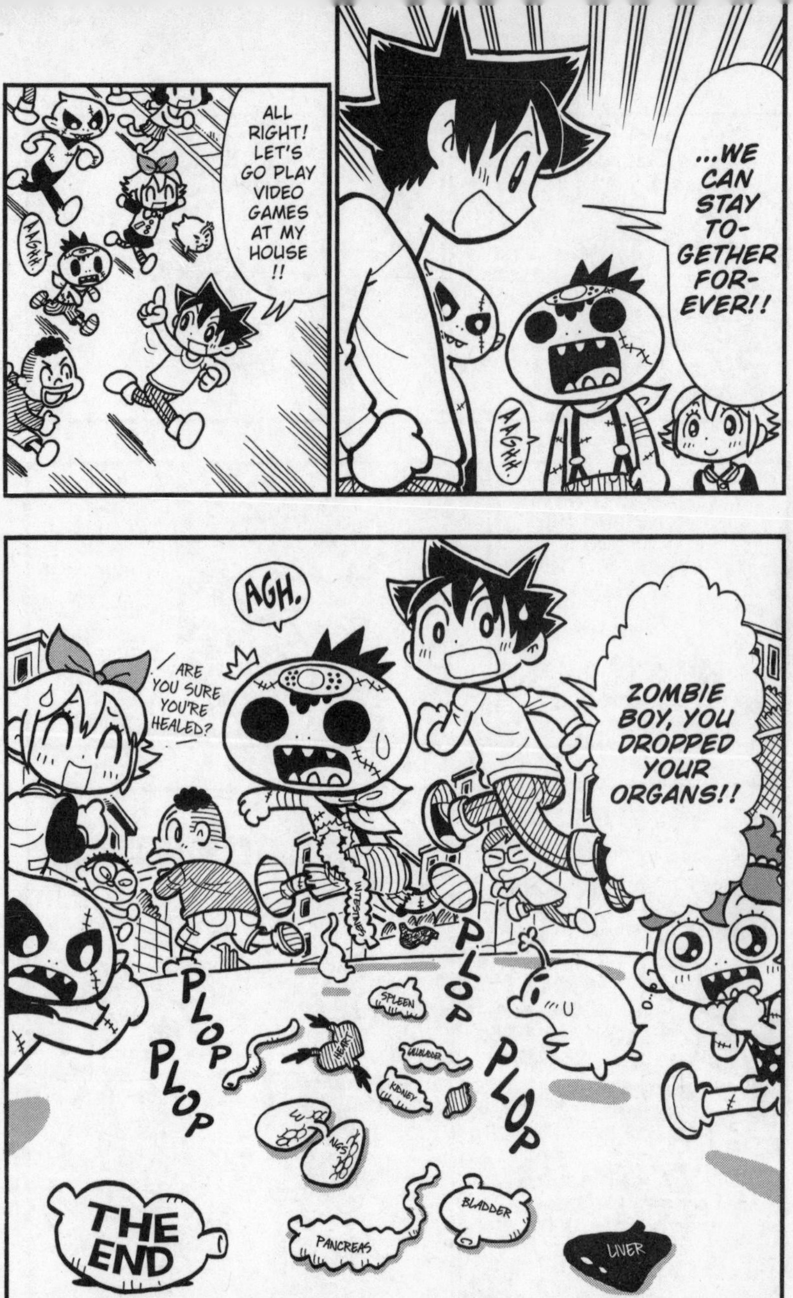
...WE CAN STAY TO-GETHER FOR-EVER!!
AAGHH.
ALL RIGHT! LET'S GO PLAY VIDEO GAMES AT MY HOUSE !!
AAGHH.
ZOMBIE BOY, YOU DROPPED YOUR ORGANS!!
AGH.
ARE YOU SURE YOU'RE HEALED?
PLOP
PLOP
PLOP
PLOP
PLOP
SPLEEN
HEART
GALLBLADDER
KIDNEY
BLADDER
PANCREAS
LIVER
THE END

COLD GERM

CO LD

SNORA

ISAMU'S UNCLE

SEE YOU!!

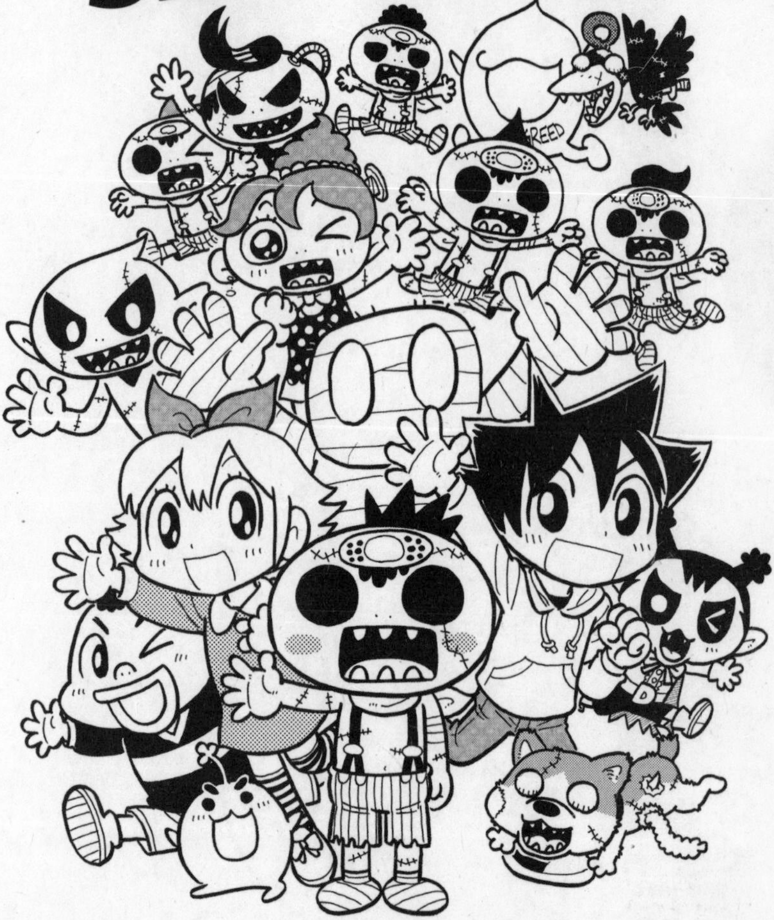
GREED

★ SEND YOUR LETTERS FOR YASUNARI NAGATOSHI TO ▼

JY
150 West 30th Street, 19th Floor, New York, NY 10001

ZO ZO ZOMBIE 11 THE END

ZO ZO ZOMBIE

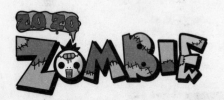

ZOMBIE 11

YASUNARI NAGATOSHI

Translation: ALEXANDRA MCCULLOUGH-GARCIA ✸ Lettering: BIANCA PISTILLO

This book is a work of fiction. Names, characters, places, and incidents are the product of the author's imagination or are used fictitiously. Any resemblance to actual events, locales, or persons, living or dead, is coincidental.

ZOZOZO ZOMBIE-KUN Vol. 11
by Yasunari NAGATOSHI
© 2013 Yasunari NAGATOSHI
All rights reserved.
Original Japanese edition published by SHOGAKUKAN.
English translation rights in the United States of America, Canada, the United Kingdom, Ireland, Australia and New Zealand arranged with SHOGAKUKAN through Tuttle-Mori Agency, Inc.

English translation © 2021 by Yen Press, LLC

JY
150 West 30th Street, 19th Floor
New York, NY 10001

Visit us at jyforkids.com ✸ facebook.com/jyforkids
twitter.com/jyforkids ✸ jyforkids.tumblr.com ✸ instagram.com/jyforkids

First JY Edition: July 2021

JY is an imprint of Yen Press, LLC.
The JY name and logo are trademarks of Yen Press, LLC.

The publisher is not responsible for websites (or their content) that are not owned by the publisher.

Library of Congress Control Number: 2018948323

ISBNs: 978-1-9753-5959-1 (paperback)
978-1-9753-3361-4 (ebook)

10 9 8 7 6 5 4 3 2 1

WOR

Printed in the United States of America